DEEP SECRET

DIANA WYNNE JONES

TOR®
fantasy

A TOM DOHERTY ASSOCIATES BOOK
NEW YORK

This is a work of fiction. All the characters and events portrayed in this book are either products of the author's imagination or are used fictitiously.

DEEP SECRET

Copyright © 1997 by Diana Wynne Jones

This book was first published in Great Britain in 1997 by Victor Gollancz, an imprint of the Cassell Group.

Edited by David G. Hartwell

A Tor Book
Published by Tom Doherty Associates, LLC
175 Fifth Avenue
New York, NY 10010

www.tor.com

Tor® is a registered trademark of Tom Doherty Associates, LLC.

ISBN: 0-812-57572-5
Library of Congress Catalog Card Number: 98-49010

First Tor edition: March 1999
First mass market edition: January 2000

Printed in the United States of America

0 9 8 7 6 5 4 3 2 1

"There is a daft and complicated multiverse presided over by an inner ring of fallible guardians, an entangling of science and enchantment, a preposterous plot, a large cast list featuring numerous characters who prove to be wearing masks over secret identities . . . a hidden savior, and outrageous juxtapositions of tragedy, farce, high melodrama, and high fantasy.

"All this is told in a deceptively breathless style, as though the words were just bubbling unchecked from the wells of imagination. A second reading reveals, soberingly, how many apparent decorative flourishes and fragments of byplay are efficiently laying groundwork for revelations to come. . . . Diana Wynne Jones not only carries all this off splendidly, but successfully shifts gears into high fantasy for a quest . . . there are plenty more secrets to be enjoyably discovered in *Deep Secret*; this seems a good time to stop and echo that."

—*Charmed Lives*

"Throughout, Jones combines strong writing, high fantasy heroics, and delightfully dark humor to sparkling effect."

—*Publishers Weekly*

"An orchestrated riot, with tangled plots, bizarre doings, headlong pace, and foaming wit." —*Kirkus Reviews*

THE SPELLCOATS

"A haunting, wonderful book." —Paul Hazel

"Superior fantasy . . . An excellent book." —Andre Norton

ARCHER'S GOON

"One of the strengths of this story lies in Jones's ability to create memorable, idiosyncratic characters with swift, sure strokes of detail. . . . Leaves readers wanting more."

—*School Library Journal* (starred review)

In the year E.K. 3413, the following files were secretly obtained from the Magid Rupert Venables and, at the Emperor's personal request, deposited in the new archive at Iforion.

ONE

I may as well start with some of our deep secrets because this account will not be easy to understand without them.

All over the multiverse, the sign for Infinity or Eternity is a figure eight laid on its side. This is no accident, since it exactly represents the twofold nature of the many worlds, spread as they are in the manner of a spiral nebula twisted like a Möbius strip to become endless. It is said that the number of these worlds is infinite and that more are added daily. But it is also said that the Emperor Koryfos the Great caused this multiplicity of worlds somehow by conquering from Ayewards to Naywards.

You may take your pick, depending on whether you are comfortable with worlds infinitely multiplying, or prefer to think the number stable. I have never decided.

Two facts, however, are certain: one half of this figure eight of worlds is negative magically, or Naywards, and the other half positive, or Ayewards; and the Empire of Koryfos, situated across the twist at the centre, has to this day the figure-eight sign of Infinity as its imperial insignia.

This sign appears everywhere in the Empire, even more frequently than statues of Koryfos the Great. I have reason to know this rather well. About a year ago, I was summoned to the Empire capital, Iforion, to attend a judicial enquiry. Some very old laws required that a Magid should be present—otherwise I am sure they would have done without me, and I could certainly have done without them.

1

The Koryfonic Empire is one of my least favourite charges. It is traditionally in the care of the most junior Magid from Earth and I was at that time just that. I was tired too. I had only the day before returned from America, where I had, almost single-handed, managed to push the right people into sorting out some kind of peace in the former Yugoslavia and Northern Ireland. But all my pride and pleasure in this vanished when I saw the summons. Groaning to myself, I put on the required purple bands and cream silk brocade garments and went to take my seat in the closed court.

My first peevish, jet-lagged thought was, Why can't they use one of the nice rooms? The great Imperial Palace has parts that go back over a thousand years and some of those old courts and halls are wonderful. But this enquiry was in a new place, lined with rather smelly varnished wood, bleak and box-like and charmless. And the wooden benches were vilely uncomfortable. The figure-eight insignia—carved in relief and painted too bright a gold—dug into my shoulders and dazzled off the walls and off the big wooden chair provided for the Emperor. I remember irritably transferring my gaze to the inevitable statue of Koryfos the Great, looming in the corner. That was new too, and picked out in over-bright gilt, but there is this to be said for Koryfos: he had a personality. Though the statues are always the same and always idealized, you could never mistake them for anything but the likeness of a real person. He carried his head on one side, a bit like Alexander the Great of Earth, and wore a vague, cautious smile that said, "I hear what you say, but I'm going to do things my way anyway." You could see he was obstinate as sin.

I remember I was wondering why the Empire so loved Koryfos—he reigned for a bare twenty years over two millennia ago, and most of the time he was away conquering places, but they persist in regarding his time as the Golden Age—when we had to stand up for the entrance of the present Emperor. A very different person, small, plain and dour. You do wonder how it is that Emperors always marry

2

the most beautiful women in several worlds and yet produce someone like Timos IX whom you would hardly notice in the street. You would glance at him and think that this was a short man with weak eyes and a chip on his shoulder. Timos IX was one of very few in the Empire who needed to wear glasses. This embarrassed me as I stood up. I was the only other person in the court in spectacles—as if I were setting up to be the Emperor's equal. In many ways, of course, a Magid *is* the equal of any ruler, but in this particular court of enquiry I was a mere onlooker, there by law to certify simply whether or not the accused had broken the law as stated. I was not even supposed to speak until after a verdict had been reached.

This, among other legal facts, was tediously made known to me in the preliminaries after we all sat down and the prisoner was marched in and made to stand in the centre. He was a pleasant-looking youngster of twenty-one or so, called Timotheo. He did not look like a law-breaker. I am afraid that, apart from registering, with some perplexity, that Timotheo was an alias and that, for obscure legal reasons, his real name could not be given, I could not force my jet-lagged mind to attend very well. I remember going back to my thoughts of Koryfos the Great. He stood to the Empire in the place of a religion, it seemed to me. The wretched place had religions in plenty, over a thousand godlets and goddities, but the worship of these was a purely personal thing. As an example of how personal, I recalled that Timos IX had, about fifteen years ago, adopted the worship of a peculiarly unlovable goddess who inhabited a bush planted on the grave of a dead worshipper and who imposed on her followers a singularly joyless code of morals. This probably explained the Emperor's pinched and gloomy look. But no one else at court had felt the need to adopt the Emperor's faith. It was Koryfos who united everyone.

Here I was jerked to alertness. The Emperor himself read out the charges against the young man in elaborate legal language. Stripped of the law-talk it was appalling, even

3

for the Empire. The so-called Timotheo was the Emperor's eldest son. The decree he was said to have broken stated that no child of the Emperor, by any of his True Wives, High Ladies or Lesser Consorts, was to know who his or her parents were. The penalty for discovering who they were was death. And death for anyone who helped an Imperial child find out.

The Emperor then asked Timotheo if he had broken this decree.

Timotheo had evidently known no more of this decree than I had. He was looking as shocked and angry as I felt. I could have applauded when he answered drily, "Sire, if I hadn't broken it before, I would have broken it when you read out my parentage just now."

"But have you broken the decree?" the Emperor reiterated.

"Yes," said Timotheo.

Catch-22, I thought. I was furious. What a charade!

The worst of it was that Timotheo was intelligent as well as pleasant. He would have made a much better Emperor than his father. It had obviously taken some ingenuity to find out who he was. He had been one of four fosterlings in the house of a provincial noble and, as the enquiry proceeded, it became clear that the other three fosterlings and the noble must have given him some help. But Timotheo stuck to it that he had done the detective work and made the discovery by himself. Then he had made the bad mistake of writing to his mother, the Emperor's First Consort, for confirmation.

"Did it not occur to you that, once you were known, my enemies might kidnap you in order to threaten me?" the Emperor asked him.

"I wasn't going to tell anyone," Timotheo said. "Besides, I can look after myself."

"Then you were intending to claim the Imperial throne for yourself," the Emperor suggested.

"No I wasn't," Timotheo protested. "I just didn't like not knowing who I am. I think I have the right to know that."

"You have no right. You are convicted of treason to the throne out of your own mouth," the Emperor said, satisfied. He looked at me on my high, uncomfortable bench. "The law is the law," he said. "Bear witness, Magid, that this man broke our Imperial decree."

I bowed. I couldn't bear to speak to him.

After that there was a great deal of palaver, with other dignitaries getting up in their grand silks and bearing witness too. It got like a pompous dance. I sat there considering when would be the best time to spirit young Timotheo away—and I blame my jet-lagged state that I didn't do it there and then. He was looking stunned by this time. Six men had just paraded past him, passing sentence of death on him, each swinging the white lining of their bright pink cloaks towards him. It was like being sentenced by a bed of petunias. I couldn't take it seriously. I reckoned the best time to act was when they marched Timotheo back to his condemned cell. He had been brought in by a squad of élite guards with a mage following for added assurance, and I assumed they would think no one could touch him through all that. I bided my time.

And missed out completely. The petunias retired. The Emperor said, quite casually, "The sentence can be carried out now." He raised a hand glittering with rings. One of them must have been one of their beam weapons, miniaturized. Timotheo gasped quietly and fell over sideways on the floor with blood running out of his mouth.

It happened so quickly that I hoped it was a trick. I could not believe that, even in the Koryfonic Empire, an Emperor would not want his eldest son alive. While I was climbing down the varnished wooden steps to the centre of the court, I was still sure it was just a deception, to make the Emperor's enemies believe Timotheo was dead. But it was no trick. I touched Timotheo. He was still warm like a living person, but my fingers told me there was no soul there.

I left at once, from beside the corpse, to make my feelings plain.

I was thoroughly disgusted, with myself as well as the

5

Emperor. As I made my way home, I told myself I had been stupid to expect compassion or even value for life in that place. And I had sufficient time to curse myself. Earth lies Naywards of the Empire, which makes the journey rather like going slowly uphill. I had to haul myself from lattice to lattice in the spaces between the worlds, and by the time I reached my house I not only hated the Empire, but also the stupid hampering robes it caused me to wear. I was just tearing the darn things off in my living room when the phone rang.

I wanted nothing more than to sit down with a fresh-brewed cup of coffee, before calling up the Senior Magid and lodging a formal complaint against the Emperor. I swore. I snatched up the phone.

"*Now* what?"

It was my elder brother Will. "Bad day?" he said.

"Very," I said. "The Koryfonic Empire."

"Then I believe you," he said. "Glad I don't have to look after that lot any longer." Will is a Magid too. "And what I've got to tell you won't make your day any better, I'm afraid. I'm ringing from Stan Churning's house. He's ill. He wants you here."

"Oh God!" I said. "Why does everything unpleasant always happen at once?"

"Don't know. It just does," Will agreed. "It's not a deep secret, but it ought to be. I think Stan's dying, Rupert. He thinks so anyway. We tried to get hold of Si too, but he's out of touch. How soon can you get here?"

"Half an hour," I said. Stan lives outside Newmarket. Weavers End, where I live, is just beyond Cambridge.

"Good," said Will. "Then I can stay with him until you get here." And keep him alive if necessary, Will meant. If Stan really was dying, there would be Magid business he had to hand on to me. "See you soon," Will said and rang off.

I stayed in the house just long enough to make coffee and fax Senior Magid that I intended to complain about the Empire, to the Upper Room if necessary. Senior Magid

6

lives several worlds Naywards and I normally make heavy weather of getting a fax through there. That day I did it in seconds. Five angry, trenchant sentences in no time at all. I was too busy thinking of Stan. I got in my car still thinking of him. Normally, getting into my car is a thing I pause and take pleasure in—particularly if I have just been away for a while. It is a wholly beautiful car, the car I used to dream of owning as a boy. I usually pause to think how good it is that I can make the kind of money you need to own such a car. Not that day. I just got in and drove, swigging coffee from the Thermos, with my mind on Stan.

Stan had sponsored first Will, then our brother Simon, then me, into the Company of Magids. He had taught me most of what I know today. I wasn't sure that I knew what I'd do without him. I kept praying that he, or Will, had made a mistake and that he was not dying after all. But one of the things about being a Magid is that you don't make that kind of mistake.

"Damn!" I said. I kept needing to blink. I didn't consciously see any of the roads I drove along until I was bumping up the weedy drive of Stan's bungalow.

A nasty bungalow. A blot on the landscape. It looked like a large cube of Stilton cheese dumped down in the flat heathland. We used to kid Stan about how ugly it was, but he always said he was quite happy in it. People who knew me, and particularly people who knew all three of us Venables brothers when we lived in Cambridge, used to wonder what we saw in a seedy little ex-jockey like Stan. They asked how we could bring ourselves to haunt his hideous house the way we did.

The answer is that all Magids lead double lives. We have to earn a living. Stan earned his advising sheiks and other rich men about racehorses. I design computer software myself, games mostly.

I parked my car beside Will's vehicle. At dusk, with the light behind it, it passes for a Land Rover. In broad daylight, as it was then, you look away and think you may have imagined things. I edged past it and Will opened the bottle-green front door of the bungalow to me.

"Good timing," he said. "I have to go now and milk the goats. He's in the front room on the left."

"Is he—?" I said.

"Yes," said Will. "I've said goodbye. Shame Si can't be found. He's somewhere yonks Ayewards and not in touch with anyone I can contact. Stan's written him a letter. Let me know how things go, won't you?" He went soberly past me and climbed into his queer vehicle.

I went on into the bungalow. Stan was lying, all five foot of him, stretched on top of a narrow bed by the window. His slightly bandy legs were in child-sized jeans and one of his socks had a thin place at the toe. At first sight, you would not have thought there was too much wrong with him, except that it was unlike him not to be wandering about doing something. But if you looked at his face, as I did almost straight away, you saw that it was strangely stretched over its bones, and that his eyes, under the high forehead left by his curly grey receding hair, were standing out like a cat's, luminous and feverish.

"What kept you, Rupert?" he joked, a bit gaspily. "Will phoned you a good five minutes ago."

"The Koryfonic Empire," I said. "I had to send a complaint to Senior Magid."

"That lot!" Stan gasped. "She gets complaints about them from every Magid who goes near the place. Abuse of power. Contravention of human rights. Manipulation of Magids. General rottenness. I always think she just puts them in a file labelled K.E. and then loses the file."

"Can I get you anything?" I said.

"Not much point," he said. "I've only got an hour or so—no time to digest anything—but I would appreciate a drink of water."

I got him a glass of water from the kitchen and helped him sit up enough to drink it. He was very weak and he had that smell. The smell is indescribable, but it belongs only to the terminally ill and once you know it you can't

8

mistake it. I remember it from my grandfather. "Shouldn't I ring the doctor?" I asked him.

"Not yet," he said, lying back and panting a bit. "Too much to say first."

"Take your time," I said.

"Don't make bad jokes," he retorted. "So. Well. Here goes. Rupert, you're junior Magid on Earth, so it's going to fall to you to find and sponsor my replacement—but you knew that, I hope."

I nodded. The number of Magids is always constant. We try to fill the gaps left by deaths as promptly as possible, because there is a lot for us to do. That was how Stan came to sponsor me as well as my brothers. Three Magids died within six months of one another, long before Will was competent to try. Before that, Stan had been this world's junior Magid for nearly ten years. As I said to Will, bad things always happen at once.

"Now there are several things I want to tell you about that," Stan went on. "First, I've got you a list of possibles. You'll find it in the top left-hand drawer of my desk over there, on top of my will. Get it out of sight before anyone else sees it, there's a good lad."

"What? Now?" I said.

"What's wrong with now?" he demanded.

Superstition, I thought, as I went over to the desk. I didn't want to behave as if Stan was dead while he was still alive. But I opened the drawer and took out the folded list I found there. "It's quite short," I said, glancing at it.

"You can add to it if you want," he said. "But look at those lot first. I spent all last month making sure you had some good strong candidates. Two of them have even been Magids before, in former lifetimes."

"Is that such a good thing?" I asked. Stan was fascinated with past lifetimes. To my mind, it was his great weakness. He was ready to believe anything people said about reincarnation. It never seemed to occur to him that nobody who said they remembered a former lifetime ever remembered

9

an *ordinary* one. It was all kings, queens and high priest-esses.

He grinned, stretching his already oddly stretched face. He knew my opinions. "Well, if they bothered to get reborn, it has to mean they're keen. But you'll find the great advantage is that they're born subconsciously *knowing* half the stuff—and usually with plenty of talent too. All my list are good strong talents though. The best untrained in the world." He paused a moment. He kept getting breathless. "And take your time looking at them," he said. "I know we're supposed to be quick, but it's not *that* urgent. Do what I did: I left *you* for nearly a year. I couldn't mostly *believe* it, that three brothers in the same family should all be Magid material. Then I thought, Why not? There has to be something in heredity. But I never told you what really made up my mind about you, did I?"

"My obvious superiority?" I suggested.

He chuckled. "Nah. It was the fact that you'd been a Magid before in at least two lifetimes."

In the ordinary way, I would have been extremely annoyed. "I have never," I said stiffly, "*ever* either remembered a former life or told you anything to suggest that I had."

"There are other ways of finding out," Stan said smugly.

I let it pass. This was not the time to argue. "All right," I said. "I'll weigh up everyone on the list very carefully."

"And don't necessarily choose the most willing. Run tests," he said. "And when you do choose, make sure you let them follow you around during a fairly big assignment before you begin instructing them. See how they take it—the way I did with you over the Ayeworld pornography and with Will over the oil crisis."

"What did Simon have?" I asked. No one had ever told me.

"A mistake on my part," Stan admitted. "Someone was doing a white slave and marriage trade, pushing girls through Earth down from Naywards and then on through the Koryfonic Empire. I let Simon see the police team the

10

Empire sent here to see me about it. Half of them were centaurs. There was no way I could pass them off as Earth people. After that I had to get him ratified as a Magid—he'd seen too much. Lucky for me he's made a good one. But don't you worry that you'll make a mistake like that."

"I should hope not!" I said.

"You won't," said Stan. "Because if you start, I'll stop you."

"Er . . ." I began, wondering how to point the hard truth out.

"I'll be around," he said. "I've arranged to be here. A Magid can work quite well disincarnate, and I plan to do that until you've got things settled."

I said, half joking and wholly disbelieving, "Don't you trust me not to balls it up then?"

"I trust you," Stan said. "But you've only been a Magid just over two years. And it used to be customary for all new Magids to have a disincarnate adviser—I found it in the records. So I asked the Upper Room if I could stay and keep an eye on you, and they seemed to think it was reasonable. So I'll be around. Rely on it." He sighed, and stared into distance somewhere beyond his flaking off-white ceiling.

I sighed too, and thought, Be honest, Stan. You just don't want to go away for good. And I don't want this to happen either.

"Mostly, though," Stan added, "it's that I can't bear to leave. I'm only eighty-nine. That's young for a Magid."

I had not realized he was much above sixty, and said so.

"Oh yes," he said. "I've kept my condition. Most of us do. Then one day you get told, 'That's it, boy. Deathday tomorrow,' and you know it's true. I've been given until sundown."

I looked out of the window, involuntarily. It was November. The shadows were long already.

"Call the doctor just before sunset," Stan said, and did not say much for a while after that. I gave him some water, got myself some more coffee and waited. Some time later, he began to talk again, this time more generally and reminiscently.

"I've seen this world through a lot of changes," he remarked. "I've helped clear away a lot of the political garbage that built up through this century. We've got the decks cleared for the changes due to come in the next century now. But, you know, the thing I take most pleasure in is the way we've managed to coax this world Ayewards. Gradually. Surreptitiously. When I was a lad, no one even considered there might be other universes, let alone talking of *going* to them. But now people write books about that, and they talk about working magic and having former lives, and nobody thinks you're a nutcase for mentioning it. And I think, *I* did that. *Me. I* slid us back down the spiral. Back to where we should be. Earth is one of the early worlds, you know—well of course you know—and we should be a long way further Ayewards than we are."

"I know," I said, stressfully watching the shadow of my car spread over his bushy lawn.

"Help it along some more," he said.

"It's one of the things we're here for," I said.

Later, when the room was getting dim, Stan said suddenly, "It was the homesickness that brought me back here, you know."

"How do you mean?" I asked him.

"I started out my work as a Magid a long way Ayewards," he murmured. His voice was getting weaker. "I chose it. A bit like Simon chose it. But I chose it for the centaurs. I'd always loved centaurs, always wanted to work with them. And as soon as I learnt that more than half the places Ayewards of here have centaurs, off I went. I thought I'd never come back here. Centaurs need a magical ambience to maintain them—well, you know they do—and they all died out here when we drifted off Naywards. And for three years I was blissfully happy, working with centaurs, studying them. I don't think there's a thing I don't know about centaurs and their ways. Then I got homesick. Just like that. I can't tell you what for. It was too general.

12

It was just that the world I was on wasn't this one. It didn't smell right. The wind didn't blow like it does here. Grass the wrong green. Small things, like the water tasting too pure. So back I had to come."

"To work as a jockey," I said.

"It was next best to being a centaur," he said. After a long pause, he added, "I want to get reborn as a centaur. Hope I can arrange that." Then, after a longer pause still, "Better phone that doctor then."

The phone was in the kitchen. I went through there and found the number carefully written on a pad laid by the phone. I remember thinking, as I punched it in, that this seemed hard on young Timotheo. I must have been one of the few people to be sorry he was dead, and yet all my sorrow was concentrated on Stan. I forgot Timotheo again the next moment. Stan had made his arrangements with care. The doctor, to my astonishment, answered the phone himself and promised to be there in ten minutes. I rang off and went back to the front bedroom.

"Stan?" I said.

There was no answer. He had fallen half off the bed as he died and he had wanted to do that in private. I put him gently back.

"Stan?" I said again, into the dead, dim air.

There was nothing. I could feel nothing.

"So much for the idea of staying around," I said loudly. But there was still nothing.

TWO

A little before Christmas, when most of the other small and large things connected with Stan's death were done, I had a serious look at the list he had given me. There were five names on it, two of which were female. The addresses indicated that one of these women was British and the other American. The males were from Britain, Holland and—I had to get out my atlas—Croatia. I sighed and tried to look forward to travelling to meet all of them on various invented excuses. At least three of them spoke my language. I could call that lucky, I supposed. Stan had also supplied the dates of birth for all of them except the Croatian. The British girl and the man from Holland were both young. She was twenty, he was twenty-four. That was a point in their favour. The other two were in their forties. I found that a bit daunting. I had just been twenty-six, and the idea of having someone so much older for a pupil filled me with apprehension.

But I set to work to find them all.

I do not wish to describe the frustrations of that search. With interruptions from my neighbour—of whom more hereafter—and my mother's natural desire to have at least one of her sons home for Christmas, I was divining, travelling or querying my various sources nonstop for six weeks. I flew to Amsterdam to find the Dutchman, Kornelius Punt, only to discover that he had won some kind of scholarship enabling him to travel. He had taken serious advantage of it too. I went down to Avignon, where he was last heard of, and found that he had gone to Rome, Athens and then Jerusalem. After a maddening four days dealing with the Greek and Italian telephone systems, I came home to find a fax from a Magid visiting Israel informing me that Punt had gone to Australia. I gave up and decided to wait for him to come back. My American contacts traced the older woman, Tansy-Ann Fisk, soon after that. I was just preparing to fly out to Ohio when all sources sent urgent messages not to bother. Fisk had gone into retreat in some kind of all-female clinic where men were not allowed. Looking up this clinic in Magid records, I was a little perturbed to find it carried the remark "Query dubious esoterica." Still, she could have entered the place in good faith for a simple rest-cure. All I could do was wait until she came out. The British man, Mervin Thurless, was equally hard to trace. Eventually it emerged that he was on a lecture tour in Japan. As for the Croatian, Gabrelisovic, I don't have to remind you that there had been a war on there. My NATO sources rather feared he was among the many who had vanished in it without trace.

I turned to hunting for the British girl with some relief. At least we were both in the same country. Moreover she was younger than me and possessed, according to Stan's list, the greatest amount of untrained talent of the lot. She was the one I secretly hoped to select. I even allowed myself very agreeable visions of her as a pretty and intelligent young woman whom it would be a pleasure to instruct. I visualized myself laying down the laws of the Magids to her. I saw her hanging on my every word. I looked forward to meeting her.

I couldn't find her either.

She had a slightly complex family history. The address I had for her proved to be that of an aunt, her father's sister, in Bristol where Maree Mallory seemed to be a student. I stood on the aunt's doorstep in Bristol, in the pouring rain, while damp children pushed in and out of the house around me. Before long, the children formed a yelling, fighting

15

heap behind the aunt. She shouted at me above the din that poor Maree had gone back to her mother in London, didn't I know? Parents divorced. Sad case. I bellowed to be told whereabouts in London. She screamed that she couldn't remember, but if I didn't mind waiting she'd ask her sister-in-law. So I stood for a further five minutes in the rain watching the aunt across the fighting heap of children while she telephoned further down the hall. Eventually she came back and screamed an inaccurate address at me. I wrote it down, with further inaccuracies caused by damp paper and blotches of rain, and went to London the next day. It rained that day too.

The address was in South London. That part I got right. But when at last I found it, it proved not to be called Rain Kitten as I had written down, but Grain Kitchen. It was a healthfood shop. The lady standing behind a glassed-in display of more kinds of beans than I knew existed was tall and slender in her white overall. The white cloth round her head revealed youthful fair hair. She was so young-looking and comely that, for a moment, I had hopes that she was Maree Mallory herself. But when I came nearer, she looked older, possibly even over forty. She could have been Maree's mother. My blotched notes said that in this case she would be a Mrs. Buttle; but the sign over the door had read PROPRIETORS L. & M. NUTTALL. I decided not to risk names. I told her politely that I was looking for Maree Mallory.

She stared at me with her head on one side, in a summing-up way I found slightly ominous. "I'm not helping you," she announced at length.

"Can you tell me why not?" I asked.

"You think too well of yourself," she said. "Posh accent, shiny shoes, expensive raincoat, not a hair out of place—oh, I can see well enough why you let her down like that. You thought she wasn't good enough for the likes of you, didn't you? Or didn't she iron your shirts to your liking?"

I know I was speechless for a moment. I could feel my face flooding red. I do, certainly, like to be well dressed, but I found myself wanting to protest that I always iron my own shirts. It was too ridiculous. I pulled myself together enough to say, "Mrs.—er—Buttle—Nuttall?—I assure you I have not let your daughter down in any way."

"Then why is she so upset and saying you *have*?" the lady demanded. "Maree's not one to lie. And why have you come crawling to *me*? Realized you let a good girl slip between your nicely clipped fingernails, have you?"

"Mrs. Buttle—" I said.

"Nuttall," said she. "I never did like men who wear cravats. What's wrong with an honest tie? Let me tell you, if I'd seen you when she first took up with you, I'd have warned her. Never trust a cravat, I'd have told her. Nor a mac with lots of little straps and buttons. Clothes always tell."

"Mrs. *Nuttall!*" I more or less howled. *"I have never met your daughter in my life!"*

She looked at me disbelievingly. "Then what are you here for, dripping all over my shop floor?"

"I came," I said, "because I am trying to trace your daughter, Maree Mallory, in connection with—with a legacy which may come her way." The idea of a legacy was perhaps a poor one, but I was too flustered to remember all the cleverer pretexts I had invented on my way to Bristol the day before.

It seemed to impress Mrs. Nuttall. It was her turn to blush. Her fair pink skin went a strong purple and she clapped both hands over her mouth. "Oh. You mean you're not this Robbie of hers, then?"

"My name is Rupert Venables, madam," I said, hoping to rub the embarrassment home.

"Oh," she said again. I assumed she was about to relent and summon her daughter from a flat upstairs or somewhere. Not a bit of it. "Prove it," she said, as her flush died down. And when I had shown her a business card, she said, "Anyone can have a card printed." So I produced my driving licence, a credit card and my chequebook. She looked at them long and hard.

"I didn't bring my passport," I said, not altogether pleasantly.

To which she said, "Well, Rupert's not much different from Robbie as a name."

"There is all the difference in the world," I said.

She returned to my business card and looked at it broodingly. "It says here Computer Software Designer. That's you?" I nodded. "And this Robbie is supposed to be training for a vet," she mused. "That is different. But why aren't you a lawyer if it's about a legacy?"

"Because," I said, "I am the executor of the will. The deceased, Stanley Churning, named me executor in his will. Mrs. Nuttall, much as I applaud your caution, I would be grateful if you would let me talk to Maree."

"I suppose I have to believe you," she said, grudgingly. "But Maree's not here."

My heart sank. "Where is she?"

"Oh, she went to her Dad when they found he'd got cancer," Mrs. Nuttall told me. "She would go. It's not my fault she's not here."

"Do you mind giving me her address then?"

She did mind. She was suspicious of the whole thing. I applauded her instinct even while I tried not to grind my teeth. Eventually she said, "I suppose if it's over a legacy . . ." and at last gave me an address north of Ealing.

I thanked her and went there. It took hours. And when I got there I found the house locked and the lower windows boarded up. A neighbour informed me that the owner was in hospital—a long way away, she couldn't remember where—and the daughter had closed the house up and left.

I drove home, seething the whole way. The M25 was at a standstill. I tried to go cross-country and there were roadworks every half-mile. Talk about a run round the gasworks! I slammed my car door viciously when I finally got out in my own yard. I kicked my back door open and then slammed it shut. I tore off my damp mac. I slammed cupboards hunting for a glass. I slammed my way into my quiet, orderly living room, poured a stiff drink and threw myself into a chair. After the first swig, I had a thought. I swore, tore off my cravat and threw it at the fireplace.

"If I'd only known what you were letting me in for, Stan!" I said. "If I'd *known*! As it is, I give up. Now."

"Why? What's the matter, lad?" Stan's voice said.

I stopped dead, with my whisky tipped towards my mouth. "Stan?"

"Here, Rupert," his voice said, husky and apologetic, from the space by my big window. "Sorry about the delay. It's—well, it's not as easy to come back as I thought. It's not like you think. There's conditions to be met. I had to argue my case with the Lords of Karma as well as the Upper Room, and Lords of Karma aren't easy. Not all of them are human. I don't blame you for not looking happy. What's the problem?"

I think if Stan had arrived at any other time, I would have had trouble accepting him. Something about that unembodied presence brought me out in cold shudders, even annoyed as I was. But I was so fed up that I drank the rest of my whisky in one gulp and told him what was the problem. And finished by yelling, "And it's all your damned fault!"

"Steady! Steady on!" husked his disembodied voice. I had heard him talk to unquiet horses the same way. "It isn't *my* fault. Another Magid has to be found. And you're going about it all wrong anyway."

"Wrong?" I said. "In what way wrong?"

"You always were prone to it," he said. "Going about it like a normal person and forgetting you're a Magid. You've got enormous powers, lad. Use them. Go after them the Magid way."

"Oh," I said. "All right. But not until I've had a square meal, another stiff whisky and a pint of coffee. Does your present state remember the needs of the body? Can you wait that long?"

"They've given me a year, these folk Up There," he said. "If you can be ready before then."

That was the Stan I knew. I laughed. It made me feel better.

An hour later, I took off my jacket. I was just about to hang it over a chair in my usual precise way when I thought of Mrs. Nuttall and threw it after my cravat. Then I rolled up my sleeves and got to work, with Stan's voice occasionally husking hints and short-cuts. It was a long evening. And a frustrating one. Thurless was thinking of staying in Japan permanently. Kornelius Punt had decided to go on to New Zealand. The Croatian and Maree Mallory were still untraceable—

"Well, they would be," Stan's voice observed, "if they want to be. They're the two with the really strong talent."

"And Ms Fisk is probably having a nervous breakdown," I added.

"That follows again," Stan said. "It's the penalty of being odd when most people are normal. We might have gone the same way, you and me, if we hadn't been picked out for Magids."

"Speak for yourself," I snapped. My mood had gone bad again after this further frustration. "I regard myself as a stable personality."

"Do you now?" said Stan. "You forget. I knew you when you were a schoolboy. This Maree. I agree with you she's the most likely one. Dowse around for her father. He'll know where she is. They say fathers and daughters are always pretty close."

I followed his advice, and it was excellent. A week later, I drove to a hospital in Kent and interviewed a tired, sagging, small man in a wheelchair who had already lost most of his hair. I could see that he had, only recently, been a fat little man with a twinkle. I could see the cancer. They hadn't done much for it. I was desperately sorry for him. I gave that cancer a sharp flip and told it to go away. He doubled up gasping, poor fellow.

"Ouch!" he said. "First Maree, now you. What did you *do*?"

20

"Told it to go away," I said. "You should be doing that too, but you're hanging on to it rather, aren't you?"

"Do you know, that's just what Maree said!" he told me. "I suppose I do—hang on to it—it feels like part of me. I can't explain. What *should* I be doing?"

"Telling the thing it's an unwanted alien," I suggested. "You don't want it. You don't seem to me to have finished what you set out to do with your life."

"I haven't," he said sadly. "First the divorce came along, now this. I'm not like my brother, you know, book after book—I have just the one thing. I would have liked to patent my invention, but, well . . ."

"Then do it," I said. "Where is Maree at the moment?"

"In Bristol," he said.

"But I went to see her aunt and—"

"Oh, she's gone to her other aunt, up the road. I made her go back, love affair or no love affair, money or no money. She's training to be a vet, you see, and it's not a thing you can stop halfway over."

"I'm afraid I wouldn't know," I said. "Would I find her through the university, then?"

"Or the damned aunt," he said. "Ted's wife, Janine. Hateful woman. Can't think why my brother married the bitch, frankly. Made even more of a mistake than I did, but Ted stuck by his—for the boy's sake, I suppose." He gave me the address, maddeningly enough in the same street as the house I'd gone to before, and then said anxiously, "It's not really true I can get shot of this cancer by just thinking, is it?"

"A lot of cancers do respond to that," I said.

"I'm not so good at thinking positively," he said wretchedly.

Before I left I did what I could for Derek Mallory. It was no good hitting the cancer when he was embracing it so fervently, so I hit a few centres in his brain instead, trying to turn him to a more cheerful way of thinking. I suspect he felt every hit. His face puckered like a baby's.

I thought he was going to cry, but it turned out that he was trying to smile.

"That helped!" he said. "That really helped! I'm all for the mind stuff, deep down really. I've often argued with Maree about it. She can do it, but she won't. Makes scathing remarks instead. She lacks belief, that's her problem."

So I went back to Bristol again. But not until a week had passed. First I had to earn my living. I had a lot of deadlines to meet that week, and I would have met them too, with time to spare, except that as I was sorting the last and most intractable problems, my fax machine began making the little fanfare of sound I had set it to make when it was bringing me Magid business. I went and picked up the sheet. It said:

Iforion 10:2:3413. 1100 hrs. URGENT
     Emperor assassinated. Come back to Iforion
Imperial Palace soonest for immediate conference.
     This message by order of the Acting Regent,
General Commander Dakros

"Oh good!" I said. "Hurrah!" That was my first reaction. That man Timos IX really had it coming, and not only because of Timotheo, either. I hoped the assassin had hurt him first. Rather a lot. Then I thought again and said, "Oh shit. No heir." Then I thought again and added, "And what am I supposed to do about that? I'm their Magid, not their nursemaid."

"Tell them to go whistle," Stan suggested. He was evidently reading the fax over my shoulder.

I faxed back that I would come tomorrow.

They faxed back:

Iforion 10:2:13. 1104 hrs URGENT
     Imperative you come now. Dakros

I faxed again:

Why? I'm busy here with Magid business.

Dakros (whoever he was) faxed in return:

We got the assassin's accomplices. We're dealing
rebellion/other chaos. We need you to find the next
Emperor. Real problems there. Only a Magid can
solve it. Please, sir. Dakros

It was the "Please, sir" that got to me. The man was a
General and Acting Regent and he was saying that, like a
small boy pleading. I faxed that I was on my way and,
since it sounded like the kind of problem you have to spend
time on, I started to pack an overnight bag. Doubtless I
could borrow stuff, but in the Empire they slept in a thing
like a hospital gown, tied up with tapes, which I dislike,
and I *hate* their razors. I could feel Stan hanging over me
as I packed, wanting to say something.

"What is it?" I said.

"Don't get too involved in that Empire, will you?" he
said.

"No fear. I hate the place. Why?"

"Because there's a sort of directive out to Magids about
it—not as strong as an Intention, more of a suggestion—
to leave the place to go to hell in its own sweet way."

"It can, for me," I said. "What directive is this? A deep
secret you forgot to tell me, or what?"

"No, it's something I picked up after I—while I was—
was over there—negotiating with the Lords of Karma and
so on," he confessed. "I had to go even higher up in the
end. It came from a long way up. Them Up There want the
Empire left alone."

"Happy to oblige," I said, hurling my washing things into
my bag. I zipped it up and set off downstairs. "Are you
coming to Iforion with me?"

There was an unhappy pause. It lasted while I hurried
from the stairs and into the living room. Then Stan's voice

husked, "I don't think I can, lad. I think I'm fixed on Earth. I may even be stuck to this house of yours."

"That's boring for you," I said.

"There's no rule that says life—I mean afterlife—has to be interesting," he said ruefully.

I sensed him hovering wistfully in the middle of my living room as I set out for the Empire. It took several moves, from lattice to lattice, with its attendant feeling of being a pawn on a chessboard hopping from square to square—but downhill, since I was moving Ayewards. I thought as I went that Lewis Carroll got it right in *Alice Through the Looking Glass*. No one had ever told me, but I have always suspected that Carroll was a Magid. It is a very influential thing to do, to write books like the *Alice* books; and influence is what being a Magid is all about. Subtle influence.

THREE

I emerged in Iforion, as before, in the small cubicle in the palace they call the Magid Gate and found myself in a roomful of dust—pungent, old, bricky dust. My eyes and nose instantly streamed. I got my handkerchief out, started to blow my nose, and then changed my mind and held it over my nose and mouth as a filter. While I was dumping my bag in a corner, two soldiers edged into the tiny room.

"Posted to take you to General Dakros, sir," the man said hoarsely.

They surprised me, and not only because they appeared so suddenly out of the dust. One was a woman and both were younger than me. Their uniforms were of a very low-ranking kind, dark blue and grey, such as I had seen only in the far distance before, herding aside those of the common people who were allowed within (or probably just beyond) shouting distance of the Emperor. Both looked deeply weary. It was in the way they moved, as well as their pale faces and dark-circled eyes. The man had clearly not shaved for several days. The woman's hair was clotted with grey-red dust.

"If you'll keep close to us, sir," she said, as hoarse as her companion. "Parts of the building are dangerous."

I saw what she meant as we set off into the fog of brick dust. Almost at once we turned sharply into a domestic-seeming corridor, a low, stone-floored passage I had never seen before. When I craned back to look at the corridor I was used to, I had a glimpse of sky there among bent and splintered girders. I could hear quite heavy pieces of masonry dropping from higher up. I jumped at the first crash, but the soldiers took no notice. It was happening all the time and they had obviously grown used to it.

"Was the place bombed?" I croaked.

"Big bomb in the Throne Room," the man replied.

"Blew a hole through the middle. Weakened the structure," the woman added. "Took out all the Chiefs of Staff and the Council too."

"And all the Imperial Wives," said the man. "Lot of important clerks killed when the service rooms caved in."

"Lot of military too," said the woman.

"Élite guard was surrounding the Throne Room," the man explained. "Nearly all got crushed."

Not to speak of the Emperor too, I thought. Bull's-eye. Nice timing, whoever you were. All the top echelons of the Empire at one stroke, by the sound of it. It made me shiver and want to laugh at the same time. I put on a suitably grave face under my handkerchief and stepped cautiously after the two uniforms. Even in this safer corridor, the flagstones had heaved up here and there. In places, the stone ceiling bulged downwards. We kept close to the walls where that happened.

At length, after a long and roundabout walk, we arrived in the doorway of an arched stone vestibule. It glared with some kind of emergency lighting, making the hanging dust into a sort of bluish pea-souper. My glasses were coated by then. I had to take them off and clean them before I could see anything through that fog. While I wiped at them with my gritty handkerchief, I was aware of my two soldiers pulling themselves into smart attention with an evident effort and snapping slightly flaccid salutes. They said, in hoarse unison, "Magid Venables has arrived, sir."

Inside the light, a tenor voice said, "Thank goodness!" Another person coughed hackingly, and a third, deeper voice said, "Great. Get him in here."

I put my streaky glasses back on and advanced. Consid-

26

ering what the soldiers had said, I suppose I should not have been surprised by the people currently in charge of the Empire. But I was. They sat, the three of them, in various attitudes of deep weariness, at a table crowded with stuff. The tenor voice belonged to a wizard—mage, or whatever they call them in the Empire—who looked younger than I was. His eyes were so red with dust that I thought at first they were bleeding. One of his arms *was* actually bleeding, or had been. He was using the pompous short cloak the Empire decreed for its magic users, very sensibly, as a sling. Its gilded Infinity sign glittered off his left elbow. The one coughing was female, a very pretty lady even through streak upon streak of soot and brick dust, most oddly dressed in a pair of striped drawstring trousers and a blouse-thing sewn with sapphires and pearls. The third one was clearly General Dakros.

He wore the blue and grey uniform of the second-grade soldiery, as far as I could see it. It was torn and dusty and, in places, burnt. Like his private soldier, he had not shaved for some time. His chin was blue-black, matching his close-cut wriggly black hair. He was evidently from one of the swarthier races of the Empire, those not selected for the élite troops or high responsibility, and though this had saved his life, it had thrust upon him the shattering demands of running the Empire. His face, as he turned to me, had a hunted, nightmare look, hollowed at the temples and with muscles clumped at the blue jaw. But his eyes, I was glad to see, looked at me and appraised me quite sanely. He was older than the rest of us, but young for a General, from which I deduced that he was good at his job.

He turned away almost at once. There was a second arched doorway across the vestibule and several figures emerged from it as I walked to the table, materializing out of the dust fog with quiet urgency. Two laid faxes on the table. One, in the gold and royal blue of the élite soldiery, but looking drab and strained, came and muttered respectfully in the General's ear. I was glad to see that respect. It proved that this Dakros really was in charge. It was some

27

urgent tal kabout a captured World Gate. While it went on, I examined the table, which carried swathes of dust-covered faxes, several portable battle computers, a mind-speech receiver (something I wouldn't have minded owning myself) and more empty plastic coffee cups than I could count.

The élite guard left and Dakros turned back to me. By this time I was coughing nearly as hard as the pretty woman. I said, "General, you *have* to get out of here before you ruin everyone's lungs!"

"I know," he said. "There's just been a new fall. We'll get out as soon as you've helped us solve our problem."

"It's in the Throne Room vault, you see," the woman said.

The young wizard put in, in a tone of fretful pride, "I *am* doing what I can to keep it all up."

He was, too, I realized when I sent my senses upwards. There were tons of masonry and it was half killing him to support it. I did what I could to help shore it up. Stan might have objected, but I didn't care. The whole broken palace seemed to be on the slide. The young wizard gave me a grateful grimace as I slid my supports in around his.

"We'd better make it quick, then," I said. "Which way is the Throne Room?"

The General heaved himself to his feet. He was a fine, tall fellow, even sagging with weariness as he was then. "We'll show you." As the other two stood up too, he seemed to recollect the manners of yesterday's Empire. "Oh. Sorry. This is Junior Mage Jeffros and this is the High Lady Alexandra. The High Lady is the only one of the Emperor's consorts who survived the blast."

At this, the High Lady gave me a shamed sort of smile, as if she'd been caught stealing the jam or something. Perhaps one would feel guilty, I thought, when others of much higher rank had died. The Mage Jeffros evidently did. As we all hurried away down another long stone passage, he told me, "I was just left sitting in the rubble. All the senior mages around me were killed. I feel really bad about that. It was so senseless that it should have been just me left."

28

The passage led us to a sort of canyon open to very blue sky. Broken building towered on either side—sliding, I could feel it sliding. I hastily did a lot more shoring. Then I looked at the canyon floor and, with difficulty, recognized the imperial Throne Room, mostly by the shattered patterns on the floor, the remains of age-old mosaic littered with its own little stones and fragments of stained glass. The remains of the dais were at the other end. There was a black bowl scooped in the dais where the throne had been. Otherwise nothing. I whistled. They must have collected the Emperor and his staff in shreds, if at all.

"How on earth did you escape this?" I murmured to the High Lady.

"I was in the toilet," she murmured back. She said it with defiance, but defiance that was in some way worn out. Poor girl, I thought. She's been having to admit to it for hours, to soldiers.

"Don't talk here," Jeffros whispered.

"And don't walk in step," the General added.

He stepped carefully into the middle of the skylit canyon and walked lightly and swiftly towards the dais. The rest of us pattered after him, stepping in blank areas that had once been priceless designs in semi-precious stones, crunching through rubble and glass shards, and setting little cubes of mosaic rolling. Meanwhile, the cliffs of masonry on either side grumbled softly and, in places, suddenly subsided, letting out squirts of dust. I found it terrifying. But halfway along I was distracted by something worse. It was the smell of—well, sewage, garbage, butcher's shop and gunpowder, I suppose, with a strong reek of ozone. I gagged quietly into my handkerchief. Ozone? I thought. Ozone is frequently an aftermath of magic. I felt about mentally, as far as I could bear to. Yes, the bomb that did all this had been guided and triggered by magic. It must have been one of the Emperor's senior sorcerers on a suicide mission, I guessed, who had done it. A brave man. Or maybe a desperate one.

We mounted the dais beside the scooped hole, where the

29

smell was nearly unbearable, and I found there was a roof over the back of the platform and a wall behind that which seemed almost intact. Though the roof bent and creaked and sifted dust on us, my instant, anxious probing revealed that this part of the building was immensely strong, reinforced with girders, granite and magic. Good. We could relax a little. If the Emperor's throne had been set just two feet further back, he could have been relaxing too.

It was dark under there. All I could make out was the black hole of a doorway, with a hugely thick door hanging out of it. Jeffros reached out with his good hand to touch a wand that had been rammed upright into a crack in the dais. It flared like a torch, and so did a line of such wands, into the distance beyond the door. I could see glimpses of some kind of installation in there. The light also showed the door to have buckled in foot-thick waves, as if it had been under the sea.

Wow! I thought.

My three companions were already climbing over the doorsill into the secure chamber beyond. I hurried after them. It felt quiet in there, and safe, and it was almost dust-free. I took my handkerchief off my face and used it to clean my glasses again. After that I could look properly at the ranks of screens, keyboards and computers which the Emperor had used to control the eleven worlds straddling the waist of Infinity.

"We're going to have to blow all these up before we leave," the General told me gloomily, "in case someone gets in and tries to use them. This one seems to be the one we need. It won't let Jeffros divine its purpose."

"And I was told he kept information about the succession separate from everything else," the High Lady Alexandra explained.

I slid into the red leather bench in front of the machine the General pointed at. It started up fairly readily. There was some kind of emergency battery in it. "Explain the problem," I said as I watched the basic programming coming up on the screen. "It's not harmed in any way. It's just told me so."

"We got that far too," the General said, with a touch of sarcasm.

"I wouldn't let him go beyond that," Jeffros said. He looked strained and ill. "You'll find it's got magic protections."

I had already seen those. They did not seem very formidable. I boxed them out and typed in a command for the names and whereabouts of the Emperor's children. Nothing. I tried "HEIRS" for "CHILDREN." Again nothing. Then, with memories of that mock trial last November, I typed "TIMOTHEO." And got a response.

MALE BORN 3392 CODENAME TIMOTHEO DELETED 3412

"Deleted!" I said. "That's a fine touch. What was his real name then?"

"We don't know," said the General.

Well, at least this did seem to be the machine that had the answers, I thought. "Tell me the codenames for the other children, then, and how many of them there are."

"Again we don't know," said the General. "We're not even certain there are any."

"Oh, I think there *were,*" said the High Lady Alexandra. "There were rumours of at least five."

I swivelled round on the red bench. "Look here. I got a fax two years ago, just after I took over as Magid for the Empire. It recorded the birth of a girl to . . . to . . . um . . . a Lesser Consort called Jaleila. That's one at least."

"Wasn't true," said the General, and the High Lady added, "Poor Jaleila had been dead nearly fourteen years then." The General gave me a look that was more than a touch sarcastic. "Beginning to see the extent of our problem, eh, Magid?"

I was. My face must have been expressive. Jeffros looked up at me from stringing lengths of flex between his wands. "This Empire," he said, "was built of planks of delusion across a real cesspit. You don't have to tell us, Magid. The

Emperor was so scared of being tossed off the planks that he did a great deal more than just hide his children."

"Hid them even from themselves and issued false bulletins about new births," Dakros said. "Cut the moral stuff, Jeffros. That's our current problem. Thanks to Lady Alexandra we're fairly sure there *are* some heirs and the question is, can you find them, Magid?"

I looked him directly in his weary face. "Do you really want to find them? Since they don't know who they are and you don't either, wouldn't it be better just to start all over again with a new Emperor? You seem to have made a start yourself—"

He had grown more outraged with every word I spoke. He interrupted me vehemently. "Great and little *gods*, Magid! Do you think I want to deal with this mess for the rest of my life? I want to go home to Thalangia and run my farm! But I know my duty. I've got to leave the Empire in order with the proper person on its throne. That's all I'm trying to do here!"

"All right, all right," I said. "It needed to be asked. But let's hope this proper person of yours has a watertight birth certificate, or a birthmark or a tattoo or something, or half the Empire is going to say he's a fraud if we do find him. Do they?" I asked Lady Alexandra. "Get some kind of mark at birth?"

"I've no idea," she said.

"Then I take it you're not the proud mother of an heir yourself?" I said.

Even in the queer, flaring light of the wands, I saw how she coloured up, and she wrung her hands in an involuntary, distraught way. Dakros made a movement as if he was going to hit me, but stopped as she answered sedately, "I never had that honour, Magid. My sense was that the Emperor didn't like women much."

"And thought he was going to live for ever," I said disgustedly.

"He was only fifty-nine," she told me.

"Oh, what a *mess*!" I said. "So what *do* you know?"

"Only rumours, as I said," she answered. She shamed me. She was being polite and she was trying to help, and here was I getting progressively ruder and more irritated. But then the Empire has an atmosphere that always gets me down, and it was worse then, in that dusty ruin with tons of masonry hanging over our heads. "I heard," Lady Alexandra said, "of at least two girls. And there may have been two boys besides the one who was executed recently. I think Jaleila may have had a son before she died, but I wasn't a consort then, so I don't know for sure."

"Thank you, lady," I said. I turned back to the computing machine. Beside me, Jeffros crawled to attach a wire to its cabinet, awkward and one-handed. He shamed me too. He was getting ready to explode the place as soon as I came up with something and all I was doing was getting waspish with the General and the lady. I had better come up with something quickly. The thing that was making me most irritable was the way I could feel the ceiling, despite its magic, creaking and faintly shifting above us.

I typed away unavailingly for a minute. The screen kept giving me the news that Timotheo was deleted. I scowled at it. Surely even a paranoid fool like Timos IX must have envisaged a situation like this. There had to be some reasonable way to locate and identify his heir. Even if he had thought that whichever Councillor or Mage also knew the secret was going to survive him, there still had to be a way. The ceiling creaked again as I tried a new way. Ah. A new message.

ENTER CORRECT PASSWORD OR PENALTY ENSUES

I tried the Infinity sign, but that was too obvious. I tried "KORYFOS," since someone had just mentioned him. No luck.

It was Lady Alexandra who had mentioned Koryfos. Something about Koryfos the Great coming back to rule the day the Imperial Palace fell.

As I tried the word "TIMOS," I heard the General say, "Stupid story."

"It isn't all down yet," Jeffros put in.

33

While he was speaking, the machine whirred and came up with another message:

THREE PASSWORDS INCORRECT. PENALTY ENSUES

The ceiling creaked once more, loudly.

"Someone find me a copy disk," I said: "Several. We need to get out of here." I could feel the magics up there shredding away as I spoke. A safety device. Anyone not in the know queried this machine and down it all came on top of him. The Emperor didn't care. If that happened, he knew he'd be dead. Of all the stupid, *selfish*—"Quick!" I said.

The High Lady Alexandra arrived at my side with a box of copy disks. She wasn't just a pretty face, then. But I had begun to realize that anyway. On my other side, the General proffered two more. I snatched one, snapped it in and commanded the machine to copy.

"Do you think it will?" the General asked dubiously.

"No," I said. "But I'm going to *make* it!"

I have seldom worked so hard or so fast as I did then. With one mental hand, as it were, I held together the unravelling magics overhead. With the other—with everything else I had—I forced that damned machine to copy its entire contents at speed, *high* speed, on to disk after disk. I had only managed four when I felt the overhead magics escaping me. I left the fifth disk in there and swung off the bench.

"Come on. *Run*, all of you!"

They had all been staring upwards uneasily. They did not need to be told why. The General left at a sprint, managing to call into his battle-com as he ran, "Clear the building. Roof's about to go." Jeffros and I took the High Lady Alexandra by an arm each and hammered desperately after him. We chased across the ruined mosaic floor with slow-motion landslides beginning on both sides of us, and tore along a stone passage that seemed endless. Long before the end of it, I was hawking for breath, far worse than the lady, far too breathless even to try to stop the palace going. I just ran, hearing the long slow grinding of a mountain of building collapsing overhead, forcing myself to run faster, swearing to keep myself in better condition if I ever got out, and running, running.

We pelted out on to a terrace of steps above a vast courtyard. All along the length of these steps, shabby uniformed figures shot out of other doorways and ran too. The General, and everyone else, wisely kept running, down the flight of steps and on out into the courtyard. We panted after them, with chunks of stone crashing and bouncing at our heels.

The General stopped in the middle of the courtyard beside the huge statue of Koryfos the Great. The rest gathered in a ragged group around him, no more than a couple of hundred or so—surprisingly few people to hold down an empire.

"The Emperor had just cut back on the Army," the General said sourly, seeing my surprise, and swung round to look at the palace.

I was beyond speech by some way. My chest burned. I could only heave up breath that hurt and stare at that huge building folding in on itself and the dust boiling up from it. Jeffros, who looked as if he felt far worse than I did, shot me a look that said, Why not? and snapped his fingers. There was a sulky boom somewhere in the midst of the vast grinding, and the dust boiling out sideways was suddenly orange with fire.

"Oh—oh!" Lady Alexandra cried out.

As the building spread itself majestically into a heap of scorching rubble, the General put an arm round her. "You'll find a new life, my lady," I heard him say through the astonishing noise of it all. And I thought that when General Dakros finally went home to Thalangia—wherever that was—he would not be going alone.

I don't know how long we stared at the palace. I remember we all seemed to want to wait for the outlying wings, each of them with a row of vast turrets, to collapse with the rest and that these took quite a time to go. More people came running into the courtyard from there, so that by the end we were quite a large crowd of shivering, orphaned, dusty folk, all staring at the end of the seat of a government we had thought would never end. I know I felt as stunned as the rest. The Empire I had loved to hate was simply not there any longer.

My breath came back by slow stages. When I had merely trembling legs and a sore chest, and the ruin in front of us seemed to have stopped moving, I turned to General Dakros and passed him two of the four copy disks. "There you are," I said. I was hoarse as a crow. "One to work on and one backup. Warn whoever works on it to have a magic user standing by. That programme is almost certainly designed to wipe if anyone tries to use it anywhere but on that machine." I pointed my filthy thumb at the rubble. "I've done what I can, but it will need reinforcing when you try to run it."

I was, to tell the truth, quite worried about that. I'd wrapped all four disks in every protection I could think of, but I didn't have exact enough knowledge of the Emperor's methods to know what to protect them from.

"What are you going to do?" Dakros asked.

"I'm going to take the other two disks home and work on them there," I said. "Could you let me know anything—anything—that you find out from yours? You have local knowledge I don't. And I'll fax you when I've got something."

He responded by pointing his thumb at the vast heap of rubble and gave me a wry look. I remembered that the fax machine to which I was tuned was somewhere under there. So was my overnight bag.

"I'll call you," I amended. "Give me your battle-com number and I'll tune it to my fax machine at home."

He gave me the number, looking doubtful. "But how will you get home now the Magid Gate has gone?"

"That was only used by custom," I said. "I can go from anywhere." He looked so surprised and respectful that I felt that I had been boasting—and I had, a little. Some places you can't make transit from. But there was no problem with the courtyard. I said, "See you soon, I hope." Then I walked out across the court, the uphill Naywards way home.

36

FOUR

The first thing I did at home was to put the two disks into plastic with magically enhanced protection and then lock them in a drawer. I did that even before going to the bathroom and coughing up what felt like two pounds of brick dust. Then I showered and changed my clothes. By that time I felt slightly less shaken, but still too shaken to get back to work. I decided to take my filthy clothes to the cleaner instead and buy a new razor on the way. I was on my way out of the house when I heard piano music, loudly, from the living room.

I opened the door. The Diabelli variations were coming over my CD player, quite thunderously. "I don't remember leaving that on," I muttered, going to turn it off.

"You didn't," Stan's voice said. He sounded slightly ashamed. "It was in there and I found I could do that—turn it on. It's the kind of brain-music I seem to fancy in this state. I can turn it down if you'd rather." The music became suddenly blessedly faint.

"It's all right," I said. "I'm going out. Enjoy yourself till I get back."

When I got back, the same CD was still playing. It finished, and started all over again, while I was in the kitchen finding something to eat. I stood it for half an hour and then went in there. "Want me to put a different CD on for you?" I asked.

37

"No, no," Stan said. "This suits me fine. But I'll lower it right down while you tell me what's been going on."

The Diabelli variations once more sank to a distant tinkling. Invitation hung in the air. It seemed pretty clear that Stan was bored. It had not occurred to me before that a disembodied person could be bored—but why not? "There was a bomb in the Throne Room," I said, and sat down and told him the rest.

"Those disks'll wipe," he said decidedly, when I had done. "If there are any kids, no one will find them and that will be that. There'll be six trumped-up Emperors in the next year, and then the whole thing will fall apart. No more Empire. Just what's supposed to happen."

"Maybe," I said. "But I'm professionally bound to try to help—even though it almost certainly means ruining a computer over it."

"You can do that in your spare time if you want," he said. "Don't forget your main job is to find a Magid to replace me. You'd better go to Bristol tomorrow."

"No," I said. "Not with a computer puzzle like this one hanging over me. I couldn't concentrate."

I did not want to say I was sick to death of the fruitless Magid hunt. I thought of every other possible excuse instead. Stan protested. We argued for the entire length of the Diabelli variations. As they started yet again, I said, to placate him, "All right. I'll write the four we know about a letter, asking them to get in touch with me. How does that grab you?"

"I'd be surprised if anything grabbed me in this state," Stan retorted. "Fine. What are you going to tell them?"

"Different things, depending," I invented. "Thurless is a writer. I can send him a fan letter. Mallory's a student. She'll want money. I've already told her mother she's got a legacy. I can write about that. Fisk sounds as if she would be interested in a new miracle cure, and Kornelius Punt . . ."

"Yes?" said Stan.

My invention, which had been flowing so freely, dried up on Punt.

38

"He's been travelling. Ask him if he's interested in doing a travel book," Stan suggested.

"Good idea!" Because I knew he'd give me no peace until I did something, I wrote the letters then and there. I was rather pleased with my artistry. Regardless of the fact that I had never even seen a book by Mervin Thurless, I wrote lyrically of the beauties of his style. To Mallory, I wrote that she had inherited £100. I reckoned I could just about afford that much. To Tansy-Ann Fisk, I was the friend of a friend of a friend who had heard she was in a clinic and wanted to tell her about the marvels of the Stanley Diet. To Kornelius Punt, I was a small publisher touting for interesting books.

"What's this Stanley Diet?" Stan said at my shoulder.

"Airy nothing, like you," I said.

"I thought so," he said. "Go on. Take the mickey. I don't care."

I posted the letters and then, at last, Stan allowed me to get on with the Empire disks. It took me the next three days.

I started by studying one of the disks by every Magid means that were relevant. When I thought I knew enough about the nature of the program and the safeguards implanted in it, I stripped down my oldest computer and started forcing it to become Empire-compatible. This was a major task in itself. The Empire used a different size and shape of copy disk, different power and a more streamlined approach to programming. I had to render the metal and plastic of my poor old Amstrad into a sort of jelly and then harden it into the correct form. I had to create a power adaptor. Then I had to programme it to reflect, as near as I could conjecture, the nature of the machine I had copied the disks from. This was the hardest and most finicky part of all. I can safely say that only a Magid could have done it. I remember remarking to Stan, "Lucky I'm in practice with this sort of thing. It's probably cheating, but I use Magid ways a lot in my ordinary programming. Did you use Magid methods with your horses?"

There was no reply. I heard the Diabelli variations *again*, coming from my living room.

"I bet he did," I murmured. There is almost no way not to. It seems to permeate everything you do, being a Magid. Sometimes it's so nebulous as to seem like intuition. Sometimes, when you hit a fierce problem, there seems no way forward without, and you push, the way I was pushing that program then.

At the end of the first full day, I was ready for a trial. I put in the Empire disk and told it to copy to the hard disk. It resisted all my attempts to make it, even when I very cautiously took the protections off it. So I sighed, put the protections back, and told it to display its files. Nothing. I pushed, unwisely.

The computer went down so comprehensively that things melted inside. Small flames played over it, and I only just saved the power adaptor. I did not want to have to make another. I swore. I had to make haste to study the fused and mangled remains while they were still hot too, which was no fun. There turned out to have been no fewer than three magical safeguards embedded in that program, two major mistakes in my attempt at Empire software, and several more in my adaptation of the unfortunate Amstrad. I spent the evening feverishly tracing pathways.

"What did that fool Emperor think he was playing at?" I said irritably to Stan, through the tinkling of the CD player. "You'd almost think he'd said, 'I can't be Emperor when I'm dead, so I'll make sure nobody else can.'"

"Maybe he did," Stan said. "But some of the other ones who were blown up must have been in the know. He maybe relied on them. It doesn't matter. You don't want to get involved."

"It's the people who matter," I said, thinking of the strained, nightmare look on the face of General Dakros. "There's an ordinary, honest man over there, trying to cope. There are millions of other ordinary people who could get slaughtered when the men of high rank in the other ten worlds start to move in on Dakros. There's going to be an almighty civil war. It may have started already."

"Don't get sentimental," said Stan. "Either the high-rankers will win, or your general will get a taste for ruling and keep the Empire for himself. These things happen."

That night in bed, I had to admit he was right. But I also wanted to solve the *problem*.

The next morning I got a letter from young Mallory. The hard-up student had replied by return of post.

Dear Mr. Venables,
           I don't mind admitting I could use a hundred quid. I shall be at this address until July, so you can send the money any time. But do you mind telling me just who left me this legacy? I am an adopted child. I know nothing of my real family, and I thought they knew nothing of me.
        Yours,
        M. Mallory.

"A graceless and slightly suspicious letter," I remarked to Stan.

"Yes. You get quite a feel of her from it," he said. "You'll know her if you see her across the street after this."

He was right. The letter was full of a personality. The paper had evidently been borrowed or purloined from the uncle. It was headed, in gothic type, *From Ted Mallory, author of Demons Innumerable*, and printed on a hideous dot-matrix printer with almost no ink. But it all breathed a very strong personality.

"A nuisance, her being adopted," I fretted. "Who on earth can her legacy be from?"

"Me," said Stan. "Say I did research and thought I was her uncle. I did have several very randy brothers, so it could even be true."

I dashed off a courteous note to this strong personality, saying that I would give her the money and explain its origin in person shortly, and got back to work on my

41

second-oldest computer, a Toshiba I had barely touched for a year.

It was hard, detailed going. And it put me under pressure, knowing that I only had the one disk left. I wished I had not left two with Dakros now. In fact I became harassed enough towards the end of that day to get through to the com number Dakros had given me and ask him to spare me another. The answer came back, a prompt and laconic fax:

Both disks melted.

Damn. And I really did not want to melt another computer. There seemed nothing for it but to cross my fingers and put the second disk in.

VIRUS DETECTED, announced the Toshiba.

I got the disk out quick, but at least I was on familiar ground here. I clicked my tongue at the paranoia of the Emperor and set about dismantling the virus. It was a magical implantation. It was like undoing old lace.

"Aren't you going to eat today?" Stan asked a while later.

I looked up to find night had come, early, since it was early in the year, but time to stop for a bit. I made a cup of coffee while I wondered what to eat. Next thing I knew, I was in front of the Toshiba again. It was after midnight. But the virus had gone when I tried the disk.

"You're getting obsessed with that Empire," Stan warned me.

"Correction," I said. "I'm obsessed with a computer problem. It's not every day I get a magical virus."

The third day, I actually got the program to copy and display. That was a relief, since I could now reshape some of my own disks and make backups. But it did me no good. All I could get on the screen was the statement that Timotheo was deleted and the perpetual PASSWORD REQUIRED. This was maddening, since I had been behind the scenes of it, so to speak, dealing with the virus, and ought to have

42

been able to bypass the need for a password. But if I tried that, I got nothing at all. And I did not dare push, Magid fashion, for fear of another meltdown.

Stan heard me swearing and drifted into my workroom. "Give it a password then," he said. "And when you've a moment, put me another music disc on, would you?"

"What's the matter with Diabelli? Have you learnt it by heart?" I said.

"Every note," he said, quite seriously. "I know Beethoven like a friend now."

I put him on a choral medley, because that made a change, and got through to Dakros again. The reply was from the mage Jeffros:

Empire passwords are usually seven letters. We didn't try many because the disks melted at every third mistake. But the High Lady Alexandra suspects the word may have been from a nursery rhyme.

A nursery rhyme! Well, Lady Alexandra was definitely not just a pretty face and the suggestion fitted, as we were dealing with children here. Empire nursery rhymes are not so different from Earth's. They are one of the things we Magids put into circulation. But seven letters, like a mad hand of Scrabble, in any one of the fourteen languages spoken in the Empire! Actually I was full of hope as I went to set up one of my other computers to run through all the possibilities. I think my only problem was surprise that Timos IX knew such things as nursery rhymes existed.

Just then I heard Stan's new music lustily bellowing, "In Babylon, the mighty city!"

It gave me a *frisson*. Babylon is one of the deep secrets of the Magids. But it was, for this reason, also a nursery rhyme. I went to the Toshiba and told it "BABYLON".

It was right.

World maps began to unfold on the screen, Empire fashion, rippling with lines like isobars on weather charts, map after map, world after world, like half of Infinity. I leant back and watched them, wondering why the Emperor had chosen this particular password from this particular rhyme. Babylon was never a place in the Empire. After a while, a moving frieze of graphics appeared, humans and centaurs passing in profile across the shifting maps. They had the look of real people taken from photographs and they all seemed to be different, but it was hard to tell if they were intended to be meaningful or just an indication that the program was now truly running. Finally, the screen cleared. Letters said TYPE KNARROS.

I typed "KNARROS."

NOW TYPE THE NAME OF MY GODDESS came the reply.

I turned frantically to the computer that held my Empire database, knowing I was going to be too late. "Stan!" I shouted. "Stan, what's the name of the Emperor's dismal goddess?"

"Can't remember," he shouted back across what seemed to be the Hallelujah Chorus. "Some damn great mouthful."

I remembered it myself—Aglaia-Ualaia—just as the disk wiped.

"And that's the man who knew every racehorse from 1935!" I said. "Well, at least I have backups."

I did it all over again. By the early evening I was ready again, this time with a list of various other gods, heroes and historical personages from the Empire, just in case. I had developed a hearty respect for the Emperor's paranoia. But it seemed that the name of his goddess was his last resort. I typed "KNARROS" followed by "AGLAIA-UALAIA" and a list came up.

KNARROS CODEWORLD LIXOS
FEMALE B. 3390 CODENAME NATHALIA
FEMALE B. 3390 CODENAME PHYSILLA
FEMALE B. 3400 CODENAME ANANTE
MALE B. 3401 CODENAME EKLOS
MALE B. 3402 CODENAME MAGRAKES
PLUS TWO MALE CENTAURS B. 3394 AND 3396

CODEWORLD BABYLON
FEMALE B. 3393 CODENAME TIMOAEA
MALE B. 3399 CODENAME JELLIERO

Each of the names was followed by clumps of letters, numbers and signs, which meant nothing to me, but which I supposed were the Empire's version of blood groups or genetic codes or some such. The two lists were followed by the statement:

KNARROS WILL SUPPLY IDENTIFICATION AND
AUTHENTICATION OF HEIR(S) ONLY TO ACCREDITED
MESSENGER ON PROOF OF THE DEATH OF TIMOS IX

"Gotcha!" I said. I opened a bottle of wine to celebrate before I endeavoured to get through to Dakros on his com number. After the fun and games of the last few days, it was a simple matter to splice him into my telephone. I got him after half an hour, sounding far-off, crackly and very tired. "Two sets of them," I said, "on two codenamed worlds." I read him what they were.

He was nothing like as jubilant. "Who is this Knarros?"

"Some kind of guardian, I imagine. He might come forward when he hears—"

"Well, he hasn't," he said. "And which bloody worlds are Lixos and Babylon meant to be?"

"You could get the Imperial Secret Service on to it," I suggested.

"I could if they weren't all mindless gangsters," he retorted. "We executed most of them yesterday. Trying to stage a coup. And," he returned to what was obviously the main difficulty, "I don't like the way it all seems to hang on this Knarros. You have to go through him for the eldest boy, even if it is on another world. What if he's untrustworthy or someone does him in?"

"Blame the stupidity of your late ruler," I said.

"I don't like it," he said.

"Neither do I," I said. The fact that the password was

45

Babylon still made my back creep. "I've faxed the list to Jeffros. Let him put people to work on it and tell him to let me know if you need my help."

"I'm bound to," he said. "This is a stupid over-secretive mess!"

I rang off, sighing. "He's going to want me to find Babylon for him. I can see it coming."

"You can't do that!" Stan said sharply.

"I think we're talking about two different things, Stan," I said. "Or at least I hope we are. Mind turning that music down? I've got a headache."

FIVE

I drove to Bristol the next day with a passenger. I had not meant to go so soon, in spite of Stan's nagging. It seemed to me that I had earned a day with my feet up. But my neighbour rang my doorbell just at the point where I had drunk enough of the wine to quench my headache.

Andrew Connick is a strange fellow, an inventor. Unlike the unfortunate Derek Mallory, Andrew has succeeded in pushing his creations out of his head into reality, and he holds several dozen patents, all for very useful gadgets. My favourite coffee-pot is one of them. Andrew gave it me to test. Like me, he lives alone—in one of the only two other houses in Weavers End, which is bigger and fancier than mine; it has a large garden with a pond in it, which I sometimes envy him for, until I think of all the digging and weeding Andrew has to do. The third house in Weavers End contains the Gibbs family: Mrs. Gibbs cleans my house, her daughter cleans Andrew's. Mrs. Gibbs tells me her daughter says Andrew Connick is a very strange man. And I believe her—though I also believe that Miss Gibbs tells Andrew that her mother says Rupert Venables is pretty strange too.

He was standing on my doorstep looking as if he was not sure why he was there. "Hello, Andrew," I said. "Come on in." I supposed Stan would have the sense to keep quiet, even though choral music was blasting out around me.

"I'll not come in," he said, in his *distrait*, Nordic way.

47

Actually I believe him to be Scottish, but I think of him as Nordic because he has that bleached, handsome head and those large bones I always associate with Scandinavians. He is very tall. I am just under six feet and he towered over me, looking uncertain. "No, I'll not enter," he said. "I just came to ask you to give me a lift tomorrow."

"Car broken down again?" I said. My heart sank. The last two occasions Andrew's car had failed him, between Christmas and New Year, I had clocked up over six hundred miles shuttling Andrew and various spare parts between here and Cambridge—and Ely and Huntingdon and St Neots, not to speak of Peterborough and King's Lynn.

"Aye," he said. "It won't be moving."

My heart rebelled against more shuttling. I had earned a rest. "I'm so sorry," I said. "I'm not going to be here tomorrow. I've got to go to Bristol."

He was silent, with his large pale eyes on the distance above my head, evidently thinking. After a while he said, "I'll come to Bristol then."

I had a mad feeling that if I had said I was going to drive to Carlisle, Edinburgh or Canterbury he would have agreed to come to any of those places too. "It's quite a way," I said, in a last-ditch effort to dissuade him. "I'm making an early start."

He thought about that too. "I can be ready by six."

"Oh, for God's sake, I didn't mean that early!" I said, giving in. "Let's say eight-thirty, shall we?"

"I'll be there," he said, and left.

So I found myself committed to driving to Bristol. "Are you coming with me?" I asked Stan. "Or do you think you might frighten Andrew?"

There was one of Stan's unhappy pauses. Then he said, "I don't think I can, lad. I seem to be confined to your house."

"Are you *sure*?" I said. "Where else have you tried to go?"

"Beyond the garden gate. Past your barn at the back. I couldn't manage either direction," he said.

I was annoyed. It had been a tiring few days. "What's the good of having a ghostly adviser, if you can't be around to advise me?" I demanded. "I was relying on your opinion about this girl."

"Then stand on your own feet for a change!" his voice retorted. "It's what Them Up There seem to want you to do."

I knew I had hurt his feelings. He did not speak to me again that night, and I heard not a word from him in the morning, not even when I arranged for him a floating stack of CDs, each one magically programmed to hop in or out of the CD player when he gave it the word. I was proud of that magic. And I considered it thoughtful too. So I was offended in my turn. I went out to my car in chilly silence and found Andrew waiting beside it.

Andrew is actually a good passenger. He does not make conversation, or talk about other motorists, or make nervous comments on how fast I drive (which is *fast*). He just sits there. This sometimes gets unnerving. When I got particularly unnerved—the first time was two-thirds of the way round the M25—I asked him about his latest invention. And he told me, in his deceptively slow and meditative way, which nevertheless described the thing—he called it a "swing-ratchet"—so accurately that I could probably have done drawings and patented it myself. Then he stopped talking.

Some way down the M4, I became unnerved again. But I felt it was my turn to tell him something. Usually when I drive him anywhere I tell him about any software problem I have lately run into. Very often he has set me on the right lines just with one of his slow, wondering questions. This time, however, my problems had been something of a deep secret. There did not seem to be any way to talk about them. Or was there? In a world tending Naywards like ours, no one is going to suspect you are talking about a collapsing Empire three universes away.

"Tell me," I said, "what would you think if you found

49

the password you needed to access someone else's program was a sort of secret codeword the programmer shouldn't really have thought of using in that way? I mean, suppose the password was something silly like Humpty-Dumpty to a very serious program—say, something about genetics—and *you* knew that Humpty-Dumpty was actually a codeword for something equally serious—say, classified military information. What would you think? Would you put it down to coincidence, or what?"

Andrew said ruminatively, "I'm told there is no such thing as coincidence."

I was told that too and, what is more, told it as a Magid, which made it very significant. But it seemed to me that Andrew was just uttering a platitude. I was disappointed.

He said, "Is there no chance the user of the password hacked into the other classified material?"

I said, "Well, it's always *possible*," to cover up what I was really talking about, and added, "but it's unlikely to many decimal places. Virtually impossible, in fact."

"If it's that unlikely," Andrew meditated, "then I reckon you have to go back in time, to some wee point where the codeword was known to someone who told it to both parties—a teacher who recited 'Humpty-Dumpty,' to take your example, and both users learnt it from him. And this teacher would have given both of them the idea that the words were somehow important, maybe—but that is not essential."

"That," I said, "is very true." I drove digesting this thought. Were Magid secrets known in the Koryfonic Empire sometime in the past? I did not think they were supposed to be known there now, any more than they should be known here on Earth. There are some things that even Ayewards worlds should not know yet. But there are always hints, vestiges of knowledge both from the past and the future, that Magids leave for people to pick up when the time is right. Babylon was certainly one of those. I suppose it worried me that Timos IX was an unlikely person to be interested in such a hint.

Here Andrew startled me, the way he often did, by saying musingly, "There is very seldom any true secret."

"Right," I said. "Things get out. Look at King Midas and his ass's ears."

I don't think either of us said anything else until we reached Bristol and he asked to be dropped by the Nails. I got lost getting him there. It was midday or after when I finally dropped him. "When do you want to be picked up?" I asked him.

"Oh," he said, and thought. Then he gave the smile that always made me realize he was not the absent-minded fool he often seemed. It changed his distraught, neurotic face quite radically, so that you saw there was a deep mind behind it. "I'll find my own way home," he said. "I don't know how long I shall need to be here."

That was a relief. It meant my time was my own. I found a promising Italian restaurant and treated myself to a good leisurely meal. Later, I was glad I did. The rest of that day was pure frustration. It was typical of the hunt for Mallory. And I still don't see how she did it, but I am sure now that it was all her doing.

First, I lost the place where I had parked my car. When I found it, it had acquired a parking ticket. Then I got lost again driving to Mallory's new address, regardless of the fact that I had been to the street before, and when I did get there, there was nowhere to park, in that street or the next. It was after three when I finally rang the bell of the tall, smartly painted Regency house.

The woman who answered the door was as smartly painted as the house. She would probably have been good-looking, in a dark, gypsyish way, if she had not worked so hard at it. Under the make-up, her face had the look of someone who dieted fiercely. Her dark hair had been enhanced with bronze streaks and her strenuous slimness enhanced by a tight black skirt and a designer jumper. The jumper fascinated me. It was one of those which have a white satin pattern, sewn with beads, randomly appliquéd to one shoulder. It was the most pointless pattern I had ever

51

seen. So fascinated was I that it took me a moment even to realize that she was too old to be Maree Mallory. She was in her mid-thirties at least.

She tapped the doorframe with a shapely red fingernail and said, "Yes?" impatiently.

"I'm sorry to disturb you," I said. "I'm looking for Maree Mallory. About a legacy."

As I spoke the name "Maree" her face hardened. It was clear she hated Maree and now disliked me by association. "I'm afraid my niece has just gone out," she said. I could tell she was pleased to frustrate me.

I said, "Have you any idea when she might be back?"

"Not the foggiest," she said, with evident pleasure. "When my niece takes it into her head to go gallivanting, it's anyone's guess how long she'll be gone." Then she added, as if it were a major tragedy, "She took my son Nick with her too." Her manner suggested that Maree had torn the infant from her arms.

"I'm sorry to hear that," I said, to both things. "Do you know where they've gone?"

"All I know," she said, with satisfaction, "is that she drove off almost the moment you rang the doorbell."

She was right to be satisfied. It is always worse to know you have just missed someone. In the normal way, that is. But for a Magid that is not such bad news. "Thank you," I said humbly. "Perhaps you could tell your niece that I called." I gave her a business card. From the way that she took it, I could tell that it would be in the wastebin, in pieces, seconds after she shut the front door. I gave a last fascinated look at the design on her jumper—the satin had scalloped edges and two beaded tendrils that impinged hungrily on her right breast—and went away.

Janine, I thought. That had to have been Janine. Poor sick Mr. Mallory had correctly pronounced her to be a bitch.

Then I dismissed her from my thoughts, jumper and all, and took out the letter Maree Mallory had written me. Everyone leaves traces of themselves in the air as they go.

These last for ten minutes strongly and can be detected for another twenty minutes after that—or more, if the person has a powerful character. In letters, traces of personality can, linger sometimes for fifty years. And Maree Mallory had left her strong character all over that letter. All I had to do was match it with any nearby traces.

They were just up the street, those traces, mixed with pungent blue smoke from a car in dire need of an oil-change. I remember at the time misguidedly finding the traces rather agreeable. They had a valiant, pugnacious and even humorous feel—as if Mallory, despite the misfortunes that had evidently befallen her recently, was holding herself together and fighting fate. And Janine had been quite accurate. The girl had been driving out of one end of the street literally as I walked into it the other end. I was—again misguidedly—delighted. I sprinted back to my car and set off in pursuit.

I followed those traces for half an hour. They led me on a tangled trail, through streets broad and narrow, under other streets, over bridges, downhill, uphill so steeply that once I stalled my engine, and out along small snaking roads across green parkland. I saw Regency terraces, pink Gothic towers, modern office blocks, cobbled alleys, Brunel's iron ship and the M32. From the map that I had spread out on the seat beside me, I reckoned, with growing exasperation, that I had seen every part of the city north of the harbour—and all without once coming within hailing distance of the car I was following. I hadn't even identified it—let alone discovered what the girl thought she was doing—but since the narrower streets where she had been were invariably pungent with oil, I guessed I was looking for a fairly old car.

Guessing is a mistake. You should keep to the traces. About this point, the trail plunged steeply down to the waterside again. Following it, I saw ahead of me a small dingy Morris with a woman driving and a child's seat in the back. Ahah! I thought. I gave chase, sending Magid messages to the driver to draw in somewhere and talk. There was no response. I pursued the Morris across two branches of river into a place where a one-way system induced mad circularities and the growing amount of traffic reduced us both to a crawl. The Morris was always three cars ahead of me and its driver refused to respond to my messages in any way. My frustration mounted with every yard. I would have given up, except there she was, so *near*.

Then the brown Morris abruptly turned off into a side road and I realized it was not the right car after all. The traces of Mallory had completely vanished. I had probably lost them from the moment I assumed the Morris was hers.

I cursed. I decided to give up and drive home. Then, with uneasy thoughts of Stan's comments, I supposed that the obvious thing to do was to drive back to the aunt's house and lie in wait there. I set out to do that, but by then, of course, I was lost again.

I fought through the ever-increasing traffic, looking for a bridge, and no bridge appeared. Instead, I found myself to my bewilderment driving steeply uphill on what was almost a country road. The traffic was appalling. We crawled. More cars came crawling up behind me. I had ample leisure to see I was driving along one side of a very considerable ravine and that the whole of Bristol was now spread out or piled up on the other side of it.

That settles it! I thought. I'm driving home. And resigned myself to having to do it via Wales or something.

But at that point, the traffic ahead speeded up, the city vista vanished behind trees and a notice by the road stated that I could turn right for Bristol via tollbridge. I turned right thankfully. And the tollbridge, when I reached it, was a perilously high suspension bridge across the gorge—a ribbon of road hung from cliff to cliff between two quasi-Egyptian towers. I put money in a slot and rumbled across it dubiously, sparing glances through its sides at a muddy trickle of river flaring in the sunset some hundreds of feet below.

Some fool had stopped a car in the middle of the road just beyond the bridge. I nearly ran into it.

I stamped on my brakes. Squeals behind me told me that a line of other motorists was doing the same. Not only was the car stopped, but its driver's door was open blocking what was left of the road. There was no room at all to get by because the road was divided by a steep kerb to stop cars going the wrong way on the bridge. Motorists were stopped on the other side of this kerb, staring. The way they stared told me that my first idea—that this was an accident—was wrong. This car had been stopped deliberately. Then I saw its driver.

She was dancing. Dancing on the sidewalk beside her car.

She was a small, unlovely woman in glasses, with a figure like a sack of straw with a string tied round it. And she danced. She bent her knees, she hopped, she cavorted. Her ragbag skirt swirled, her untidy hair flew and her spectacles slid on her barely- existent nose. Beside her, her passenger also cavorted. Both of them waved their arms. Both bounded about. He was a teenage boy, dark and startlingly handsome, and he towered over her in his dancing, rather sheepishly. He had the air of one who was only dancing because she was not going to drive on unless he did. I exonerated him. As for her . . .

I put my thumb on my hooter-button and held it there. I was not the only one.

The woman stopped twirling, but only to bend at the knees and shoot out her fingers—those fingers were adorned with nails long enough to be classed as murder weapons—flick, flick, flick, towards the road. It was a totally contemptuous gesture. The boy did the same, self-consciously. I could see they were both singing, or chanting something, as they flicked. Then, calm as you please, they both went back to dancing.

I was angry enough to augment the sound of my horn with a blast of magic. It fair bellowed. Behind me, the bridge was jammed solid and half the cars on it were hooting too.

The boy at least noticed. He looked unhappy. But the

woman went on dancing and he obediently imitated her. They did another flick, flick, flick of the fingers, this time in the direction of the rocky bank. And then they danced some more. I lost my temper.

I took my thumb off the hooter. I turned off my engine, pocketed my keys and got out of my car. They were doing another flick, flick, flick as I reached the woman's car. Her keys were inside it, dangling from the ignition. I nearly slammed the door on them—except that then she would have had to pick the lock to get in and no other car would be able to move until she had. Instead, I stalked round the bonnet of her car and confronted the capering pair on the pavement.

"Luck, luck, luck," they were chanting. Flick, flick, flick.

"Do you mind holding your Sabbath somewhere else?" I said. I had meant to say much more, but I had got so far when the traces of her personality hit me. She was Mallory. Of course. She had done nothing but lead me a dance all along.

She stopped dancing. She turned to me as if I had just crawled out of a sewer. Then, with immense disgust, she put one of her outsize fingernails to the bridge of her glasses and looked me up and down all over again.

Two can play at that game. I took my left lens between my finger and thumb and focused the look right back at her. "Maree Mallory, I presume," I said contemptuously, before she had quite got round to speaking.

"Get lost," she said, as she had been meaning to say all along. She had an unpleasingly loud, gloomy voice, with a sort of sob embedded in it. Then, belatedly, she registered what I had said. "You may know me," she retorted, "but I don't know you and I don't want to." Beyond her, I saw the boy—who must be Nick Mallory and not the infant Janine had implied—looking as if he wanted to get down and lie under her car.

I was angrier than ever. It was the sob in her voice, I think. "Rupert Venables," I said—or rather, snapped. "I wrote to you." I let go of my lens and brought out my wallet. "I've been looking for you all over town to give you your wretched legacy. Here you are." I held out to her in a fan the ten ten-pound notes I had made ready to support my story.

She looked dumbfounded. And, as I had hoped, she automatically put out her hand for the money. I counted the ten notes into it with angry ceremony. There began to be yells, whistles and cheers from the motorists watching across the road, and from some of those behind, who were now either hanging out of their windows or standing irritably beside their cars. Mallory's face turned a dull, furious red. Her cousin's dark face was redder still. Mallory's chin bunched and her hand flinched, as if she wanted to throw the notes into the road. But the money meant too much to her. She hung on to it.

"Ten," I said, "making a hundred. Now will you please get into your bloody car and drive it out of my way!"

She did not answer, just strutted haughtily to her open door, to further hoots and cheers from the line of motorists. The boy folded himself in through the other door with the speed of an early silent film.

"Was it worth the money then?" the driver of the car behind mine called out, as I went back to my own car.

I wanted to say it was indeed worth £100, just to be able to wash my hands finally of Mallory and her family, but I could hardly explain why. I simply shrugged and smiled and got behind my wheel as Mallory started her car with a leap and roared away in a cloud of blue oily smoke. Her car was nothing like as elderly as the brown Morris. She just didn't look after it, evidently.

I was glad I did not have Andrew with me on the way back. I was able to swear the whole way home. I arrived still raging.

"What's the matter now?" Stan asked from my dark living room, over the remorseless rhythm of a Bach fugue.

"Mallory," I said, snapping on the light. "If anyone wants to make that girl a Magid, it will be over my dead body!

57

She's . . . unspeakable! And ugly with it. Besides being mad." And I angrily described my day's adventures.

"Hm. Did she show any talent at all?" he asked.

"I'm sure she has bags of it," I said. "Enough to keep me away from her all day. Which is where I want to stay! I don't want any part of someone who uses their talent to hold up rush-hour traffic by dancing widdershins in the street. Not even ashamed of it, either! At least her teenage cousin had the grace to look embarrassed."

"Look on the bright side," Stan said. "Mallory can't behave like a Magid. So you've eliminated one candidate. Now you can start thinking about the other four."

"What fun!" I said savagely, and stormed into the kitchen. I said to myself as I tore open the fridge, "And how am I supposed to look at four people when they're scattered all over the globe? Japan, New Zealand, Bosnia, Ohio—oh, *fun*!"

Stan had evidently followed me. His voice said at my shoulder, "I've been thinking about that."

I slammed the fridge shut. "Don't *do* that!"

"When you've had something to eat and cooled off a bit, I'll tell you," he said.

SIX

It took me another two hours to simmer down. That only happened when I admitted to myself that not only had I been hoping that Mallory would turn out to be Magid material, but I had also, on the basis of her personality trace, been building up a picture of a brave person in considerable adversity. She had a broken home, she had been jilted by this man Robbie, she had no money and was forced to live with a bitchy aunt, and on top of this her father (adoptive father, I supposed) was dying of cancer. I had been prepared to be wonderfully sorry for her. But all that went when I saw her grotesque baglike figure prancing at the side of the road. Then, after the way she had first ignored and then looked at me, I wanted to go and shake the hand of that ex-boyfriend and tell him he was well out of it. I was well out of it. It was worth a hundred quid—cheap at the price.

"Ready to talk now?" Stan asked.

"Yes," I said.

"What you want to do," he said, "is collect all your candidates in one place and interview them for the job. Am I correct?"

I had been brooding with my chin on my chest. I sat up. "But how?"

"The extreme way," he said. "Tweak their fatelines. Bring them to you."

"Is it permissible?" I said. I had thought that way was

only for emergencies. Anything that involved meddling in someone's personal life without their permission was to be considered only in extreme need.

"Yes, you're allowed to do it if you're choosing a new Magid. That's important," Stan said. "You'd be doing it anyway by appointing someone, if you think about it."

"OK, but not tonight," I said.

What Stan was suggesting was a fairly arduous process. I have always thought it lucky it is so difficult, or Magids— and other people—might be tempted to do it for trivial reasons. Done often, it could bring chaos to more than one world. It can also bring chaos down on the Magid who does the working, unless it is done carefully, with proper safeguards. If you don't get it right, you can tangle your own fatelines disastrously with those of the people you are trying to influence. A Magid is supposed to be a free agent. One of the things which is done when you become a Magid is that your personal fatelines are freed from those of the rest of the multiverse. Rather a lonely state, actually.

Anyway, I knew it was going to take days and I didn't want to be interrupted. The next day, I finished all my ordinary business (somewhat late, but too bad—Mallory's fault) and then disconnected my phones from this world and the others. I shut down all the computers, including the one devoted to Magid business, and hung what amounted to a "Do Not Disturb" notice on that one.

I was a little irritated to find a series of faxes from General Dakros had come in overnight. The first said triumphantly that his experts had deciphered the genetic codes on the two lists: they would be able to recognise all the heirs when they found them. The second told me that Knarros was still untraced; the third that Jeffros thought Knarros was hidden by magic. The fourth asked me outright to come and discover Knarros for them.

I faxed back briskly that I saw no reason why they should maintain the Emperor's secrecy, and suggested that they advertise for Knarros in the media. Then I unplugged the machine.

"See?" I said to Stan. "Not sentimental at all."

Then I set to work with a large globe of the world, pins and strands of cotton. It was important to find a point in this country to which it was best to summon my four candidates. Because this was fateline work, the place had to be a node of power (there are a surprising number of these nodes in the British Isles) and the distances between this place and each of the four people had to satisfy mathematical laws. It also had to be somewhere where any of them might naturally expect to go. Even though they would be tugged to this spot by a series of Magid-made accidents, I could not stretch the laws of probability too far for fear the three I did not select would notice.

This was why I ruled out all solitary nodes like Stonehenge, or most castles, or that hidden valley in Derbyshire, and looked mainly at towns or at country places where there were conference centres. Before long, I was sitting in a heap of guidebooks and information leaflets, darting between these and the globe, and then to the detailed maps spread out on the floor. I needed a mundane, normal-seeming node. Stan was a great help here. As a jockey, he had rushed all over the country to racecourses in every corner of it, and he knew hotels and nodes I had never heard of.

Myself, I had hoped to bring everyone together in London, but that did not satisfy the numerical conditions. Annoyingly, it would have been fine had Mallory still been in the equation. I found I was interrupted here by a great rush of anger and exasperation at Mallory. How *dared* she lead me such a dance! How dared she go *on* doing so, even when I had eliminated her!

Stan recalled me by suggesting we considered some of the nodes in the Midlands. There are some good strong ones there. I wondered about Nottingham, but the numbers were off there too.

"Pity, that," Stan said. "Nottingham's a place where everyone goes sooner or later. All sorts of reasons. You want a lot of reasons. Concerts, conferences—or a race-course would do it."

"There are reasons for going to Birmingham," I said, "but the node there's only a pinprick. How about Stratford-on-Avon?"

"Too many tourists," he said. "Is Wigan any good?"

Wigan was numerically wrong. After hours of discussion and measuring and reading brochures, we settled on a medium-sized town called Wantchester. We both knew it. Stan said there were at least two good hotels there because of the racecourse. The guidebooks claimed there were conference facilities and a factory that made small-arms. These were clearly new since Stan's day, and mine. Stan remembered a pleasant, sleepy town. My memories were from a summer holiday there with my family, and I mostly remembered the river. There had been a fishing competition there for children. I had been in the grip of a fishing craze—I suppose I would be about nine at that time—and I had eagerly enrolled in the competition. I fished all day without the slightest luck. I was, I remember, disentangling my line from a willow tree for at least the fortieth time when my brother Will arrived and wanted to try his luck too. He never wanted to be outdone by his younger brothers.

The supervisor must have been very good-humoured. He gave Will instructions and Will borrowed my rod, and the supervisor left us to it. Will, in his usual way of always succeeding at everything, almost instantly hooked a fine fat fish. He struck at precisely the right moment and landed it perfectly. Then there was terrible trouble, because Will couldn't bear to kill it and neither could I. It flopped about madly. We shouted for the supervisor, but he was out of hearing, and we were forced to deal with it ourselves. Between us, we succeeded in getting the hook out of its mouth and we threw it back in the river, where it floated on its side, convulsing and obviously dying. Will realized he had half-killed it. He burst into tears, even though he was thirteen. I felt awful. I kept trying to get the fish out of the river again and I couldn't. We were in this state when our brother Simon wandered by. Simon hates killing things, so he had kept away from the fishing. When he saw us, Will in tears and me white and dithering, he simply waded into the water, fetched out the fish and whacked its head on a stone. "There," he said, and went on his way. I gave up fishing after that. Will never tried again.

Later on, these memories of Wantchester struck me as decidedly inauspicious. Maybe they did even at the time. If so, I dismissed them, because I was tired of looking. Wantchester fitted our requirements. Stan and I both knew the town. That was sufficient.

"Wantchester it is, then," we said.

The next step was, of course, to go to the place and check it out. "I wish you could come too," I said to Stan.

"You don't need me to help you look at a town," he said, threatening huffiness. I was beginning to see that Stan got irritated whenever I went somewhere without him. I said no more.

The next day I drove up to Wantchester and found the place still very pleasant, despite a one-way system and the cold wind of late February. I even took a walk by the river for old times' sake. There were willow trees, currently bare, and brown water swirling under the bridge, just as I remembered, but the river walk was curtailed since that far-off holiday by the new factory built on the riverside. So I walked back into the town, to the large hotel I had seen standing across the end of the main square. The hotel I remembered dimly, although we had stayed in a guest-house, but my chief memory was of the way the square was more like a very wide street, with a market in it. To my joy, the square (or street) was full of stalls that day too, and I stared at crockery, fruit and clothing, much as there had been when I was a nine-year-old, all the way to the hotel.

I was rather disconcerted to find it was called Hotel Babylon.

There is no such thing as coincidence, thought I, and

pushed through the large glass doors. Inside it was large and hushed and a queer mixture of modern décor with traditional market-town habits. There seemed to be mirrors everywhere and the receptionist was foreign, but the place was filled with huntin'-and-fishin' types who were here for the horse sales, and lunch was traditional and nourishing, served by staff with local accents. As I ate chicken and mushroom pie among the mirrors, I realized that the building was actually on the node. Better and better. After lunch, I enquired about booking a room for the Easter weekend. Stan and I had settled on Easter because that is a powerful time-node.

I could get no sense out of the foreign lady. I asked to see the manager. His name was Alfred Douglas, but that was not his fault. Easter weekend? he said. He was very sorry, but all the rooms were taken by a convention over Easter.

I nearly went away. Possibly I should have done. Things would certainly have turned out very differently if I had. I was within a whisker of deciding to try another town when it occurred to me to ask what kind of convention—expecting the reply to be Freemasons, Social Workers or some kind of Business Training.

A book-lovers' convention, Mr. Alfred Douglas told me. Science fiction and fantasy—or he believed the term might be speculative fiction. That kind of area, sir, anyway.

There is no such thing as coincidence! I thought, marvelling. Mervin Thurless *wrote* science fiction. According to my American contacts, Fisk had once taught a course about writing it. I didn't know how Punt and Gabrelisovic felt about the genre, but here were half my candidates at least ready to fit in. Two of them could come here in the most natural manner possible.

"But that's just what I was looking for!" I said.

Deeper enquiries elicited the fact that the convention guaranteed to fill the hotel for five days and did the booking for its members. But Mr. Alfred Douglas was happy to let me have the name, address and telephone number of the organizer. He was called Rick Corrie. I phoned him from the hotel.

He was very pleasant. I liked at once the voice that answered, "PhantasmaCon hotel liaison here." We had a very agreeable conversation, in the course of which I discovered that Corrie, like me, worked with computers from his home. Certainly I could join the convention, he said, and named a modest fee—that he apologized for: it seemed the sum had gone up after Christmas. He would, he said, send me the details and the hotel booking-form, and urged me to get it back to him quickly because the hotel was already quite full.

I gave him my address. "What happens if I send my form back but you find the hotel is booked solid?" I asked.

"Oh, we try to fit everyone in," he said cheerfully. "A lot of fans sleep on the floor—don't tell Alfred Douglas that—but I've got the Station Hotel lined up to take the overflow if there is one. But you'll want to be in the Babylon if you can. That's where the action will be."

I promised to get my application back to him by return of post and rang off. Then I did a small amount of adjusting before I left, to ensure that I and my four candidates would indeed have rooms here. And—perhaps it was the thought of a letter by return of post—I found myself once more interrupted by a surge of rage against Mallory. So, as an afterthought, I did some more adjusting, to make sure that Mallory could have nothing to do with this. Then I went home, rather pleased with my day's work.

There followed a time of intense, detailed labour to wind the fatelines in exactly the right way. Almost the only communication I had with the outside worlds was when I received from Rick Corrie a bundle of highly peculiar stuff. Opening it, I wished that Fisk, Punt or Thurless had replied to me anything like so promptly (in fact, none of them ever replied: either my letters went astray or they did not strike any of the three as important) and was once again seized with irrational rage at Mallory. My fingers quivered with fury as I examined Corrie's bundle.

Some of it was the booking-forms he had promised me. That concerning the hotel was normal enough—except that I was required to state whether or not I wanted mushrooms for breakfast—but the booking-form for the actual convention was full of curious passages. I read: "Fans wishing to enter the Masquerade should state in advance whether Animal, Human or Other. We're having three classes this year" and a little further on: "PhantasmaCook entries must be checked in on arrival. The hotel manager has asked that no actual construction of green slime etc. be done in the hotel bedrooms" and right at the end: "We regret having to ban explosions, but after last year the cost of insurance is now too high."

Wondering what had happened last year, I turned to the thing labelled *Progress Report III* and stared at it. My face was probably a study. Stan demanded to know what was the matter.

" 'Hobbits will be mustering under Gandalf as usual in the Ops Room,' " I read out to him. " 'Esoterica with the Master Mage is in a dimension yet to be fixed . . . Filking will be in Home Universe this year . . . Writers' Circle is rounding nicely in the hands of Wendy the Willow but there are rumours of another. Watch this space . . . Bumpkin has agreed to handle Games and Games Workshop . . . No charges of fraud in the Tarot classes this year, please. Our new reader is a genuine sensitive . . . There are still a few places in the Dealers Room. Apply to Eisenstein . . . Security will be handled by HitlerEnterprises and all swords are to be in their charge until Sunday . . .' Stan, who *are* these people?"

"Ordinary folks having fun, I expect," he said. "Nobody's really normal when you come down to it. But I'll tell you something—they can't draw." He was right. The brochure—if that's what it was—was decorated with blurred portraits of wizards, witches and girls wearing little but jewellery. All were extremely badly drawn.

"Oh, well," I said, and sent the man Corrie a cheque.

A week later he sent me a receipt and a certificate to say

I was now an official member of PhantasmaCon, with a room booked in the Hotel Babylon to prove it.

Otherwise, as I said, I was hard at work, both in the house and in the shed at the end of the yard. The shed is one of the reasons I bought the house. It is big and airy and someone had already laid a smooth wooden floor in it. I have added heating. That floor means I can chalk symbols and figures at need. For fateline work, you need, among other things, a double spiral Eternity, which is the very devil to get drawn right. Shortly after Corrie's certificate arrived, I was crawling on the floor in my barn, dressed in my oldest clothes, chalking and rubbing out and chalking again, when I looked up to see Andrew standing in the doorway.

He gave no sign that he thought I might be doing something out of the ordinary. He said, in his vague, deadpan way, "I was wondering when you might be ready to give me a lift."

I had forgotten his car had broken down. I got up, dusted my knees, and devoted the rest of the day to sorting him out. I remember that some time while I was driving him— either to Cambridge or to Huntingdon or back—I said airily, "I do a lot of programming on my knees. It helps to see it all spread out."

He said, "I do a lot of my thinking walking over the fields."

I assumed all was well, but I took the precaution, when I went back to work next day, of putting heavy prohibitions round the barn, and round the house, the yard and my strip of front garden too. Then, confident that I could not be disturbed again, I went back to chalking and crawling.

By the early evening, I was ready to walk the spiral. It takes immense concentration, because you are pulling four people's fatelines with you—not to speak of your own— and you can do a great deal of harm, to those people and to the rest of the world where their lines connect to everyone else's, if you get it wrong. I was shuffling forwards along the chalklines, with my arms spread to keep the world

67

in balance, when I looked up to see a figure straddling the loop at the far end. I couldn't see the person clearly because he was silhouetted against the stream of orange sunlight slanting from the high window of the barn. Chalk dust and motes from the barn itself were catching the light too and standing round him like rays. He looked vast.

You know that feeling when your stomach seems to drop away, leaving you cold and empty. I felt that. But I couldn't stop. That would have been really dangerous. My first thought was, At least it isn't Mallory! I wouldn't have put it past her. Then I thought it might be Stan, made visible by the dust. But the figure was too huge. I had to shuffle on for another five minutes, until I came to a place where the sunlight lit him sideways from my point of view. Then I could see it was Andrew. He was just standing there, staring. He seemed totally bemused, but I could see his eyes watching me.

"You shouldn't be here," I said to him, when I could spare the attention.

He smiled. It worried me, the way that smile made him look so intelligent. But he seemed to be in a sort of trance-state in spite of it. I could feel he was, when I got close to him. Since he was across my chalk marks, I had to take him by the elbows and move him aside. He moved just like a zombie and stood where I put him. I shuffled on past and round the spirals at the top of the loop, hoping for the best. But when I had rounded the curve at the top to face the other way, I found Andrew had moved again while my concentration was elsewhere and was now standing straddling the loop at the opposite end. From there, the sun shone yellow on his blank, austere face.

Damn! I thought, and shuffled on. I had to face the fact that Andrew had somehow got himself entangled in the fatelines I was manipulating. *He* had no idea of it, of course. He must have wanted to borrow some sugar or something, and arrived at just the wrong moment. When I had finished, I took him by one arm, led him across the yard in the gloaming, and let him out of the gate.

He came to himself as soon as he passed my prohibitions. "Thanks," he said, as if he had now borrowed the sugar. "I'll see you." And he walked off beside the hedge to his own house.

"Look on the bright side," Stan said when I told him. "It wasn't Mallory."

"God forbid!" I said. "But what do you think I've *done* to him?"

"Lord knows!" Stan said. "I've never heard of this happening before, but it may be just that Magids didn't mention it. It can't be too serious. I hope. Probably the worst that can happen is for our Andrew to take a whim to report to Gandalf as a hobbit."

"I just hope that's all," I said.

SEVEN

From Maree Mallory's
Thornlady Directory, extracts
from various files

[1]

OK. So I've been behaving badly to Janine. As usual.

Janine was furious when I had to move in with them. She was so poisonous that I said to her, "*You* try living with your husband's sister down the road! *You* try to write essays that are supposed to count towards your degree with seventeen children yelling round you!" My Dad's sister Irene has five kids of her own and two from her latest husband, but she finds life too quiet unless each of them has at least one little friend staying the night every night. Fortunately, the last thing my little fat Dad did before they carted him off for chemotherapy—apart from giving me his car, that is—was to get on to his brother Ted and make Ted promise to house and feed me. So I told Janine to take her objections to Uncle Ted.

She said, "What's wrong with university accommodation?"

"No room," I said. "I was in a flat, but it was let over my head."

That's actually not quite what happened, but I wasn't going to tell Janine. Robbie was sharing the two rooms with me (that I had used all my money paying for in advance) and then he just coolly moved his new bint Davina instead of me. Or he said I could sleep on the sofa, I believe,

70

though I may be wrong because I was too angry to listen at the time. I stormed off to Mum's in London, swearing never to come back. And I meant it, too, until Dad made me. He made me go back and I had to spend one glorious month in Aunt Irene's house. And I told Dad, "Never again!" about that too, which is why he fixed things up with Uncle Ted.

Janine looked daggers at me. But she doesn't go against Uncle Ted. If she did, he might notice the way she manages him. She's going to bide her time and wait to work Uncle Ted round to thinking I'm impossible. So she did that thing she does, of pulling down the sleeves of her sweater so that her gold bangles jangle. Tug. Tug. Toss impeccable hair. Go away, *clack, click, clack*, to start phoning the unfortunate girls who mind the clothes shop she owns up in Clifton. She's still sacking them for practically no reason. I heard her say to the phone as I went upstairs with another load of my stuff, "She'll have to go. I've had quite enough of her." She gets those awful sweaters she wears through that shop of hers. The one I hate most is the one she was wearing then, that looks as if she'd spilt rice-pudding over one shoulder. Nick says he hates the one with the bronze baked beans most.

And Janine thinks I'll corrupt Nick! Or steal his affections or something. You couldn't. No one could. *Nothing* can influence Nick unless he wants it to. Nick is sweetly and kindly and totally selfish. It says volumes that I never once set eyes on Nick while I was living just down the road with Aunt Irene. I asked him why when I was bringing my stuff into Uncle Ted's house.

"That house is full of *children*!" he said, surprised that I should wonder. Nick himself, I should point out, is all of fourteen. He stood with his hands in his pockets watching me unload boxes and plastic bags from Dad's car. "You've got a computer," he observed. "Mine's a laptop. What's yours?"

"Old and cranky and incompatible with almost everything—just like me," I said.

71

He actually picked it up and carried it to the top of his parents' house for me. I think he was doing me an honour—that, or he was afraid I'd break it. He has a low opinion of women (well, so would I have with a mother like Janine). Then he came down again and looked at Dad's car. "It's quite nice," he said.

"It's my Dad's," I said. "Or was. He said I could have it after I passed my driving test."

"When did you pass?" he said.

"Hush," I said. "I don't take it till Monday."

"Then how did you get it to Bristol?" he wondered.

"How do you think?" I said. "Drove it of course."

"But—" he began. "All alone?" he asked.

"Yes," I said.

I could see I had awed Master Nick. This pleased me. You have to keep someone like Nick suitably humble or you end up washing his socks while he walks barefoot all over you. (Robbie was the same, but I didn't manage to awe him for long enough.) Nick has both his parents just where he wants them. I was delighted and highly chuffed to discover that Janine actually washes Nick's socks by hand for him, because Nick claims to get sore feet if she doesn't. Uncle Ted hands Nick ten-pound notes more or less whenever they pass on the stairs. And Nick has the whole basement of the house to himself. His parents have to knock before they come in. Honestly. He showed me his basement after I'd got all my things to the attic. I think that was another honour. It's like a luxury flat down there, with all-over plum-coloured carpeting. And as for his sound system! Yah! *Envy!*

"I chose the carpet myself," he said.

"Lovely funereal colour," I said. "Like a bishop's vest with mildew. You could spill whole jars of blackberry jam here and never notice."

Nick laughed. "Why are you always so gloomy?"

"Because I've been crossed in love," I told him. "Don't push me about it. I get dangerous."

"But you're always dangerous," he said. "That's why I like you."

Yes, Nick and I are getting on very well. Maybe this is why Janine objects to me. We seem to have been able to take up our old relationship exactly where it stopped when my parents divorced and moved to London. It goes way back, with me and Nick, to the time when Janine used to pay my Mum to take care of Nick most of the time for her. The trouble was, Mum doesn't go for babies (though she's pretty good with teenagers, I'm here to tell you) and she used to push Nick off on to me as soon as I got home from school. Some of my earliest memories are of reaching up to push Nick's great tall pushchair up the hill to the Downs, and when I'd toiled all the way up there, I used to fetch him out and we'd sit on the grass and invent stories. My first really bitchy row with Janine was when I was twelve and Nick was six and Janine discovered that Nick would rather be with me than go anywhere with her. She said I was putting fantasies into Nick's head. I told her Nick was inventing most of them himself. She said he didn't know truth from reality because of me. And I said that yes he did, because he knew he would be bored going out with her.

I suppose it helps pick up the old relationship that Nick is still exactly the same startlingly good-looking child he was when I wheeled him up the hill and old ladies used to stop me and say what a beautiful little brother I'd got (and I always said, "He's not my brother, he's my *cousin*"). Except that these days he's about a yard taller and I have to crane upwards to see his face. He says I haven't changed either. He's right. I haven't grown since I was twelve. And still the same round face, like a badly drawn heart on a school Valentine, and my nose never grew either, so my specs slide off all the time like they always did. Same mousy mane of hair, same lack of figure. And I did a lot of comfort-eating while I was with Mum (like a fool, I thought health foods were invented to *stop* people putting on weight) so now I'm truly FAT—and I always was on the plump and dumpy side. I looked in the mirror before I wrote this and wondered how Robbie ever fancied me . . .

(2)

. . . told me I'd failed the driving test. Well, it's not *my* fault Bristol is so confusing. I don't think he should fail me just for getting us lost, though I did end up running backwards down Totterdown (I think the gradient is 1:5 there) because I couldn't seem to remember how to do a hill start. Now I shall have to wait another month before I can take the test again. Pah.

I relieved my feelings by storming into the Vet Dept and applying to change to Philosophy. They said I was doing quite well and did I mean it. And I said yes. If they thought I was going to stick around watching Robbie Payne make sheep's eyes at Davina Frostick, they thought wrong. They said that wasn't a good reason to switch subjects. I said it was the only real one. So they ummed and aahed and said it wasn't possible until after Easter, or maybe even until autumn, and obviously assumed I'd have changed my mind by then.

I WON'T. I'd let my fingernails grow while I was looking after Dad. Now I swear not to cut them for a year. They can't make me do work on animals with six-inch talons. So.

Oh FRUSTRATION!!! Applying for a new driving test took nearly all the money I had left. I had to tell Uncle Ted I'd pay him for my bed and board every six months. He took it well. He's pretty rich anyway. And Janine seems to be made of money.

But God those two are so *boring*!

I don't blame Nick for diving away into that basement of his every evening. Before I got it sorted out that I could go away to my attic and pretend to work, I spent several centuries-long evenings sitting in their living room with them after supper (hm. Supper. Janine doesn't cook, you know. She has what she calls her menus in the freezer, pre-packaged slenderizers. Nick and Uncle Ted eat them with ten-inch-high piles of reconstituted potatoes. She and I just eat them. I keep myself awake rumbling with hunger every night, but it *must* be worth it). They never go out after supper. Apparently Uncle Ted once got struck with an idea for a book in the middle of the Welsh National Opera and they had to leave so that he could go and write Chapter One. Janine is opposed to wasting money like that, so they stay in now. They almost never watch television because it interferes with Uncle Ted's ideas.

So there we sat. Now you'd think that a world-famous author like Uncle Ted would be really interesting to talk to. The very least you'd expect was that he'd discuss the vileness of his latest demons (*no one* does demons like Uncle Ted: they're really horrific). But not a bit of it. He doesn't talk about his work at all, or anything to do with it.

I asked him why, the second evening. Janine looked at me as if I'd remarked that the Pope was into voodoo. And Uncle Ted said he saved that kind of talk for public appearances. "Writing's a job, like any other," says he. "I like to come home from the office and put my feet up, as it were." (He works at home of course.)

"Well, it's a point of view," I said. Actually I was scandalized. *Nothing* to do with the imagination should be just "a job." My opinion of Uncle Ted, whom I've always rather liked and admired, went screeching downhill almost to zero.

Then it went down again, in a steady depressed trundle, like a sledge on a very small slope, because Uncle Ted started talking about the house. And money. Looking very satisfied with how much money he'd made lately, he told me just which bit of redecoration or alteration he's paid for out of which book. And Janine nodded enthusiastically and reminded him that Nick's basement came out of *The Curse on the Cottage*; and he retorted with the fitted bookcases out of *Surrender, You Devil*; and they both told me that after *Shadowfall* they were able to afford an interior decorator to revamp the living room. I thought that was an *awful* way to look at a book. I thought a book was a Work of Art.

"But we left the windows in all the rooms as they are," Uncle Ted added. "We had to."

Now I had been fascinated by the glass in the windows. I remember it from when I was small. It waves and it wobbles. When you look out at the front—particularly in the evenings—you get a sort of cliff of trees and buildings out there, with warm lighted squares of windows, which all sort of slide about and ripple as if they are just going to transform into something else. From some angles, the houses bend and stretch into weird shapes, and you really might believe they were sliding into a set of different dimensions. From the back of the house it's just as striking. There you get a navy blue vista of city against pale sunset. And when the streetlights come on they look like holes through to the orange sky. With everything rippling and stretching, you almost think you're seeing your way through to a potent strange place behind the city.

I knew Uncle Ted was going to destroy all the strangeness by saying something dreary about his windows, and I terribly didn't want him to. I almost prayed at him not to. But he did. He said, "It's genuine wartime glass from World War Two, you know. It dates from when Hitler bombed the docks here. This house was caught in the blast and all the windows blew out and had to be replaced. So we leave the panes, whatever else we do. The glass is historic. It adds quite a bit to the value of the house."

I ask you! He writes fantasy. He has windows that go into other dimensions. And all he can think about is how much extra money they're worth.

Oh, I know I'm being ungrateful and horrible. They're letting me live here. But all the same . . .

Nick at least has noticed about the windows. He says they give you glimpses of a great alternate universe called

76

Bristolia. And, being in some ways as practical as his father, he has made maps of Bristolia for a role-playing game . . .

(3)

. . . a low time. I ache inside my chest about Robbie. I go into the university but I just mooch about there really. One's supposed to get over being crossed in love. People do. It was *months* ago now, after all. I don't seem to be like other people. I don't know what I'm like. That's the trouble with being adopted and not knowing your real parents. They have little bits of ancestry you don't know about, and aren't prepared for, and they come up and hit you. You don't know what to *expect*.

And my money has dwindled away to almost nothing . . .

(4)

Well, what do you know! I got a letter from someone called Rupert Venables. I suppose he's a lawyer. No one but a lawyer could have that kind of name. He says a distant relative has left me a hundred quid as a legacy. Lead me to it!

Those were my first, joyous thoughts. Then Janine put the kibosh on them by asking sweetly, "What distant relative, dear? Your mother's, your father's, or your own?"

And Uncle Ted chipped in, "What's this lawyer's address? That should give you a clue."

Practical Uncle Ted again. The man Venables writes from Weavers End, Cambridgeshire. Mum's family comes entirely from South London. Dad's is all Bristol. And none of them have died recently as far as we know, not even my poor little fat Dad, who is still hanging on in there, out in Kent. That only leaves real, genuine relatives of my own, who could have traced me by mysterious means. I was almost excited about it until Nick said he thought it was a cruel hoax.

Nick gave his opinion an hour after the rest of us had stopped discussing it. It takes Nick that long to stop being his morning zombie self and become his normal daytime self. He got his eyes open, collected his stuff for school and picked up the letter, which he subjected to powerful scrutiny on his way out through the back door. "The address doesn't say he's a lawyer. The letter doesn't say who's left you the money. It's a hoax," he said. He threw the letter back at me (it missed and fell on the floor) and departed.

Hoax or not, I can use the money. I wrote to the man Venables saying so. I also suggested that he should tell me more.

Today he wrote back saying he'd come and give me the money. But he didn't say when and he didn't say who'd left it to me. I don't believe a word of it. Nick is right.

(5)

. . . and said I had passed my driving test! I was feeling so pessimistic by then that I didn't believe him and asked him to tell me again. And it was the same the second time round.

I wonder if test examiners aren't used to being kissed. This one took it sort of stoically and then climbed out of the car and ran. I vaulted out. I tore off the L-plates, shot inside the car again and drove off with a zoom. I felt a bit guilty about leaving Robbie's friend Val standing on the pavement like that, but he had only sat beside me for the hundred yards or so between his flat and the test centre. Besides, Val gives me the feel that he thinks he's going to get me on the rebound from Robbie, and I wanted him to know different. I drove to Uncle Ted's and screamed to a stop, double-parked outside. Nick had some sort of free day off school and I wanted him to be the first to know.

Unfortunately Janine was there too. I think she runs that clothes shop entirely by phone. Uncle Ted was in London that day, so she had come back to make sure Nick had some lunch, even though she never eats it herself. A study in Sacrificial Motherhood (actually Nick, when left to make lunch for himself, tends to drape the kitchen in several furlongs of spaghetti, and I almost see Janine's point of view on that). She was in the kitchen with Nick when I burst in.

"So you failed again, dear. I'm so sorry," she says. How to replace joy with anger in eight easy words.

"No. I passed," I snapped.

"Excellent!" says Nick. "Now you can take me for a drive round Bristolia."

"Says you!" I said. And Janine put her hand on my arm and said, "Poor Maree. She's far too tired after all that concentrating. You mustn't pester her, Nick."

At that, I realized that Janine was really here to prevent me risking Nick's neck in Dad's car. "Tired? Who's tired?" I said savagely. "I'm on top of the world!" I wasn't by then. Janine had put me in a really bad mood. "You just think I'm not safe to drive Nick anywhere."

"I didn't say that, Maree," she said. "But I do know I only started to learn to drive *after* I passed my test."

"That's what they all say, but it's different for me," I said. "I practised beforehand and ruined your fun."

"Maree, dear," she said, "I know you love breaking all the rules, but you really *are* no different from everyone else. Cars are dangerous."

Well, we argued, Janine all sugary sweetness and light and me getting more and more inclined to bite. That's Janine's way. She expertly puts you in the wrong and never loses her temper. Just smiles sweetly when she's got you hopping mad. Nick simply watched and waited. And at the crucial moment, he said, "You know she's been driving that car for years, Mum. Maree, if you're not going to drive me, I may as well go and see Fred Holbein."

"No, no. I'll drive you. I'm coming now," I said.

"Nick, I forbid you to go," said Janine.

He grinned at her, meltingly, and simply walked out to the car. That was it. Master Nick had decided he wanted to show me Bristolia and the womenfolk did as he wanted. Actually, I felt quite honoured, that he trusted me both to drive him and not to laugh at his Bristolia game. It put me in a much better mood. "Where to?" I said.

Nick unfolded a large, carefully coloured map. "I think we'll start with Cliffores of the Monsters and the Castle of the Warden of the Green Wastes," he said seriously.

So I drove him to the Zoo and then past the big red Gothic school there. Then we went round Durdham Down and on to Westbury-on-Trym and back to Redland. After that, I don't remember where we went. Nick had different names for everywhere and colourful histories to go with every place. He told me exactly how many miles of Bristolia we'd covered for each mile of town. I did my best to keep an intelligent interest, but Dad's car was not behaving very well. Perhaps it believed what Nick said. After he'd told me we'd gone seven hundred miles to the Zoo, it began making grinding noises and stalling on hills. I was a bit preoccupied with making it go. But Nick went on explaining eagerly, even though some of my answers were a bit vague and sarcastic. I don't think he noticed. I was rather touched, to tell the truth, because we used to play games like this (but on a smaller scale) when I was fourteen and Nick was eight. And I would have died rather than hurt his feelings.

We were going steeply down towards the Centre, and Nick had just told me we'd now clocked up two thousand miles of Bristolia, when he suddenly said, "Just a moment. I think we're being followed."

I very nearly said, "Is this part of the Game?" and I am glad I didn't, because I was suddenly quite sure he was right. Don't ask me how. I just knew someone was behind us, looking for us, with serious intent to find us. It was not a nice feeling. I supposed Janine must have sent someone

80

to make sure I didn't kill her Nick. So I said, "What do you suggest we do?"

"Keep going towards Biflumenia—I mean Bedminster," Nick said, "and I'll tell you what to do then."

Traffic was pretty thick by then. It was very useful to have someone with Nick's encyclopedic knowledge of the place to tell me what turning to take. We both dropped the Bristolia game for a tense quarter of an hour or so, while we zipped up the opposite hill across the river, came back down another way, and took the road up to the suspension bridge. The creepy feeling of someone behind us trying to find us left us on the way. Nick sat back with a sigh.

"That's it. We lost him. Now we're in Yonder Bristolia where most of the magic users live."

"Yes, but I wish we weren't in line for the suspension bridge!" I more or less moaned.

"It's all right. I've got money to get across," Nick said.

"But it's the place I have my bad dreams about!" I wailed. I really didn't want to go there. My bad mood was back. It was thanks to Janine. She'd stripped the joy about passing my test off the underlying misery and, though I'd forgotten it a bit during the tour of exotic Bristolia, it was still there, as bad as ever.

"I was hoping I'd stopped you being so gloomy," Nick said.

"I can't. I've been crossed in love," I said. "And there's my Dad—not to speak of the dreams."

I suppose it's not surprising Nick got the wrong idea of the dreams. Clifton Suspension Bridge is notorious for suicides. "You mean you dream about jumping off?" he said.

"No," I said. "They're weirder than that."

"Tell the dreams," he commanded.

So I told him, though they were something I'd never mentioned to a soul before. I almost don't mention them to myself, apart from calling this journal Directory Thornlady just to show I know about them really. They're too nasty. They go with a horrible, depressed, weak feeling. I've been having the dreams for over three years now, ever since we moved to London and Mum and Dad split up, and they make me wonder if I might be going mad. I was sure Nick would think they were mad. But there is something about driving a car that makes you confiding—like a sort of mobile analyst's couch—and after Nick and I had shared the feeling of being followed, I felt as if we'd shared minds anyway.

In the dreams I am always at the Bristol end of the bridge, and I go up the steep path that cuts into the bank by the footpath there and find I'm on a wide moorland by moonlight (not that I ever see the moon: I just know it's moonlight). I walk until I come to a path. Some nights I find I can dig my heels in and refuse to take that path. Then I get punished. I get lost in the dream, wandering about in beastly marsh-like places, and wake up feeling incredibly frightened and guilty. If I give in (or can't dig my heels in) and simply follow the path, I always come to a sort of horizon, where the sky comes right down to the moor, and there is a solitary dark bush in the middle of it. That bush is an old woman.

Don't ask me how. Nick asked me how. I couldn't tell him. She isn't made of twigs. She isn't the sky showing through the bush. She isn't even exactly *in* the bush. But in my dream I know that the bush is the same thing as a narrow-faced severe old woman who is probably a goddess. I don't like her. She despises me. And she's brought me here to tell me off.

"Don't ever expect any sort of luck or success," she says, "until you stop this aggressive approach to life. It's not ladylike. A lady should sit gracefully by and let others handle things." She always says that sort of thing, but recently she's been on about Robbie too. At first it was the immorality of living with him, and now that seems to be over she says, "It's degrading for a lady to go pining after a man. You won't have any luck or worth in your life until you give up university and marry a nice normal young man."

"And *don't* tell me it's my subconscious talking!" I said to Nick.

"It isn't. It's not the way you think or talk at all. It's not you," he said decidedly. "I think she's a witch."

"I call her Thornlady," I confessed. Just then it dawned on me that Dad's car was making incredibly heavy weather of the hill up beside the gorge. We were crawling. The engine was going *punk, punk, punk.* And when I looked in the mirror (which I'd forgotten to do while I told Nick about the dreams), I could see a whole line of cars snorting and toiling and crawling impatiently behind us. The road behind us between the hedges was full of blue fumes. "Oh God!" I said. "What's wrong? We're breaking down!"

"You could try going into another gear," Nick suggested.

I looked down and found I was in fourth. No wonder! I slammed us down into second and we took wings. The car gave a grateful howling sound as we hurtled round the last bends and swooped along to the bridge. Nick produced a lavish handful of coins and paid the toll machine.

"It's an omen. You may have changed my luck," I said as we shimmied across the gorge.

"I've been thinking about that," Nick answered. "We ought to break that dream. Why don't we—"

I knew what he was going to say. We both shouted in chorus, *"Do the Witchy Dance for Luck!"*

I stopped the car as soon as we were across the bridge. I vaulted out. Nick unfolded out, and we both rushed to the pavement beside where the path went up. The Witchy Dance was something we had done often and often when we were kids—we were convinced then that it worked too—but we were both a bit out of practice. I got into the swing of it fairly quickly. Nick was self-conscious and he took longer. We were into the third flick, flick, flick of the fingers before he loosened up. After that we were both going like a train when people began honking and hooting horns at us.

"Take no notice," I panted. Flick, flick, flick. "Luck, luck, luck," we chanted. "Break that dream. Luck, luck, luck!"

The horns seemed to get louder, but I had a strong feeling the Witchy Dance was really working—Nick says he had too—so we simply went on dancing. Next thing I knew, the man in the car behind me had climbed out and marched round to the pavement in front of me.

"Go and hold your Sabbath somewhere else!" he shouted. Oh he was angry. I *looked* at him. I *looked* at his great silver car and then back at him. He was a total prat. He had a long head with smooth, smooth hair, gold-rimmed glasses, a white strappy mac and a *suit*, for heaven's sake! And instead of a tie he had one of those fancy silk cravat things. Businessman, I thought. We've made him half a minute late for an appointment. I took a glance at Nick to see what he thought. But Nick can be a real rat. He was busy injecting acute embarrassment into every pore of himself. He stood there and he cringed, the rat! It wasn't *me*, sir! She *made* me do it, Officer! The woman tempted me and I did eat, Lord! I could have smacked him.

So I fought my own battle as usual by pushing my glasses up my nose with one finger in order to point a truly dirty *look* at the prat.

Unfortunately he was a tougher nut than he looked. He held his left lens up against his left eye and gave me the dirty look right back. In spades. I was about to resort to speech then, but the prat got in first. "I am Rupert Venables," he snaps. "I've been looking for you all afternoon to give you this." And he fetches out a hundred quid and counts it into my hand.

I was too gobsmacked even to get round to asking how he knew it was me. For that, blame the other motorists. There seemed to be several hundred cars lined up going both ways by then, and they were all gooping. When they saw the money, they began to cheer. I don't think they thought the prat was paying me to move my car, either. Oh I was FURIOUS. And Nick was overwhelmed with genuine embarrassment as soon as he heard the name and saw the money, and he was no help at all. We simply got into Dad's car and I drove us away. Rather jerkily.

After a while I said—between my teeth—"I hope for

both our sakes I never meet that prat again. *Murder* will be done."

Nick said, "But the Witchy Dance has worked."

That inflamed my wrath further. "What do you mean, you rat?"

"You got a hundred pounds with no strings attached," he pointed out.

"They're probably forged notes," I said.

"What are you going to buy with them?" Nick asked.

"Oh don't ask—I need almost everything you can name," I said. I suppose I was mollified. I know I haven't felt nearly so depressed since.

EIGHT

Rupert Venables for the
Iforion archive

Once the various fatelines were moving the right way, I could keep them in hand without too much trouble. I took the blocks off my communications. Instantly the phone rang. The answering-machine flashed furiously. Two computers put up MESSAGES INCOMING and the fax machine put out paper after paper.

"Well it's nice to be needed," I said to Stan.

About half the stuff waiting was requests or enquiries from the software and games companies I work for. Two recorded calls were from Magids elsewhere in the world wanting to know why I had let the beef crisis get so much out of hand. I swore. I hadn't realized it had. And it was too late to do anything by then. The current phone call was a girl I know in Cambridge who wanted to know why I hadn't been seen or heard of since Christmas. I told her an old friend had died and left me a lot of unfinished business.

"That's right. Blame me," growled the voice of that same old friend from behind me.

One of the computers was full of regular e-mail. I let it wait and turned to the other. It was my channel for Magid business and wouldn't wait. Months can pass without Magid communicating with Magid, but when they do communicate there is an urgent need-to-know.

The first message was from my brother Will. WHAT'S HAPPENING? THULE IS SWAMPED WITH REFUGEES FROM KORYFONIC WORLDS.

The next was from a Magid called Zinka on the other side of the Empire from Will. DID YOU KNOW KORYFONIC 10 & 12—I.E. ERATH AND TELTH—HAVE DECLARED INDEPENDENCE AND ARE MAKING WARLIKE NOISES AT MY LOT? The third message said much the same, only about Koryfonic 9 and 7. The fourth was from my brother Simon: RUMOURS HERE THAT THE KORYFONIC EMPIRE IS BREAKING UP. IS THIS INTENDED? IF NOT, DO YOU NEED HELP? INTENDED OR NOT, IT SEEMS HARD ON THE PEOPLE THERE.

I said to Stan, "Well? *Is* it Intended?"

"Probably," he replied.

Gloomily, I went through the faxes. Two-thirds of them were from General Dakros. Typically, he said nothing about war, or worlds seceding from the Empire. To him, this was military business and nothing to do with a Magid. The first few faxes were jubilant. He thought he was on the track of Knarros; he had found him; through Knarros he now had a line on the Babylon heirs. By the sixth fax, he had found two more people claiming to be Knarros and the number of putative heirs had trebled. After that it was exponential. Lost Emperors had poured in on him while I was otherwise engaged—hundreds of them, and several score Knarroses. The latest fax said,

> I've weeded it down to eight men who may possibly
> be Knarros. The Empire would appreciate your help
> in this.

"What do you think I should do?" I said to Stan.

"Lad, I'm supposed to be advising you about sponsoring a new Magid, not about this," he answered. "What do *you* think?"

"I . . . think . . ." I said slowly, trying to get at the right gut feeling on this, "that the Empire is breaking up as was Intended all along—and this is why they always put the newest Magid on to it. He or she will make mistakes. *I've* made mistakes. I could have saved that poor sod Timotheo—OK, OK, Stan. It's done. I won't beat my breast

87

about it any longer. But to judge from the history of *this* world, when a big Empire breaks up, there's usually one or two last rulers at the head of it who are either very weak or very young, to, to . . ."

"Sort of guide it down the drain?" Stan said.

"Exactly," I said. "So I imagine it's my job to go and pick a Knarros—any old Knarros—to provide Koryfos with a weak ruler. Stan, this is the part of being a Magid that's not pleasant."

"I know," he said. "I've done some dirty things too."

I got through to Dakros, sighing rather, and was directed to meet him in a distant suburb of Iforion. Just arrive in the road, he said. Someone would be looking out for me.

They were.

I stepped out into a chilly, rubble-covered street between two rows of small houses, and something went *whee* past my head and *whang* into a low brick wall. In fact, whatever-it-was only missed me because I stumbled on the rubble as I arrived and twisted my ankle. I dived into the garden behind the low brick wall, ankle and all, and crouched there, watching the opposition retaliate. One of their queer beam-guns yammered from the next house along from my garden. A flaming bundle with arms but no legs toppled from behind a chimney across the street and plumped down somewhere out of sight. The stench of it streamed across me. I felt ill. I *know* this kind of thing happens all the time in my world—in most worlds—but I still felt sick, and weak, and hot round the eyes. I also wondered, with some earnestness, which side was whose.

General Dakros settled that by coming out of the next door house at a run. "Are you alive there, Magid?" he shouted. He looked like the Big Bear in the Goldilocks story, coming out of that small house in a great furry hooded coat which did not look like army issue.

I managed to smile at his bearish look. I rolled on to my knees and shouted back that I was fine.

"Sorry about that. We never get to the bottom of the sniper problem," he said. He came and helped me scramble over the wall and hobble into the house. The air smelt horribly of soot. I thought it was from the dead sniper, until he helped me through into a back room. This street of houses was built on a hill. Through the back window was what ought to have been a fine view of the city. Now it was a panorama of drifting smokes, high buildings with black empty windows, two ruined bridges and one stately climbing cloud of fresh new grey-blue smoke with a tower burning in the midst of it. There were bright red rags of flame in the rolls of smoke. "Insurrection in the city," Dakros explained as he put back his furry hood. He had lost weight. He looked far more tired and harrowed than when I had last seen him. "The poorer classes don't like the way everything's getting so expensive." He ran both hands through his black wriggly hair, which had definitely become thinner since the Palace fell. "I can't understand it myself," he added. "Money just seems to be worth nothing suddenly. I've had to issue a list of what things are supposed to cost—bread and so on—with penalties for overcharging, but it's made no difference. Goods just vanished overnight. Some of them have to be sold in secret or bartered, but I don't see why at all."

I felt acutely sorry for him. Things like this might be Intended, but Dakros was the one who had to cope with it all. "Inflation," I said, "happens when times are unstable. The Emperor kept things stable, if only by consuming most of the valuables he could get his hands on."

"Then let's get another Emperor quickly!" he said, with vehemence. "I'm sick of all these frauds, Magid. Did you know there were over a thousand of them?"

"What have you done with them all?" I asked him.

He was surprised I should wonder. "Executed them."

"Bad idea," I said.

"They committed treason and fraud," he said. He shrugged. "You can't let people get away with that."

"True," I admitted. "But there *are* alternatives. Talking of which, where are all these other people who say they're Knarros?"

89

"Oh, I've got them all lined up for you in the next room under guard," he said. "I'll have them marched in one by one and you can look them over in here. That suit you?"

The straightforward, soldierly method, I thought. It did not surprise me that things were falling to pieces here. Still, I was glad that I was not going to have to travel about the place to interview the claimants. The chances of getting shot seemed quite high. And my ankle still hurt, and both knees, where I had hit the ground. "Wheel them in, then," I said.

I do not wish to dwell on those eight interviews with eight doomed men. They were all middle-aged and all looked rather imposing. You felt each of them must have looked in the mirror at some point and thought, I look like someone the Emperor would trust. One was more or less in rags, one in the soutane of one of the travelling religions, and one seemed to be a minor noble. Two of them were schoolteachers. God knows why those two had put themselves forward, unless it was looking in a mirror, as I said, and knowing they had care of the young—so why not the Emperor's young? The other three were a grocer, a farmer and a poet. All these were mad. So, I discovered after a while, was the preacher. The one in rags was a sly rogue, the noble a blatant one. Most of them looked bewildered or shifty when I asked them about the youngsters supposedly in their charge, though the noble talked glibly of "the Emperor's five fine boys."

It did not take very deep Magid work to ascertain that every one of them was another fraud. And the worst of it was I could *not* bring myself to pretend about any one of them. I looked at Dakros's strained face. I looked at the poet as they marched him away. I could not *do* this to him. Bugger the Empire. Bugger what was Intended. Dakros deserved some honesty.

"Sorry," I said, when the door had shut behind the poet's escort. "None of them is Knarros. But you could do yourself and the Empire a bit of good if you put them on trial publicly. Let justice be seen to be done. Expose them.

90

Prove the mad ones are mad. Then imprison the sane ones and put the loonies in an asylum."

It did no good. Dakros had not been raised to think in this way. He ran his hands through his decreasing hair again and said, "I'm sick of taking strong measures." This did not mean he was considering what I said. It meant that he was going to take the strong measures, and he was fed up with doing it. I think the only reason he didn't order a firing squad out into the back garden straight away was that he guessed I would find it offensive. He added, "I'm only saying this to you, you understand, because I can't say it to anyone else. I'm sick of this whole thing. I keep wondering why *I'm* the one who's been landed with it, and I want it to stop."

"I understand," I said. "Is High Lady Alexandra not with you?"

"By all gods, *no!*" he said. "I've sent her away to Thalangia. At least there's no fighting there. I wish I was there too."

I was sure he did wish it, since he had chivalrously sent the one person he might have talked to there. "Is it far to Thalangia?" I asked, and wondered whether, if I advised him to go there and let the Empire go to hell, he would listen to me. It was hard to see someone under such stress and not offer help.

"Far?" he said. "It's two worlds Ayewards from here. And you can be sure I've got my best unit guarding that world gate. Those gates are so damned vulnerable, you know. The Telth gate went down in seconds." Seeing me looking searchingly at him, he added, "I'm from that world—from Thalangia. Empire policy was that no soldier served in his or her world of origin. I had to come and serve here. But I'd go home tomorrow, except I know damn fine that hell would break loose in Thalangia too if there was no one at the head of things."

"You're certainly right there," I said soberly. Then, as a last stab at getting things to go the way they were Intended,

I said, "You could still solve that by taking the throne yourself. Why not?"

He gave me a long expressionless look. It almost seemed a look of hatred. "I'm not even tempted, Magid. There's men on Telth and Annergam with much better families than mine, and they've taken power there, but they've not called it a throne, and they've not dared to call themselves Emperor. They know. I know. I'm not tempted."

"All right," I said dejectedly. "All right. Then you'll just have to keep on looking for Knarros."

He sighed deeply. "I know. Eight more dead."

"Eight more poor fools dead," I told Stan when I arrived home with a black ragged hole in one trouser-knee and my hands covered with sooty mud.

"Seven of them would have been anyway," he said. "You know what the Empire's like." He was listening to Scarlatti harpsichord sonatas that week. He had gone through all Bach while I worked on the fatelines. Now it was Scarlatti. *Tinkle, tinkle, tinkle.* There are over five hundred Scarlatti keyboard sonatas. I only had a few. In self-defence, I went and bought Stan three more CDs full of them that afternoon, in order to have a different *tinkle-tinkle* to listen to while I took another look at the Emperor's disk.

I was hoping there was a clue to the whereabouts of Knarros somewhere on it. The Emperor had brought himself to make this secret record after all. Being Timos IX, he must have felt he was shouting the facts from the Palace roof. So why not go a bit further and put in *all* the facts? Even he must have realized that he might not be there to explain the program. I had hopes that there might be something hiding behind the lists. There was an awful lot of space left on that disk. But there really seemed to be nothing. And the darned thing was designed as a loop. Like the continuum itself, it kept bringing you back to the beginning. Babylon, I thought uneasily. First you got the graphics, with the worlds arranged like isobars, waving from one configuration to another, and then, superimposed on these, the semi-animated drawings of men, women and centaurs of both sexes.

The drawings were all in side-view and had, as I said, the look of having been taken from photographs of real people. I stopped each one and studied it, but I was none the wiser. They were all different unknown beings, except that two—a human girl and a young female centaur with rather similar features—occurred twice, but this seemed to be because the programmer had slightly botched the loop and put them in at both start and finish by mistake. The girl and the centaur-woman both had the strong-arched nose and the almond eyes you find on Greek vases and Minoan wall paintings, but this told me nothing, except perhaps that the graphics had stylized the real picture to conform with a fashion of beauty. Funny to think that the Koryfonic Empire was already flourishing when Greece and Minos were new. High time it broke up, really.

I froze each of the linear, isobar-like worlds then and looked each one up laboriously in my Magid database. They were a loop too, starting randomly with a different Empire world each time, and making a circuit of the Empire and forty-one neighbouring worlds, Ayewards and Naywards both. Apart from the fact that I incidentally learnt the Koryfonic isobars for Earth, this told me nothing.

"I give up!" I said to Stan.

"I think that's what you're supposed to do," he said. *Tinkle, tinkle.*

All this put me in such a pessimistic mood that I was quite surprised when my fatelines started to draw in beautifully. They drew in all through the rest of March, just as I had planned. At least I got *something* right! I thought after NATO stepped in and sorted out the former Yugoslavia, and my Croatian candidate came to light manning a gun emplacement in the mountains there. Kornelius Punt returned to Holland. Fisk came out of her retreat (or clinic, or whatever) and seemed to be making plans to come to Britain soon; and my remaining British candidate flew in from Tokyo a week before Easter. When Rick Corrie or one of his colleagues sent me a sheaf of updates on the convention, I began to think I had wrought better than I knew. Mervin Thurless actually figured in it as "hopefully making a guest appearance." The rest of the stuff was almost too strange to contemplate, but I hoped I could make sense of it once I was there. Almost the only other part I understood was the statement that the Guest of Honour was now confirmed to be "world-acclaimed writer Ted Mallory, the Grand Master of black humour." For some reason, the name rang no bells with me. I went into Cambridge and bought a paperback by him called *Shadowfall* and fell asleep over it repeatedly.

I was preoccupied at that time with a premonition. This told me I needed Stan with me in Wantchester, and Stan couldn't leave my house. We experimented. He could not go out through the front door at all. He could go a foot or so beyond the back door, but not as far as the barn. At the sides of the house, he tended to get sucked back in through the windows.

We gave up experimenting the day Mrs. Gibbs arrived to find me leaning out of my bedroom window, calling to empty air, "Where are you now, Stan?" I don't think she heard the croaked reply of, "Round near your car. I just— oh bugger!" but we didn't want to take any more chances.

"This is *ridiculous*, Stan!" I said, when Mrs. Gibbs had safely gone, leaving the house scented with bleach and detergent. "The Upper Room sent you back expressly to help me choose your replacement, but they won't let you come and do it! Do you think you could go back and point this gently out to them?"

"I could *try*," Stan husked, after one of his unhappy pauses. "They don't sort of think in these human terms, though, do they? As far as they're concerned, I'm back and that's it."

"Go and explain," I said. "I *know* I'm going to need you."

"Precog?" he asked.

"Yup," I said. I had absolutely no doubt.

"All right then," he said. "But I may be away for some time, I warn you. It may take an appeal to Higher Up—not to speak of the way time goes odd that far outside the continuum."

And before long, Stan was gone. It was a slow fading, nothing sudden. By mid-afternoon, the Scarlatti tinkled to a gentle stop and the house felt empty.

For the rest of that day, I enjoyed the sense of peace enormously. It was a relief not to have an invisible presence likely to look over your shoulder whatever you happened to be doing. It was a relief not to sense silent disapproval at my work on behalf of the Empire. Above all, it was a relief not to have to listen to Scarlatti all the time. The next day, I tried to enjoy the same feeling of relief, and even told myself I *was* enjoying it. The following day, the Wednesday before the convention, I couldn't settle to anything. I told myself I was nervous of going to this strange gathering to make a selection on which the future of worlds depended—but it wasn't that: it was Stan's absence. On Thursday morning, I sat having breakfast and feeling truly desolate. It seemed to me that I had lost Stan finally and for ever, by my own insistence. Them Up There don't like you trying to change their decisions (which never seems to stop us Magids trying, but there you go). They tend to say, "If you don't like it, you can do without," and turn their backs on you. I opened my newspaper, but I couldn't concentrate on it.

The back door opened. Icy wind blew in.

I whirled round. I don't know what I expected—Stan, in some way more incarnate, I suppose—and I hope the smile of delight and welcome didn't freeze on my face too obviously when I saw it was only Andrew. He was standing there, on my threshold, with that tranced look again. Damn! I thought, and told myself I should have been expecting this. Andrew had somehow got himself tied in with the other fatelines. He had been bound to turn up.

"I'm sorry, Rupert. I need you to drive me again," he said.

"And *I'm* sorry too, Andrew," I told him. "I can't. Not today. Not till Tuesday. I'm going to be away till then, leaving this morning. But come in and have some coffee anyway."

Andrew advanced a step, then stopped. "I can be ready whenever you want," he said. "Where are you going this time?"

"Wantchester," I said, "for a conference—I mean, convention."

Andrew stood there with that air he has of consulting parts of his brain so distant that it takes time to reach them. Then he smiled and his face looked intelligent again. "I'll come with you to Wantchester," he said. "Thanks."

"Andrew," I said, truly exasperated, "this is a convention for readers of fantasy, *and* you have to book in advance."

"It doesn't sound like your cup of tea," he remarked. "It's not mine either. But I'd like to see round Wantchester. You can drop me off in the centre of town somewhere. I shan't be in the way."

"All right," I said. What else *could* I say? "I'm aiming to start at twelve-thirty."

"I'll be there," he said and went out and shut my back door, cutting out the icy blasts of wind, to my relief. It had been an unusually cold Spring. April had come in with snow. I poured myself some coffee that had cooled considerably despite Andrew's patent pot, and muttered things about Andrew as I tried to drink it.

Stan's voice said, "He was a fool not to have some of that coffee. It smells good. I wish I could have some."

"Stan!" I said. "They let you come!"

"With conditions, Rupert. With conditions," he said. "They'll let me come with you, but I shall be bound to your car, just like I am to this house. When you want to talk to me, you're going to have to come and sit in the car."

"Why? What are they afraid you'll do?" I said. "Haunt people?"

"It's not that, lad. Wantchester's one of the really potent nodes, and they don't want any more trouble than they can

96

help. They're pretty nervous about you choosing it, as it happens. They say things could blow up in your face if you're not careful. I got torn off a strip for letting you choose it. They said I should have reminded you of your Roman lore, and I said I couldn't, could I?, when I'd forgotten it myself. It wasn't," Stan said, "a comfortable meeting."

I should have remembered Roman lore too. Any town whose name ends in -chester will have been an ancient Roman camp. And the Romans always built these on nodes if they could. It was like plugging into the power-points of the country they were conquering. Roman survey teams had augurs with them as a matter of course, and most of these could divine a node at least as readily as a Magid can. I have always suspected that their chief survey-augur may have *been* a Magid: he was so accurate. And if there was a choice between one site with a lesser node and another with a greater, you can be sure he chose the latter.

"Ah well," I said. "It's too late now. We'll just have to be careful. At least I've got a sound system in the car. Let's get you a stack of Scarlatti tapes."

NINE

[1]

I haven't had the Thornlady dream for two weeks now.

The ten-pound notes were genuine. I have been renovating my appearance with them. I had my hair cut and bought some clothes. Some of my old clothes were so terrible that I wasn't even going to take them round to Oxfam, until Nick said he didn't approve of throwing away clothes, because there had to be people who were worse off than me, so why not mix them with a bag of things he had grown out of? And I was glad I did. I found a really good leather jacket in Oxfam for only £5! I suppose it was too small for most people, but it looks good on me. And I've kept my old specs as a spare, even though I can hardly see through them since I've been wearing the new ones. I hadn't realized how much my eyes had changed since I was sixteen.

[2]

Uncle Ted has been making the air loud with grumbles and indecision. It seems he was invited to a conference of some kind—last year, he says, when it didn't seem real and, for all he knew, the world would end before a year as improbable as 1996 ever occurred—and now it's only a week or

98

so away and he doesn't want to go. At least once a day, he thinks of a new excuse for not going. "I shall ring up and tell them Maree's got meningitis," was his latest one.

"Don't be silly, dear," Janine says. She says that each time. "You're Guest of Honour. You'll let them down terribly if you cancel now." Janine is very keen for him to go because she wants to bask in reflected glory. And she's already got new clothes for it. Nick wants him to go because he's going to fill the house with his role-playing-game friends while they're away. I am the only one who's neutral.

"Not cancel it," Uncle Ted said. "They want me to confirm that I'm going. They keep asking. They're getting quite neurotic about it, if you ask me, but of course I can't go if Maree's ill."

"I refuse to fake meningitis," I said.

"But you don't understand!" Uncle Ted howled. "It's interrupting my life! It's interfering with my work. If I have to go and say things about the way I write, I shall end up thinking I mean them and not be able to write at all."

"You always enjoy conventions once you get there," Janine persuaded. "You meet a lot of people. You sell a lot of books."

At this point I went away to a lecture (Robbie never goes to things where people just talk, so it was safe) and when I came back in the evening, rather depressed again, Janine had won. But at a cost. Uncle Ted had confirmed he would go to the convention on condition he was bribed with a weekend in Scotland playing golf. This doesn't count as interrupting his life apparently. And Janine is a very keen golfer too. So off they both went, leaving me in charge of Nick "as an experiment." Usually when they go away, they park Nick with one of Janine's friends, but now they can use me. It's just like the way Janine always used me when we were small. She left a list as long as my arm of things I had to do pinned to the kitchen board. I feel like Cinderella.

(3)

The whole thing was a disaster.

For one thing, I can't cook—and anyway I draw the line at cooking for seven—so Nick did it. He ignored all Janine's lists and Janine's freezer-menus and made several hundredweight of spaghetti. For another thing, Nick decided to have a dry run for the convention weekend and invited all his friends. For a third thing, they got bored with role-gaming and had a party in the living room instead. Nick wasn't about to have a mess in his basement, not he! So they used the living room and invited more friends and everything was rather noisier than the sort of thing I'd left Aunt Irene's to avoid. Aunt Irene's kids aren't into pop music yet. I never thought I'd miss anything about her house! And for the fourth and worst thing, the weather in Scotland was lousy and Janine and Uncle Ted came back after a day.

They arrived about an hour after I'd come down from the attic and read the riot act. I mean enough is *enough*. Even most of my fellow-students don't get as drunk as those kids were.

I was standing on the stairs, bawling orders, sarcasm and abuse, while great big lads ran humbly about with empty bottles, carpet cleaner, pans of broken glass, sleeping bags, disinfectant and the furniture they'd moved to other places. I still wonder how I'd got them so thoroughly cowed. They were all a foot taller than me. But I was *furious*. I knew I was the one who'd get the blame. And Nick had *promised* me that nothing like this would happen. And the mess was—or had been—phenomenal. Even then the whole house smelt of sweaty teenage boy—with detergent, alcohol and disinfectant coming in as poor seconds. I RAVED.

And broke off sharpish when I saw Janine and Uncle Ted in the hall.

I thought they were about to turn me into the street there and then. I swore I saw it in Janine's eye. I had time to visualize myself wrapped in a blanket, shivering in a shop doorway along with Bristol's other homeless, and not even a dog to provoke the pity of passers-by, when I realized that by some miracle most of the abuse was not being directed at me. Nick's friends were kicked out almost instantly—but they had homes to go to, so that was all right—and I had to help Nick clean up the rest of a mess I hadn't made—but that was all right too—and it was Nick that Uncle Ted went for. I hadn't realized what a sense of justice Uncle Ted has. Janine made one or two efforts to stand in front of Nick and blame me, but they were not her best efforts, until she went into the kitchen and found it draped in pasta, and recognized Nick's touch. Then she went, "Poor Maree," she went, "Maree's not up to this sort of responsibility!" she went. And then she joined Uncle Ted in shouting at Nick.

I let the injustice of that go, I was so relieved still to have a roof over my head. To hear Janine, you'd think she hadn't heard a word of my Sergeant Major act on the stairs. And I'd got it all more or less under control by the time they came home.

Nick was in deep shit for nearly twenty-four hours. Much of it was Janine or Uncle Ted snapping criticisms of every single thing he did or said—which form of nagging Nick avoided any time he wanted by going to ground in his basement—but some of it was Uncle Ted angrily totting up how much of his whisky Nick and his friends had drunk and demanding to be paid for it. For some reason, this was the part that truly upset Nick. That boy doesn't know he's born. He's had to sell two CDs to pay for the booze and he was nearly in tears over it.

I kept out of the way of all of them as much as I could. So this Monday evening I was quite shattered to find I was being punished along with Nick. We are both being made to go to this thing of Uncle Ted's over Easter. The Injustice! The Inequity. The Pettiness. It's Janine. Janine sticks to her line of me not being cut out to look after Nick. She won't even trust me with the empty house while they're away. I ask you! It's not as if I'd invited *my* friends in! And Uncle Ted says, "Nick's proved he's not responsible enough to be left with anyone. He's going to stay in Wantchester under my eye. And you, Maree, are to come to keep Nick off drink, drugs and smashing the furniture while I'm busy doing my act."

I protested. Janine said, "Well, dear, you *have* got a certain amount to prove, you know."

Uncle Ted said autocratically, "There's no argument. She's rung up and booked you in, both of you. You come and keep Nick in order, Maree, or you can find somewhere else to live. It's a simple choice."

Damn! And I'd hoped to earn some money over Easter— enough to afford to go and see my Dad in hospital at least. I'm divided between thinking that Uncle Ted so hates being a guest artiste that he's determined we shall be miserable with him, and thinking that Janine is the one who wants me there, bored and penniless and running round after Nick. She looked so smug while Uncle Ted delivered his ultimatum. I suppose she wants to queen it and not have to spend time making sure Nick survives in the mornings.

And damn again! I had the Thornlady dream again on Monday night. The woman in the bush told me to search my mind and work out why I couldn't cope with normal life. Cheek, I call it. Sitting in a bush and making other folk feel one-down.

[4]

END OF TERM!!! Perhaps I shall be a philosopher when we start again. Robbie . . .

. . . Sometimes Uncle Ted can be quite reasonable. These last few days he's been really woebegone, sitting in his study composing what he calls his State of the Art to the Masses speech, which he has to give at the convention next Sunday. Every so often he trudges out, grabs whichever of us happens to be passing, and demands to be told a word that's on the tip of his mind, only he's forgotten it; or a joke—*any* joke.

Janine just shrugs. Nick supplies jokes. I seem to be so good at coming up with the word or thing that Uncle Ted wants that he's started to call me his peripatetic encyclopedia. *Not* the snappiest of job descriptions. The last time he did it—"Maree, for God's sake that constellation with the belt and the sword—fellow who rode on the dolphin's back—*you* know"—and I told him, "Orion," he stopped as he was going back into his study and wrote *Orion* on the back of his hand so as not to forget it again. Then he said, "Maree, do you have *any* money at all?"

"No," I said. The hundred quid is gone now and not for worlds am I going to go and beg Robbie for what I paid for our flat. "Not until next term," I added hastily, remembering I am supposed to pay Uncle Ted rent. It wasn't quite a lie. After all, some other prat might make me a present of another £100. Who knows?

"Then you'll need some for the convention," he said. "They can be quite expensive." And he gave me this wad of money. When I counted it, it was £75. All he had in his back pocket. Then he went on—I nearly fainted—"And I'll pay your petrol if you're driving there. After all, it's my fault you're going to have to be there." Then he rushed back into his study before I could even start to thank him, muttering, "Orion. Orion."

Well, well. Poor Uncle Ted. He's so dreading making this speech that he seems to have forgiven me for Nick's little caper. He's forgiven Nick too. Nick has his usual lavish pocket money. I shall go and buy a spare pair of jeans. Then I can wash these I have on.

(5)

Poor Uncle Ted. On the Thursday—I started writing this when it was still Thursday, but it's turned into Friday now—he was pale and trembling and kept having to dash to the loo. He couldn't pack—at least, he did pack, but he left all the clothes out except for a sweater and half his pyjamas—and Janine had to do it again for him. He left his speech all neatly piled up on his desk and got into the car without it. Janine had her hands so full of him that she seemed quite relieved when I said I was driving myself to Wantchester in Dad's car (I didn't mention Uncle Ted had paid for the petrol). Nick promptly said that he'd come with me. I think Master Nick hoped, or thought, that this meant we'd be skiving off and staying at home, but apart from the fact that I'd promised Uncle Ted that I'd FAITH-FULLY listen to his speech and applaud it at the end, I was intrigued. I wanted to know what kind of event could make him so terrified.

Well, now I know. To some extent.

Nick and I set off about an hour after his parents. This was because I filled Dad's car with all my worldly posses-sions. Nick wanted to know why.

"Other people have security blankets," I told him. "I have a car filled with everything I own." I didn't like to confess to him that I keep having this strong feeling that I am going to be homeless after Easter. No—worse than that: it feels as if the world is going to end then, and I have to carry every thing around with me and make sure that, when I'm crouching in a cave after Armageddon, I at least have my computer and my vet-case to hand (both of which will be very useful, of course). I don't know what's making me feel this way. It could be the Thornlady dreams. It's not my Dad. I've rung him and he swears he's improving (ex-cept I know he's saying that to make me feel better). It's just that I have this gloomy conviction that's settled on me like a rainy week. I even phoned Mum about it. She was her usual cheery self.

"Ah, Maree," she says, "you want to take notice of a premonition like that. I know, because it runs in my family too. My mother foretold the very day and hour she was going to die, and she wasn't even ill when she told me."

Thanks a bunch, Mum.

Anyway, I loaded in my stuff and Nick got into the car saying, "I won't say anything. My father made me promise not to keep winding you up."

"What do you mean, winding me up?" I said, starting the car with a roar and a swoop. It always seems to do that when I'm a trifle irritated.

"He means the way we usually go on—he calls it sparring for dominance." Nick said placidly. "He doesn't understand that I have to do that or you'd walk all over me."

"Oh, spare me!" I said. It took me half the drive to simmer down after that one. Uncle Ted no doubt meant well and I knew he'd had a private talk with Nick yesterday, but Nick had no business to spill the beans to me. It annoyed me even more that I knew Nick had said it on purpose, to make me angry instead of gloomy. News for you, Master Nick. A person can be angry *and* gloomy. That seems to be my permanent state at the moment. And I detest being *managed*.

Arriving in Wantchester didn't exactly improve my state of mind. Nick fetched out the map the convention had sent Uncle Ted, that Janine had photocopied for us after breakfast, and said, "Here it is. Hotel Babylon, right in the middle of town. Easy. Why do you think it's called Babylon? TV show? Burning fiery furnace? Hanging gardens? Go straight ahead here."

"What *are* hanging gardens?" I said, taking the road he pointed at. "It always makes me think of rows of gibbets in a park."

"Trees in the air, I think of—go first right," said Nick.

"We'd notice those," I agreed, going where he said, "or

a furnace. Or a dirty great tower broadcasting in a hundred languages. Tower of Babel. That was in Babylon too, wasn't it?"

Ten minutes later, we both noticed it—a large sign above the houses that said HOTEL BABYLON—but the town has a one-way system to beat any other town I know and it took us on past at a distance. I drove on, grinding gears about, and after a while we saw the sign again, going past on the other side. But there was no way to get to it. We saw the Cathedral, a shopping precinct, the Town Hall and the river. We crossed the river, because there seemed no way not to, and next thing I knew we were entangled in an open space full of long glass arcades like tunnels to nowhere, that Nick identified belatedly as Whinmore Bus Station. Much too late. By that time I was having to back out of the place, bonnet to bonnet with a double-decker bus, whose driver was *not* pleased to see us there.

I drew into a bus stop to recover from that. From there we saw the Hotel Babylon sign quite clearly, about a hundred metres away, behind the glass arcades. The only way I could see to get there was to drive through the bus station and risk another double-decker bus.

"The place is trying to stop us getting to it," I said. "It's like an evil spell. Perhaps I should try driving to it widdershins, the wrong way round the one-way system."

"You'll get arrested," Nick said. He was perfectly happy. By this time he had a map of Wantchester set up on his laptop and was filling in all the places that we passed. The bus station, I saw, had just gone in as "Glass Maze with Monsters."

"Nick, are you doing this to me on purpose?" I demanded, with menace.

"No way. Try turning left at the next lot of traffic lights," he said.

Since a bus was trying to get into the bus stop where we were, I drove on. And after that I really did feel as if something was trying to stop us getting to the hotel. I said so to Nick after we had accidentally visited a small factory and were doing a brisk tour of the suburbs. I could see we were almost out of town by then. There were fields and bare trees on one side of the road.

Nick grinned. "Then we say the spell to stop the spell." Naturally we both began chanting:

> "How many miles to Babylon?
> Three score miles and ten.
> Can I get there by candle-light?
> Yes, and back again."

And then I felt much better and turned in someone's driveway and we drove back into Wantchester from the other side. I can hardly describe the hilarious mixture of laughter and misery and anger that I was feeling by then. I said, "And on top of it all, I keep having the Thornlady dreams again!"

"Why didn't you *say*?" Nick said. "We should have done the Witchy Dance for Luck in the garden at home. Now we'll have to do it the moment we find a place to stop."

"Are you sure?" I said.

"Positive. Urgently," he said. In a hilarious, not-quite-sane way, we both knew it was true.

And seconds after Nick spoke, we turned a corner and saw Hotel Babylon standing across the distant end of a great wide street in front of us.

"The spell worked," Nick said.

"Just as well," I said. "It's going to be dark soon and I'm not sure how the lights work. Now conjure me up the car park and we'll get dancing."

"Hey presto," Nick said, calmly shutting down his laptop.

Sure enough, there was an archway in the wall beside the hotel, labelled HOTEL CAR PARK GUESTS ONLY. I turned into it, saying, "Why the hell are you always so *lucky*, Nick? It's bad for your personality. It's not fair. I've had bad luck ever since I can remember."

"Witchy Dance," Nick said, throwing open the door on his side.

So I stopped the car just inside the archway and jumped out too, and we began the Dance at once: step-shuffle-step-hop-hop-step—stop. At every stop we did the flick, flick, flick, and chanted, "Luck, luck, luck!" My fingernails have now grown into great long yellow spikes, so the flicking was really satisfying.

And it was odd. The car park was pretty well full. I saw Janine's car parked nearest the hotel as I hopped and turned. There was no sign of her and Uncle Ted. But there were people at at least half of the other cars and the vans, unloading things—suitcases, guitars and video equipment—and most of them barely glanced at us. There was an old van almost beside us where three people with waist-length hair and a baby went on unloading bags, bundles and the baby's cot without even looking at us. You got the feeling they saw much odder things than the Witchy Dance every day of their lives.

This was rather encouraging. "Luck, *luck*, LUCK!" Nick and I roared, and danced and twisted like dervishes. I *did* hear a car hooting, but I honestly thought it was out in the road—well, it almost was, because it was halfway through the archway I had blocked by stopping Dad's car—but I didn't notice a thing until its driver came and screamed at us.

"Get this load of scrapiron out of my way, you stupid bitch!"

"Screamed" is the right word. He had a thin tenor voice. He had a little pointed beard. His face was mauve and his nose was pointed too, and pinched with fury, so that white marks came and went on the sides of it.

Nobody calls me a bitch and gets away with it. Even Robbie only tried it once. I calmly pointed a flick! at his mauve face and turned to look at his car. It was a horrible old banger, covered with rust, and it was blocking the archway. I could see at least one car angrily backing away from behind it. I looked at Dad's car. True, it was in the way, and it's a bit weather-beaten these days, but nothing to the heap that *his* was.

"Same to you," I said. "In spades. Bitch and scrapiron."

"MOVE it!" howled curly beard. "I am a guest at this convention."

"Me too," I said. "For my sins."

"I am Mervin Thurless!" he screamed.

"Then you need a deed poll," says I. "Can't help you there."

He screamed I was a bitch again. I told him, "Once more, my good man, gets you pins in a wax image, or worse. I'd do it now, and curse you into the bargain, only I'm crossed in love and haven't the energy. Now *you* get out of *my* way." I pushed past him, climbed into my car again, and drove with immense dignity to the free space where Nick was now standing beckoning. Typical Nick, that. Brisk vanishment at the first sign of trouble. Nick waved me into the space with great flourishes to disguise the fact that tears of laughter were pouring down his face.

"How is it that this happens every time we do the Witchy Dance?" I said to him.

"This one forgot to pay you," he giggled.

"Yes, but it was *much* more satisfactory," I said. "I actually got a word in edgeways—several in fact—this time."

That space turned out to be the last one empty. Clever Nick. Mauve Mr. Thurless was forced to back out through the archway and drive away. That gave me great joy. I watched him doing it from under one of my arms while I was unloading the bags with our clothes in from the boot.

TEN

From Maree Mallory's
Thornlady Directory: file
twenty-three

We entered into a large space full of suitcases and confusion. People in jeans and T-shirts were rushing everywhere, shouting things like "Tell Rocker to go straight to the Ops Room!" or "Hasn't Jedda got those bloody files copied yet?" or simply "Slime Monster!" and hugging one another, men and women alike.

"Well, well," I said to Nick. "They did build the Tower of Babel here after all!"

We ploughed our way through it all to the Reception desk near the back. I jumped the last clump of suitcases to find Nick saying to the harassed hotel-lady at the desk, "We're Nick and Maree Mallory. I think we've got rooms booked here."

Someone behind bellowed while Nick was speaking, "The badge machine's broken again, I tell you!" Maybe this caused the girl to mishear Nick or something.

The girl's neat little brooch said she was Odile and she had a permanently worried look. She punched things on her computer. "I'm sorry," she said in a foreign accent. "That room is already taken."

"It *can't* be!" I shrieked across the noise. "Anyway, it wasn't one room, it was two."

Odile, looking fractionally more worried, punched buttons some more. "Mr. and Mrs. Mallory," she said. "One double room, already taken. That is all there is on the computer. No doubles left. Sorry."

"We *aren't* Mr. and Mrs. Mallory," Nick attempted to explain.

And I probably made things worse by adding, "We're cousins. Those Mallorys are his Dad and his Mum. We want a single room each."

"I'm sorry," Odile intoned. "All rooms have been taken by the convention."

She obviously hadn't understood a word we said, but we still tried to behave as if she was rational. "We know," we said in chorus. Nick said, quite slowly and loudly, "Two of those rooms are for *us*."

Odile looked blank. She punched more buttons. "One double room for Mr. and Mrs. Mallory is already taken by the convention. Sorry."

By this time, we were both leaning rather desperately over the desk, as if we could get through to Odile if we got close to her. Nick said, "Look. Look at us. Do we look as if we're married?"

Odile shot him a blank, worried look. Perhaps where she came from people do get married at Nick's age. Anyway, she said, "It is in the computer."

So I had a go. I said, "Listen, Odile. Try *single* rooms in the name of Mallory. Please? As a favour."

Without altering her blank, worried look, Odile went back to pressing buttons. The suspense was too much for both of us. We sort of turned away, and Nick muttered, "I think she's a robot."

"Android anyway," I muttered back. Then I discovered that the ceiling of the hotel foyer was a mass of mirrors, large and small. The entire confusion of folk was reflected there, upside-down, milling about, sort of hanging there mixed up with trees in urns and piles of suitcases. There were the three people with the baby again, passing the baby chair round from one to another so that they could hug someone they had just met. I could see Nick and me. We rippled from one mirror to another as I moved my head—

one tall dark good-looking teenage boy and one short girl who looked surprisingly like a normal human being. It gave me a queer feeling, as if I was reading the future in the sky. It caused an anxious thought to strike me. "Nick," I said. I could see from the ceiling that he was looking at the three with the baby, cautiously and sort of sideways, trying to see which of them was female and which male. It wasn't easy to tell. Two of them could have been either. I jabbed his elbow with my longest fingernail. "Nick, who actually booked our rooms? Janine or Uncle Ted?"

"Oh—Mum did," he said.

As he said it, a little of the blankness faded from Odile's face. We both spotted it in the ceiling and turned to her eagerly. "Mallory," she said. "The computer has one single room booked for Nick Mallory."

"Oh *fun!*" I said. "Dear Janine."

"Look some more," Nick said to Odile. "There should be one for Maree Mallory too."

The blankness descended on Odile again, but she pressed buttons. I suddenly couldn't bear to look. I thought I was going to cry. I mean I know Janine hates me, but to have it publicly demonstrated like this was almost too much— and the thought of driving all the way back to Bristol in the dark was definitely too much. I looked firmly at the ceiling, where the man the three with the baby had been hugging was now moving upside-down across the foyer, greeting this person and that. He stood out for his very white T-shirt with a row of large flat badges on it, and he had some sort of equipment clipped to his belt. But his stomach bulged and hid most of his belt. And then he went all blurred. In order not to cry, I rounded on Odile again. She was shaking her head.

"Oh look here!" I said. It came out booming. "There has to be a room for me if there's one for Nick. My uncle's Guest of Honour at this convention. He was *told* there would be rooms for his family!"

The man in the white T-shirt came up beside me. "Having trouble?" he said.

We both jumped. It was odd to find him real, as well as upside-down in the ceiling beside my small shock-headed figure. One of his row of badges said COMMITTEE, and when I pushed my glasses up my nose, I could see the name beneath that: RICK CORRIE. The rest of the badges said things like ALL POWER CORRUPTS BUT WE NEED ELECTRIC-ITY and DYSLEXIA RULES KO, and the thing clipped to his wide waist was a radio phone. He had a black streaky beard and a round pleasant face.

"This robot-woman thinks I don't have a room booked," I told him. I was ashamed of the angry, booming sob in my voice.

"Happens all the time," Rick Corrie said cheerfully. "I'm supposed to be Hotel Liaison. Let me see what I can do." He pushed me gently aside and started talking rapidly to Odile in a foreign language. Odile's face turned from worried robot to the face of a human being and she began pushing buttons again with a will. Rick Corrie turned to Nick. "What was your name again? We're trying to get your sister a room next to yours."

"Cousin," Nick said. "I'm Nick Mallory. She's Maree."

A great smile split Rick's beard. "Then you're the great man's family! In that case we must definitely do a bit of room-juggling." He leant back over the counter and ex-changed more foreign talk with Odile. In under a minute, he was turning back and holding a key out to each of us. "Here you are. Rooms 534 and 535. Just sign these forms and then I'll take you up to register with the convention."

We signed, me at least in a wash of gratitude, and picked up our bags and followed Rick up the nearby stairs. I had a last glimpse of us in the ceiling, looking flurried and glad, and me a shock-headed scramble of legs as I caught up with Rick. "How did you work that?" I said.

"Easy," he said. "I told her to give you a room that some-one hadn't turned up to claim."

"But won't he mind?" I puffed. The stairs were short but steep.

Rick shrugged his plump shoulders. "Too bad if he does.

113

He hasn't arrived when he said he would, and the Opening Ceremony's coming up in half an hour. A lot of the programme items have already started. He's late. Or he's not coming and hasn't bothered to cancel."

There were more mirrors at the back of the wide landing the stairs led to. We watched ourselves advance as Nick asked, "What language did you speak to the robot-woman in?"

"Finnish," said Rick. "More of an android really. The hotel hires her cheap because she wants to get programmed in English."

"Then this *is* the Tower of Babel," I said.

"Yes," he said feelingly. We arrived into a crowd on the landing and had to wait our turn at a long table there. He said, "It's caused a lot of trouble already. The Romanian fans arrived without their luggage, the Russians can't find their interpreter, and the Germans don't like the plumbing. At least the Americans speak English, even if there was a muddle about their rooms—you're not the only ones."

We broke through to the long table then, where a big hand-painted notice said PHANTASMACON REGISTRATION. Several people were sitting behind the table, half hidden by boxes with teddy bears propped against them. Rick Corrie led us up to a blue teddy with a large M under it. A notice hung round the teddy's neck said I AM SOCRATES. I ♥ CONVENTIONS. I looked it in its mournful button eyes and wished I hadn't. I was not sure I was going to heart anything about this weekend at that stage.

"Mallory," Rick Corrie said to the fat girl behind the box. Her badge said WILLOW, but Rick called her Wendy. "The rest of the GOH family party, Wendy."

Wendy gave us a hasty smile that lifted her cheeks into lumps like tennis balls, and then lowered the lumps to say to Rick Corrie, in a strong, whining voice, "Rick, I hope someone's going to relieve me here soon. I need to get into con-clothes for the Ceremony."

"Not my problem," Rick told her cheerfully. "Speak to Magnus or Parabola."

Wendy muttered something and searched through hundreds of plastic bags in her boxes. It took her a while, because her long hair kept falling over her massive shoulders and she kept stopping to hurl it back. When she at last discovered two bags and leant forward, smiling tennis balls again, to hand them round Socrates, her vast bosom pooled on the boxes in cushion-sized lumps. I saw Nick look hastily away. I think he thought she was some kind of cripple.

"Here you are," she said. "Programme and breakfast-tickets, lucky number and badge. Please wear your badge at all times. We're having trouble with gate-crashers."

Nick took his bag sort of sideways. I took mine. "Right," said Rick Corrie. "I'll take you up to your—" His radio phone began yelling. He unhitched it and listened to the agitated quacking coming out of it with growing dismay. "But we weren't expecting anyone from Croatia!" he said to it. "All right. I'll be down in two seconds. Out." He was on one foot ready to run by then. "Hey you," he said to a pale young man loitering by the end of the table. "You take these two to rooms 534 and 535, will you. I have to go," he said to us. "See you at the Ceremony." And he left at a sprint, taking the stairs in threes.

The pale young man solemnly held out a hand for my bag. "The lifts are just along here," he said. He had hair so fair it was greenish, almost matching the colour of his T-shirt, which had words on it in a strange language. Finnish? I wondered, while he was pressing the lift button for us.

I was going to ask, only a tremendous noise broke out behind us. A tenor voice was howling, "I *insist* on satisfaction! I'm a guest at this convention!" and other voices were clamouring, trying to soothe it.

Luckily the lift arrived just then. Nick and I both hopped in and then looked anxiously out as the door slid shut. Sure enough, Mervin Thurless was leaning over the long table, beard jutting, mauve with rage again. "I bet I know what's happened," I murmured to Nick.

"Not your fault," he murmured back as the lift started upwards.

"I am Dutch," remarked the young man. "My name is Case. That is spelt K-E-E-S. It is short for Kornelius." And he spelt that too.

"Oh," I said.

"Ah," Nick said.

There was a mirror in the lift too. It showed us both staring cautiously at Dutch Case.

"I'm Maree," I said. "This is Nick."

"Pleased to meet you," said Case. "You are not Old Nick and I am not a nutcase. There is a Dutch joke for you."

"Ah," I said.

"Oh," said Nick.

We were both glad when the lift stopped and the door slid away to show a board with arrows. It said

← ROOMS 501–556   ROOMS 557–501 →

"I think we can find our—hang *on*," Nick said. He took another look at the notice.

"Precisely," Case said smugly. "It is not so simple. Also a Committee member has told me to take you and I must do what he says. I am a Gopher."

"Gopher?" we both said together as we all turned left. "Oh, I get you!" I said. "You go for—"

But Case told us anyway. He was that kind. "It is spelt G-O-P-H-E-R and it means people who fetch and carry and whom the Con cannot do without." We pushed through swing doors and went down a long, long corridor. "People who run errands," he said. "No doubt it began as a joke, meaning 'Go for this' or 'Go for that,' but now it is an institution. Round here." We turned left again and went down another corridor. Case said, "At PhantasmaCon it is also an institution that the Gophers are known as Hobbits." We turned another left-hand corner. There were mirrors at each of these corners. They produced a very odd effect, a brief illusion of us coming and going, and wheeling elsewhere.

As we wheeled round the fourth left-hand turn, I tore my eyes off the mirrors and said politely, "Your English is very good."

116

"Thank you," said Case. "I am rather proud of it."

The numbers on the doors we passed now said 523, 524, 525. "It can't be much further, surely?" Nick said.

"You may be wrong," said Case. "This is a very peculiar hotel. I think it is straight out of Escher. Escher was a Dutch artist, you know, who drew things so that they look as if they go up when they go down, but when you look closely they do both and you cannot tell."

"Er . . . yes," said Nick. The numbers on the doors were in the forties now. And believe it or not, we turned left again and I really think that was five right angles by then. Nick said uncertainly, "We'll be back at the lift again at this rate, won't we?"

"I think not," said Case. "Yes, in most hotels. But here you can turn five corners and still not make a square."

And, you know, he was right! Nick muttered things about this building *must* be built in a sort of Greek key-pattern and it wasn't *possible,* but I'm here to say it *was.* We turned left yet again and had to walk most of the way down a long corridor lined with red carpet before we came to room 534. I felt it was quite lucky that room 535 was next to it. At that rate, it could have been *anywhere.* All the same, we were both quite sure that Case had taken us the long way round and that the lifts must be just round the next mirrored corner. We suspected another Dutch joke, and we each decided, quite independently, to go that way when we went to look for this Opening Ceremony.

Meanwhile, Nick tried to get even with Case. Case announced that, well, he would love us and leave us now. Nick held the door of his room propped open on one foot and leant backwards out of it. "I hope you won't mind my asking," he says, very serious and polite, "but what does your T-shirt say?"

Case looked smugly down at his narrow chest. "It says," he said, "I AM A HOBBIT." He bowed and walked away. "In Elvish," he added as he left.

That round was Case's, hands down.

We didn't stay long in our rooms, just long enough for

me to look in the placcy bag I'd been given. It had a smiley face and "PhantasmaCon" on the outside, and a mass of bumf on the inside, one item of which was a whole glossy magazine with a story by Uncle Ted in it; but there were appeals for AIDS victims and ads for things called Swords N'Attire and . . . anyway, I found the badge with my name on it and threw the rest away. In this I was less than clever. Master Nick had had the sense to notice that the scruffiest bit of paper was in fact the programme to this madhouse. It was all organized in columns labelled "Parallel Universe One," "Mallory World," "Home Universe," and so on, and it made no more sense to me than the hotel corridors. But Nick had it worked out. He said. He said the Opening Ceremony was in Home Universe and that was the first floor in the big function room. So we tried to go there.

We went the other way, expecting to get to the lifts any moment. And we didn't. I lost count of the corners we turned, but I remember Nick saying they were all right-angles, which meant that by now we had walked round two and a half squares at least, and it didn't make *sense*. I said we ought to have met ourselves, or walked into a new dimension or something, but all we did was get to the lifts, in the end.

Downstairs it ought to have been simple. There were even notices with arrows, saying HOME UNIVERSE, but I suppose the trouble was that we didn't know what we were looking for. And everyone seemed to have gone by then, so we couldn't ask. Anyway, we wandered for a bit, until we came to an official-looking door, and we opened the door and looked round it.

We found a small, rather dark room, where a dozen or so people were clustered round a blackboard. Every single one of them wore a long robe with a cowl to it—like mad monks. You couldn't see any of the faces at all, not even the face of the one who was writing on the board and turning to explain to the others. He was writing symbols that made my stomach feel queer after only one glance. *Really* queer. At the moment we looked in, he was saying, "For the strongest effect, you should visualize all these written in fire on a background of flames."

Nick and I, with one accord, backed out and closed the door very gently. After that I let fly a giant burp, because of the funny way my stomach was feeling. "Which universe do you think *they* were in?" I whispered.

"Somewhere very alien," Nick said decidedly.

We continued our search by going along to the next door and opening that. I was saying, "If Uncle Ted was wanting to punish us, I think he's succeeding," and Nick was agreeing, "But not quite in the way he—" when we found we were in a vast hall full of faces all turning to look at us. We were there. It was like a bad dream, but it was the Opening Ceremony right enough. We slid into the back row of seats with hot faces.

It was just starting. There was Uncle Ted in the act of taking a seat on the far-off platform, along with ten or so other people we didn't know, and Janine being shown to a seat in the front row. As we sat down, a glossy-faced youngish man in a T-shirt, with a great deal of wriggly blond hair, sprang up and began welcoming everyone to PhantasmaCon. But he'd only got as far as ". . . pleasure it is to have with us as Guest of Honour . . ." when the door that end burst open and a high tenor voice cried out, "I'm sorry, I'm *sorry!* I know you're just starting and I haven't come to stay!" and Mervin Thurless rushed in and rushed up on to the platform. "I just wanted to tell you it's a disgrace," he said. "I'm a guest of this convention and you've put me in the Station Hotel!"

Half the people on the platform sprang up. Rick Corrie sprang up too, out of the audience. He bounded to the platform, seized Thurless by one arm and hurried him aside, where he talked to him in urgent whispers. Thurless was not placated. In the end, Rick hurried him outside and the door banged on Thurless shouting, "I don't care! I insist on a taxi!"

"That was Mervin Thurless," said the blond, glossy man gravely.

119

The audience, to my surprise, clapped and cheered. A lot of people laughed. They were like that, the people at this convention—surprisingly good-humoured and in a holiday mood: as if they had come to enjoy themselves as much as listen to writers talk about books. I spent the rest of the very boring Ceremony looking around at them.

My first thought was that the police would be in trouble here, if there had been a crime and they needed descriptions of the man on the scene. About nine-tenths of the men had beards and wore glasses. Otherwise there were people of all ages, from the eccentric-looking old man with the deaf-aid to the long-haired people's baby (which had to be carried outside crying around then) and quite a number of children. There was also more than a fair share of achingly glamorous young females. But there were also more than usual numbers of Wendy-shaped fat ones. There was a whole row of them, male and female, just along from Nick and me, and I stared fascinated at their huge tightly stretched T-shirts, each with something clever or weird written on it. They made me feel pleasantly slender for a change. The men were none of them my types, fat or thin. I don't go for beards and glasses. But I thought I could quite fancy one or two of the willowy types in paramilitary gear, or the dark one in black leather and mirror shades sitting beside Uncle Ted on the platform. But I know what *really* struck me: the hall was full of people I'd like to get to know. An unusual feeling for sulky, solitary me, that. This feeling extended particularly to the large sprinkling of shy-looking middle-aged ladies (much to my surprise). I found myself looking at the skinny greying one nearest—she was in a bright patchwork jacket—and thinking that whatever she did for a job, it bored her, and she didn't get on with her workmates, so she clearly lived a passionate life among books instead. And I would have liked to talk to her about some of the things we'd both read.

By the end of the Ceremony, I was thinking that the punishment was not really a punishment at all. Ha, ha. That was before Janine swept down on Nick with "Come along, darling. We're going to eat with the other guests," and whisked him away.

I was left on my own for the rest of the evening.

It was a bit like your first day at school or college. I didn't know anyone and I had no idea what to do, and everyone was charging and bustling around me, knowing exactly where they were going and who they were going with. So I pushed my specs up my nose, squared my shoulders and went to my car to bring my most valued things up to my room. I did the first load unhindered—or unhindered by anything except the weird effect of those mirrors on the corners of the corridors. And there were five right-angle corners. I counted. There and back, going to the lifts both ways. And I was standing waiting for the lift to go down for the next load when I happened to look back at the nearest corner. And I saw the MOST FABULOUS MAN I'd ever seen in my life. Tall and Nordic and slim, deep-set eyes, no beard, no glasses—just *staggering*. To die for, as Robbie's bint Davina would say.

He was just at the junction, reflected in all the mirrors, so I could see he was fabulous from every angle, and at first I thought he was coming towards me, to the lifts. My knees felt weak at the thought of actually sharing the lift with him. But he was really going the other way. The four images of him I could see wheeled to the right—I *think* it was to the right—and walked off the mirrors. I was smitten enough by the sight of him to run back to that corner to get another look at him as he walked away—he had the sexiest walk—but he must have gone into one of the nearest rooms, because by the time I had tottered over there the cross-corridor was empty. All I saw were multiple versions of myself, looking small and lost.

Then the lift came and I sprinted back and got in it. Further mirror, showing Maree looking glum and frustrated. Still, I'm bound to see him again. And I ask myself what has become of my feelings for Robbie, that I could be so knocked sideways by a total stranger. But it was all right. As soon as I looked inside me, I was as raw as ever in the

121

place where Robbie was torn away. Yet I still feel weak thinking of that fabulous man. I must be very odd.

I was coming back through the foyer with another load, watching the image of myself in the ceiling dangling bags and clutching my VDU to my tummy, when I was accosted by Dutch Case. "Let Case take your case—this is what I am here for!" he cries, and whips my vet's bag out of my straining fingers. "Where to?" And he set off for the lift anyway.

I went after him at a panting trot. Dad proudly gave me that bag—and it's never been any real use, bless him!— and I didn't trust Case with it one bit. When we got to the lift, he tried to wrestle the VDU out of my grip too, but I hung on to it and he only got the carrier bag with the flexes in.

"Let me take it all. I am an excellent beast of burden," he said.

I said no, I could manage the rest, thank you. So we went up in the lift protesting at one another, and then he said was I a computer freak? And I said no, I just used it.

"But I am a great freak, in all sorts of ways," he said. I believed him. "I can do tricks with viruses," he says. "I once made every computer in Rotterdam display the same nonsense rhyme on the stroke of midday." He recited the rhyme in Dutch. It took four floors.

"Very clever," I said. We left the lift and started the trudge round the five right-angles.

"We will set up your computer and then you will eat with me," he said.

"No thanks," I said.

"But you must. I will make it a Dutch treat," he said beguilingly. "Dutch joke."

"No money," I said.

"But I have no money either!" he exclaimed. "So let us have a Barmecide's feast and drink warm water together!"

"I have work to do," I lied.

When we got to my room, he tried to stay and set up the computer. I was quite determined he wouldn't. I didn't trust him not to fill my software with Dutch jokes. I didn't trust him, period. I more or less kicked him out. He leant back in round the door and smiled meltingly. "Such a strong mind!" he said. "Call on me if you change it. I am room 301."

"Go away," I said.

After I set up the computer, I was hungry. I found the service stairs, just in case Case—oh God, another Dutch joke! It's catching—was hanging about by the lift. I don't know what it is about that boy (or perhaps I do) and anyway, I've been crossed in love and Case is a bit of a come-down after that fabulous Nordic type, so I went down the stairs and found the dining room. The prices posted on the board outside made my hair curl. So I went to the bar, hoping they did sandwiches. I was afraid I was going to have to starve until breakfast.

Mirrors again there, too, not only behind the bar, but the whole end wall, so the place looks huge. They did the most expensive ham rolls I have ever eaten. I bought half a pint of orange juice and found a place to sit.

That bar was crowded with strange conversations. Some Americans next to me were avidly discussing something called a "shared world" (I thought it was something we had no choice about sharing), and someone just behind me kept saying, "It's no skin off his nose if I filk his filk!" A highly hairy man in front of me was complaining, "It's his inker that lets him down every time!" Then I heard a girl scream-ing out, up by the mirror end, "Come to the Gophers' Orgy! I'm just starting it now!" to which several people yelled, "Oh, shut up, Tallulah!"

I turned to see who was shouting and saw, of all people, that prat Venables!

I don't mean he was shouting. He wasn't. He was sitting on a tall bar stool, chatting to the blond glossy man. Because of the mirror up that end, I had him in front and back view, so there was no mistake. From behind, there was the long, smooth head, and in the mirror there was his long, smooth face with the gold-rimmed specs—and the face was just turning away from me with much the same horror on it that I was feeling, seeing him. At least he wasn't wearing a suit this time, but he had on a smart suede jacket and a pristine polo-neck sweater. Altogether he was out of place. I'd have bet large odds he'd ironed his jeans.

"Ouch!" I said, and jerked my eyes away. This was lucky, because it showed me in the mirror that Rick Corrie was standing doubtfully looking down at me. "Oh, hello," I said to him.

"Hello. Is nobody looking after you?" he said. "Can I get you a drink?"

I said yes please, I'd like a vodka, if he would. He looked so dismayed that I realized he thought I was Nick's age. A lot of people do. "I'm twenty," I told him. "Honestly. Do you want to see my birth certificate?"

"I think I don't want you to push your specs up your nose at me like that," he said. "I can see it means trouble."

Then he fetched himself massive amounts of beer and me a vodka, and we talked for a bit. He loves Uncle Ted's demons too. I said my favourite was the blue three-legged one that kept pushing its face through bedroom walls to see what people did in bed. *His* favourite one was the one that was just a pool of saliva that took the skin off your ankles. And we both agreed that the demon that came up at you out of the loo was a bit too close to real fears for comfort. Then his beeper went. He left his beer and pelted away to deal with a crisis. I was sorry. But I could see that in ordinary life Rick Corrie would arrange to be called away by beepers too. He was one of those people who find it hard to talk to anyone for very long. I think a lot of the people here may be like that.

But it was a shame, because it left me to the mercy of an awful woman who was just the opposite. While I was talking to Rick, I noticed her drifting up to the Americans in the next seats, and that they all said, "Hi, Tansy-Ann" and then turned their backs on her. I can see why. And the moment Rick left, this Tansy-Ann creature pounced on me.

"Tell me *all* about it!" she said. "I'm Tansy-Ann and I'm a healer." When I stared at her rather, she added, "Your

124

aura is one big grey psychic cloud. Let me give you a back-rub. It'll stop you being so sad and tense." And she pushed me forward in my chair and started sort of kneading at my shoulders. I didn't like it. Neither did I like her. *She* was the big grey psychic cloud, *if* you like. She was biggish and plumpish and her face somehow retired behind her large, probing nose. And she was dressed in something orange and shapeless covered with millions of little cold dangling pieces of yellow metal that jangled when she pounced, and I didn't like that either. I wriggled away from her probing cold hands and said I didn't feel like a back-rub just now.

"A hand-massage then!" she exclaimed, diving and jingling round in front of me. "I'm real good at massaging hands. It's the most soothing experience in the world. You'll love it!" And, blow me down, she grabbed my hands and started squeezing and bending them about.

I took them away and sat on them. I said I was all right. Thanks. Tansy-Ann.

"You need to sort out your sex life!" she cried. "You're British. That's what's wrong with you. *I know!* Let me set you straight." Then she leant over me and talked. And talked. After a while I didn't listen. Tantric sex came into it, and karma, and auras. But then, somehow, she seemed to be talking about widow spiders and the joys a rat felt running in a maze. I just sat there and decided that it wasn't that her nose *was* that big. It was just that it sort of probed at you as she talked. It seemed to poke about greedily for something she could get off me. Maybe she was a vampire. Possibly she was cuckoo. But I still didn't have to like her. I made several attempts to get up and go. She just pushed me back down again and went on talking. She had got on to Tarot at some stage. She said she would sort me out by doing a reading.

I was rescued by the sweetest lady. She was shortish and plumpish and darkish, with a rosy sort of innocent face, and she simply came up behind Tansy-Ann and murmured something to her.

125

Tansy-Ann leapt backwards from me, yelling out, "Is that so?" Then she was off like an orange juggernaut through the bar, hitting tables and spilling people's drinks and yelling out, "Excuse me! I have to go see to my exhibit!"

The lady smiled at me and went away. She was wearing a long crimson robe thing and lots of necklaces, which ought to have looked as strange as Tansy-Ann's orange, but it didn't. There was all the difference in the world. The crimson robe looked natural, somehow, as if the lady deserved to wear it and usually did wear it. I wondered who she was.

(Later: I found out she's called Zinka Fearon and everyone I asked says she's marvellous.)

As soon as Tansy-Ann's yells died away into the distance, I fled back here to my room and started writing this. Widow spiders! I thought to myself as I came up in the lift. Rats! Massage! How the hell does she think she knows rats enjoy mazes? And what has Tarot to do with any of it?

Nick banged at my door and came in a while back. It was after midnight by then. And we both said, "Where the hell have you *been*?" at the same instant, which made us both laugh. Then he said that I didn't miss much, not eating with the guests—it was dead boring, and one of them was a man called Something White he's always hated. He'd escaped before the end and looked for me, because Universe Three was showing *The Princess Bride* and he wanted to see it with me.

"But you've seen *The Princess Bride* three times already, to my certain knowledge!" I said.

"I still wanted to see it," he said. "I went by myself in the end. But that wasn't what I came to say. That prat with the silver car who gave you the money—he's here."

"I *know*!" I said feelingly. "I've been wondering if we summoned him up by doing the Witchy Dance. It just seems so unlikely—here, of all places."

"Well," Nick said, looking rather odd, "you could be right. I'll tell you—I was just coming out of the lift just now, and I saw him standing up at the end of the corridor where the mirrors are—"

"About ten reflections of him. I know," I said, thinking of the fabulous Nordic type.

"No," Nick said. "No, that was one of the odd things. There was only him. No reflections at all. But then the walls and the mirrors started turning round him. Like a wheel. I mean, I saw the edges of the mirrors as they went round past him. Honestly."

We stared at one another queasily. Nick doesn't say things like that unless they're true. And I could see he was not having me on. "Remind me never to do the Witchy Dance again," I said.

"I think it's this hotel," Nick said. "It's the weirdest place."

"And full of weird folk," I agreed.

That was over an hour ago at least. I kept plugging away at the keyboard because there is a disco going on downstairs. Another weird thing about this hotel is that you can't hear a *thing* from any of the people chasing about in it, but you can hear the disco loud and clear through four floors. But I think it's stopped now. I might get some sleep, with luck.

ELEVEN

(1)

From the account of Rupert
Venables

Scarlatti played in my car all the way to Wantchester. I
bore it. I even changed the tapes myself so that Andrew,
sitting solidly beside me, should not notice there were three
of us. Andrew was remarkably cheerful. He looked out at
the wintry landscape and smiled as if it were high summer
and blue sky, instead of bare fields under sulky grey rolls
of snowcloud. He had just designed the perfect vacuum
cleaner, he said. New principles. Should last through the
twenty-first century. He asked me to drop him outside the
Cathedral in Wantchester. This I did. He ducked out of the
car briskly. And then ducked back in to look at me gravely.

"There's a presence in this car," he said. "Does it worry
you?"

"No," I said, somewhat thunderstruck. "It's quite be-
nign."

"How about *that*!" Stan said as I drove on up the empty
market street. "The man's a psychic empath!"

"I suppose he had to be, or he wouldn't have got into the
barn that evening," I said, slowing down to swing into the
hotel car park. "But it's unlikely that I—*What* the—?"

A horribly battered car blocked the archway. At the moment when I swung in behind it, its driver hurled open his
door and rushed, waving and gesticulating, upon a car

stopped just beyond the entry. Against that car, two heads were bobbing, one high and dark, the other low and like a lion's mane—that lion having been dragged backwards through a hedge recently, of course. I did not even need the sight of two hands, spiked like stilettos, coming into view with a memorable flick, flick, flick, to know what I was seeing here.

"I don't believe this!" I said, and backed away in a howling half-circle.

"What's going on? What's up?" Stan wanted to know.

"Mallory," I said through clenched teeth, as I went forward on the other lock. "At her tribal dances again in the car park. What's she *doing* here? I put an exclusion round my working after Andrew walked in, I *know* I did! I put an exclusion on Mallory particularly!" On the other side of the road there was a much smaller archway, which I remembered from my last visit. This proves how useful it is to inspect a site before doing a working in it. The notice on this smaller archway said HOTEL STAFF ONLY. I drove through it like a bullet. Beyond, as I had hoped, was a smaller car park, only half full. "Let's pretend I'm the chef," I said, and roared over to the far corner.

"Steady, steady!" Stan said. He was treating me like a horse again. He said soothingly, "That writer fellow on your programme—he's called Mallory. Must be some relation. Must have been fixed up months ago. It can't be anything to do with the working."

I put my chin on the steering wheel, the better to feel my teeth grind. "There's no such thing as coincidence, Stan. And the fact remains that she ought not to *be* here!"

"Yes, but she is and you have to live with it," he said. "Just keep out of her way. Better put up a Don't Notice round this car if you're going to leave it here. I don't need the manager sniffing around me."

I put a blanket of modesty round the car as I unloaded my bags. When I walked away from it, even I could have taken it for a dismal, ordinary, slightly battered car like Mallory's, like all the other cars around it. I hurried in

129

through the Staff door. I wanted to get hidden in my hotel room before Mallory finished her fandango. I could still hardly believe she was here. Perhaps, I thought, I had made a mistake, and it was somebody else dancing beyond that archway.

I got to the foyer. The placid, stately area I remembered from my last visit was bedlam. Beards. Embraces. Heaps of luggage. Everyone in T-shirts. A roar of greetings. The only other person wearing a suit besides me was also wearing a floor-length cloak. While I waited for the maddeningly slow Finnish receptionist to find my key, I saw, upside-down in the ceiling mirrors, a row of robed and cowled figures processing through the crowd. People drew back from them and pulled luggage out of their way, but otherwise failed to look at them. I could see why. Even upside-down and in reflection, they gave off a strong smell of—well—power that was unright.

Still, they were nothing to do with me. I took a look in the mirrors again as I finally got my key. Mallory and her young relative were just coming in through the glass doors of the main entrance. It was definitely them. Damn, I thought, and sped up the stairs. Here I was again delayed, this time by a row of people dispensing membership badges. The girl on the V-section clutched a teddy bear to herself and wanted to know what I wished to be called on my badge. A perspiring pair of lusty youths behind her were wrestling with the machine that made the things. They looked up expectantly.

"My name's Rupert—" I began.

"Rupert Bear," said the girl with the teddy. "*Love* it!"

"He looks more like Rupert of the Rhine," said one of the lusty operators. A female, I realized.

"But he's too cuddly!" said the teddy carrier.

"Venturesome as well," said the operator firmly.

"Rupert Bear has lots of adventures," the teddy carrier argued, injured.

The argument went on for some time. I was so unused to being discussed like this that I stood for a while, dumbly turning my eyes from speaker to speaker, until a loud, low voice with a sob in it, that could only be Mallory's, sounded behind me on the stairs. I pulled myself together.

"Wrong, both of you," I said. "Have you never heard of Rupert the Mage?"

They had not—which was not surprising, since I had only just made him up. "Who *is* Rupert the Mage?" asked the teddy one as she wrote it on the unmade badge.

"The *preux chevalier* of magicians," I invented. "The books were all written in the twenties, so you may not have come across them."

"Oh. A sort of magical Bertie Wooster!" the operator panted. She and her companion leant mightily on the machine to force it to make my badge.

I thought of Stan. "With an invisible butler," I said. "Thanks."

As I received my badge, Mallory advanced on the table for hers. I fled to the lift, where I rode to the top floor with a beautifully dressed transvestite boy, trying to think just where in my working I had let Mallory in instead of excluding her. I remembered those bursts of rage I had kept having about her. Those, I suspected, were the crux. They had caused me to be too preoccupied with her. Now, it seemed, I had to face the fact that I had entangled Mallory's fateline with my own, and Andrew's, and those of my four candidates. What a mess!

The beautifully dressed boy bowed gravely to me when we reached the top floor. I bowed back. He set off striding on spike heels one way and I in the other. The marvel of it was that we did not meet round the other side. I turned corner after mirrored right-angle corner on my way to my room. Seven of them. The room was near the lift on the other side. At the time, I was too bemused by what I had done to the fatelines to recognize the peculiarity of this. I simply slung my bags on the stand, noted that it was a fine, large room with a cocktail fridge and a big bed, and tastefully decorated for a hotel room, and changed into the most casual garments I had with me. I feared I was not going to be happy in the forthright weirdness of this convention. Now Mallory was here, I wished I could go home.

But I had work to do. I pinned on my badge to prove I was not a gate-crasher, studied the Alice in Wonderland sort of pamphlet that said "Read Me" under a portrait of a coy-eyed dragon, and discovered I was already late for the Opening Ceremony in Home Universe. I sped back downwards.

I missed some kind of interruption that happened at the beginning of this. The chairman, a guy called Maxim Hough, who wore his curly blond hair cut in the manner of an ancient Egyptian wig, was apologizing for whatever it was when I slipped into a seat in the vast room. The event was otherwise prodigiously boring. I studied the folk on the platform, and those in the audience, with equal misgivings. Ted Mallory was the only one who looked halfway normal. He was a larger, healthier edition of the poor cancer-ridden man I had met in Kent, and this made it certain there was a family connection with Maree Mallory, as Stan had suggested. To confirm this, I spotted the Mrs. Mallory who had opened the door to me in Bristol sitting in the front row, looking attentive. Her jumper, this time, had a bundle of pink satin roses sprawled down its left side. I played with the notion of tapping her on the shoulder and whispering that she was being attacked by man-eating sugar mice.

I would never have said such a thing, of course, not even to a third party. But people say this kind of thing at conventions. I was surprised and highly delighted when one of the very agreeable Americans I met over supper opined that Mrs. Mallory seemed to have had an accident with some strawberry ice-cream.

"No, no," said her husband. "You didn't examine them closely enough. Those are parasitic sea anemones."

We talked of all sorts of other things as well. By the time we all got to the bar, where I met Rick Corrie and, through him, Maxim Hough, I was actively enjoying myself. I think it was on slightly false pretences. Maxim seemed sure I

132

was some sort of hidden celebrity, and my friends from supper had obviously decided the same, but I am not sure that was important. My main feeling by then was annoyance with myself—exasperation that I had chosen to live so much out of the world. I hadn't, until that evening, remembered the value of congenial company. True, I need privacy for my Magid work, but one can have that without isolating oneself.

Rick Corrie, who had rushed away, now rushed back, very much out of breath and aggrieved. "That was Thurless again," he said.

"Oh what is it *this* time?" said Maxim.

"I think he's settled now," Corrie said, "but it cost the convention forty pounds—"

"*Already? How?*" Maxim wanted to know. "The bloody man's only *been* here four hours! That's ten pounds an hour, Rick!"

"Well, you know I let Maree Mallory have Thurless's room," Corrie explained. "Her fool aunt forgot to book for her. She looked as if she was going to cry when I got to her. And Thurless was late, so I had to find him a room at the Station Hotel, because all the other empties are needed for publishers—none of them have turned up yet, by the way—and I took Thurless down there myself in a taxi along with that unexpected Croatian and a Russian or so. And I went and *looked* at all the damn rooms and they're OK. Just as good as the ones here. But next thing I know, Thurless arrives back here in another taxi, insisting his shower won't work and demanding that we pay for his taxi. So I sort that one out, and back he goes in the taxi again—"

"Hang on," I said. "It's only about a hundred yards from here to the Station Hotel."

"It's longer with the one-way system," Maxim pointed out. "Still—but forty *pounds*, Rick! How often did he come back and forth in that taxi?"

"*And* Thurless has got a car," Corrie said. "It was because I'd given his room away, you see. I didn't feel I should argue too much, and to tell the truth I've lost count

133

of how many times Thurless turned up in that taxi. Ten times? Something like that. I just gave the driver a cheque in the end. Thurless turned up this time saying he was late for Esoterica and wanting the taxi to wait for an hour and I thought I'd better scotch that."

"If he wants a taxi to go back in, tell him to come to me," Maxim said. "Tell him I'll find him a bicycle."

Corrie nodded and flitted away again. I looked idly after him in the mirror at the end of the bar. And there was Maree Mallory again. She had seen me too. To do her justice, she looked horrified. The feeling is mutual. I looked pointedly away. She was looking rather glum—which I suspect is her natural expression: it goes with that irritating sob in her voice—but otherwise she had neatened up considerably from the witchy bag-lady I had encountered in Bristol. She was wearing a nice leather jacket and jeans and had obviously made efforts with her hair. It was now in quite a stylish bush, though still a bush, and I think she had new glasses. Evidently my hundred quid had wrought quite a change. She looked almost human. I watched Rick Corrie dart up to her, converse, dart away, and dart back with drinks. I got the impression he fancied the woman in his shy way. There is no accounting for taste.

"Is Thurless generally such a pain?" I asked Maxim, with some anxiety.

"Nearly always," he told me. "The trouble is, he's not that good a writer and he thinks he *is*. I've never known him quite this dreadful, though. There must be something else biting him. I'll get someone to—Oh, Zinka! You're the very person! Have you heard about Mervin Thurless?"

Zinka is not that common a name. I turned stiffly on my stool, unbelievingly. And there, coming up to about my waist, stood the well-known crimson-robed lovely ample shape of Zinka Fearon. Fellow Magid. One-time lover. Last heard from messaging me about Koryfos several worlds Ayewards from the Empire. I couldn't think what she was doing here. While Maxim was ordering her the pint of cider she always drinks, I bent down and asked her.

134

"And I love you too, Rupert," she said. "I'm here on holiday. I always have my holiday here at PhantasmaCon. I close down. I put everything on hold, and I have a rest. Your brother Si's handling any emergencies out there for me. Are you here working? Yes, I can see you are. It's not exactly quite your usual scene, is it?"

"I'm beginning to enjoy it rather," I admitted.

"Oh good," she said. "If ever I knew anyone who needed to unbend . . . ! But don't ask me to lift a hand to help you in any way. I'm off duty. I mean it."

Maxim turned back with her cider then, and we had the tale of Thurless all over again, including the way he had made an ass of himself at the Opening Ceremony.

"Male menopause," Zinka said decidedly. "I'll sort him out."

I sincerely hoped she could, or I was one candidate short. Thinking this, I raised my eyes to the mirror, and saw Maree Mallory bent back in her chair, trying to avoid the great beaky gabbling face of an appalling female dressed apparently in an orange tent.

"Who is that dreadful creature in orange?" I asked.

Zinka looked in the mirror too. She slammed her tankard down on the bar. "Damn! Tansy-Ann's caught a neo again. Back in a moment."

She was. The woman in orange fled yelling, Mallory vanished too and Zinka was back, unruffled.

"Tansy-Ann?" I asked her apprehensively.

"Fisk. American," she told me. "Not exactly nasty—just a well-known pain. Can you lend me ten pounds?"

"Probably," I said. Damn. There, by the looks of it, was another candidate down the drain. "Why?"

She looked, to be sure Maxim was safely talking to someone else (and he was: bellowing into a deaf-aid) and muttered hurriedly, "I've almost no Earth currency until I sell some stuff in the Dealers Room."

So I gave her a tenner. It is a problem a Magid can face quite often. All in all, it was a very pleasant evening, except that before it ended I seemed to be two candidates short. I went up in the lift knowing that my spirit rebelled at the thought of having Fisk for a pupil—unless she turned out to be one hundred percent more reasonable than she looked, of course. Of the two women, I almost preferred Mallory. Which was saying something. Mervin Thurless, I hoped, might be still possible, if one supposed that he had been unbalanced by having the sort of gifts that make a person a potential Magid. It is bad, having those gifts and not knowing how to use them. I know I was pretty difficult myself as a student because of this. My brother Will has described me then succinctly as "a little shit" and I suspect I was. But then, I thought glumly, the same could apply equally well to the dreaded Fisk.

I had walked round at least one mirrored corner on the nearest way to my room before I realized that I had not yet reached it. It was literally not where I left it. It should have been just beyond the lifts. But, according to the numbers on the walls, rooms 555–587 were somewhere round the next corner. My room was 555.

I stopped. I thought. Then I turned round and retraced my steps to the corner just beyond the lifts. It was extraordinarily hard going, because I was now walking clockwise, and whoever had been using the power node had set about it anti-clockwise—widdershins, the direction of bad magic. I was not happy about that at all. I had to strive around yet another corner before I came in sight of the lifts, too. Someone had set something going and not bothered to stop it. Sloppy practice. In this case you could even end up with a vortex. This node was powerful. I stood at the corner and considered it.

The node was centred on this hotel. It spread through quite a bit of the town too, but the strong centre was almost where I stood. That ought to have meant that things were relatively calm here—like the eye of a storm—but someone had come along not long ago and disturbed it, violently. Two someones, in fact. I could detect two different sets of recent activity from where I stood. And the node had responded violently to violence because it was so exceptionally strong. The Upper Room had been right to feel concerned.

I put everything back and stilled it as gently as I could. Then I went to bed.

(2)

From Maree Mallory's Thornlady Directory, file twenty-four

Thornlady dream again. Biting moonlit comments about my antisocial nature. Why don't I ever dream I bring matches and set fire to her damn bush?

Got up feeling disgruntled and went to see after Nick. I do this most mornings, particularly on schooldays. Janine is usually happy enough to leave him to me. Nick really is a total, genuine, sleep-walking zombie for at least an hour after he gets up. I have never met anyone quite as bad. Nick is capable of putting clothes on, more or less, but it stops there. I don't ask if he washes or cleans his teeth.

When I went into his room, he was sleep-walking into walls with his sweater on backwards. He could only speak in a blurred sort of blaring mumble. I turned his sweater right way round, found his room key and led him to the lift. He had still not opened his eyes when we got to the ground floor. This had its advantages. I couldn't find the place where they were serving breakfast, but Nick could. His nose flared to the smell of bacon and toast and he shambled along that way, dragging me.

A bright young waiter-man met us at the entrance. "Two, miss?" he says. "Not much room at the moment, I'm afraid. This way." He gave us both menus and Nick promptly dropped his. This alerted the waiter-man to Nick's condition. He peered at Nick's face. Then he retrieved the menu and gave it to me, looking Nick in the face again in a sort of hushed, respectful way, as if he thought Nick might be dead. He led the way past tables where most of the fat people were already eating, and quite a few of the shy middle-aged ladies too—you could see these ladies had been trained all their lives to eat breakfast punctually at eight—and over to a table near the window. It was the only semi-empty table in the room.

I don't believe this! I thought.

The Prat Venables was sitting at one end of it reading a newspaper and drinking coffee. He twitched the paper aside as I sat Nick down, saw it was us, and put it up again like a shield. Too bad. I got on with ordering us both breakfast.

"To start?" says the waiter-man, pad poised.

"Ner—yah!" says Nick.

"He means not yoghurt," I said. "Cornflakes for both of us, please. And to follow—"

"Ner—bah—bah—ez—bay!" Nick stated.

"He doesn't like beans, but he does like eggs and bacon," I translated.

"How about sausages, tomatoes or mushrooms?" the waiter asked courteously. I swear he was experimenting to see what noise Nick would make for these. Nor was he disappointed.

"M'sha, m'sha, m'sha," Nick went.

"Mushrooms, but he doesn't want sausages," I explained. "He wants tomatoes. Fried bread, Nick? Toast?"

"M'fee," said Nick.

"He says toast but not fried bread," says I. "To drink—"

"WOOORF—EEH!" Nick proclaimed.

"Yes, we want the biggest pot of coffee you've got," I explained hastily. "It's urgent. His mind's working perfectly, you see, but he can't see or speak properly until he's had at least four cups of coffee."

The waiter peered respectfully at Nick's face once more. Nick's eyes were still shut and sort of bloated. "And for you, miss?"

"The same," I said.

He wrote it all down and whizzed off, whereupon Nick blared, *"M'feeyert."*

"Oh God," I said and raised the tablecloth to look at his feet.

"M'bertowswash!" Nick wailed.

"It's all right, you fool," I said. "You've got your shoes on the wrong feet again, that's all." I got down under the table and changed his shoes over. As I went to my knees, I thought I heard newspaper crackle. When I backed out from among the chairs and got the cloth off my head, I caught a glimpse of a gold-rimmed lens hastily retreating behind the *Telegraph* again. The Prat, like the waiter, was fascinated, but pretending not to be.

I'd just got sat down again when the waiter dashed back with a coffee-pot half the size of a gasometer and poured some of it out for both of us, with reverent curiosity. "Milk, miss?"

"Thanks," I said. "No, *he'll* have the first four cups black."

The waiter stood and watched and poured and watched while Nick drained the necessary four cups, still without opening his eyes. The newspaper in front of the Prat noticeably shifted so that he could watch too.

The waiter had obviously spread the news of Nick to the rest of the staff. A waitress arrived with cornflakes for both of us. She, and the waiter, and the Prat (with a corner of his newspaper bent back for the purpose), all watched fascinated while Nick ate a whole bowlful and absorbed two more cups of coffee without looking at any of it. His eyes were open in slits by then, but he was still at the state of staring ahead at nothing when another waitress rushed up with two plates of cooked breakfast. Another waiter arrived with a rack of toast, and the four of them stood there expectantly while I put a knife into one of Nick's hands and a fork into the other and said to him, "Eat."

Nick obeyed. They watched wonderingly while Nick somehow managed to spear a brisk slippery mushroom he couldn't have known was there and get it into his mouth. Then they watched him cut bacon and eat that. Their eyes turned to the egg. I wondered if they had a bet on that Nick couldn't eat an egg without spilling some of it. If so, they lost. Nick put the whole egg in his mouth at once, dangling perilously from his fork by one corner. Not a drop got away.

Here the Prat stopped pretending he wasn't watching. He folded his paper and asked me, "What happens if you put another plate of breakfast in front of him when he's finished this one? Would he eat that as well without noticing?"

The waiters and the waitresses looked at him gratefully. I could see they had been dying to know this too.

"Yes, he would, just like a zombie. I've tried," I told them.

"Eyenose cuzzedin lyebins," Nick added.

Everyone looked at me for a translation. "He's saying he noticed what I'd done when he discovered he was eating beans for the second time," I explained.

"Dinlye furstye," Nick agreed.

Before I could translate this, I was swept aside by Janine and Uncle Ted. I mean literally swept aside. Janine cried out, "Oh, my poor Nick!" and pushed me off on to the chair opposite the Prat's, while Uncle Ted said, "Morning, morning," as he sat down by Nick, and both waitresses and one waiter fled. The first waiter fetched out his order pad, rather sadly.

"Order for me, Ted," Janine said. "Poor Nick's helpless in the morning." She began tenderly buttering toast for Nick. She had a new sweater today. The shoulder of it that was turned to me had a golden splash on it, as if someone had broken an egg over her. I wish someone had.

The Prat looked as disappointed as the waiter. But he politely pushed the marmalade nearer Janine and said to me, "Can't he butter his own toast by now?"

"I usually let him try," I said. "Some mornings he butters the plate and tries to eat it."

"He looks rather to have reached that stage," the Prat said. Shrewd of him. Nick always makes his worst mistakes when he's almost awake.

140

But this conversation caused Janine to notice the Prat. She leant forward and read his badge. So did I. It said RUPERT THE MAGE. "Rupert the Mage," Janine said. "You must be one of Gram White's esoteric circle in Universe Three."

"Strictly freelance," he said. "I believe we met in Bristol the other day, Mrs. Mallory."

I never heard how this not very promising conversation developed—or even if it developed at all—because Uncle Ted shouted at me. "Maree!" he shouted imploringly from the other side of Nick. "Maree! I've been put on a panel at twelve today. What do I *say*?"

"That depends what it's on," I said soothingly. "What's it about?"

"God knows," he said, despair all over him. "Promise me you'll come along and nod intelligently at me from the front."

"Senzyou murain fanzy," Nick said.

"Eh?" said Uncle Ted. He never could understand Nick's morning talk.

"He's telling you about the panel," I explained. "He says it's on—"

Then we got interrupted again. This time it was a long thin fellow dressed like a soldier who came up and loomed over Uncle Ted. His tall cheekbones loomed too, over his hollow cheeks, as he said, "Mr. Mallory. Sir."

His teeth showed under a fierce black moustache after that. I *think* it was a smile. I *hoped* it was, for Uncle Ted's sake. Uncle Ted sort of sank down in his chair and looked as if he hoped so too. "What can I do for you?" he asked the man.

"I come to embrace you," the man said. Uncle Ted flinched. "I am—" The man said some foreign name none of us could catch. He was too tall for any of us to read his badge. Then he said, "I come from fighting for my country. From Croatia. I come to say that you have saved my life and my sanity, sir. The guns would have killed my mind. But by reading your great book daily, I kept my courage and fought for my country."

141

"I'm glad to hear that," said my uncle. "Er—which book?"

"Your so great history of King Arthur, his riders and the saintly Graal," said the man.

"Er," said Uncle Ted, "I think you've got the wrong Malory. The one you want has only the one L. And he's been dead quite a while, I'm afraid."

He might as well not have spoken. Staring into the distance—like Nick was also, except that this man's eyes were wide and mad—the Croatian went on, "It is a book that inspires the heart to greatness. To serve. To fight against odds. To crush the enemy. To smite so that blood bursts from the nose and the ears. I have two English books of great inspiration with me as I fight. Both folded in my breast. Both stop several bullets. I have your book and the great Tolkien's. But they tell me Tolkien is not here. So I come to you to thank you. Thank you, sir." He ducked his long cadaverous face at Uncle Ted and marched away.

"I think he may be what they used to call shell-shocked," Uncle Ted said ruefully. "*What* name did he say? All I heard was Balkan gabble."

"Million Gabblevitch," Nick said, almost normally. "Tower of Babel. Dutch joke."

"Eh?" said Uncle Ted. He never gets Nick's jokes, either.

Something made me look at the Prat. He was staring after the tall Croatian striding away from us, and he was looking utterly fed up and disappointed, as if the Croatian had somehow let him down badly.

TWELVE

(1)

From Maree Mallory's
Thornlady Directory, file
twenty-five

Nick deserted me halfway through this morning, the rat,
but not before we had done quite a bit of exploring together. We were trying to disentangle Mallory Universe
from Home Universe and the other ones. Couldn't be done.
The Hotel Babylon, true to its name, wants everything mad
as the man who ate grass or mixed up like the Tower of
Babel—particularly the last, particularly Russians and Germans. There was a huge crowd from both countries in a
room upstairs called Ops, shouting one another down in
both languages, with squirts of bad English in between. Ops
is supposed to deal with crises. This was clearly a crisis,
but no one in Ops knew if it was one combined crisis or
two separate ones.

People kept explaining things like this to us. Or if there
wasn't a crisis, people chatted or gave us friendly smiles.
They all seemed to know who we were without looking at
our badges (nobody looks at badges anyway). The three
long-haired people with the baby kept grinning at us as we
went up and down the corridors, even the baby. Nick remarked that it was the most unpunishmently punishment
his parents could have devised, and I kept saying how nice
everyone was. But that was before we found a room la-

belled Press Office, where people in more than usually wordy T-shirts were just running off this morning's news sheet. Apparently they do several each day of the Con. They gave us one each and we went and sat in the Grand Lobby to read them.

Everyone sits in the Grand Lobby. It is pretty big, but it looks *enormous*, because there are mirrors in one wall reflecting large windows in the wall opposite. It is full of armchairs and tables and small children running about in little cloaks or small-scale Batman gear, and all the adults sitting around in bundles. At that moment it was pretty full because a whole lot of new people had just turned up. Most of them were rather smartly dressed and had a sort of urgent, I'm-working look, which some of them clearly felt placed them in a class above the rest of us.

"Don't despise them," fat Wendy said, flopping down next to us. Nick had to look away from her again. "Those are the publishers. They'll all be giving parties this evening."

So I didn't despise them and looked at the news sheet instead. But Nick really can't take someone the size and shape of Wendy. He sprang up. "I've got to go. Games Universe is just starting," he said. "I'll look for you here or in your room at lunchtime." This was a blatant lie. I *knew* the Games didn't start yet, and I could see him hovering over by the far door, but the fact was that he had *deserted* me—deserted me just as I hit the para in the news sheet that said: "Fans please take note of Ted Mallory's niece, Maree. This small orphaned-looking lady is going about with a broken heart. Any fan happening upon Maree needs to be nice to her."

I was so angry and so embarrassed that tears came into my eyes. My face felt sort of blue-hot. Wendy said something to me, but I couldn't hear or answer or look at her. She was probably only talking to me because the news sheet told her to. I made a kind of low howling noise.

"I said," said Wendy, "was there anything interesting in the news sheet? I haven't read it yet."

144

Then I hated myself for being hypersensitive. I looked up and pushed my sliding glasses up on my nose. And behold. *Lo!* WONDERS! The tall Nordic type I had seen the night before was walking through the Grand Lobby. He was every bit as beautiful as I remembered—better, if possible. Such wonderful slender hips, and such a *walk*! And—shame!—he just went striding through, past armchairs, past tables loaded with cups, past kiddies swirling little cloaks, past people sitting on the floor, past huddles of publishers, and went out the other end without looking at anyone, followed every inch of the way by my eyes.

I wasn't the only one. A well-dressed publisher lady got her legs in a corkscrew trying to watch him and almost fell over. Beside me, Wendy said, "Oh my God! Look at that! Look at him! Have you ever seen anything quite so beautiful?" When I managed to tear my eyes away from the archway where the man had vanished, I saw she was staring after him too. Her hands were clasped under her enormous bosom and her face was all funny colours.

"Fabulous," I agreed. My lower half felt weak.

Then I saw Tansy-Ann bearing down on me waving a news sheet. I gave a sharp cry and managed to get up and run, weak legs and all. People were going into the big hall by then for Uncle Ted's panel and I went in with them, where I flopped down on a chair near the door and began thinking that I seriously might be getting over Robbie. I'd never felt like that over *him*.

After that, a certain amount of sanity came to my rescue, and it occurred to me that you feel like this about pop stars and other people you never expect really to meet, and the fever went off enough for me to start wondering who the man was. Then I started wondering angrily about the news sheet and who might have done that to me. I was disposed to blame Uncle Ted. He might not have meant to punish me, but it would be very like him to have dropped a jovial word about me over supper last night. But it was even more like Janine. Or it could even have been Dutch Case or Rick Corrie, thinking they were doing me a kindness. And I still haven't found out whose fault it was. Whoever it is is going to get themselves bitten, savagely, in the fleshy part of the calf.

When I came-to a bit, a good looking woman in publisher clothes was introducing herself as Master of Ceremonies—I think she's called Gianetti and runs a chat show on TV—and then telling us that Uncle Ted was Master of Black Comedy, and that some woman beside him wrote funny stuff too, and Mervin-Thurless, who was sitting up there with them, was renowned for his wit (well, you could have fooled me) and they were all going to discuss "A Sense of Humour in Fantasy."

I have to hand it to Uncle Ted. You'd not have known he hadn't had a notion what he was supposed to be talking about. He just took hold of the microphone and talked about it. "Writing a book is just a job, like any other job," he said. I hoped he wouldn't go on that way, but he did. Shortly he was saying, "Consider the job as if I were building a bicycle instead. I'd have to plan the frame—call that the plot—and put on the wheels—call that characters and their motivation—and then I'd put in the gears. Now the jokes are the gears. You have to get them just the right size and configuration, or you wind the pedals and—hey presto!—the chain falls off." That got a good laugh. "So I always plan my gags in detail and in advance," he says. "The whole book is like a machine, planned in detail in advance and well oiled with a smooth writing style."

There was quite a bit more like this. Then Mervin Thurless upped and said yes, he agreed in every particular, except he thought humour was more like planning spices for a sauce. Then the woman upped in her turn and said she agreed with both of them, it was utterly mechanistic, but she said (as if she was very ashamed to admit it) sometimes her jokes made her laugh.

At this, Uncle Ted seized the mike again and said he *never* laughed: it was fatal.

And Thurless said it was bad form anyway, to laugh at your own jokes.

146

By this time I was really depressed. I thought of Uncle Ted's wobbly windows, and I began to think he must really, truly never look *through* them or anything else. Coming on top of everyone being nice to me just because the news sheet told them to, it was just too much. Can't anyone look out there and see that you need not think of everything in terms of what works, or what they ought to do?

To do the Ceremonies lady justice, she began to look a trifle glum as well. At length she said, "But what about that extra factor, the miracle ingredient? Isn't there a moment when everything stops being like a machine? Doesn't a joke ever take off on its own for any of you? Let me stick my neck out here. What about inspiration?"

"No," says Uncle Ted. "To work, it has to be all hard graft. You can't afford to get carried away, or your book becomes a dangerous, out-of-hand thing and it may not sell."

"I'll go further," says Mervin Thurless. "If there *is* a miracle ingredient, it's money."

"Precisely," says Uncle Ted. "It's how much you get paid for using the right formula."

I got up and went out. I didn't care if the door did crash behind me. I felt totally let down. Machines. Bicycles. FORMULA. Bah!!

As I stood there with sort of gloomy thunder and lightning playing round my mind, the door behind me clicked quietly and the Prat crept out and closed it gently behind him. He looked, to my surprise, just like I felt.

"Money!" I said to him. *"Bicycles!"*

"Yes, I know," he said. "What price imagination, let alone integrity? And for God's sake don't push your glasses up your nose at me like that. You make me feel I've got to defend those three, and I don't want to. How about some coffee?"

So, to my further surprise, I found myself having coffee with him in the corner of a corridor somewhere, at a glass table. I think the Prat was fairly surprised himself. He had a wondering look behind the gold-rimmed glasses. But, just to be on the safe side, I asked him if he had read the news sheet. At this, his wondering look increased and he said, "What, do they have a news sheet as well as all the rest? They work pretty hard, don't they?" Then I was satisfied he was not giving me coffee out of kindness and, as I was still fulminating, I told him angrily about Uncle Ted's wavy windows.

"And all he could say about them was they added value to his house!" I said. "Gah! Phooey!"

"Possibly it's the only way he can convince himself to talk about them," the Prat says fair-mindedly. "They must have some kind of effect on him. He said 'value,' after all, even if he put it in terms of money. It may be quite hard for him to talk in public about things that strike him as strange or wonderful. He may be afraid people will think he's soft."

"He should *try*," I said. "And you said you didn't want to defend him."

"I know," he said. "But there's this—I know that in my work, I don't get very far forward unless there comes a moment when everything suddenly rushes together in an exciting sort of explosion in my mind. Then it all seems wonderful and ideas just pour in. Your uncle and the others—*they* must have times like that, or they couldn't do what they do. But it's awfully hard to describe. So they fake it, and say what they think people want to hear."

"Nice try," I said. "But describing things is what they're supposed to be *good* at. They fell down on the job, in my opinion. What work do you do?"

"Oh, I—er—design computer games," he said.

"What? Killing aliens? Pzzwat, pzzwat?" I said. "I like shooting aliens."

"I thought you might," he says. "You get to do a lot of other things too, with mine. They're fairly sophisticated. It's an odd thought that quite a few of them are based on books that are on sale here in the Dealers Room, so I'm told, and I haven't actually read one of them."

"Then you should have read them!" I said. I was quite

scandalized. He protested that he just worked on specs from the distributors and I told him that that just wouldn't do. As soon as we'd finished the coffee, I took him along to the Dealers Room. I'd not dared to do more than drool in the doorway before this. I knew if I wanted to eat anything apart from the free breakfast, I shouldn't get in among all those books. But it was all right if somebody else was buying them—it took the fever off me, so that I didn't need to buy any myself. Well, almost. I made him buy all the basics (believe it or not, he hasn't even read *I, Robot* or *The Lord of the Rings!*) and one or two of my special favourites, including the latest by three or four writers I really like. I intend to borrow those off him. We also looked at jewellery and dragons and comics (they had an old *Sandman* I hadn't got, but the price was horrible) and then at stalls of painted things. Zinka Fearon was selling some beautiful stuff, but there was another stall full of glass aliens that were *yurk!*

"Reminds me of your aunt's jumper," says the Prat. "She is your aunt, isn't she? The one with the custard on her shoulder."

"I thought it was an egg," I said. "Yes, that's our Janine." That reminded me of breakfast, and I tried to get out of him why he had looked that way at the crazy Croatian who thought Uncle Ted wrote about King Arthur. But I had forgotten what a cool customer he is.

He said, "Poor fellow. I suddenly saw what war can do to people."

I *knew* that wasn't the truth, but that was all he'd say. Strange. I can't help connecting the way he looked at that Croatian with what Nick says he saw last night.

Anyway, we went on to the Art Show after that. By this time I was thinking that, if anyone had told me yesterday that I'd be standing in front of pictures chatting amiably with the Prat, I would have blacked their eye and called them a liar. It must be something in the air of this con, I think. And there were some *very* naughty paintings by Zinka Fearon we were just discussing, when Dutch Case comes zooming through the Art Room. The Prat takes off after him at the double, grabs him by the arm and says, "Found you at last!" he says. "Care to come and have lunch with us?"

With *us*? I thought. No way, not with Case—quite apart from the fact that the Prat has money and will go and expect me to buy lunch in that expensive dining room. And I went off in the opposite direction, fast.

I ran into Nick near the lifts. Nick was looking like the cat that had the cream. "They loved Bristolia!" he proclaimed. "And my new Wantchester game! I'd got some twists on both of them that no one had come across before. They're saying I ought to get them made into proper computer games. Only I don't know who to ask about it."

"I do. Start talking to the Prat," I said. Nick stared at me. "Honestly," I said. "He's just been telling me he designs the software. He seems to know most of the distributors and manufacturers."

"Wow!" says Master Nick. "Let me at him!"

(2)

From the account of Rupert
Venables

I find that the notes I made at the time scarcely mention the hour or so I spent with Maree. I seem just to have jotted down *Bought an unconscionable number of books*, followed by *Mallory uncomfortably shrewd*, by which I certainly didn't mean her uncle. I have seldom heard such drivel as he talked on that panel. What I meant was the awkward moment Maree gave me in front of Zinka's paintings. Zinka does exquisite, delicate portrayals of humans copulating with various kinds of ribby-winged beings. Mostly they are the people you find in increasing numbers as you go Ayewards from the Empire. Though I have never

150

myself met the horned men she had painted, I've met quite a few of the other winged ones in the pictures—but clearly not as intimately as Zinka has.

Maree said, staring, the sob growing in her voice, "You'd really think these were painted from life!"

I tried not to jump. "Zinka has quite an imagination," I said. At this, Maree pushed her spectacles up her nose and looked at me. She seems to have an instinct for when I'm covering something up. Shortly after, she disappeared while I was flagging down Kornelius Punt, and I hardly knew whether I was relieved or aggrieved. Possibly she didn't like Punt. I don't exactly blame her.

I didn't dislike him, or like him either. This is not a consideration for a new Magid anyway. What I was looking for were certain qualities that are necessary. Kees, as he told me he liked to be called, certainly had some of them. He had the brains. The travelling scholarship he had won was for outstanding achievement at university, and he told me he had been selected from thousands, all over Holland. But it was a while before I could get him to talk about this. He was incredibly hyped—I think it was contact-high from the convention—and would keep making inane jokes.

"You must give me a Dutch treat," was the first thing he said. "I have no money."

"That means we both pay half," I said.

"And so we will!" he said, his voice going up into a delighted shriek. "You will contribute the money and I will give the pleasure of my company."

"Fine by me," I said. So he proceeded to order the most expensive things on the menu, while I tried to get him to talk sense.

When the food came, he said, gobbling up scampi, "I have decided it is a fine joke to be in love with Maree Mallory. They say she has a broken heart, so there is no danger to me."

I felt my face heating with anger. "I wouldn't be too sure of that," I said.

"Oh I know. She will bite me. Or scratch," he said glee-

151

fully. "But then I am a masochist so that is all right." I think I would have cut in angrily here, only it dawned on me that Kees was trying to get a reaction out of me, having seen me going about with Maree. I was sure of it when he added, cocking his eye to see how I responded, "And she is a chip off the old block. Probably she is one of her uncle's demons in disguise."

I ignored this, but I was very mortified. Probably the reason I made such few and curt notes on the morning was that I was increasingly exasperated to find that I infinitely preferred Maree, whom I had discounted, to any of the candidates left. If only she did not speak with that *sob* in her voice . . .

Meanwhile I got irritated with Kees Punt. He seemed to be a confirmed jester. It would in a way, I thought, be quite good cover for a Magid, never to be taken seriously, except that Punt was drawing attention to himself all the time—his voice kept rising to a shriek as he made yet another outrageous pun—and it is not a good idea for a Magid to do that. If people notice you for one thing, they tend to notice the rest. But Kees was young. I had hopes he could grow out of it. There must be a serious man in there somewhere, I thought, while he shouted that he was great joker and then told me in a shriek that the words on his T-shirt were Elvish.

And I still feel I may not have done justice to Kees, because while he was blithely laying into his Woodcock Supreme and I had just got him to talk about his travels, we were both distracted by turmoils among the other eaters. From the table behind me, Ted Mallory said loudly, "Well, why *should* I have denied it, for fuck's sake? He'd made a total mess of it. I simply took it and improved it and I'm not ashamed to admit it! Books are public property—and he'd no business to be so damn rude!"

Kees's pale face lit up and he raised a hand to make sure I was attending to this. "I am a great gossip," he said gleefully, "and a nosy parker. Listen. There is some scandal here."

From the table behind him, one of my American friends was saying, "Why, if that guy thinks he's been robbed, how is he going to handle shared world writing? There, you make a gag, someone else takes it up, and next you know it's being bounced around every single story. That's all Mallory did. Thurless is an asshole."

From across the dining room, I could now hear Thurless himself, practically screaming. "It's shameless plagiarism! I've a good mind to sue Mallory for this!"

I looked at Kees, his pale excited face and raised hand. He had the ability to be a Magid all right. I could feel him raising the sound level of all the voices around, so that we could hear even the distant Thurless without missing a word. "It is a scandal!" he said delightedly.

Evidently Maree and I had left the panel just before the fun started. Thurless had suddenly rounded on Mallory and accused him of having stolen all the funniest bits of *Shadowfall* from a novel Thurless had published the year before that. Mallory had blandly confessed it was so. "If I find the cog I need lying around in somebody's botched machine," he was saying behind me, "I feel quite justified in taking it and using it properly." Well. That certainly fitted his philosophy. But it was clear there had been a flaming row, and not everyone had enjoyed it.

Under Punt's manipulations, I could hear the MC, Tina Gianetti, saying tearfully to Maxim Hough, "I couldn't *stop* them! I thought they were going to *fight* across me! And I don't like to hear language like that in public, Maxim."

"What language?" Kees wondered delightedly. "Double Dutch consisting of four-letter words? Let someone tell us, please!"

Now he was actually pressuring Gianetti and the Americans to repeat what had been said. I said to him, rather sharply, "Kees, do you always do this to people?"

"Only when I need to know," he said happily. "For gossip and exams and so on."

"It's a misuse of power," I told him.

"Yes, you are po-faced," he said. "I have noticed. But where is the harm?"

"It amounts to cheating if you do it in exams," I pointed out.

"*Everyone* cheats," he said, "if they can. I would not do it for something serious like a parliamentary election or anything like that. And this is juicy gossip."

It left me with considerable doubts about the man's ethics. I *think* he truly intended no harm to anyone, but that was not to say he would still be harmless in ten years' time. I was doubtful about him, enough to be quite glad when he looked at his watch and said he had to go and gopher for the publishers.

"You need not pay for a dessert," he said. "I am sweet enough." And left.

I left as soon as I could flag a waiter and get my bill signed. I hefted my four bags of books and made my way across the room. Thurless was at a table by the exit. I had been hoping to snag him next, but he was clearly still in a fury, to judge by the way he was stabbing the roast potatoes on his plate. I could almost see him thinking of them as Ted Mallory's kidneys and heart. His beard wagged with rage. Even so, I would have stopped and had a word with him, had not the other man at the table looked up at me as I approached. It was the most unloving look I have ever received. It was delivered at me from pale eyes that were yellow where they should be white and fat lips that parted in a snarl shape amidst a brown and grey beard.

The fellow was a total stranger. His badge said GRAM WHITE, which rang a faint bell. Mrs. Janine Mallory had mentioned that name at breakfast, that was all I knew. But it was clear he had pretty strong magic, about equal to Thurless. I could feel it in both as soon as I was near. And he hated me. And was warning me off. I simply walked on as if I had not noticed. I saw myself in one of the hotel's ubiquitous mirrors stride on and push at the exit door with a couple of my bags of books without batting an eyelid or changing my expression, for which I silently commended myself. It was not until I was past the door and puzzling about the way the fellow had looked at me that I recalled that there had been a grey hooded cloak thrown across the back of this Gram White's chair. *Then* I placed him. He was the leader of those monk-like figures that everyone drew back from in the foyer. And, having been near enough to sense the character of his magic, I thought I knew why he had glared at me. He had been one of the ones using the node. He must have realized that I was the one who had stilled it.

I went straight to the Dealers Room. "Gram White?" I asked Zinka.

She was sitting among her mirrors, boxes and winged models eating a large hot dog. "Bad news," she answered, one cheek bulging. "Local resident. Runs an arms factory in Wantchester. Always comes to this con and always teaches Esoterica in Universe Three. Don't touch him with a bargepole, or even something longer than that."

"Thanks," I said, and left her to her lunch.

I went to my car then. I came out through the kitchen entrance into a surprisingly biting-cold bright day, in which snow was drifting like pollen, and stowed my carrier bags in the boot before climbing into the car.

Scarlatti went from loud tinkle to faint tinkle. "About time!" Stan said. "Your phone keeps going off, but I can't seem to manage that like I can manage the tapes. I just had to let it ring."

"Sorry," I said. "I was busy. Stan, where exactly did you get that list of possible Magids from?"

"Senior Magid," he said. "Handed down to her from Above about the time I knew I was dying. Why?"

"Upper Room, or higher up?" I asked.

"Well, it *came* to her through Upper Room, like most things," he said. "But the details were so vague, I got the feel it could have come from much higher up. Cost me a lot of work, to get you a list with names and addresses out of it, I can tell you."

"I thought so," I said. "We are being Intended, Stan. And

155

I don't like it. I can't see what they're *playing* at! *None* of these candidates is right. Punt is the best, and he'd do anything for a laugh. I think the Croatian is deranged. Thurless has been throwing scenes like a prima donna ever since he appeared, and I suspect he's into the bad magic too. Fisk is *awful*, and you know my opinion of Mallory. I think we'll have to wipe that list and start again."

"Steady on. I must have been given it for a reason!" Stan protested. "Have you talked to all of them now?"

"Not to Fisk or Thurless," I admitted, "and not properly to Gabrelisovic."

"Then one of them's got to have hidden depths," Stan said. "Don't judge until you've done a proper—"

Here my phone clamoured. It was Dakros. The sound was unusually distant and crackly, but Dakros's voice came out of it joyously. "Got you at last, Magid. Sorry about the interference. I'm in a landcruiser on my way to the Thalangia World Gate. We've found Knarros. High Lady Alexandra found him."

"She did?" And not just a pretty face, I remembered. "How did she do that?"

"You remember I sent her to Thalangia?" Dakros's crackly voice asked. "To the farm my uncle manages for me? Well, she got talking to my uncle and his people there, and my uncle happened to mention there was a religious colony up on a hill about ten miles away; and somebody else remarked they were thorn-worshippers like the Emperor was. So Alexandra made quiet enquiries. And it appears there are children, or at least young people, up there, but everyone told her that the head of the colony won't let anyone near the place unless they come on business, and won't let them talk to the children if they do go with deliveries and so forth. So she asked some more. And today someone told her that the head of this colony is a strict brute of a centaur called Knarros. She called me up at once."

"Knarros is a *centaur*!" I exclaimed. Then there *had* been a clue in the graphics.

Dakros laughed joyously amid the static. "Yes, no wonder all the humans were frauds. As I said, I'm on my way to Thalangia in a cruiser, with as many men as I can spare. We'll be at the farm by tomorrow evening. Can you join us beside that hill, Magid?"

"Well, I've got rather pressing business—" I began.

"If he's a centaur, it's going to take a Magid," Stan put in, in my other ear. "Tell him yes, and put things on hold for an hour or so here."

"All right," I told Dakros, sighing a little. "Give me node points and references for the hill. What hour?"

We settled on six in the evening and I hung up. "What do you mean, it's going to take a Magid if he's a centaur?" I asked Stan.

"If you know centaurs," he said, "it stands to reason. This one's in a position of trust and he hasn't come forward. That means he's promised not to, or probably only to come forward under certain conditions. Centaurs like that are real sticklers. You're going to have to convince him the conditions are met. They listen to Magids, if they listen to no one else. And he could be a magic user himself. That would make sense in the—"

"All right. I'm convinced. I'm not a centaur," I said. "I'll go and argue with Knarros tomorrow. Meanwhile, I'd better make some arrangements here."

I got out of the car, into the stinging snow, and hurried to the Dealers Room again. I was not about to do as Gram White seemed to have done and leave a major working set up unattended in a strong node like this one in Wantchester. I had four people's fatelines woven into the Hotel Babylon—no, more like seven, if you counted my own and Andrew's and, as I strongly suspected, Maree Mallory's too—and there was no way I could wind all that down before Saturday night. I had intended to spend most of the following week doing it.

Zinka had finished her hot dog by then and was drinking tea. Luckily there were very few other people in the room. I panted out my problem to her in a hoarse whisper.

"No," she said. It was quite pleasant. It was also like running full-tilt into an iceberg. "Leave the Empire to stew, Rupert. Word's out that it's Intended to fall apart anyway. I'm on holiday. I told you."

"But you said you would in an emergency," I pleaded.

"This," said Zinka, "is not an emergency. This is you trying the kiss of life on a week-old corpse. I repeat: no."

"I can't leave a full-scale working unattended!" I more or less wailed.

"Then don't," she said. "Or get someone else in. What's wrong with Stan?"

"He's dead," I said. "Dead and disembodied and in my car at this moment."

"Oh," she said. "Then I am sorry. I hadn't heard."

The signs were that the iceberg would have melted then, except that, unfortunately, my Croatian candidate came and loomed over us. Suddenly, before I could say any more. His hollow, haunted face bent down between us. Zinka and I both drew back from it. "You two have the wrong smell," Gabrelisovic said. His large mauve hand, marked with lumps and white nicks, came between us also, forming one of the more violent of the signs against witchcraft. "Such as you," he said, "have I killed with the bare hand and buried in the mass grave many times in the mountains of my country." He stood up and retreated. "I hunt by smell," he said. "Beware. You disgust." And he strode away.

"Gosh. Wow!" Zinka said. "Long time since I encountered a genuine witch-sniffer. He must have added quite a dimension to their war! He's mad as a hatter as well, isn't he?"

Knowing what a good healer Zinka is, I said wistfully, "Is there any chance you can make him sane again?"

"No," she said, staring after Gabrelisovic as he strode from the room. "No way. Not after he's killed people bare-handed, there's no chance. And he'd go for me if I tried." Then, as I opened my mouth to continue pleading about my working, she added, "And no to that too, Rupert. I

158

always know when I'm needed and I'm not needed now. Go away."

I took myself off, wondering what to do. The answer seemed to be, to finish my work here—at least I needn't now interview Gabrelisovic—as far as I could, and then ask Will, as the nearest off-world Magid, to stand in for me while I dealt with Knarros. Will was easier to reach than any other Magid currently on Earth. It sounded so simple, put like that. I went off to do it.

THIRTEEN

From Maree Mallory's
Thornlady Directory, file
twenty-six

I'm entering this quite late at night, after I left the publishers' parties and dragged Nick away with me before he got too drunk. One of the parties must still be going on. I can hear distant drunken hooting, and somewhere there's just been a huge crash of broken glass. Someone turned the wrong way at a corner and tried to walk through a mirror probably.

Actually I left because a) my fabulous Nordic type wasn't at any of them (Wendy was hunting for him too); b) Rupert is furious with me; and c) Janine came in while I was sitting on the floor between Nick and Wendy and bitched about what a sight we looked. She can talk. She was wearing a black thing with a golden snake wrapped round it that made her look like an advanced version of one of Zinka's pictures. The snake had two heads and one head was—well anyway, I couldn't stand any more and came away.

But I really meant to write down the extraordinary thing this afternoon.

What happened was that Nick was desperate to talk to Rupert—the Prat—about computer games. "Desperate" is an understatement. Nick wouldn't let me do anything else but help him find and snabble Rupert Venables. Of course we couldn't find him at first. Then we ran him down in the bar—naturally at the precise moment he got caught by the dreadful Tansy-Ann. He was with her for ages.

Nick kept saying we should go and rescue Rupert, why didn't we? He said we would earn the man's undying gratitude. And I told him he had no idea what Tansy-Ann was like. She was quite capable of catching us and holding us in thrall too. And even Nick agreed she did look a bit that way. So we sat and waited. Somebody bought me some Real Ale because they said I looked as if I needed it—I blame that news sheet again—and Nick got bought a Coke he didn't like. And we watched Rupert avoid having his back massaged by Tansy-Ann and get his hands squeezed instead, while Tansy-Ann pushed her beak into his face and talked for a good hour. I was getting almost sorry for the Prat, when Nick and I looked up after not looking for a second or so. And Rupert was gone. Tansy-Ann was alone, looking startled.

"Told you so," said Nick. He had done no such thing. "He's just like me. I can always get away from people if I want to. He's probably in the gents."

He wasn't. Nick went in and looked. So we hunted all over the hotel again.

This time we found him with Mervin Thurless, but not until we'd hunted through all the downstairs places and most of the public parts of the first floor—not to speak of asking everyone we met. Rick Corrie went bounding past and sent us up to the first floor. Someone else sent us down again, where we met Wendy, who said she wouldn't know Rupert if he came up and hit her. Then a great huge man with a fringe of black beard round his face and FANGS! written on his T-shirt came up and slammed into Wendy and hugged her. It made a truly massive embrace. And he told us over Wendy's shoulder that Rupert the Mage was in Ops looking for Mervin Thurless. So there we went, and a man in battle fatigues who was trying to canoodle with a carroty girl told us wearily that he'd only just come on shift, try the Press Room. So we did that. And got handed another news sheet full of stuff about Uncle Ted pinching ideas from Mervin Thurless, and Tina Gianetti refusing to have both of them together on the same panel ever again.

"I bet he did take stuff from Thurless," Nick said, reading all about it as we went along the corridor.

"I'm sure he did," I said. "He told me he couldn't bear to see ideas lying around not being used properly. And I wouldn't trust a person like Thurless to use an idea properly if it was handed to him on a scroll from Heaven."

"It says here," said Nick, "that Thurless is running the Writers' Workshop tomorrow in place of Wendy Willow. I should think she'd be better at it, wouldn't you?"

By this time it was quite late. People were appearing changed into fine clothes ready for the parties. Maxim Hough hurried past wearing a velvet patchwork jacket, beside two achingly slender girls in glittery dresses. And coming towards us were two fabulous women in long tight black leather dresses that laced up all over with red thongs. It took me a moment to recognize that they were two of the long-haired people with the baby. Their hair was piled up in glossy hairdos and their false eyelashes stuck out a good inch.

Nick recognized them at once. "Wow!" he said. They were delighted. They struck poses and Nick admired them. "What have you done with the baby?" he asked.

"Larry's looking after him," said the one on the left. "Loretta, I mean."

"She's got ever so maternal since she changed sex," the one on the right explained.

Nick became speechless. I asked them rather despairingly whether they'd seen Rupert.

"Rupert the Mage?" they said in their lovely husky voices. One of them added, "I love that man—he's so *straight*!" and the other one said that he (or she) had seen Rupert going into the Filk Room, just along there. Then they went swaying off—they both had shiny black boots on with six-inch heels. I wondered how they could walk at all, in those tight black leather skirts as well.

162

Nick said, "I know one of them has to be a man! Can you tell which?"

"*Darned* if I know!" I said. "They're both so beautiful. But that baby's surely having a weird upbringing!"

Nick said, in a vague way, "*All* upbringings are weird." He had his con map out, looking for this Filk Room. "It's down the end of this corridor."

It was a medium-sized empty room with bits of sound equipment strewn about in it, mostly flexes snaking all over the floor. Rupert Venables and Mervin Thurless were sitting on the only two chairs in there, talking deeply. But Thurless swung round and jutted his beard at us as we put our faces round the door. When he saw it was me, he looked savage.

"So you think you're going to take *this* room away from me as well, do you?" he snarled. "Go away. Go and voodoo-dance somewhere else!"

We shut the door hurriedly and went and sat by the wall in a sort of lobby outside. Nick said, "It's all right. We can catch Rupert the Mage as soon as he comes out."

I wailed, "Oh dear! It *was* his room Rick Corrie gave me!"

"It's not your fault," Nick said.

We sat for some time. Nick was quite happy. He got out a notebook and set to perfecting his Wantchester game, bringing it up to Bristolia standard, he said. I was pretty restive. It was an unrestful spot. Waiters and waitresses kept coming out through a door disguised as a mirror, carrying glasses and boxes of bottles for the publishers' parties. They all seemed to be talking about music. The waitress who had brought Nick his cornflakes hurried by saying, "It's not that I *mind* music—it's not that. I just want to know where it's coming from."

And the waiter who had brought the coffee said, "Yeah, I know. It's creepy. Music in the air."

A few minutes after they had gone, I heard music too. It was coming from behind the closed door of the Filk Room. It didn't strike me as creepy, but it seemed unlikely

163

that Rupert Venables and Mervin Thurless had both suddenly started playing guitars. "Nick . . ." I said.

Nick looked up, listened and said, "Oh *no!*" The guitars had now been joined by a sweet soprano song.

We both jumped up and Nick tore open the Filk Room door. The three women alone in there looked rather startled. "We were just having a bit of a rehearsal," said the one who had been singing. "The filking doesn't really start until eight."

Nick spotted the door at the other end of the room, where the women must have come in and Rupert and Thurless gone out. "Sorry," he said, sprinting for it. "Looking for someone." We crossed the room like an army crossing the stage, with the women gaping at us, and crashed out the other side into a shabby passage where the service stairs were. Nick seemed to have no doubt that Rupert had recently gone up those stairs. He went up them at a gallop and I panted behind, thinking that, even if Rupert *had* gone that way, he was long gone by now. There was a fire door at the top, saying it led to the Second Floor. Nick pushed it open, looked, and beckoned me on with a large excited sweep of his arm.

I panted up to him to see a long corridor ahead, with the usual mirrors at the corners, and Rupert Venables just turning left at that end. We raced after him. I was almost as frustrated as Nick by then. I'd wasted a whole afternoon and I was *determined* to catch him this time. We whirled round that corner, me on Nick's heels, only seconds behind Rupert.

It was only when we had run some yards down a passage lined with mirrors, but the glass all faint and dark, like the reflections of reflections, that I had a clear memory of the hotel corridor and knew something was very wrong. There hadn't been a cross-corridor. There never was this side of the hotel. There was always only a right-hand turn. There was no way we could have turned left without crashing into the wall. But we had.

Nick realized all this too, a second later. "Where are we?"

"In the soup," I said. "Run. Keep him in sight."

Rupert Venables was still ahead, calmly walking along there in the dim distance. I was fairly sure that if we lost him we were lost for good. If I looked over my shoulder— and I did, about six times, in increasing panic—there was, well, not the hotel. A sort of fuzzy strangeness. Nick looked once, too. Then he seized my wrist and we ran. And that was another thing about this strange experience. Rupert Venables just walked, a bit jauntily, swinging along as if he knew where he was going, but not walking fast. We fair pelted. But he was always the same distance away.

I was going to type, "It was hard not to panic," but the fact is we *did* panic. Running and running and not making any difference is like your worst dreams. Hot and horrified and nightmarish, we ran. And shortly it was *exactly* like my worst dreams, because there, just to one side, was the bush with my thornlady in it—or that she was part of, or whatever. She said to me, sneeringly, "What good do you think *this* is doing you?"

"Oh shut up!" I told her.

I don't think Nick heard her or knew she was there. He went trampling and crunching through one side of her bush, bellowing, *"Rupert the Mage!* WAIT!" with his voice roaring and cracking with panic. The bush whipped about with indignation. She was *furious.* But I had no attention for that, because Nick was dragging away at my wrist and Rupert Venables just walked on and didn't seem to hear us yelling.

We seemed to be mostly out in the open air by then, on a hillside of steep slanting banks, going downwards ahead of us. But there were regular dreadful places where it was all fuzzy sliding instead, where what was *almost* hillside, but not quite, moved giddily this way and that. There was hillside sliding overhead in those places, and we had to duck under, with our stomachs squirming with vertigo, and then jump over the fuzzy slidings underfoot, because we neither of us dared touch those bits. And the relief of get-

165

ting to grassy slope again would have been inexpressible, except that Rupert was always just that bit ahead and we had to go hurtling, shouting, ducking and jumping down after him again. In the grassy bits, the sky kept changing, from cloudy to blue, to near-dark, to sunset, and back to blue with white clouds. It made me feel sick.

The nightmare ended in a lovely Spring afternoon. Rupert jumped down ahead of us, and we jumped down after him, from what seemed to be the bank of a hedge, into a dirt road. He walked slantwise across the road to a shabby white gate in the hedge opposite. We scuttled over after him for dear life.

"Stop! Wait!" Nick croaked.

"Help!" I added.

He had his hand on the gate latch, but he spun round and stared at us. I have never seen him look so utterly outraged and angry, not even when he interrupted the Witchy Dance. "What the *hell* are you two doing here?" he said. His voice had the sort of cold clank to it of someone chipping stones.

Nick quailed. "I—er . . . I wanted to speak to you," he quavered.

"We sort of followed you by mistake," I apologized. "We did shout, but you didn't seem to hear. And we didn't dare lose you."

Rupert said nothing. He simply did that thing of taking hold of his left lens and pinning us with it, like vile germs on a gold-rimmed slide. I began to get angry myself at that. I remember thinking it was *ridiculous*, us all humble and him glaring at us for something we couldn't help, in a spot like that. There were violets and primroses growing on the banks by the gate, and a clump of tiny daffodils to one side. I could hear distant, gentle country noises, sheep bleating and hens clucking and so on, and it seemed quite out of place and stupid for him to stand glaring and blaming us for being there.

Nick was completely crushed by the lens treatment. That surprises me whenever I think of it. Until then I've never known Master Nick crushed by anything. He said, "Sorry!" and looked like a dog with its tail between its legs.

That made me even angrier. "I'm sorry too," I said, "but it was an *accident*. Nick wanted to talk to you about computer games, so we ran after you. There's no call to fry us on your lens for it!"

Rupert breathed in. I could see he was going to say something that would blast me. But the gate opened out of his hand before he could speak and a tall, untidy, farmerish man in green wellies looked out at us all. "Hello, Rupe!" he said. "What's going on here?"

"Oh—hello, Will," Rupert said, rather let down and wind-out-of-sails. "You seem to have some uninvited guests, is what's going on. Nick and Maree followed me here somehow."

The man Will grinned sweetly. I could tell he knew Rupert was furious. "*You* weren't invited either," he said, "but that doesn't mean I'm not glad to see you."

"It's not the *same*!" Rupert said. He didn't exactly stamp his foot or even yell particularly, but the way he said it was doing both those things, and I somehow understood from it that Will was his elder brother and had had *years* of experience in winding Rupert up.

"Is your name Venables too?" I asked Will, testing my theory.

"That's right." He grinned even more sweetly. "Do you know my brother well?"

"NO," Nick, Rupert and I all said in chorus.

"Shame," said Will. "He quite often improves on acquaintance. Why don't you all come in?" He held the gate open invitingly and we all three trooped in past him.

Beyond it was a low white house against a hill of ploughed fields. I could see the roofs of quite a large village at the top of those fields. But I didn't pay much attention to the view, because the space beyond the gate, which was a garden of sorts, was just such a mass of creatures. The majority were pale fluffy chicks, all running about and cheeping. They sounded like a chorus of mobile phones.

167

They must have been several different kinds of chick, because the adult birds goose-stepping about amongst them were some strange sort of hen and peculiar ducks and a number of tall grey birds with long pink legs. But there was a peacock too, which flew up into a bare tree with a shriek and a whacking of wings that made Nick jump and clutch hold of me. A large silky dog appeared then, out of nowhere, pushing her nose lovingly into Rupert's hand—and then doing the same quickly to Will, in case he was offended—and she was followed by four cats and a whole gang of kittens. Meanwhile a flock of white creatures—I couldn't tell if they were odd sheep or unusual goats—was coming galloping from mid-distance baying with interest. Since they had fairly sizeable horns, Nick was not happy to see them and got behind me quickly.

But that was as nothing to Nick's dismay when the door of the house burst open and a string of little girls—six of them, I gathered later—came rushing out screaming. "Rupert! Rupert's here!" and flung themselves in a mass upon their uncle. The smallest had come out in such a hurry that she was only wearing her vest. Two of the kids had heads of hair even bushier than mine. I could see they got it from Will. He had bushy hair that wriggled. He was standing there grinning broadly at our reaction to his livestock, and he more or less laughed when the inrush of little girls caused Nick to yelp, "Oh help!" and retreat towards the gate.

I would have expected Rupert to behave the same way, but he surprised me by greeting his nieces as enthusiastically as they greeted him. He let himself be grabbed and dangled from and then dragged off to see the new swing and slide, looking as if he loved every minute. Before he had been dragged many yards, though, a fantastically good-looking woman in jodhpurs and pink bedroom slippers appeared at the house door waving a small pair of red leggings.

"Vendela's trousers!" she shouted. "Put them on her, Rupert."

She threw them and Rupert caught them, laughing. Then he was dragged away, scattering chicks and kittens and halting the charge of the sheep-goats, who stopped dead when Rupert and the children all rushed past their noses. The woman came up the path towards us, smiling, to find out who we were.

"My wife, Carina," Will said. It was like someone saying, "And here are the Crown Jewels."

"We're Nick and Maree Mallory," I explained, "and we're here by mistake, I'm afraid."

"I'm just in the middle of getting a meal," Carina said. "You'll stay and have something with us, won't you?"

"Rupert won't like it," I said. "But——"

"Rupert can lump it," said Will. "Have we got enough food, Carey?"

"Eggs to burn," Carina called, on her way back to the house. "Sponduley and Cash both started laying today, as well as all the quacks."

"That's all right then," said Will. "I hope you both like eggs."

"Yes, and we didn't have any lunch," Nick said.

"Then that's settled then," said Will. Then, in the most natural, casual way, he took us on a tour of the livestock while he got out of us what had happened and then gave us an explanation (which we certainly wouldn't have got out of Rupert). I had been dying to take a look at the strange hens, not to speak of the birds with the long pink legs. Will trudged casually in among the little running, cheeping birds in his great boots, picking one up here, and another there, and upending them for me. "A quack chick," he said. "Female, look. Most of these are Buktaru quacks. Good layers. Nice feathers too. See, this one's getting her blue tailfeathers already. She'll be different blues all over when she's fledged. We sell a lot of these, but we make pets of the sollyhens. Here. This one's a sollyhen—unless it's a cock. They're hard to sex at this age. What do you think?"

I peered at the upside down rear end of the placid yellow

169

handful he was holding out to me and mustered all my despised vet-learning. "It's a cock," I said.

"Yes, I think you're right," he agreed.

I could tell I had gone up in his estimation, so I risked saying, "But I never heard of a sollyhen. Are they the ones that look like herons?"

"No, those are butes," he told me. "You don't have those in your world, or sollies either. Butes are a bit like guinea-fowl to eat, but they're much quieter to keep. They only shout if there's a fox near. When they shout, we turn Petra out." He patted the head of the silky dog. "Petra eats foxes for breakfast, don't you, lady? Sollies, now, they're a bit like bantams, but they have lots of these little spotted feathers. And their combs are orange. Come and see the goats."

He trudged away into an orchard-like section of the garden, followed by Petra, followed by me, followed by several butes, followed by Nick, looking bored and traumatized. The white, horned flock did not please Nick, although he pleased them. They bustled and butted around us, then concentrated on Nick and left drool on his jeans.

"They're very intelligent," Will observed, "and perverse as hell. They're teasing you, Nick. Look pleased to see them and they'll leave you alone."

I was fascinated by the creatures, so of course they avoided me. They were so like sheep, except for the mad goats' eyes. Will told me they kept them for milk and for wool. We caught one and ran our hands through the silky, curly pelt, which he said made the most wonderful sweaters. Beautiful. I felt myself relaxing, in a way I hadn't for years. I remembered all over again why I had decided to become a vet. The air of this place had something to do with it. It was wonderful—even laden with goat-smell—fresh, mild and light. Being in the hotel all those hours had given me a headache I hadn't noticed until then, when the air melted it away. I think it was having the same effect on Nick—unless it was the distant sound of Rupert being mobbed on the other side of the orchard. That seemed to please Nick, and it certainly pleased me.

Anyway, as we went on into the vegetable plot, where wire runs held about a hundred rabbits, I told Will how I hoped to be a vet and he told me that he had almost trained as one too. He said they lived off the land here as far as possible. Then Nick and I both told him about the nightmare way we had followed Rupert here.

"I thought you both looked pretty upset," Will said. "Transit from world to world can be unsettling, even if you know what you're doing. And Rupert wouldn't have been able to hear you shouting—or see you, unless he was deliberately looking. He was a universe ahead of you the whole time, you see."

"You mean," Nick said challengingly, "that there really are other worlds?"

"Infinite numbers," Will said cheerfully. "This may look like England here, but it isn't. It's a country called Albion, on a world—well, they call it The World, the people who live here, but we Magids call it Thule."

"What," I said, "are Magids?"

"So Rupert hasn't mentioned it to you?" Will asked, unhitching a gate to a hillside paddock. "I'm surprised. Or perhaps not. Earth is far enough Naywards that you have to be fairly cautious who you tell. The ones who don't believe you try to lock you up, and the ones who *do* try to exploit you financially. But I should have thought he could have told you two. My brother's a bit of a stickler sometimes."

The paddock contained a family of donkeys and several horses. We held the rest of the conversation walking in among big grey and brown bodies, pulling stiff ears, smacking necks or stroking large pulpy noses, and pausing from time to time to comfort Petra, who was convinced she was far more interesting than a mere horse. At least, I did all this. Nick found the horses too big and the donkeys highly unpredictable and contented himself with petting Petra.

"Right. Magids," said Will. "I am a Magid, Rupert is a Magid and so is our brother Simon. It's actually fairly unusual, having three in the same family like this, but we all

171

had the correct abilities and Stan, our sponsor, said he wasn't going to let it worry him when three vacancies came up, one after the other. There are always a fixed number of Magids, you see."

"How many?" Nick wanted to know.

"Good question," Will said, digging in the pockets of his old green coat for sugar. "Old beliefs put the number at thirty-six or thirty-eight, but that was before it was confirmed that the number of worlds really is infinite. We think there may be as many Magids as there are worlds. But I only know forty or so. But then Rupert probably knows a slightly different forty. Simon will know another very different forty. That's because he's in a world a good long way off from here."

"So there's one of you on every different world, is there?" I asked, wondering whether to point out that the fawn-coloured donkey was lame.

"No, she's not lame, she's just faking it for sugar, aren't you, Milesia?" Will said. He and the fawn donkey went forehead to forehead, possibly thrashing the matter out telepathically. It seems certain to me that *one* Magid ability at least is a measure of telepathy. But Will was talking to us at the same time. "No," he said. "We live where we like, as long as we can conveniently get to the places where we're needed. Some worlds have ten Magids. Earth does, because it's comfortable. Thule only has me. Then there's the Koryfonic Empire. That has none—everyone hates the place, all eleven worlds of it."

"But what do you *do* exactly?" Nick said.

"Not easy to put into words," Will said, posting a second lump of sugar into Milesia. "No, that's your lot, girl. Basically we're people who can control the currents that run through the worlds. Time currents, space currents. We can push history the way it needs to go, or people, or things, if necessary, and you can see that means we have to have pretty strict rules to—"

"Are you talking about *politics*?" Nick said, suspicious and sceptical. "Or some kind of magic?"

172

"Both," Will said, after thinking about it. "But I don't think any of us are politicians. It's too hard to stay honest. And we have to be honest. No, we mostly work with magic. There are so many different kinds of magic, though, that half the time I'm not sure *what* I'm using to work with. It's quite unusual for one of us to stand up and summon a thunderstorm, you know. We'd only do that if there was nothing else we could do. Mostly we do the quiet things. You'd probably find it quite disappointing if you saw me at it."

"We saw one of you go from world to world," Nick said. "That was fairly striking."

"And it was meant to be secret," I said. "Why? And who controls you, or do you just do things?"

"Earth is what we call Naywards," Will explained, "which means sceptical—like Nick here—and averse to being pushed about, and *very* antipathetic to anything that can be called magic. Magids do tend to be secretive on Earth, though a lot of us come from Earth, because you have to be damn strong to work magic there. If we weren't secret there, we'd disable half the things we try to do. As to *what* we do, well, we have a fairly wide brief to keep things running on the right lines, and we work largely on our own initiative, but we are directed. Each group of worlds has a Senior Magid to keep the rest of us in order, and they hand down what are called Intentions. From Up There." He pointed to the pale blue Spring sky above us, and then began to trudge back to the paddock gate, avoiding Nick's disbelieving stare—and maybe mine too.

I kept up with Will and so did the horses, hoping for sugar again. "Look," I said, squeezing between the bay and the grey, "do you seriously mean that? Is what they do Up There a good thing? My Dad has cancer. From out of the blue. From up there. If they do exist, they either don't care, or they're pretty vile."

Will stopped by the gate, waiting for Nick to nerve himself up to come through the horses after us. "Cancer's on *our* level," he said, "the human or animal level. Part of the

173

conditions of existence, like you tearing your nice jacket or stepping on a mouse. Even they can't do much about that sort of thing, though you can ask, and they will try. They mostly deal in larger units. And their aims are right and good in the long term. Promise."

"How do you *know*?" I demanded.

"They explain it to you when you get sponsored as a Magid," Will said, "and again from time to time. It's part of the wisdom you take on when you take on the job. You swear to work for the good of the worlds, and you get told things in return."

"What things?" Nick asked. He had come sidling up along the hedge.

Will laughed at that. "What we call the deep secrets," he said.

"So you can't tell us?" I said. I felt scornful and disappointed.

"Not," said Will, "in so many words. But some of them are things you more or less know anyway. If I were to tell you some, you might laugh—I know I did—because a lot of the secrets are half there in well-known or childish things, like nursery rhymes or fairy stories. I kid you not! One of our jobs is to put those things around and make sure they're well enough known for people to put them together in the right way when the time comes. Or again," he said, swinging the gate open, "some of the secrets are only in parts. These are the dangerous secrets. I've got the memorized parts of at least seventy of them. If another Magid has need of my piece of a secret, he or she can come and ask me, and if the need is real enough, then I put my part together with his or hers. It acts as a check. We only do that in an emergency."

"Is that why your brother's here? To ask you a piece of a secret?" I asked.

Will laughed again. "More likely he needs a favour. I'll find out after the girls have had their go at him. Let's go in. I want my tea."

I suppose Rupert did get to speak to Will at some time

during that crowded and noisy meal. I wouldn't know. I was busy helping Carina put at least one egg in front of each child and then holding six conversations at once while I shared out bread and tomatoes. My fingernails caused much comment. Lion-headed Venetia wanted to know why they were so long. Smooth-haired Vanessa demanded to be told why they grew so yellow. Fair-head Vanda speculated that I must hurt myself when I scratched, and her carrot-haired twin Viola wondered why her own nails always broke before they were anything like as long as mine. (Yes, they were all V. Venables. Nice idea *now*, but there'll be problems when they're teenagers and getting letters from boys.) Little-lionhead Valentina was the one who kept shrilling to be told what *use* my nails were.

"Endlessly useful," I told her. "I'll show you." And I caused much amazement by nipping the top off her egg by digging my nails through its shell. Then of course I had to do the same for five more eggs. In addition, I acquired a kitten on each knee every time I sat down. My good jeans are all pecked and pulled on the thighs now.

We all sat round a crowded table in a room with a low ceiling and sunset light coming in through a window lined with geraniums in pots. I enjoyed it, but poor Nick was not happy. "Free-range livestock," he said to me feelingly. "Free-range cats, free-range kids! I wish I was in a cage." Well, I know how I felt in my aunt's house, so I shouldn't blame him.

And, just so that I wouldn't think Carina and Will were living in any sort of a superhuman idyll, they contrived to have a short loud spat halfway through tea. I don't know how it started, but Carina suddenly screamed, "Oh don't be so damned superior, Will! Stop looking so *smug*! Rupert's quite right!"

To which Will roared, "Bloody hell, Carey He's *my* brother!"

I could see Rupert at the far end of the table trying to look as if this had nothing to do with him. Nick looked alarmed. His parents never shout. But the six kids went on chatting at the tops of their voices. I could see they were quite used to it. Venetia grinned at me and yelled in my ear, "You should see them when they throw *eggs*! It's really funny. We get under the table then."

The row passed. Rupert eventually stood up and said we'd got to get back to the hotel. I made some comment that it would be polite to help with the washing-up. Rupert gave me one of his stony glares. So did Nick. Dishwashers were invented for people like Nick, but I could see Carina and Will didn't have one. Will said, in his most expansive, benevolent way, that the dishes were his chore—and then contrived to look gentle and tragic so that I knew he was being saintly.

Will, and Carina too, were both covering up for the way that Rupert was still so obviously furious with us. Carina said she'd really enjoyed meeting us. So we were all three able to go up the garden, where the various fowls were all in or under bushes, roosting for the night, and out through the gate, seeming as if we'd taken part in a normal social visit. But nothing really disguised the fact that Rupert was utterly pissed off with the pair of us.

Out in the road the last of the daylight seemed to reflect up from the white surface. Rupert glowered at us in the gloaming. He said, in his clipped, stone-chipping, furious voice, "Don't expect to be able to babble about this jaunt to everyone at the convention."

"We wouldn't dream of it!" I said.

He turned his white-reflecting spectacles on me. It was worse than seeing his eyes. "You're right," he said. "You won't be able even to dream of it. Now, in order to make sure you get back less stupidly dangerously than you came, you'd better hang on to each other and to me." He held out his hand to Nick. Somehow he made it plain that he could bear to touch Nick—just about—but not me.

We meekly took hold. I think we both felt he was justified. After all, we had intruded on his private, family life, even if we hadn't meant to. He towed us up the bank opposite—not in exactly the same place as we arrived: I saw a luminous-looking clump of primroses that I had not seen when we came—and out on to the hillside with the fuzzy places. It was incredibly hard work, climbing the grassy banks in between the fuzz. Nick and I were both puffing and scrambling and using my free hand to help us up, though Rupert marched on ahead, dragging the pair of us as if there was nothing to it. And it was somehow nothing like as alarming as when we came. The sliding misty spaces between bank and bank were hardly there: we could step over easily from one slope to the next. I couldn't help seeing that there was something Nick and I had not done quite right on the way out, and I tried as I clambered to work out what Rupert was doing that we hadn't. I think I see.

It wasn't straight climbing, just as it wasn't straight rushing downhill when we came. We had been *doing* something, Nick and I, that moved us from world to world, and though I couldn't possibly describe it, I would know how to do it again. It's like the way you never forget how to whistle or ride a bicycle once you learn how it should feel. And I'm afraid I'm determined to do it again. Nick hasn't said anything to me, but I know he's just as determined, in spite of what Rupert said. It's like being hooked.

Quite soon and quite suddenly, we came off the hillside into the corridor of dim mirrors. I nearly stopped as a realization struck me. "Oh!" I said. "The Thornlady wasn't here this time. What a relief!"

"Don't stop! Don't let go!" Rupert snapped. "You're still somewhere quite different. At the very least, you'd be stranded for life. You don't seem to realize what a stupid, dangerous thing you went and did!"

"But we got there," Nick panted. He hates being told off.

"Because you were following me," Rupert retorted. "It was rank idiocy. Don't dare do it again!"

"Why was it idiocy?" Nick said.

"Because you could have thrown several worlds out of kilter, as well as getting yourselves killed," Rupert snapped. "If you'd happened to have stopped between world and world, you would have fallen in two halves. If you'd got

the transit wrong, you could have weakened the wall between universes. All sorts of things. And I'm not telling
you any more. Just take my word."

"Mysteries. Secrets," Nick muttered disgustedly.

We suddenly popped into the hotel corridor, as he muttered it. Rupert let go of him and rounded on him. "Be
thankful there *are* mysteries!" he said. "They keep you safe
in your silly ignorant little life!"

That got me mad. I could feel my finger pushing at my
glasses. I said, "Oh yes? And who keeps everyone ignorant? Rupert Venables, the secret ruler of the world!"

I think it was the unforgivable thing to say—well, I knew
it might be, or I wouldn't have said it. Rupert sort of drew
himself up. He didn't even pin me with his lens. He just
stood. Icily. "I don't know exactly what Will said to you,"
he said, "but you couldn't have misunderstood it more!"
Then he swung round and went stalking away down the
corridor.

The heavy, scented, indoors air of the hotel seemed to
close round me as if it was trying to drown me. I stared
after his angrily marching back, wishing I hadn't said that.
I wish it even more now.

Heigh-ho. I think the only thing I really mind about is
my little fat Dad having cancer. I don't even mind about
Robbie any more. I just wish I wasn't me. That's all.

FOURTEEN

Rupert Venables, for the
Iforion archive

Looking back on things, I see I was more concerned about
what those two had managed to do, almost unaided and
wholly untaught, than I was about the failure of my attempt
to find a new Magid. Even when I think about it now,
months later, my scalp rises. They broke all the rules for
mobile workings, they used no safeguards, they had no idea
what they were doing, they simply went. And to make it
worse, I had a strong feeling, both coming and going, that
somebody had set traps out round the power-node for them.
But they seem simply to have avoided those.

I hoped I had said enough, savagely enough, to stop them
trying again. But in my heart of hearts, I suspected I had
overdone it. The trouble with pretending outrage and anger
is that your body responds to the gestures you make and
your fake emotions start becoming real. I was quite angry
even before we waded in among Will's chickens. When,
during tea, Will told me—looking his smuggest—that he
had seen no reason not to tell them all about Magids, I
almost hit the beams in his ceiling. Thule is *not* Earth. I
was glad Carina agreed with me. I was so furious with Will
that I wished I had not already arranged for him to take
over from me at the hotel while I went to see Knarros. I
would have asked someone else. Gladly.

What I should have done is to have sat carefully down
and let my precognition work on why I was so furious and
alarmed. But I was quivering all over and angry with Will

too, and I confused those feelings with my exasperation about Fisk and Thurless. Possibly I confused Stan too. But his precognition was never as acute as mine.

I didn't get to talk to Stan, anyway, until the Saturday morning. Every time I looked out into the staff car park, there seemed to be at least four of the hotel employees out there, wandering from car to car. They appeared to be looking for something. Since I had no wish to draw attention to my illicitly parked car, I went indoors again. But Saturday morning, when I tried once more, there must have been a good twenty people out there, including the hotel manager.

I heard him say, "No, I don't know where the devil it's coming from either, but I know it's Scarlatti."

Oops! I thought and dived indoors again.

It took me twenty minutes, sitting unobtrusively on an old tubular chair outside the kitchens, to persuade them to stop their search for the source of the music and go back to work. They were convinced the staff car park was haunted. And, being natives of Naywards old Earth, they were not going to leave until they had found a rational explanation instead. I put the explanation before them. I dandled it. I waved it enticingly. And they still rightly suspected a ghost.

Finally I got to work on the manager himself and persuaded him to give up in disgust and send the rest about their business. One of the chefs went in past me, saying, "Well, all I can say is that if it *is* a car radio, why is it always the same music?"

The waiter with him agreed. "Thirty-six hours, it's been going. Any car would have a flat battery by this time."

I went cautiously out to where my car sat disguised as a B-reg Ford, drawing power from the sun and exuding a faint far-off tinkle of Scarlatti. I could understand why the hotel staff were spooked. Unless you knew, the sound didn't seem to be coming from *anywhere*.

"Stan," I began as I unlocked the door.

"What's going on? What were all those people hunting for?" he wanted to know.

"You," I said.

He was very chastened when I explained. "You mean I've got to go without music even?" he said piteously. "What am I supposed to do?"

"Can't you make yourself psychic earphones or something?" I demanded. "I've got enough on my mind without you terrifying the hotel staff."

"I never thought of that. Psychic earphones, now," he mused. "Let's see . . ." I was about to point out to him, rather acidly, that he was not here to learn all five hundred-odd Scarlatti sonatas by heart, when he said, "You're going to wipe that list then?" and I realized he was just kidding me.

"It's more or less wiped itself," I told him. "Fisk massaged my hands for an hour while she told me my aura was like a grey psychic blanket, but unfortunately the greyness is hers. She's swathed in it. She can't see outside it any more. I don't know what she's done to herself, but she smells of the bad stuff. Thurless too. He—"

"Hang on. What do you mean, 'smells'?" Stan interrupted.

If the mad Gabrelisovic could describe this sensation as smell, then so could I, I thought. "You must know the feeling, Stan. It's like acid indigestion to your soul, or as if someone were sponging your mind down with strong bleach. You get it when black practitioners start to talk to you. Or in bad cases, when they just look at you."

"Oh, I get you!" Stan said. "Mindburn, I used to call it. Thurless has it too?"

"Much stronger than Fisk," I said. "I talked to him for quite a time, while he gave me a dreary history of all the times people have let him down, or insulted him, or pinched his ideas, or persuaded publishers not to take his latest book—in the end, I asked him straight out if it might not be his own fault. I asked him if he'd ever gone out of his way to be nice to anyone, or had a kind or an affectionate

181

thought. And he didn't know what I was getting at, Stan. And by then this—mindburn, was it?—smell was coming off him so strongly that I felt ill and had to go away. And then—"

"The Croatian?" asked Stan.

"Mad," I said. "Certifiable. And—"

"Then what about Punt?" said Stan.

"He's even more irresponsible than Mallory. He sees himself as Court Jester to the world, I think. But let me tell you about Mallory's latest caper." I told him about the way I had set off to see Will, and my horrified astonishment when I arrived at Will's gate to find Maree and her cousin running after me. "The boy, Nick, said he wanted to talk to me. I've no idea what about. *Nothing* could justify the risk, Stan! They could have got themselves stripped. Will and I could have spent the evening picking pieces of them out of five different worlds!"

"I take it they weren't to know that, though," Stan remarked.

"They weren't to know *anything*," I said sourly, "except that Will then went blandly ahead and told them all about Magids. All I could do after that was pretend to fly into a rage and put embargoes on their telling anyone else."

"Pretend?" asked Stan.

"Yes, I am still pretty angry," I admitted. "With Will as well."

"Seems to me," Stan said musingly, "that our Will must have had a reason for telling them. I admit he's a tactless bugger, always shooting his mouth off, but he's surely got to have thought they were Magid material after what they did. Was it just the girl who transferred them both, or did the boy do it too?"

"Both of them," I said. "That boy's pretty gifted in a quiet way. But for one thing he's too young, and for another he's about the most self-centred kid I've ever met. I don't think Will thought at all. And yes, I'm going to wipe that list and start looking all over again just as soon as I've unwound this working."

"Then you'd better lay in a load of Palestrina and Monteverdi," Stan observed. "I'll be on to that next. What about the working? Is Will coming here?"

"Middle of this afternoon," I told him. "I don't have to meet Dakros until around six, so there'll be plenty of time for Will to take hold. Meanwhile—I'm sorry about this, Stan—could you seriously think of a way to listen to Scarlatti without all the hotel staff hearing it too?"

"I'll try," Stan said dubiously. "It won't be easy, but I'll do what I can."

I left him to try and went back into the hotel. There was a panel on at midday on "What Makes Good Fantasy," and I thought I might pass the time by going to it and finding out. In the meantime, I bought one of Hotel Babylon's excellent pots of coffee and took it into the Grand Lobby to drink.

The area was, as usual, crammed with people, some in strange attire and most of them looking thoroughly hung over after the publishers' parties the night before. Ted Mallory was sitting in one corner, looking more hung over than anyone. His wife sat beside him, obviously bored, in a new and startling jumper. At a quick glance, it looked as if someone had thrown a pint of blood at her right breast. Whatever the red stuff was, it glistened like a raw wound. I looked hastily away and spotted Maree and Nick Mallory perched on a bench at the side of the area, under one of the long windows. It occurred to me to wonder, as I made my way over to them, at the way the elder Mallorys took almost no notice of the younger ones. I had realized at yesterday's breakfast, of course, just how acutely Janine disliked Maree, but I did marvel that, apart from buttering one slice of toast for him, she had never to my knowledge done anything maternal for Nick. Maybe it was simply that Nick didn't let her. People of fourteen are touchy about mothers fussing around them. But Nick seemed to rely heavily on Maree instead. The marvel of it, to me, was that Janine tolerated that. She did not strike me as a woman who tolerated much.

I suppose I speculated this way to disguise from myself the fact that I was going to talk to them. I planted my coffee tray on the windowsill and found I was saying, "Coffee, either of you? I got the largest size of pot."

They were both looking thoroughly dejected. I know my heart smote me. I suppose I wanted to make amends. That it was mostly my fault they were so dejected was plain. They both looked up warily, almost relieved I seemed friendly, but not sure I was. Maree went a little pink and said, "Nick's still awash from breakfast, but I'd love a cup."

The hotel had provided four cups, to go with the size of pot. Nick eyed them. "Me too. Who's the fourth one for?"

"Nobody," I said. We settled, sort of amicably, along the bench, looking out into the mirrors that lined the far wall. "I'm sorry I lost my temper," I found myself saying.

"So am I," said Maree, with the gloomy sob prominent in her voice. "I've been thinking I probably said the unforgivable thing."

"I wanted to make quite sure you didn't believe it—that we secretly rule the world," I said. This seemed to be the real reason I had sought the two of them out. That surprised me. "It caught me on the raw, because we do indeed do a fair amount of guiding and pushing and persuading when the need arises," I said. "Sometimes we do tread a mighty thin line between persuading and ruling."

"I thought you had to," Nick said. "You must have to have rules about it."

"Very strict ones," I said.

"I wish I could make a computer game out of it," he said wistfully. "But I bet I couldn't. I tried to mention you to Dave—he runs the Games here—as an experiment, and I couldn't. You did something to stop us. It wasn't just threats, was it?"

It turned out that the reason they had run after me was Nick's passionate desire to sell a couple of games he had invented. I have come across games submitted by kids before. They stink, frankly, and I had no reason to think

Nick's inventions were any different. But I was still wanting to make amends. I gave him a few names and addresses, which he wrote down rapturously.

While he wrote, Maree said, "There must be times when you can't guide, or you know you mustn't. It must have been like that in the World Wars. How does that work? It's been worrying me."

"It can be agonizing," I said, thinking of my current dealings with the Koryfonic Empire. "You just have to stand aside. Sometimes you get a directive to leave things alone, but sometimes you have to work out for yourself that there's nothing you can do. There are times when you even have to go in and make things worse, knowing that millions of people—"

I stopped, because she had stopped attending. Her face was bright red and she was staring, one finger to the bridge of her glasses, at something across the room. Around us, the buzz of talk had died down considerably. I could hear gasps and murmurs. I looked at where Maree was staring and I know my mouth fell open.

Andrew was walking through the room—walking in that way of his, vague but single-minded, looking neither to right nor left, but somehow avoiding all obstacles, even people sprawled in his way, gazing up at him, and small children zigzagging across his path.

"Oh God!" Maree gasped sobbingly. "The fabulous Nordic type again!"

It looked as if every female in the place was saying, or thinking, the same. Even Janine had both hands clasped to her bleeding bosom and stared with the rest. Andrew certainly seemed healthier than when I last saw him. There was better colour in his face and he strode with a swing. But I never have the least idea what makes a man attractive to women. To me he was just my neighbour in a surprising holiday mood. I hadn't realized he had meant to attend the Convention, but he had clearly paid at the door. He was even wearing convention-type clothes, more so than mine— a matter of a knee-length embroidered jacket in red and

185

brown, and brown baggy pants that seemed to be cross-gartered. At any rate, red criss-cross bindings flashed forth with each of his purposeful strides, from knee to foot.

"Wonderful!" said Maree.

Nick jabbed my arm with his pen. "Look in the mirrors."

I looked, up beyond Andrew, to Andrew's reflection striding parallel through the reflection of the crowded room. Nick had noticed something I should have noticed myself. In the mirrors, Andrew wore a sort of navy blue battledress nipped in at the waist with a broad white canvas belt.

"It was like that when he came through yesterday," Nick murmured. "Only it was ordinary clothes here, and a long overcoat like a tramp's in the mirrors."

I was dumbfounded, for more than just one reason. Maree, beside me, moaned, "Oh. I wish I knew who he was!" and I realized that the reason I was not going to tell her had changed. When I first saw Andrew, I was not going to let on that I knew him out of pure, simple jealousy. Now I was not going to tell her because there was something very strange about my neighbour which it was my business as a Magid to investigate. Both reasons, and the fact that they were both true, held me rigid and dumb and staring, while Andrew strode on and strode out through the other end of the Grand Lobby.

Then I was galvanized. I leapt up and rushed after him.

I could not see Andrew anywhere. I could not even sense his presence. And I never learnt what makes good fantasy. I was too busy roving over the hotel hunting for him and trying to come to terms with that double realization. Kicking myself. Why had I not realized that I had been wildly attracted to the sense of Maree that I had followed all over Bristol that time? Because she had annoyed me by mad behaviour that didn't live up to my romantic expectations, I suppose. I had let that totally mess up my search for a new Magid. And on top of that, Andrew had been my neighbour for two years and I had not noticed anything wrong with him. I had had to have it pointed out by a teenage boy!

Such was my distraction that the nearest I got to the panel I had meant to attend was when I edged through an agitated knot of people outside the main hall clustering round Tina Gianetti.

"I tell you it's a migraine!" Gianetti was yelling. I remember she looked very unwell.

"Nonsense, darling. You should know a hangover when you see one at your age," said a man in a suit next to her—her agent? boyfriend? both? "Take another aspirin."

"I tell you I am incapable of chairing this or any other panel today!" Gianetti screamed. "They're all futile anyway. All they do is bitch."

"Why not go in there and see how you do, Ms Gianetti?" Maxim was suggesting in the soothing tones of pure desperation, as I edged by.

Later on in my rovings, I learnt that this was what she did. I met Kees Punt in the sandwich bar. "And that was just about *all* she did," he told me with his mouth full. "She leant back in her chair and let the speakers get on with it. It was a great joke, because each of them bobbed up and said that their own book was the only good fantasy ever written—except for the great Ted Mallory, who said he was not going to compete."

"He had a hangover too, I think," I said.

Hangovers or not, both Tina Gianetti and Ted Mallory happened to be in the hotel foyer that afternoon when Will made his unintentionally dramatic entry.

FIFTEEN

I went down to the foyer to meet Will, still trying to digest my discoveries of the morning. I was not happy with myself. There was still no sign of Andrew and, as for Maree, I found I was actively avoiding her. I had seen her in the distance several times and had deliberately gone the other way. I checked the foyer anxiously as I came down the stairs, in case she was there. At first sight, the place seemed empty of anyone but the doll-like Finnish receptionist, Odile. Outside the big glass doors, the wide space of the market street was likewise empty. Will was to arrive immediately outside those doors. I put myself where I could be sure of seeing him the instant he came, ready to make a diversion in the unlikely event of Odile's noticing something strange about his arrival, and then checked the mirrors in the ceiling for hidden observers.

And there they both were. Tina Gianetti was crouched in a chair behind a potted palm tree to one side of the foyer, undoubtedly hiding from her suited boyfriend. She seemed to be holding an icepack to her forehead. Ted Mallory was asleep behind a fern on the other side. I winced a bit, by association, at the sight of Mallory, but I didn't think either of them was capable of noticing much. I strolled about, hands in pockets, waiting, unworried by anything but the oddness of Andrew and my trouble over Maree.

Almost at once, the long-suffering Maxim Hough bounded down the stairs into the foyer area, saying loudly,

188

"OK, OK, we'll have it out here, Wendy. I don't want the whole con stirred up again."

He was followed by a large lady, whining belligerently. "There's nothing to have out, Maxim. I was clearly told I was running my women writers' workshop now in Universe Three."

She was followed by Mervin Thurless, who was yelling, "I don't care what you decide! Just get this obese dyke out of my workshop!"

"I'm not standing here to be insulted, Maxim!" Wendy trumpeted.

Ted Mallory sat up and scowled. Tina Gianetti curled down further in her chair. Maxim ran his hands through his blond Egyptian curls and got himself between Thurless and the large Wendy. "It's a clear case of double-booking," he said, raising and lowering both hands in imploring chopping motions.

And there was an almighty squeal of tyres from outside the glass doors. Next second, something large and four-legged banged through those doors, crossed the foyer too fast for me to see it clearly and vanished up the stairs in a spatter of blood. The receptionist came to curiously robotic life. She swung round, pointing stiffly, and cried out, "No horses allowed in this hotel! No horses in the hotel!"

"My God!" said Thurless. "Someone just rode a horse through here!"

In the overhead mirror, I had a sight of Tina Gianetti, bolt upright and staring from dark-pouched eyes. At the same moment, I was seized, fiercely and tremulously, from behind. I spun round to find myself nose-to-nose with Ted Mallory, who was staring much like Gianetti.

"Tell me I haven't got DTs, man!" he said chokingly. "Tell me I didn't just see a centaur come through here!"

A *centaur*! I thought. Oh my God! Simultaneously, I realized that Wendy had fainted. She was in a rather large heap on the floor, with Maxim and Thurless crouching over her. In a moment of panic and inspiration, I remembered things I had not even known I had read in today's conven-

189

tion programme. "It's the masquerade tonight," I told Ted Mallory. "Someone's in costume already."

"But it was pouring with blood! I thought I saw it pouring with blood!" he said.

"Tomato ketchup," I told him soothingly. "Tomato ketchup."

The glass doors clashed again behind him. Will staggered through them, white as a sheet, and stared at me beseechingly. Beyond the doors I could see his pseudo-Land Rover crookedly stopped half-way up the shallow steps outside. For a nasty instant I thought Will was injured too.

"It's all right," I said to Ted Mallory. "I'll take care of it. I'll look into it, I mean. You go and look after Gianetti and the receptionist." I pushed him that way. Gianetti was now laughing in a way that sounded like oncoming hysterics and Odile was green.

He shambled off. I dashed over to Will. "A centaur!" Will said. "I hit a centaur, Rupert! We both came through at the same spot at the same moment and I *hit* him, Rupert!"

"It's all right," I said. "I'll go and find him, see how badly he's hurt. You get that vehicle out of sight in the staff car park and then come to my room—number 555."

Will nodded shakily and staggered for the doors again. I avoided the efforts of Maxim, Thurless and Ted Mallory to grab me and demand explanations I couldn't give, and sprinted up the stairs.

It was not hard to track the centaur. He was bleeding quite badly. The carpet was printed with small neat crimson crescents, widely spread in a panicked gallop, accompanied by a red trail to the left of them that glistened like Janine's jumper. I raced along it, wishing more and more devoutly that I was any real good at healing, followed it as it veered sideways—the waiter who had been pushing the tall trolley that caused the veer was still there, and stared at me as piteously as Will had. "Masquerade. Tomato ketchup," I told him as I swerved round him and his trolley—and found myself in the main function hall.

There had been a panel in progress here and this was

now in total confusion. But at least, I thought as I sprinted amongst the milling audience, these people, as befitted fantasy fans, were reacting with amazement rather than panic. "Masquerade," I told a large man with FANGS! on his T-shirt, who accosted me with questions. "Slight accident. Horse bolted."

"What a *marvellous* costume!" cried a small lady with OOOK on her shirt. "This has made my day!"

Well that makes one of us! I thought. "Good. Great," I gasped, zigzagging along the trail, giving out soothing cries of "Tomato ketchup! Masquerade!" as I went.

No one seemed to have tried to stop the centaur. Probably just as well. Someone could have been kicked. The trail swerved to the far doors, in a speckle of crimson and a smallish red handprint, and out into the corridor beyond. I raced round leftwards after it, among mirrors and round a right-angle turn, along again and round, and then round two more corners. Too many right-angles. I swore as I ran. Someone had been messing with the node again. Finally I whirled into the area above the foyer again where the lifts were. The nearer lift had smears of blood on the door. Its door was shut and the green arrow indicated the lift was in use, going up. The hurt centaur seemed to have gone to ground in the lift. It was hard to blame him, but someone losing blood like that had to be in urgent need of attention. I rammed my thumb on the call button and started hauling the lift back downwards, Magid-fashion.

It was seriously hard to haul. I was sweating with the effort and the lift was merely creeping down when Will panted up beside me, looking thoroughly distraught.

"The centaur's in there?" he gasped. I nodded. "You've got to get him down then," Will said. "They hide away to die when they're hurt bad."

"Then *help* me, damn you!" I snarled.

"Sorry," Will said. He clapped his hand rather tremulously over mine and we both hauled. The centaur was apparently an extremely powerful magic user. We had to

191

pull madly for a while. Then the lift came down with a rush. Its door swept open. We stared.

Maree and Nick Mallory were in there, supporting the centaur, one on either side. I am not used to centaurs. There was a moment when I saw a small bay horse with its head hanging down out of sight, wedged sideways across the lift, and its black tail swishing almost in my face, while its rider sat on the horse's neck with one thin brown arm over Maree's shoulders and the other arm held by Nick. The rider's head was resting against Nick's chest. Long black hair draped over Nick's supporting hands. The human head was outlined against Nick's shirt, Asian brown and exquisite in profile, and a large dark eye, almond-shaped and fringed with long black lashes, rolled sideways at us in terror. Though the face was larger than a human face all over, I think my first thought was, What a beautiful boy! *Two* beautiful boys. Nick, though he was much paler-skinned, had the same sort of dark good looks.

Then things snapped into focus. Horse and boy became one being, with a lot of blood on the lift floor. Maree jabbed at her glasses and raised her chin across the centaur's bowed back. "I'm a trainee vet," she said. "We *were* trying to get him to my room for first aid until you two fools interfered."

"Take him to *my* room," I said. "It's nearer the lifts." I hauled Will in behind me and wedged us both into the lift alongside the centaur. Will jabbed the button marked 5 and we shot upwards at an unholy speed. "Will hit him with his car," I explained.

"Then he'll be horribly bruised too," Maree said. "Shit."

The centaur's head stirred against Nick's chest. "Knarros sent me," he said. He had a pleasant husky voice. "I was to come here because the Emperor's dead."

"That's all right," I said. "I'm the Magid in charge. You came to the right place."

The centaur became agitated at this. One rear hoof lashed the lift door and the husky voice cracked as he said, "You don't understand! I have to fetch the right person! Knarros is forbidden to talk to anyone but the right person!"

"Steady, steady!" Maree said. She sounded like Stan putting a stopper on me.

I said, "Don't worry about it. I've arranged to go and talk to Knarros this evening."

That was all there was time for before the lift banged to a halt on Floor 5. And it was just like our current luck that, for the first time ever, there was quite a crowd of people waiting to go down. About half of them were already in costume for the Masquerade. I stared out at a towering papier-mâché and plastic alien, a gentleman in Tudor court dress, two young men in almost nothing but boots, basques and bras, a slender girl apparently clad in a bead curtain, and at ordinary people clustered among them.

As Will and I edged out of the lift and Maree and Nick carefully manoeuvred the centaur round so that he could come out forwards, all these people broke out cheering and clapping.

"*Excellent*!" they shouted. "Fantastic costume! Never thought of hiring a horse!"

Possibly this was because, as the centaur turned, his unwounded side was always towards them. The hurt side was towards me. Flaps of living horsehide hung down from it. I felt hurt too, with a terrible sympathetic soreness, and rather sick. At least the bleeding seemed to have stopped, although the lift floor was a marsh of blood. I slammed its door shut behind us all, sealed it Magid-fashion, and made sure that lift would not move from this floor until I was ready to deal with it. Will hurriedly brought the other lift up instead. The centaur was near fainting by this time. His hooves staggered and his legs splayed. Since the variously dressed folk getting into the other lift were all staring over their shoulders at him, Will said, smiling inanely, "He's got to go away and practise, you know."

"Well done, Nick!" the alien said, bending to enter the lift. He seemed to have conflated the centaur and Nick, regardless of the fact that the two were side by side. I thought, as I

193

passed Maree my room key and got under the centaur's left arm in her place, that it was the clearest case I had ever seen of someone simply not believing their eyes.

But Nick was highly annoyed by the confusion. He said, in an angry blare, "Before this, I thought the people at this con were the only ones I'd ever met who *understood* when things weren't ordinary. But they're just as bad as *anyone*."

Will took a look at Nick and decided that Nick was even more shaken than he was himself. He took over supporting the centaur's right arm. "Everyone has limitations," he said.

"They can't help it if they're not all superbrains like you, Nick!" Maree snapped. She was looking vainly along the corridor for my room number. I remembered the extra right-angles I had sprinted round downstairs. I clenched my teeth and dragged everything back into place.

"What's up?" asked Will.

"Someone keeps fooling with the node here," I said.

Maree made no comment. She just gave me an approving nod as the door labelled 555 slid to a stop in front of her, put the key in, opened it and took charge. "Oh good," she said. "Lots of space. Nick, you belt off to my room and fetch my leather vet-case. Rupert, go and collect my kettle and any others you can and get them all full of boiling water—but first think of some way to keep him standing up. He looks as if he's going to fall over and I can't get at him if he does."

In mere instants, we were all flying about at Maree's commands. Will and I dismantled the trouser-press on the wall and, by hasty Magid means, got it to act as a tall shelf-like table, so that the tottering centaur lad could rest his forearms on it. This he did, gratefully. His glorious brown features were all dragged out of shape by pain and he had begun shaking. While Will and I were growing the legs of the padded stool in front of the dressing-table, Maree put her hands on the centaur's quivering arms. "I never caught your name, sweetheart."

"Robbios," he answered. "Rob usually."

"Oh, not another Robbie!" she said.

"Rob," said the centaur. "Not Robbie."

"OK," Maree replied. "Now, Rob, I'm going to have to take a close look at your side. I'll do my best not to hurt you, but I can't promise. No. Higher," she said, as Will and I tried to slide the by-now tall stool under the centaur's horse-body. "I don't want him slumping if his legs give."

I left Will to elongate the stool and flew off for kettles. Some room doors were open and the rooms still being serviced by a weary-looking chambermaid. I unscrupulously took kettles from the rooms she was not actually inside. Nick and I arrived back together to find Maree in the middle of what struck me as a most efficient and gentle examination of Rob's flayed and gaping side. Nick looked, turned extremely white, and bolted for my bathroom. I crawled about finding places to plug kettles in. Will finally got Rob supported from underneath by the stool and backed away looking as bad as Nick. It finally dawned on me why Will had so suddenly given up his boyhood ambition to become a vet.

Maree, on the other hand, seeming quite unmoved, finished her inspection and walked round to look at Rob's face. He was leaning his head in his arms, in a tumble of straight raven hair, on top of the transfigured trouser-press. He turned his face to see her. "First the good news," she told him. "It's not as bad as it looks. Most of it's your hide, but there's skin damage underneath and a couple of muscles torn. We got the bleeding stopped in the lift, but it wasn't from any of the really big blood vessels, so you aren't going to lose any more blood. The bad news is that I'm going to have to stitch you. I haven't got any local anaesthetic and it's going to hurt."

Rob gave a little howl and a gulp. "I can manage."

"We could get him drunk," I suggested, pointing to the cocktail fridge. "There's whisky and brandy and vodka in there."

"Hm," said Maree. "Rob, how do you behave when you're drunk?"

Rob said, muffled in his arms and his hair, "No, no—I can't. I cry."

"*That*'s all right," said Maree. "I just don't want you violent. OK, Rupert." She eyed Rob's bulk, calculating its weight, which must have been twice mine, though he was, I suspected, rather small for a centaur. "Try two double whiskies for a start." She then turned away, holding both bloodstained hands in the air, and commenced kicking at my bathroom door. "Nick! *Nick!* Come out of there! I need to get this blood off and then scrub up."

As Will opened the fridge and passed me a cluster of little bottles, Nick emerged, gazed at Maree's fingernails, each one spiked with blood, and clung to the doorway, moaning.

"Don't be such a *wimp*!" Maree told him. "Come back in here and get those soapdishes loose for me. I'll need them to sterilize things in."

Rob sniffed at the opened bottle I offered him and shuddered. "I—I can't."

"Yes you can!" Maree commanded from the bathroom.

"The boss says you've got to," Will told him. "Come on. Drink up."

Between us we coaxed one and a half little bottles down him. Then Maree emerged, opened that leather case of hers and said, "Damn. I've got antibiotic powder but no antiseptic. Rupert—"

"I'm on my way," I said.

I caught up with the chambermaid just as she was wheeling her service trolley away. "What do you want it for?" she understandably wanted to know.

"The Guest of Honour's son has been a little ill," I told her truthfully.

"He isn't the only one!" she said. "I think half the rooms up here were drunk last night. That's why you're lucky to catch me. That, and Maureen leaving because of that ghost playing music in the staff car park."

"Oh it's not *still* doing it!" I groaned, and then felt bound to add prudently, "I saw everyone looking for it this morning."

"Yes," she said. "Still at it. I mean, if it was pop, you'd *know* it was a car radio. But it's always classical stuff. All tinkly."

"Then it has to be a ghost—I see what you mean," I said sympathetically, wondering what I could do to Stan to stop him. "It is a bit much, I agree."

I came back with an armload of various disinfectants to a room thick with the steam from four kettles and the smell of blood and horse. Will and Nick were humbly arranging implements and thread in soapdishes, cups, saucers and the lid of my silver shaving kit. There were now three little empty bottles in front of Rob. His face looked healthier because of the warmer brown flush to it. Maree stood among it all with a pair of scissors.

She accorded me an approving nod. "Good. Thanks." *Snip*, went the scissors. *Snip, snip.* Pieces of long yellow fingernail flew across the steamy room. "Bring those disinfectants into the bathroom and I'll show you how to scrub up properly. There must be all sorts of bugs in this world that Rob's system isn't used to and I'm not taking any chances."

I saw that I had been volunteered for nurse-attendant. It was fair enough, considering the state Will and Nick were both still in, but I had got by so far only by carefully not looking at Rob's left flank, and I was not at all sure I could manage.

"Come along!" barked Maree, disposing of her last fingernail. *Snip!*

"Yes'm," I said.

She caught my eye and grinned at me. "Sorry." In the bathroom, she confided in a whisper, "This is the first time I've *done* anything like this. I'm nervous."

"You could have fooled me!" I said. She pushed her glasses up and gave me a proper smile at that. It made me as warm as the flush on Rob's face. I began to feel that it was worth being volunteered, if it meant that Maree was starting to approve of me a little.

Shortly, we were all set to go, Maree in the one surgical mask she happened to have in her case, her hair tied back in my hand-towel and her newly manicured hands in rubber gloves; and me with one silk cravat over my lower face, a second round my head like a turban, and her other pair of rubber gloves.

As we went over to Rob to start, someone knocked on the door.

"Don't anyone answer it," I mumbled through the cravat.

But the door opened, in spite of being still locked. Zinka stuck her silky brown head round it. "Ah," she said. "I thought it wasn't just a costume. *Hello*, Will! Rupert, is this beginning to be an emergency, or what?"

"It's more or less under control," I said. "But I would be grateful if you could do something about the lift. It's full of blood and I had to fix it on this floor until I could see to it."

"Can do," Zinka said cheerfully. "I'll do it at once—people are grumbling. What did you use to stick it here?"

"Just a fairly strong stasis," I said.

"Consider it unfixed," Zinka said, and went away.

The door snapped shut and Maree got down to work. Rob flinched, gasped and took his head off his hands in order to grip the trouser-press so that his fingers turned grey-white. Will and Nick flinched too and both hastily went to sit on my bed, where they could not see exactly what Maree was doing. They stayed there more or less the entire time, only moving reluctantly when Maree commanded one of them to bring me the saucer with the ligatures, or the stuff in the cups. The first time Will sat down again, he sprang up almost instantly. "Oh help," he said. "I clean forgot them!" and felt carefully in the pockets of his large rough jacket. He brought out two yellow fluffy handfuls that cheeped faintly. "Orphan quack chicks," he explained. "I meant to leave them at home."

198

"Biscuits over by the kettles," I said, holding the saucer out to Maree.

Nick and Will fed the chicks crumbs on my duvet. At least this gave Rob something to watch. I wondered how he could bear it without screaming. I said to Maree, "This looks worse than your aunt's jumper."

She said, busy with little tiny stitchings, "Yes, I thought she'd cut her breast off for a moment." Then we both came to a little and said simultaneously, "Sorry, Nick."

"Why?" said Nick. "I thought it was hideous too. I don't have to like it just because she's my mother, do I?"

Rob gave a throaty yell.

"Fetch him some more whisky, Nick," Maree said. "And talk if you can, Rob. It'll take your mind off this. Talk about this dead Emperor. I want to know."

So Rob talked. He leant on the trouser-press with his face periodically twisted in pain, talking, talking. No doubt the whisky helped him to babble, but I think he was also a naturally garrulous person. I could rather easily imagine him in happier times cantering around with his friends and chattering until those friends told him, "Oh do shut up, Rob!" And it was curiously memorable, that young husky voice talking on and on as Maree worked and, every so often, breaking into a squawk when Maree dragged another piece of his hide into place.

Much of what Rob said was well known to me, if not to the other three, but not all of it. I remember him saying, "The Emperor has three grades of wives, you know. It used to be just two, True Wives and High Ladies, and they all lived with the Emperor in the Imperial Palace, but this Emperor—I mean, he's dead now, I keep forgetting—Timos the Ninth, had a third grade just called Consorts and he didn't regard them as important enough to live with him. Knarros says that this Emperor has—had—a passion for grading everything. He graded the High Ladies and left gaps in the grading, in case he got new ones who ranked higher than the ones he had already. He never filled rank eight, but he had a nine and a ten. Of course he graded all the children he had by them too. Knarros has charge of that scheme, but he doesn't have charge of children of lower grades. If he had, he said he'd never have let that one who was executed write to his mother like that. But Consorts' children were always farmed out to people in quite humble circumstances a long way away from Iforion . . ."

So, I thought, this was why the Emperor had so casually executed young Timotheo. He was the son of a mere Consort. Expendable. And he might have been a nuisance later, since he was technically the eldest. I found myself remembering that varnished new courtroom and young Timotheo's incredulity when they pronounced the sentence of death on him. I missed quite a bit of what Rob said next, and I am not sure how he got on to the subject of the colony on Thalangia.

"Knarros is my uncle," he was saying, when I could attend. "That's why I'm there—me and Kris, we're both his nephews. We're the only ones who are allowed out. There's very strict security. Kris and I spend half the year there and half with the rest of our family, and we're not supposed to talk about Knarros when we're outside. I shouldn't really be saying this—aagh!—but the Emperor's dead, so I suppose it doesn't matter now. Anyway, as I was saying, Knarros has charge of the children of the True Wives and knows how they're graded and what their real names are, and how to identify them when the time comes. The children themselves have no idea who they are, of course."

It was not easy to interrupt Rob now he was talking. I tried to at this point. If Rob himself knew which Imperial child was which—and it sounded as if he might—it would make my task that much easier. But he talked through my attempt to interrupt him and Maree was the one who broke into his talk, frowning, while she took another threaded needle from me.

"What a crazy idea!" she said. "A kid's got to be an Emperor and he's no idea even who he is, and not the least idea what it takes to govern a country, and he's never even been outside this colony of yours. It makes no sense! Does your uncle educate the heir in statecraft at least?"

"No of course not," said Rob. "That wouldn't be safe. As he is, he's safe. And the Empire's safe from the sons trying to overthrow their father, or unscrupulous people using the sons to—"

"Piffle," Maree said. "Piffle and propaganda. Nick, didn't someone try that here? The Ottoman Empire, or one of those?"

"That's right," Nick confirmed from my bed, studiously not looking Maree's way. "And it didn't work. I can't remember which Empire it was either, but I do know they shut all the heirs away in a sort of palace-prison. And when they let the new Sultan out, he hadn't a clue, and he was scared of everything. They were dreadful weak rulers."

I sighed. So I went and let the new ruler out and *this* was how the Empire fell to pieces. As was Intended. I was fairly sure Nick and Maree had got their facts right. I seemed to recall something of the kind, too.

"Knarros has trained them all in the right kind of ethics," Rob protested. "And blood will out. The new Emperor is no coward and he's no one's fool, you'll see."

"Do you know which he is?" I managed to ask at last.

"No. Only Knarros knows that," Rob replied. "I wash—was shpeaking generally." His head slumped down on his arms. "Ish—is it going to take mush—much longer?"

"Nearly done," said Maree.

This sudden collapse of Rob's was understandable, and probably genuine, but I was fairly sure he was letting it happen because he thought he had said more than he ought to have done. I did not pester him. I would be seeing Knarros myself soon enough.

Rob remained with his face in his arms until Maree tied off the last stitch and said, "There. Done." Then it was clear that Rob was truly in a state of collapse. It took all four of us to support him on his sliding, folding legs over to my bed, where we laid him carefully down on his good side. Luckily it was a large bed. He filled most of it.

Maree leant over him to say, "How about your top half? I think you've got a cracked rib there, but I can't do much for that."

Rob muttered something we took to mean that he would be more comfortable with his shirt off. It was a sleeveless blue jerkin with no fastenings. We managed to ease it off over his head. He muttered again, anxiously.

"You're all stitched up," Maree said, leaning over him again. "There was no skin missing, so I could match it all together almost perfectly. With luck, it really won't show very much when the stitches come out."

"I hope it won't," Will said. "He's such a beautiful kid." This was true. With his shirt off and a gold medallion with the Empire crest on it glinting against his brown neck, Rob was practically perfect. Even with dark smudges of pain and shock under the one eye we could see now his head was on my pillow, even with one side of his horse-body laced with stitching and grey with powder, he was beautiful. The young human torso flowed like a harmony into the shapely horse-body.

"He can hear you. You'll give him a swelled head," Maree said.

Rob had certainly heard. There was a faint, satisfied smile on his ravaged face. He knew he was beautiful all right. I suspect he had been terrified, as he rushed round the hotel, that his beauty had been spoilt for ever. Now, reassured, he visibly relaxed and fell asleep.

We covered him with the duvet and wearily cleared up.

"God!" said Maree. "I'm pooped! I'm going to lie down. Nick, come with me and make me some coffee."

The two of them departed, taking one of the kettles. It was very convincing. And I had enough on my mind. It never occurred to me, or to Will, that there was any duplicity.

SIXTEEN

Will and I made some cardboard-flavoured Earl Grey and sat at the other end of my room so as not to disturb Rob. Here Will fed the quack chicks the last biscuit but one and made himself a badge like mine out of the last biscuit, while I briefed him on the current state of the fatelines. As I was definitely going to wipe that list, it was really only necessary to hold the lines as they were until I had time to do something about the puzzling behaviour of Andrew.

"Very strange, that," Will mused. "It sounds almost as if he might have been stripped."

"I'd thought of that," I said, "except that stripped people are usually dead."

"Not all of them," said Will. "There was a mage in Thule who went round as two people for years."

"Yes, but if Nick's right, Andrew's *four* people at least. I saw two of him myself," I said. "No, I don't think that can be the answer. God knows what is, though. Anyway, keep firm hold on his line—and if you find someone's been messing with the node again, just put it quietly back. I think it's a fellow called Gram White who's doing the messing. I'm going to put a stopper on him tomorrow if I can."

"The sooner the better," Will agreed. "Amateur mage, is he? Probably hasn't a clue what he's doing. What do all the people at this convention think when they don't find their rooms where they left them?"

"They all say this hotel's very confusing," I said, "but they mean they think they just keep getting lost."

"There's why I don't live on Earth," Will said. "Everyone always has to have the rational, scientific explanation for something, even if it's so obviously wrong you could scream."

Rob was deeply asleep when we got up to leave. He was another matter I was going to have to deal with later. Meanwhile, to make sure that no one from the hotel or the Convention happened to barge in on him, I put the strongest possible wards round the room. It would be difficult for people to find a rational, scientific explanation for Rob, not if they met him face to face in my room, hard though they had all tried earlier. Will promised to keep checking up on him. He left the quack chicks running about in there on the carpet. This, he said in his blandest way, would help him remember to keep coming up here. Typical Will, that. I think he does things like that because he knows I like to be orderly. At least, if he had got round to winding me up, it meant that Will was recovering from the shock of hitting Rob. I was glad about that.

We went down in the same lift Rob had come up in. Zinka, bless her, had expunged the blood, but the thing seemed to be running now at half speed. Another thing I had to see to later. When we finally reached the ground floor, I left Will in his false badge mooching inquisitively along to the main function hall and went out to the staff car park. Scarlatti met me just outside the hotel door. It was—perhaps—fainter than before, but you could hear it everywhere. To say I was angry is an understatement.

The sonata stopped with a guilty *tink* as I opened the car door. "Stan!" I said.

"What?" he said jauntily.

"You know very well what!" I told him, flinging myself into the seat and starting the engine. "It's probably the last straw. Don't say a word. Don't excuse yourself. Don't speak to me. I have just had to assist someone to sew the skin back on a half-flayed centaur and I am probably at the end of my tether. I want to throw up. I want to scream. But because Will and Nick both did that—or more or less—I was the one who had to be sensible. The story of my life! No, don't *speak*!" I yelled, as we screamed out through the narrow archway.

"I was only going to ask where we're going," Stan said humbly.

"Thalangia, in the Koryfonic Empire," I told him. We were already on our way. By car, the way looked like a bumpy unpaved lane, running sharply downhill.

"Hey, you can't *do* that!" Stan cried out. "The Upper Room didn't say I could go anywhere but Wantchester!"

"I am sick of the Upper Room," I said, "and all of Them Up There into the bargain! They've thrown everything in the book at me lately. If they don't want you on Thalangia, they can come and take you away personally. That will stop you terrifying the hotel staff just as easily."

"Is that why you're doing the transit by car?" Stan said. "I never knew you could."

"Will always does it," I said. "No. I'm going by car because last time I went into the Empire, someone shot at me. With any luck, this time they'll disable the car and I'll have the perfect excuse to leave *you* there!"

By this time, we had reached Thalangia. A car is that much quicker. We drove into an incredible spread of evening light, and I found I had miscalculated slightly. I was not used to making transit at such a speed. I could see a wooded hill something like a couple of miles ahead and a walled place on top of it. Over to the left of it, there was the strong gleaming of more than one Empire troop carrier, where Dakros was presumably waiting. The carriers were probably more like three miles away, across a flattish plainland cross-hatched with vineyards. There was no direct route to them from where I was, but the vineyards had mud roads running hither and thither among them, and I supposed I could get there eventually if I zigzagged often enough. I set off along the likeliest mud road, bumping slowly in second gear and raising such a cloud of golden dust that I could see next to nothing in the rear-view mirror.

"Ah, 'come on, Rupert!" Stan said. "This is the first I've

heard of any of this—shooting and centaurs and all. Give us a break and explain a bit. All I know about is that blasted hotel car park, hour after hour."

I simply turned down another rutty golden lane without answering.

"Please!" he said. "OK, I'm sorry about the music. That do? I did try to tone it down, but they were all so worried by it that it was amusing to spread it around a bit and get them really scared. I know it was wrong. Please?"

"That's better," I said. "I was beginning to think your conscience died with you. And?"

"I won't do it again," he said, rather sulkily.

"Good," I said and, as we wove from lane to lane in an ever bigger cloud of dust, I told him what had been going on in the hotel.

"I wonder why Knarros thought he needed to send this centaur for you," Stan remarked. "He must have known that whoever was in charge was going to scream for a Magid anyway. Maybe it was the sight of those carriers sitting under his hill. They make *me* feel threatened. How many of them *are* there, for goodness' sake?"

We were now near enough to guess that there were at least six. This does not sound many by Earth standards, but this is because we have nothing like them. Probably the nearest military thing we have, in terms of firepower and size, is an aircraft carrier—if you can imagine an aircraft carrier on land. Empire carriers are even more powerful, however, and much more variously armed. They cost a bomb too. Usually there are only two or three deployed on any one world. Dakros had brought six or so to show he was in earnest. But he had very carefully not surrounded the hill. The carriers all sat in a cluster to the west of it, huge shiny things, blaring orange sunset light off the armour intended to deflect beam-guns. Round the base of them, I could see small dark figures bustling in numbers, and one or two smaller vehicles that were probably only four times the size of my own car.

One of these vehicles now set off towards me in a dustcloud of its own. I realized, uneasily, that I was well within range of the smallest weapon on those carriers and that my car was not equipped to deflect it. I stopped and prudently got out. The oncoming vehicle acknowledged I was recognized by flashing its several oddly placed headlights, and roared on towards me in a rising streamer of dust.

"Keep your door open," said Stan. "I want to hear this."

Accordingly I leant on my open door and watched the vehicle come towering in over me and stop. Dakros jumped down, followed by Lady Alexandra, who was now wearing complete battledress and looking very good in it. I felt more than a twinge of envy for Dakros. She smiled at me as they came towards me and I found myself reflecting that, according to Rob, she was only a second-class wife (and wondering what number she was graded at), and also speculating that, if this lady was only second-class, what incredible beauty it must take to be a True Wife. Or maybe those were chosen politically. When it came to High Ladies, the Emperor had probably been able to please himself—and he evidently had.

Next to jump down was the Mage Jeffros, whom I had not seen since the day the palace fell down. He looked awful, ill and sallow, as if he had had no chance to recover properly from that wound on his arm. That gave me the measure of how hectic things had been in the Empire. But he gave me a smile, although it was a worried one. He was followed by various military types, each with a big-barrelled hand-beamer ready at their belts, and closed, wary faces.

"We weren't sure if it was you in that dustcloud, Magid," Dakros said. I took it as an apology for the armed guard. "Are you alone?"

I wondered what he, or even Jeffros, would say if I said, "No, there's a disembodied mentor with a taste for Scarlatti in my car too," but I answered sedately, "Yes, there's only me. I came in the car because of that sniper the other time." They looked at the car, all of them, with a slight, puzzled contempt that riled me a little. But I went on just as sedately, "Now, what's the position here? Knarros sent me a message this afternoon. Have you had any dealings with him?"

Dakros took off the official-looking soft hat he was wearing and ran a hand through the wriggly lumps of his hair. "Well, thank goodness he's done *something*! We're completely deadlocked so far. He's standing us off—barely even talking." I looked at him as he raked worriedly at his hair, and I suddenly knew why it was that I kept on trying to help Dakros. It was not just that he was valiantly struggling with a job because it had to be done. It was because he reminded me of Will. They had the same sort of hair. In Dakros it was dark and woolly and in Will it was light brown and woolly, but the resemblance was there. Will had been similarly overburdened when he first became a Magid. Will had settled to his burden, but I was much afraid that the burden Dakros carried was too great for anyone.

"Knarros says he'll only speak to a Magid," Lady Alexandra explained. "So Panthendres told him you were coming, and all Knarros would say is that you have to go up the hill and prove it." Panthendres? I thought, who? Oh. Dakros of course. Dakros was his surname.

Jeffros said, "The blasted centaur seems to mean that only a Magid can break the defences he has for that hill. *I* certainly can't. I did try, but whoever the Emperor employed as mage here was too good for me." He added, looking weary and fretful, "It even deflects beams. We tried that too. We got annoyed, frankly."

"*I* got annoyed," Dakros said. "I told him Lady Alexandra was here and would help the heir in his duties. And he said a High Lady wasn't adequate."

"The arrogant bastard!" I said. Lady Alexandra was flushed and unhappy. I said to her, "If I was the heir, I couldn't imagine anyone nicer to teach me the job."

She looked up at me with one side of her face smiling. "Thank you, Magid. I will give it my best try." Very ruefully, she added, "Besides, I'm the only one left who can."

"You'll be fine," I said. "Well, how do we go about

sorting this centaur out? I can't understand what he's playing at. He sent for me himself."

"Wants you to prove you're you, I suppose," Dakros said. "Has instructions to proceed with utmost caution and so forth. Jeffros will tell you."

There was a path up through the wood. Jeffros had tried to go up that and also up among the trees, but the ambient magics had defeated him. They were assuming I could do better. They said that *if* I got to the top and *if* I got inside the walls of the colony and *if* I then persuaded Knarros to relinquish the Emperor's son, I could signal to them and they would do the rest; but I could see they had no real doubts about it. I felt slightly less confident. It seemed to me that Knarros was behaving oddly. But I put my doubts down to the pressure of their faith in me and pinned my own faith on the fact that Knarros had, after all, sent Rob to get me.

Dakros said, "If the heir turns out to be on another world . . ."

"I think that's one possibility we don't have to worry about," I said. "The messenger strongly implied that Knarros looks after all the children of the True Wives. What are you planning to do with the rest of the children?"

This had been worrying me. Empire paranoia could well mean that Dakros would have the kids executed in order not to confuse the succession. Lady Alexandra said eagerly, "Give them the life they *should* be living, of course! They're being brought up like rustics up there. It makes my blood boil."

Dakros and Jeffros nodded, to my relief, equally eagerly. I looked from face to face, Magid-wise, and found they were sincere. "Fine," I said thankfully. "Let's get going."

They gave me one of the fat-barrelled handguns which had been adapted to fire a signal light and showed me how to fire it. I was to fire one shot if I was successful. If Knarros refused to deal with me, I was to fire two. In the unlikely event of real trouble, I was to fire three times and armed support would attempt to break through the protections and come to my assistance. Again I looked from face to face. They had real faith in me. I felt pressured.

I rode to the base of the hill in their tall vehicle, leaving my own car sitting beside a vineyard with one door hanging open. I thought Stan would prefer that. And it was unlikely anyone would try to steal an offworld vehicle that didn't even run on Empire fuel. Lady Alexandra sat beside me during the short, dusty journey, telling me her plans for the imperial children. "I'm glad some of them are girls," she said. "I'm going to enjoy giving them pretty dresses and nice things. But I think the main thing I want to give *all* the children is more children their own ages. I want them to be surrounded with fun and life for a change—though it worries me that they may have been walled up on that hill so long that they'll just find everything too big and terrifying outside. I shall have to go slowly and get them used to court life by gentle stages."

She seemed to me to have the right ideas.

They dropped me off by the path and drove off along the road at the base of the hill to wait by the carriers for my signal. I stood on a dirt road in a golden evening contemplating the cart track that led up through the wood. The stuff on it was fierce. I set one foot on it and hastily backed off again. Seldom have I met such inimical magics. I couldn't help admiring the craft of it. By its nature, and judging by the wheel tracks on the path itself, I could tell the working could be lifted or lowered at any time, even by someone who knew no magic. That takes skill. But unfortunately, it had to be lifted from within the walls uphill. I doubted if I could touch it from here. But it seemed to me, as I stood and thought the working through, that the embargoes and preventions were far fewer among the trees of the wood. When I moved about ten feet aside from the track, things seemed much quieter. I made sure I had the thickest shielding I could and went up through the trees.

It was very steep going, but otherwise very pleasant at first—allowing for the fact that I was pushing aside a new prohibition with almost every step. The trees were evergreens, green-black ilexes and various kinds of pine, and the golden light struck through them in dusty fingers smelling of incense and rosemary. Restful. As I climbed, I realized that I was pretty weary anyway after the afternoon dealing with Rob. Emotionally exhausted. Having to go and argue with Knarros on top of it was a real nuisance. I wanted to go home. I wanted to go away and rest and be *done* with the Empire. As the hill got steeper and I had to duck my way under thicker and thicker branches, I grew more tired than ever. I was panting like a person sawing wood. The beam-gun dragged in my pocket and my shielding felt like plate armour. And, as the sun went lower, it grew confoundedly cold. Far from sweating with my efforts, I was actually beginning to shiver.

The cold alerted me. A strong, permanent working has to get its energy from *somewhere* and this, unlike the magics of the path, was a permanent working, neatly designed to drain the energy of intruders by using their own metabolism against them. I stood still, and my knees nearly buckled. My teeth chattered. And I saw that I had not even been going uphill, but slantwise around. Stan would have laughed his head off. He had taught me all about this kind of thing. I felt my face heating with sheer embarrassment, as I realized that the path was nowhere near and the gate to the colony somewhere above and to the right.

I said, "*Sod* this for a game of soldiers! Knarros, you *sent* for me!" and I simply drove a path to the gate through all this nonsense and followed that path angrily. Anger has its uses. The hill was not really very steep and there were far fewer trees than I had thought. I reached the rough stone wall and the unpainted gate in it within about a minute. The wall was about twelve feet high, the gate an elderly splintery double slab of wood. I hammered on it.

"Open up! This is the Magid!"

I heard shuffling on the other side. The voice that answered reminded me of Rob's. It was husky, but younger than Rob's, and cracked on the last word. "What do you want?"

211

"I want to speak to Knarros of course! Urgently, on Empire business."

Another voice answered, "*Prove* you're a Magid."

"Then you'd better stand clear of the gate," I said. There was further shuffling. "*Are* you standing clear?" I called out.

"No," said at least three voices in chorus. The husky one went on, "Knarros said no one was to come in."

Then why the hell did he send Rob for me? I wondered. As it was evident from the sounds that at least three youngsters were bracing themselves against the gate from inside, I gave up the idea of forcing it open and went in over the top. It was nearly a disaster. I hate levitating (it's one of my least secure skills) and there was some kind of magical protective dome over the place—this was certainly what had deflected Dakros's beams—which I hit and nearly bounced off. I clawed hold just in time. Then I had to hang there and tear my way through, clawing with my fingernails and kicking with my feet, while the three youngsters inside gazed up at me hanging and struggling above them with their mouths open.

I landed beyond them, rather clumsily, and turned to face them. One was a young centaur, not as comely as Rob, but with a family likeness in the dark hair and aquiline nose. The other two were human boys about twelve and eleven years old. Neither was much to look at, but then Timos IX was not much of a looker either. Both had their long hair in an untidy pigtail down their backs. They wore grey woollen smocks and large home-made-looking shoes.

"How did you do that?" said the elder. He was the one with the husky voice.

I gave him a slight bow. He was, after all, almost certainly the future Emperor. "Levitation. You asked me to prove I'm a Magid. Now will one of you please direct me to Knarros."

"Kris will get him," piped the younger boy. "We have to stay here on guard."

212

"Nothing like shutting the stable door," I said. "As you please."

The young centaur frowned at me as he trotted past. I did not feel like standing humbly by the gate waiting on the pleasure of Knarros—I was too irritated—so I followed him, but more slowly. The protection spell which I had torn through was draping around me and clinging to my shoes. It occurred to me that when I came to fire the signal gun, the stuff would probably deflect the flames back into my face, so I proceeded to get rid of it by kicking it loose and bundling it ahead of me with my arms as I went.

The walled space was largely a stony yard, dome-shaped because it took in the top of the hill. In the middle, at the summit, there was some kind of dark bush and an altar. Of course, I thought, they worship the Emperor's dreary bush-goddess here. Otherwise the place was very barren and domestic. A few small stone houses were built against the circling walls, little more than stone huts really. There was a well and a line of washing, which I heaved my growing bundle of protection magic over, and very little else. My opinion of the late Emperor fell, if possible, even lower.

I had just passed the well when three girls came hastily out of one of the stone houses and stared at me. Apart from the fact that their hair was in two pigtails, they were dressed identically to the boys.

"What are you doing?" asked the youngest one.

"Taking down your protection. There's no need for it now," I said, and hoiked the bundle over their heads. It was fairly heavy by then, about the equivalent of a roll of carpet, only long and lissom and bendy. I thought, as I heaved it up beyond the three, that Lady Alexandra was going to have a sad time with these. The elder two might have been pretty enough in the right clothes, but they were what my Yorkshire grandmother would have called gormless. The youngest, a fair little waif of about ten, gawped like a child half that age, and her nose was running. It could, I supposed, be the result of their evidently Spartan upbringing, but I doubted it. "You'll be leaving here soon," I explained.

213

"Leaving? Knarros never said anything about *leaving!*" one of the elder ones exclaimed. And, as if my statement had rendered me undesirable, she hastily propelled the other two back into the stone hut again.

I shrugged and went on, bundling the spell stuff uphill ahead of me, until I reached the altar-stone. It was just a small, plain stone, slightly stained with fruit and pips on top. The bush was the unpleasant thing. I disliked it acutely. It was greyish, barbed and spiny, and it stirred and crackled at my approach, giving out the feeling of a deity half-manifested—a small deity, but not a pleasant one. I tried not to look at it, thinking that it was an unfortunate thing that the link between the Emperor and Knarros should be something as barren and unpleasant as this.

And Knarros was on his way now. I heard the shrill battering of hooves on stones, coming up the hill from my right. The sun was very low by then. When I looked towards the sounds, I could see blue sparks from the centaur's iron shoes. I remember thinking that one of the tradesmen allowed up that cart track had to be a farrier. Rob and Kris were properly shod too, better shod than the imperial children.

Then Knarros hove up the hill in front of me and I found myself gulping slightly. He was enormous. He towered over me like a mounted policeman over a riot. I heaved the spell-bundle over the altar and the bush and let it slide its own way down the yard on the other side. The bush-deity whipped about angrily as I turned to face Knarros. And here was another thing I had not realized about centaurs. The skin colour of their human torso is the same colour as the skin under their horse-coat. I had been misled by the fact that Rob and Kris were both light bays. Knarros in his horse part was dark iron grey. So were his face, his beard, his hair and his arms. He wore a grey sleeveless vest. The effect was like being confronted by a huge living granite statue. The expression on his face was in keeping with that. I have seldom faced a being who looked less friendly.

"I'm told you're the Magid," he said. His voice was a hard, deep rumble.

"That is correct," I said. "And you're Knarros?" The granite head bent in a curt nod. "Good," I said. "Then you'll know I'm here on Empire business. According to the files the Emperor left in Iforion, you have the imperial children here—those of the True Wives at least, I gather. As you must have heard, the Emperor, Timos IX, was assassinated about six weeks ago, so now I must ask you to hand over the new Emperor, together with proof of his birth, and any other children, by High Ladies or Lesser Consorts, with similar proofs, so that I can convey them to those people who are temporarily in charge of the Empire."

Knarros simply stood like a statue.

"Oh come now," I said. "The record the Emperor left states that you have details of all the heirs, including those placed on the world codenamed Babylon."

The granite statue reacted to the word "Babylon." A flank flinched as if a horsefly had stung it. The hard voice rumbled, "I'm sorry. I can tell you nothing unless I am assured that you are indeed a Magid. I cannot be assured of Magid good faith on your word alone. I must request you prove your status."

This seemed fair enough. From the centaur's point of view I could simply be a rogue mage with designs on his charges. I summoned a little-used skill and caused the golden Infinity sign to appear floating between us, softly glowing and rotating around its own figure-of-eight substance in the correct way. It was very beautiful, and very bright in the gathering twilight.

Knarros looked at it unmoved, except that the golden light glittered in his great dark eyes. "A mere mage could do that," he rumbled. "There's more, if you are a Magid."

"You mean," I said, "you want the whole ceremony?"

"I do," he grated.

It seemed a bit excessive to me. I have never met the mage, mere or not, who could summon Infinity correctly, but then my experience is not as wide as many, and Knarros did have an important charge to relinquish. I sighed, beckoned Infinity to stand over my head, and went slowly and carefully through the ritual I had last performed when Stan sponsored me to the Upper Room. I had to concentrate. I had not done this for nearly three years. And I was distracted by the caustic rasping of the deified bush and, too, by my own growing feeling that this was not only excessive and slightly ridiculous, but wrong in some way. Something was wrong, didn't fit, didn't quite add up.

Knarros simply stood and watched. The only sign of life he gave was a slight irritable shifting of the off rear foot, until I finished and bowed. Then he gave another of his curt nods. "I accept you as a Magid," he rumbled. "What is it you want?"

I ground my teeth and politely went through my request for the second time: the Imperial heirs, their names, dates of birth and proof of identity, and the same for the children on the world codenamed Babylon.

"I have all this," he said. Then he quenched my relief by adding, "But you have been slightly misinformed. The true heir is a human female, the Emperor's eldest daughter. She is not yet here."

"When will she arrive then?" I said.

"At sunset," said Knarros. He and I both looked northwestwards across the bush. The sky there was red-gold in streaks with the merest fiery slice of Thalangia's sun showing. "The Empress will be here any moment now," Knarros said. "If you wait here, I will go and fetch you the proofs you require."

"Thank you," I said, and thought, And about time too!

Knarros turned about, battering more sparks from the stones of the yard, and set off downhill towards a building at the back of the enclosure. He did not hurry himself. I had plenty of time to realize that my bundle of protection-spell was lying in his way and probably impenetrable. I should have left it. But I was sick of all this hanging about. I slipped across to it, got the heap of it on my shoulders, and gave it another upwards heave so that Knarros could pass underneath it. Then I gave it a sort of heaving throw that sent it away downwards and across the roof of the building he was making for. I had a notion that the bush-deity tried to prevent me doing all this, but I was irritated enough to ignore that. And as I heaved the bundle to my shoulders the first time, I could have sworn something hit the bundle hard—hard enough to make me stagger. I assumed it must have been a stone spurting from under Knarros's hoof and I ignored this too. I also ignored Knarros's command to wait where I was—all out of pure, cussed irritation, I may say. Instead, I went back over the top of the hill, past the altar and on down towards the gate, intending to ask the boys there who they had actually been told to wait for.

I never got there. A few steps past the altar, I heard a dullish *crack-boom* from behind me. I turned and ran back that way, past the threshing bush and downhill to the building where Knarros had gone. My feet made a frantic noise on the stones of the yard. Stones clacked together and made blue sparks in the twilight. I could not think what the *crack-boom* had been, except that it had sounded horribly like blasting in a quarry, and I know I was quite surprised to see the building still standing there unharmed. My thought, I suppose—if I did think—was that I had removed the protection spell just as Dakros had run out of patience and opened fire.

It was a bigger, slightly better building than the others, with a wide, high doorway to accommodate a centaur. I dashed inside it, into virtual darkness, and nearly fell over something stretched across the doorway. My fingers touched harsh warm hair as I tried to save myself. That sent me leaping backwards, to collide with the side of the doorway, where I stood just long enough to smell smoke and tepid butcher's shop. At that, I raised light—another of my less secure skills—and when the candle flame finally rose high enough on my palm to show the stone space inside, I gagged at the sight of Knarros lying on the floor, with one leg that had broken as he fell doubled under him. He was

217

no longer granite. He no longer had much of his face and was still pumping out steaming red blood from his neck. But centaurs do that, because of having two hearts. He was most definitely dead. One large grey hand clutched the revolver he had shot himself with. At the back of the room was the primitive-looking wall-safe where presumably the information I needed was still locked.

As I stared at the safe, with the twirl of light trembling on my hand, its thick door slowly swung open. I could see it was empty. I looked down at what was left of Knarros again. He used a *revolver*! I thought stupidly. It seemed to take an age for me to put facts together. Actually I think it was one of those times when things only *seem* slow.

"Jesus!" I said. I dashed out through the doorway, hauling the flame-gun out of my pocket as I went—an Empire gun with a wide barrel to direct a beam and not a bullet— and fired as soon as I was outside, into the air, once, twice, three times. Then I went pelting round the base of the yard, following the circle of the wall, hoping and hoping I was not too late. Halfway round, I was joined by the young centaur Kris, who rushed out of another wide-doored building demanding to know what was wrong.

He looked to be about fifteen. It was always possible he had shot Knarros, but I didn't believe he could have done it with a weapon from Earth. "Did you hear anyone run past?" I gasped at him as I ran.

He came alongside me at an easy trot. "Not this side," he said. "But I heard people running on the other side of the yard."

"Oh hell!" I groaned. "Are you sure it wasn't me?"

"No, I heard you running down the back at the same time," he said. "*Please*, what's happened?"

"Someone shot your uncle," I panted. "Knarros was your uncle, wasn't he?"

"I'm sister's son to him, yes," he said. "But what . . . How . . . ?"

"No breath," I gasped, and ran grimly. Not for worlds was I going to send him on to the gate on his own. And I

218

knew I was right as I pelted into sight of it. Beyond the sparks his feet and mine were kicking up in the half-dark, I could see the dark gap in the wall where the gate was now standing open. Low down against the darkness were two small light-coloured lumps. "Too—bloody—late!" I panted. I slid up in a spray of blue sparks and turned the nearest lump over. The elder boy. His pigtail wrapped stickily into the big open gash across his throat as I turned him. The pool of blood under him squelched and stank faintly. He was still warm. I left the other pathetic little lump to lie and rounded on the young centaur. "Someone came through this gate," I said, "someone you know, and they told you to keep out of the way, didn't they?"

His hands were clasped under his mouth. His hooves trampled. There was still light enough to see the tears pouring down his face. "Yes, but," he said. "Yes—but—"

"But nothing," I said. "Who was it? *Who?*"

His tail slashed. He looked down at the small corpses and back at me. The tears ran across his mouth. "I—I can't *say!*" he said. "I really can't say!" Then, while I was still thinking that all the things Stan had told me about centaur loyalty were entirely true, he hurdled the two small heaped-up bodies and vanished out through the gate in a wild thudding of hooves.

I ran again, round to the other side of the yard this time, until I came to the house the girls had gone into. It was dark inside and seemed empty. I crashed through its door, raising light as I went. There was one miserable little room in there with three narrow beds in it. The corpse of the youngest girl was curled up in the space between them, and a long stream of her blood made shiny puddles in the uneven floor. I looked down at the poor kid and swore. At the sound, to my acute astonishment, one of the older girls put her head out from under the nearest bed. The second emerged from under another.

"Who did this?" I said to them. "Did you see?"

They stared at me, almost like animals. Probably it was shock. And as we all stared, light slanted into the room and there was a strong thudding drone. Leave this to Lady Alexandra! I thought with huge relief and dashed outside again. A small hover was just landing in the yard. To my extreme pleasure it came down right on top of that unpleasant bush. It could have been accident, but my bet was that the pilot worshipped a different deity. Other hovers were rising up into the yard from all round. Dakros jumped down across the altar stone and ran to meet me.

"I'm sorry," I said to him. I seemed to have gone shrill and hoarse with the horror of it all. "God, I'm sorry! The only survivors are two girls in a state of shock."

"What went wrong?" he snapped.

It was hard to watch the way his shoulders sagged as I told him—as if the weight of seven or more worlds were landing there. But he was very good at his job all the same. He barked orders and several of the hovers instantly took off to look for the young centaur. The rest landed and efficient police-like troops scrambled out of them, unreeling arclights. We went on a glaringly lit tour of the disaster, of which military men and women efficiently took pictures. Lady Alexandra had not been included in the expedition, but I was glad to find that several soldier-women almost at once took charge of the two girls, sat them by the well and began trying to coax out of them what they knew. Dakros strode about in the middle of it receiving reports from all sides. I was impressed that, faced with this almost total destruction of all his hopes, he never once seemed inclined to blame me. I would have done, had it been the other way round. I was feeling bad—vile—and would have welcomed any kind of reprimand. And the worst of it was that, though I knew it was the act of a rat to leave Dakros with this disaster in his lap, I was going to have to. The people who did this were from Earth. Apart from anything else, I had the ignoble fear that the murderers could be at this moment stealing my car.

I tried to break some of this to him about quarter of an hour later. We were standing outside the hut where Knarros still lay and someone had just handed each of us a paper cup of strong Empire coffee. "Whoever killed Knarros used a weapon from my world," I said, "and I suspect they've gone back there with whatever they took from his safe—"

"Excuse me, General Dakros." A woman trooper came up beside us. "We found this gripped in Knarros's other hand, sir. We've got pictures, but the Captain thought you ought to see it straight away."

It was a corner of a thick, official manuscript, raggedly torn off. I could see it was fluted with the grasp of Knarros's powerful fingers. Dakros took it and eagerly shone his big flashlight on it. It was written by hand in the fine slanting official script the Empire used and most of it was numbers and letters that meant nothing to me. All I could pick out was a name, or part of a name: *Sempronia Marina Timosa Th*, that had survived in the widest part.

It meant something to Dakros however. "DNA, blood group, ocular scan," he said. "There may be enough of this to match with one of those girls. Well done, trooper." He turned to me, but was at that moment interrupted by some sort of message coming in from one of the carriers. "*When* did they give you the slip?" he demanded into his com. "Oh, I see. No, that's all right. They have to be sightseers then." He turned back to me. "Sorry about that. We keep having country folk coming to stare. Not used to seeing carriers in Thalangia. For one happy moment, I hoped we might have got the murderers. Pity. Anyway, Knarros must have hung on to this certificate when he realized he'd been deceived. Do you read it that way, Magid? Maybe they had to shoot him to get it. They must have kidded him they were bringing the true heir in—you did say it's a girl, did you? That's odd. Knarros ought to have suspected that, with two boys in his charge. We always take the boys first in succession in the Empire. And they must have come on foot at sunset, so we couldn't spot them, and somehow persuaded Knarros to stall everything until then. Then they steal the details so they can fake themselves an heir and make sure we've got no heirs except their fake. Must have been something like that, don't you agree?"

I stood swigging coffee in the luridly lit yard and thought about it. I did not think it was like that at all. One thing which particularly did not fit was the heavy thump I had felt while I was lifting the protection spell to let Knarros get past it. That had been a shot. It had been a shot from the same revolver that killed Knarros. I was sure of it now. And as soon as I realized that, my mind went to that time on the outskirts of Iforion when the sniper only just missed me. How stupid not to notice that this had been an Earth-type projectile weapon too! How *stupid*! And, following this trail of violence further back, it occurred to me to wonder about the exact nature of the explosion that had killed the Emperor.

This was *planned*! was my thought, from the bomb in the palace onwards. Whoever planned it assumed I knew things that Knarros also knew. And Knarros had stalled me—*lied* to me. I had thought centaurs never lied. This was something I was going to have to ask Stan about. But I could see now that Knarros had kept Dakros off until I arrived, then taken the magical embargo off the path so that the murderers could use it. That nonsense with the Magid ceremony was purely to give them time to get into position and keep my mind off anything else. Then he had taken care to leave me standing by the altar, against the skyline, nicely placed for a shot. Luckily for me, whoever did the shooting had taken his time, no doubt trying for a perfect shot, and I had quite accidentally thwarted him by moving and lifting a bundle of impermeable protection spell into the path of the bullet. Then I had put myself out of range by running the other way. The murderer had then cut his losses by simply shooting Knarros. I had no idea if he had always meant to shoot Knarros, or not, but I knew I had been very lucky. Very, very lucky.

My hands were shaking as I passed my paper cup to the waiting trooper. In fact, tremors were running up both my arms and affecting my knees too. "Yes, I'm certain Knarros was deceived," I told Dakros. The tremor had got into my voice too. "But the most important thing is that the killers are from Earth. They're probably back there by now. If you don't mind, I think I'd better get back there too and get after them. Could one of the hovers take me over to my car?"

Dakros agreed, and we made the usual arrangements to contact one another. But there was one thing he was emphatic about. He wanted the killers brought back to the Empire to be tried and shot. So did I. There was no evidence against them on Earth. "And we may have to take this fake Empress of theirs," he said ruefully, "unless we can prove a claim for one of those two girls. I hope you can trace the rest of that document, Magid."

I didn't think there was any chance of that, but I promised to try and climbed tremulously into a hover. It had a neutral metallic smell inside, which lifted the horror from me slightly. I realized that it was truly urgent to get back home. In the artificial light glaring across the devastated colony, it had felt more like running away, but as the hover swung out over the woods of the hillside I began to see round the edges of my narrow escape and even round the cynical killing of those children. I looked down at the trees and saw that my duty as a Magid was to find these people. For one thing, they knew too much about me for comfort, and for another, they were assuming I knew more than I did about them. But the main thing was that they were using a Naywards world as a base from which to attack an Ayewards one, and that was just not on.

SEVENTEEN

As the hover left the hill and droned the short distance
across the plain, I was surprised at how much light there
still was out here. The golden, dusty soil and the lighter
criss-cross of the lanes were quite clear to see, and the
orderly black lines of the vines against the yellow ground.
Out in the distance, the lights of the hovers hunting for the
young centaur looked like dots stolen from the yellow sky.
I was not sure they were going to find Kris out there. People
who planned things this thoroughly would surely have been
waiting for him in the woods. Kris knew who the murderers
were. The peculiar thing was the way they had left him
alive at first. And Rob almost certainly knew too much as
well. I was suddenly urgently worried about that, and for
Will's safety, if Will tried to defend Rob. And about my
car. They could so easily have stolen my car. And Stan, of
course. That would make problems I didn't want to think
about.

But the car was there, standing in the lane where I had
left it. I was so relieved to see it that I thanked the hover
pilot hastily, dropped down into the stinging whirl of dust
the hover raised, and sprinted for my lovely sleek silver
vehicle.

Its door, which I had left open, was now shut. I nearly
stopped. But as the hover swept above and away, taking its
drone with it, I could hear Scarlatti tinkling in the gloaming. Maybe all was well. But in case it was not, I readied

224

a fairly massive stasis and came on at a run as if I had not noticed any difference.

The driver's door started to open. I slammed the stasis on. The door stuck, half open, with someone's hand on its edge and someone's foot appearing below. The Scarlatti stopped in mid-phrase. But I could hear Stan shouting as I covered the last few yards and pulled the door open, preparing to do things that hurt.

Nick Mallory toppled out sideways and fell to the ground, still in the forward-leaning crouch of someone getting out of a car. Dust rose around him, white in the feeble shine of the courtesy light, and pattered back on his already dusty clothes. I was particularly astonished at the way the dust made crusty streaks out of the tears on his face. Nick Mallory had never struck me as a boy who cried.

Here Stan's hoarse croakings got through to me. "Blimey, that was fierce! It's OK, Rupert. It's OK, honest! Let him up and let him talk. There's something real bad going on and he's not the one doing it."

"How do you know that?" I said.

"Things I saw and heard," he said. "Come on. Let him up."

In the normal way, I would have taken Stan's word for it, but this was not the normal way. I stayed where I was, holding the car door, half astride Nick. "Tell me what you saw and heard first."

"If that's your attitude . . ." he said. "Oh all right. I *think* I saw this kid arrive—must have been in the other car— but I didn't take much note of it, just a dust trail over in the distance that I thought must be someone tending a plantation. The first thing that really shook me up was around sunset. Red sky and all that. From up on top of that hill. Two shots."

"*Two* shots?" I said. "Thanks." Now I knew I was not being paranoid.

"Yes, two," Stan said. "Rang out real clear from here. Then about half a minute after, there were three squirts of red fire from up there—looked like a signal gun."

"That was me," I said.

"I thought it must have been," said Stan. "People around those troop carriers started acting like a stirred-up ants' nest, hovers popping out of things' bellies, lights, folk running. And the hovers sit there, half up in the air, grinding, troops running to get in them, panic. Took an age for them to get airborne and go howling away up to that hilltop. Looked as if your signal took them by surprise."

"Yes," I said. "I think they assumed I was omnipotent. What then?"

"Nothing for a while," said Stan. "Then there was this sheet of fire—"

"Sheet of *fire*?" I said.

"That's right, but only for a blink of time, over to your right, quite near that wood. Them in the carriers may not have caught it. It was round the hill from them. I only caught it because in my state it's like having eyes all round. And I was on the alert anyway, wondering if you were in trouble," Stan admitted. "Frustrating being pinned inside this car. I kept trying to think if there was anything I could do. But there was nothing going on for a while, and then a whole lot of stuff. First this kid comes bursting out through that vinefield there, acting like he'd run himself legless, and makes for this car, glad like. But just as he gets here, all the hovers start going off in different directions off the hill, like pips squirting—"

"That would be when I told Dakros about the young centaur," I said. "Did you—?"

"See him? Yes, I did," said Stan. "And I'll tell you about it as soon as you let that kid up. He'll be right royally bruised, falling the way he did, and there's no need to give him cramp as well. And my word on it, he's not part of this. He was coming to this car for *help*, Rupert. What's his name, by the way?"

"Nick," I said. I looked down at Nick's sizeable curled-up figure. Stan was probably right. He would be getting cramp. I compromised. I eased the stasis a little and levitated the boy back into the seat of my car in a rattle of

226

dust. The effort brought back the tremors in my legs. "That's as far as I go," I said. "Now tell me about the centaur."

"Then let me tell it in order," Stan said. "You need to know it all. This Nick here doesn't want the hovers to see him for some reason. This car's sitting here with one door open and the light on inside, the way it is now, and instead of getting into it, he dives on his face and crawls under between the front wheels. And I think, Aye, aye! Thinks they're looking for him, does he? Using the warm engine to hide body heat, is he, in case they use detectors? Well, well. But I don't think they do use detectors, or they'd have found the centaur kid by now, and I can see them still looking."

I turned to see over my shoulder. The very distant lights were now bright, droning hither and thither far out over the dark blue flatness. The sky was dark blue too with only a few pale streaks to the west. "Damn. No, they haven't found him. What happened next?"

"Well," Stan said, "I took a bit of a hand then, knowing the free way they have with executions in this Empire. I put a real strong Don't Notice round this car. Lucky I did, too. It's thanks to me you don't have your tyres shot out. Young Nick hadn't hardly wriggled out of sight when this centaur of yours comes by like a bat out of hell. Talk about go! They *can* go. Two hearts, two pairs of lungs. Beat any racehorse hollow. And this one had good reason to go. First, he goes flying up this path, and next thing I know there's a car, normal Earth-style car, screaming round the corner of that vineyard there, shimmying sideways, clouds of dust, and roaring flat out after the centaur. Man and a woman in it, woman driving. She sees the centaur, puts on her full headlights, pins him as he gallops, and the man leans out of his window and starts firing a pistol at the centaur. *Bang, bang, bang*. Centaur jumps sideways like a goat and then hurdles the hedge into the vineyard on the other side. Man missed, I think. I hope. Jumped like a bird flying, that centaur."

"Did you see the people in the car?" I said urgently.

"No, too dark, what with their headlights on," Stan said. "Man was on the other side, so I only caught a glimpse after they went past. Head, elbow, flash, crack—you know. Woman was just a shape."

"Did she wear glasses?" I demanded. If Nick was here, then that car was almost certainly Maree's.

"Don't think so," said Stan. "Anyway, they're long gone now. They stopped where the centaur went over the hedge, brake lights, *squeal*, more dust, and the man starts getting out. Anyway, his door opens and I know he's seen this car too. They were both magic users, so they were bound to see it in the end. And I start thinking quick, What can I do to stop him coming back and making a mess of this car, and maybe finding Nick as well? Not a lot, frankly. Then luckily one of those hovers spotted them and comes bawling down this lane, straight overhead of me. I was more or less yelling at them to go and beam their tyres, but they'd got no orders to do that, so they just sit in the air overhead of the other car. Man gets back in. Woman drives off, and they make transit as they start up, and hey presto! Gone. The hover goes back and forth a bit, and they don't see this car, or maybe they know it's yours, and anyway they're after the centaur, but by then they've lost him too. So off they drone. Then, after a bit, when things are quiet again, young Nick crawls out from under, gets in the driving seat, shuts the door and more or less cries his eyes out. He was so upset, I wondered whether to speak to him, to tell the truth."

"Why didn't you?" I asked.

"He thought he was alone, see," Stan explained.

"I see." I looked at Nick, curled up on the seat of my car, and felt slightly ashamed of my suspicions. "The people in that car," I said, "murdered three children and another centaur up on that hill. The first shot you heard was aimed at me."

"In that case," Stan said, "you've every right to be paranoid. But I reckon it wasn't this kid."

"You're probably right," I said, and took the stasis off.

Nick, because of the strength of the stasis, had no idea there had been an interval. He went on with the motions he had been making and scrambled frantically out of the car. "Thank God you're back!" he said. His voice brayed and squawked with hurry and misery. "*Please* come quickly! My mother's gone and stripped Maree!"

"What? Opened a world gate through her? Are you *sure*? Where?" I snapped. Of all the hundred questions I wanted to ask, these seemed the most urgent.

"Yes I *am* sure! I was *there*!" Nick brayed. "Over on that hill with the wood, in the lane. Oh *please* can you get there quickly?"

"Get in," I said, "at once. Give me directions." While Nick scrambled round the car and tumbled into the passenger seat, I was in the driver's seat and had the car moving before the doors were shut. If someone has been stripped by being in the exact place where a way of transit between worlds is made, you have to get to them quickly, before the two bodies they have been split into lose touch with one another. And Maree must have been split nearly half an hour ago now. As I snapped on the headlights and zigzagged among the vineyards to Nick's directions, I cursed my stupid, suspicious delay. "Was your mother alone?" I said to Nick.

"No. She was with a man called Gram White," Nick said. "They didn't see me. I kept out of sight. But I couldn't do a thing to help. Then a centaur boy came out of the woods and shouted they were murderers, and all I could think of was to get to your car while they were all yelling at one another. I just ran through vinefields and hoped you'd be back when I got there. Turn right again here."

I turned in a slew of dust and raced along the lane that ran along the foot of the hill, between the green-black slope of the wood and a bare black hedge, with my headlights lurid on the yellow surface of the track. There was no mistaking the small white body in the distance.

"There! There she is!" Nick shouted.

I screamed up to it and stopped in a slide of gravel. Nick and I both jumped out. "Keep back!" I warned him. "I have to see exactly where the gate opened."

He obeyed without question. He more or less tiptoed behind me as I went carefully up to Maree, keeping to the side where the wood and the hill loomed over the lane. Maree lay with her feet towards our blazing headlights, with her head on one arm, almost as if she had gone to sleep in the road. I guessed she had thrown that arm up as a reflex when the gate opened.

"Describe exactly where they were, those other two," I said. "Better still, move carefully to where you think your mother was and then guide me to where White was standing."

Nick nodded, a little bleak tremble of the chin, and went sidestepping gently out into the lane, almost to the bare hedge on the other side. He stopped about a foot to the rear of Maree's motionless white shoesoles and some six feet to one side of her. "The man was pretty well exactly opposite," he said, "the same distance away."

"You sure?" I asked.

"Yes," he said. "I know because I can see the marks where we left Maree's car, just over by the wood there, beside you. Maree was going to unlock the door and they came out round the back of the car."

"Where were you?" I said.

"More or less where your car is, only in the hedge," he said. "I was having a pee."

"Thanks," I said. He had been pretty accurate. And it was fortunate that it was now dark. The strong white glare of the headlights from my car threw shadows from every pebble and every dip in the surface of the lane, magnifying even the very faint straight groove in the sand that ran for about a yard on either side of Maree's ankles. It would have been almost invisible by daylight. I went down on hands and knees and enlarged the mark with my fingernails along its entire length. It was only then that I dared try to move Maree—or what was left of her.

She was still breathing—shallow, faint, infrequent breaths—but as I rolled her on to my left arm in order to get that arm under her shoulders, I found she was very cold. I hoped, fervently, that this was only because she had been lying on the ground at nightfall. It had become very cold here at sundown. The air now had that still, frigid feel to it that promised frost before midnight. And Maree, as stripped folk do, looked as if the frost had struck her already. Her shaggy hair, which had been a sort of mid-brown, was now silvery blonde. There was no colour at all in her face. Her black leather jacket had become the palest of greys and her one-time blue jeans, I saw as I got my other arm under her knees, were nearly white.

It was no trouble to lift her. Her body weight was exactly half what it should have been. I stood up with her easily and was puzzled to discover that holding her like this, light, limp and frost cold, was one of the most sexual experiences I have ever had. I also had to fight myself not to cry.

Before I could lay her down again where I needed her, Dakros's hover came hurtling down the hill at tree-top height, pinned me with its spotlight and plunged to a landing on the other side of the hedge. I heard mature vines crack and splinter under it and wondered how much he was going to have to pay the owner in compensation. Or maybe he owned the vines himself. His searchlight blazed through the hedge, casting long criss-cross shadows of empty branches over Nick and me and pretty well obliterating my carefully scraped mark.

"Is there some more trouble, Magid?" his amplified voice boomed.

Oh go away! I thought. I did not need Stan's urgent croak from the car, "Don't tell him!," to decide on my answer.

"Yes, but it's trouble to do with my own world this time!" I shouted. "I've got the problem well in hand!"

I might have saved my breath. Dakros was already crunching through the broken vines. Shortly, he was leaning through the hedge above Nick. I supposed one could hardly blame him. "What is it this time?" he said.

"The same killers," I said. "They seem to have stripped this young lady in order to steal her car. Do you mind turning your searchlight off. I can't see my mark."

Dakros spoke an order into his com, looking keenly at Nick while he did so. As the great beam flicked off, he said, "You're one of those two sightseers who gave Jeffros the slip, aren't you?"

Nick had no more desire than I had to confide in Dakros. While I laid Maree carefully in the right place alongside my now visible groove, Nick said, "Yes, I'm sorry. We had no idea it was a military operation. We just followed him here—Rupert. It was a silly jaunt. I explained to Jeffros. And we thought we'd go when everyone got busy. But—but it went wrong."

"Damned right it did," Dakros agreed. "You were told to stay by the carriers. The Magid's had enough trouble already, boy." And he stayed, leaning into the hedge, watching, while I stepped back from Maree and performed the working that unfastened just a scrap of the walls between universes.

The place was weak anyway. White, or Janine, had only sealed it perfunctorily. It burst open in our faces in a sheet of roaring red flame. Dakros and Nick both cried out and ducked. Even Maree's tepid half-body flinched. I held one arm over my blistering face and worked like a madman to get that gate properly closed. It seemed to take for ever. I heard the hedge frizzle and a tinny *smicker* from my car as its paintwork blistered, before I managed to drag the broken edges of Infinity back together and seal them down in place. I put extra sealing on them for safety and then tottered to lean on the hedge for a moment.

"Phew!" said Dakros. "What was that?"

The lane was filled with smoke, sharp singed smells and a stink of sulphur. I slapped at a burning spot on my trouser-knee and told him, "The inside of a volcano. Fool amateurs make these mistakes." But I didn't think it was a mistake. It felt to me as if the area around where Maree had lain had been carefully staked out.

"But," said Nick. "The other half of Maree—"

"Doesn't exist any longer," I said. Nick stood, half pointing to Maree's white remnant, so obviously stunned that I added, "We'll have to think of some other way, Nick." There *was* no other way, except one so strange and risky that I hoped he would come to accept what had happened and not ask. "We'd better take her home now," I said.

Nick simply turned and trudged to my car, where he opened the rear door.

Dakros said, "I'll be in touch quite soon, Magid, about the new Empress. We need to hold a serious discussion. And I still want those murderers handed over to the Empire."

"You'll get them," I said, "if it's the last thing I do."

I bent and picked up Maree's sad remnant again. This time I felt only strong sorrow. Though she was still alive after a fashion now, it was not for long. The stripped half of a person fades very quickly on its own. What I was picking up and carrying to the rear door of my car was a virtual corpse. Nick received it from me so carefully and laid it so considerately along the back seat that I rather feared he was still thinking of Maree as alive.

Poor kid, I thought and, with that, remembered Rob and my fears for him too. "Let's go," I said.

Nick obediently scrambled in beside me. I waved to Dakros and we went, further up the lane, around the same moment as the hover took off back to the hilltop.

And I muffed it.

I suppose I had excuses. We went from a different place, facing another direction. I was certainly in a state of shock after all that had happened, and quite tired. Magids are human, after all. And Maree's attackers had staked out Wantchester the way they had staked out the area round her car. I think that, having failed to shoot me, they were trying to make sure I did not come back. But Magids are chosen for their ability to carry on regardless of difficulties, mental, physical and magical. It was only a question of homing on to the place I had set out from. I am still kicking myself.

At all events, we were booming uphill Naywards, with the headlights kicking back on puffs of silvery mist between world and world, when thorn bushes began to appear in all directions, more and more of them, cluttering the hillside. The final slope was a total thicket. I went into bottom gear and drove on through, hoping a stray thorn didn't do for the tyres. Twigs crunched and thwacked underneath and squealed clattering across the doors. The wheels juddered about on the springy growth. Maybe that threw my direction out just the significant fraction. At least we made it to Wantchester. I felt us get there. I was sure we were there when I saw the dim orange of distant sodium lighting—very few places but Earth go in for that kind of lighting—but we arrived with an almighty rending *clang* on both sides. The orange light broke into murky ripples overhead. And my expensive, reliable, carefully maintained car stalled, coughed, and gave up. I could hardly blame it. It was lodged between two sets of strong metal railings almost exactly its own width apart.

The railings formed a sort of lane. I could see it ahead for yards. Overhead, the lane had an arched lid made of white corrugated plastic. I swore, with the inventiveness of helpless fury.

Nick said, subdued, "I never heard *that* expression before."

"What's happened?" Stan demanded. "Where the bloody hell are we?"

"Whinmore Bus Station, I think," Nick answered politely. "We're in one of those long shelters where people are supposed to queue."

Nick was correct, of course. We were wedged halfway along the thing, and the only good part of the situation I could see was that the bus station was pretty well deserted. It was around eight o'clock on the Saturday before Easter Day. In a town like Wantchester, that probably meant that the last bus had left half an hour ago. But even so, I felt it was all too much. I put my face down on the steering wheel.

"Then I can't see us getting out in a hurry," I heard Stan say. "We're in too tight to open the doors, aren't we?"

"Yes," Nick agreed. "And there doesn't seem to be anyone about at all. Would it do any good to shout?"

"Don't try it. They'd wonder how we got here," Stan reproved him. "And it will take heavy cutting equipment to move us. Since it's Bank Holiday on Monday, I shouldn't wonder if we aren't here till Tuesday."

"Oh, *surely* . . . ?" Nick said, not used to Stan's lugubrious style of joke. "Couldn't Rupert just go back into another world and then come out on Earth again in the right place?"

"That he couldn't, lad," Stan said. "You have to be moving to make transit, see. If you're not moving, you get stripped."

Which was possibly what our killers hoped would happen, I thought. I sat up. "What I'm going to have to do, Nick, is to force these two sets of railings apart, and stretch the roof with them, until there's room to drive out of here."

"Oh," said Nick. "Er. Rupert—who is the invisible person in here?"

"It's Stan," I said. "Stanley Churning, Nick Mallory. Stan used to be a top jockey and a Magid, Nick, before he was disembodied."

"Er," Nick said again. I could feel him decide that it might be impolite to ask if this meant Stan was a ghost. He settled for "Pleased to meet you."

"Same to you," said Stan. "Cheers."

"Yes, and now shut up, the pair of you," I said, "and let me get to work on this bus shelter."

There was instant respectful silence. I worked. Hard work, too, and I was weary. I set the principles of growth upon the sets of metal rails. I showed them how life started among minerals not so different from theirs, how it came from small beginnings and took force and direction, and

.suggested the direction that their growth might take. Then I turned to do the same for the rippled plastic roofing. And as I did so, because of the way I was working with growth and force and life, I had one of those moments that Ted Mallory and his fellow-panellists claimed not to have. Ideas, thoughts, explanations, notions, hit me and drenched my mind like the surf of a huge Atlantic roller. Rolled me over among them. I went down at first, and then sprang up and rode the wave with growing and enormous excitement. Everything I knew about what had been happening today assembled itself beneath me, as if the pieces had been lying around hoping I would see them and put them together. And I thought I knew what was going on, and why. As I reminded the lifeless chemicals of that roof of the small beginnings of life, I was sure that I did.

There was complete silence from Stan and Nick, while I worked and thought, thought and worked, but to my surprise, as I set the suggestion of a forest canopy upon the plastic, I heard the faintest of mutters from Maree, and a very slight stirring. Either there was more life to her than I had realized, or—which was more likely—I had managed to set the principles of life and growth on her too.

Finally I finished. I sat back. "This is going to take about half an hour to work," I said. "I think it's talk time."

EIGHTEEN

"Stan first," I said.

"Me?" said Stan. "Mother of pearl, why me?"

"Because you know about centaurs," I said. "Tell me if I've got this right. I've been told centaurs are incredibly loyal. If they've sworn friendship or made a contract with another person, then they won't ever let that person down."

"We-ell," said Stan. "Yes. Roughly."

"So what happens if they have equal loyalty to a centaur and a human?"

"The centaur always comes first," Stan said. "Racist lot. They'll let a human down in favour of another centaur any day. Mind you, so would we, the other way round, if you think about it."

"OK," I said. "What about loyalties among themselves?"

"Always family," Stan said decidedly. "They don't go for chiefs and kings and so forth. Don't have them really. But they'll do anything for a relative, and the closer the relative, the more they'll do. The difficult bit is the way most of them don't pair up for life, the way humans do; so they're always hard at it watching whose son has a child by whose daughter and working out if that gives them a family obligation to the child. They call themselves cousins when they do. A lot of them waste half their time following bloodlines. Bore you stiff with it. 'I'm his cousin but not hers.' All that stuff."

"What is the closest family obligation?" I asked.

"Mother to child," said Stan. "Next to that, it's a man-centaur to his sister's children, then a woman-centaur to children she's sure are her brother's—not so easy to be certain of that, you see—and then you get sisters and brothers, and then what *we*'d call proper cousins. Father to children he knows are his comes trailing in in sixth place. He'll always look after his sister's kids before his own."

"Right," I said. So far, this was fitting in perfectly. "Now I've always heard that centaurs never lie. Is that true?"

"Mm," said Stan. "That's the official truth. And you'll never get a centaur telling you a *direct* lie, like saying black is white or anything like that. But they're all of them quite capable of *bending* the truth, if they see the need. Like they'll tell you two things that don't go together and make it sound as if they do—or they'll add in a little word you don't specially notice, that makes what they *really* say into the exact opposite of what you *think* they say. I've been had by that a number of times. Smart people, centaurs. You should never forget that even a stupid centaur has more brain than most humans."

"I won't forget," I said. "I'll remember that when I talk to Rob—if he's up to talking, that is."

"He will be," said Stan, "and up to bending the truth too. That's another thing you should remember. Centaurs are tough. Stuff that would lay you and Nick here out for a fortnight, they get up and walk away from."

"I'm beginning to wonder, after all this, why centaurs don't rule the multiverse!" I said.

"Well, they can't live for long in half of it," Stan pointed out. "They need magic to survive. But mostly, they just don't go in for ruling. It doesn't strike them as sensible."

"I thought that too," I said. "But it's odd. The next thing I want to ask you is, would a centaur ever want to be Emperor? There's nothing in the laws of Koryfos to prevent it, as far as I can see."

"Only if that centaur didn't mind being on his own apart from all other centaurs anywhere," Stan declared. "The strict ones would disapprove of him and the others would laugh and call him mad. They'd only obey him if he had their personal loyalty for family reasons."

I thought of Knarros, who certainly seemed to be isolated from most other centaurs and who had, equally certainly, bent the truth to me, and I wondered. But Knarros was dead now. And I was fairly sure that Knarros had been loyal to the Emperor and then to the Emperor's assassins for other reasons than the obvious human ones. One reason had to be that they all worshipped the same dreary bush-goddess. I must ask Stan about that. But the other reason was more pressing.

"Stan, can centaurs interbreed with humans at all?"

As I said this, I thought I heard a faint gasp from Nick— unless it was another murmur from Maree.

"That's not thought terribly decent," Stan said, "but it *can* happen. You get physical problems with it, of course. Most crossbreeds die stillborn, and you'd never get a human mother getting that far with a centaur's child. They mostly miscarry fairly early on. If they do go to term, the foal's too large, you see. But the other way round, human father, centaur mother: that does get to happen occasionally. I met the odd one or two. They tend to be a bit small. And the thoroughbred centaurs are *painfully* nice to them. Fall over backwards to make clear it's not the *foal's* fault— you know."

That was it, I thought. We're dealing with centaur sisters' sons here. And their cousins, of course. "Thanks, Stan," I said. "Nick." Nick gave a startled, guilty movement beside me. "Nick, what's your actual full name?"

"Nicholas," Nick said. "Mallory."

"Oh?" I said. "Not, for instance, Nickledes Timos something else?"

"Nichothodes," Nick said irritably. "Actually."

I nearly laughed. Everyone always hated you to get their name wrong. Stan did chuckle a bit as I asked, "And Maree's?"

"She wouldn't ever tell me properly," Nick said sulkily, wretchedly. "But I know Maree's short for Marina."

Sempronia Marina Timosa, I thought, on a bloodstained handwritten scrap of a document clutched in a centaur's hand. *I* wouldn't have liked to admit to Sempronia either. "And what else?" I said.

"What do you mean, what else?" Nick answered. "Nothing else."

"Well, for instance," I said, "how you came to know about stripping people. You told me, quite accurately, that Maree had been stripped, but you didn't get the word for it from me. I remember exactly what I said about cross-world transit to you, when I was trying to persuade you it was dangerous, and I know I never once used that term."

No reply. Nick sat hunched forward, staring into the sodium gloom, to where the railings were now perceptibly growing thinner and beginning to lean outwards.

"For instance again," I said, "I would very much like to know if you were really in the hedge, or whether you helped with the stripping."

That galvanized him. He bounced round to face me, and his voice began booming, squeaking and blaring out of control as he shouted, "I did *not*! I was in the hedge! And I wouldn't know *how* you strip someone anyway! I feel guilty as *hell* about it, damn you! But it all happened so *quickly*!" This last word, almost inevitably, came out as a high squeak. I could see Nick hear how silly he sounded and saw him try to get a grip on himself. He had my sympathy there. I hate being ridiculous too. "If you must know," he said, in a careful monotone, "I was up on the other side of that hedge, like that soldier who came and talked to you was. We were arguing. I didn't want to leave. It was all so *interesting*—those landcruisers, or whatever they were, and Jeffros had this assistant who showed us round, and he had *wings*. Honestly. And I wanted to know more. I was arguing with Maree about staying nearly all the time we were coming down the lane. And Maree said we'd been arrested once, and it was pretty clear we weren't going to be able to go up the hill because something on the path stopped you. So she said we ought to go before someone told *you* we were here. And I said that Jeffros and his people had been perfectly nice to us ... Anyway, I got into that vinefield and said I wasn't coming, if you must know. And Maree said in that case I'd have to ask *you* for a lift home, and she hoped you tore lumps off me, and she stormed off down the lane to her car, waving her car keys. I sort of went along on the other side of the hedge, not saying anything and hoping she'd change her mind. But then—then Mum and Gram White suddenly came out round the car and Mum said something about 'So you turned up at last, Maree!' and they—they never even looked up at me. I don't think they knew I was there. Honestly."

"Yes," I said. "I think I believe you. Getting into a hedge is the sort of damn fool thing one does when arguing with one's elders. But what about all the rest?"

"We were lucky about the dust," Nick said. "We nearly broke our necks getting to the car when we saw you were going in yours and Maree said you were bound to have seen us if you hadn't been raising a duststorm behind you. When you turned towards the carriers, we sort of peeled off down another lane."

"But what else?" I said.

"After we tried to go up the path on the hill and couldn't, we walked to the carriers and soldiers came out and arrested us almost at once and—"

"No," I said. "I mean all the rest."

"What rest? Oh, you mean that centaur—" he began. I cut him off.

"Nice tries. No, I do not mean the centaur. I mean all the rest of your young life. I mean what sort of stuff has your mother been feeding you all these years?"

"I—Not for at least two years now," Nick said, aggrieved and defensive. "Not since I told her I didn't believe a word of it. I mean, it was so peculiar that I used a lot of it for my Bristolia game."

He broke off on a rising intonation and turned to look at me hopefully. Was he, I wondered, totally selfish, or simply just young? Whichever he was, bribery might help. "All right," I said, sighing slightly. "If you tell me what you've been told, I'll take a look at your Bristolia game and see if it has possibilities. That do? I can't promise more than that."

I could see in the orange light that Nick's face was vividly flushed. The light made him pale indigo briefly. "I didn't mean—It's just that I do mind about—Oh shit. Thanks. All right, but it's not much really. Ever since I can remember Mum's told me Ted Mallory isn't really my father, and about two years ago I got fed up with that idea and decided I'd adopt Dad anyway because I quite *like* him, and Mum never would tell me who my real father was. All she ever said was that he was terribly important and I'd be important too one day when I got my inheritance. That's not a nice feeling. I mean, he could be anybody, and it makes you feel snooty, and then you turn round and think, Why am I feeling so snooty about someone who may be horrible and may be a pack of nonsense anyway? But you can't sort of shake it off. I'd rather be you. You've got real secrets to be snooty about."

Stan smothered a chuckle. I said, "She must have told you more than that."

"Most of it was about things like stripping and that there were hundreds of other universes and lots more magic in half of them," Nick said dismissively. "Stuff about magic gives her a buzz. She was on a high Friday night about things Gram White had been telling her and she kept wanting to tell me until I said it was all boring nonsense and went away."

Ruthless child. I was almost tempted to feel sorry for Janine, murderess though she was. Still, I remembered being like this myself at Nick's age. My own mother survived it. "Has she known Gram White for long?"

Nick frowned. "I—think so. It was funny—I thought I'd never seen him before when we all went to supper on Friday, but halfway through, he said something and put his head sideways, and I realized I had seen him, quite often, when I was small. He didn't have a beard then. He used to come to our house a lot. But I don't think Dad liked him, and he stopped coming."

"Did he—Gram White—tell you the same sort of things as your mother?" I asked and then held my breath. Rather a lot of my ideas hung on Nick's answer to this one.

Nick frowned again. "I—don't remember. But I do remember Mum talking like that in front of him—how I was going to be important and about magic and so on—and he never stopped her, or told her it was nonsense like most people would. I think. But I was very young then."

"And Maree," I asked. "How much of this did Maree—?"

Stan interrupted me. "Rupert, I'm afraid this girl's not on the way out quite yet. She keeps moving about. And I think she's even trying to say something."

That lost me Nick's attention completely. He scrambled round to kneel on his seat and stare anxiously over its back at Maree. I adjusted the rear-view mirror so that I could see her too. My stomach kicked and sank at the sight. My inspirational workings just now had definitely affected her. She was shifting about, tiny, fretful movements of her hands, head and hips. Behind the blank moon-circles of her glasses, her eyes seemed to be half open, pallid as the rest of her, and small murmurs came from her colourless lips. I watched, wretchedly wondering how much I had prolonged this semi-life of hers. A few hours? A day? More?

"Say that again," Nick said, bending down to her.

It was unkind of me, but while his attention was elsewhere I tried him with another question that seemed important. People will answer absent-mindedly, with things they might otherwise not say, when their emotions are concentrated on something else. "Nick, did your mother ever tell you why Earth was codenamed Babylon?"

"Someone with a name like Chorus or something got stripped here. She laughs about it. She says he was trying to conquer Earth and made the Tower of Babel instead," Nick replied. He was thinking almost purely of Maree. He leant down across her and said, slowly and clearly, "No, it's all right. He's not giving it until tomorrow afternoon. You haven't missed it."

So that was all right. The codename was nothing to do with deep secrets. It was one of the versions of the death of Koryfos. There *was* some evidence that he had tried to conquer Earth before he died. "What is she saying?" I asked Nick.

"She says she's promised to go and listen to Dad give his Guest of Honour speech," Nick said. He scrambled round to face me, a different boy, galvanized with hope. "She's going to be all right, isn't she? She's going to grow her other half back!"

I stared at him, wondering how to say it. I was astonished at how much I hurt. Feelings I had been carefully trying not to admit to blocked my throat and tore at my chest. It was a dry, strong, physical ache, as if someone had forced me full of the little broken pieces of concrete. I was not sure I could speak through it.

To my intense gratitude, Stan answered for me. "No, lad. It doesn't work that way. The most that happens is that the strong ones, the ones with the big personality, can carry on a bit like this. Your sister's one of the strong ones, that's all."

"Not sister—cousin," Nick said. "*How* long?"

"I won't kid you," Stan said gently. "Sometimes they can drag on for years."

With another scramble, Nick was glaring into my face. The orange lights of the empty bus station caught the darkness of his eyes so that they shone into mine like spots of red agony. It was like having my own pain glare into me. "You said there was another way!" he blared at me. "What are you waiting for? *Do* it—do it *now*!"

"I'm not sure I . . . it's a deep secret," I said wretchedly.

"I won't say a word," Nick said. "Just *do* it!"

"It isn't that," I protested. "It takes quite a time. It might not work. I've never done it. It needs at least one other Magid and someone to go with her, and I'm not sure we've got—"

"You don't *understand*!" Nick roared in my face. "I wasn't *alive* until Maree came to live with us! She makes that kind of difference—she's that kind of *person*!"

"I *know* she is," I said. "But we may not have—"

"Rupert," said Stan, "the lad's right. Use the Babylon secret. You have to get this girl back because the more I see, the more I think she's Intended to be your new Magid."

How was I to tell him that I was hesitating mostly because I wanted so badly to do it myself? Half the way I hurt was because I wanted to use Babylon. You are not supposed to use a deep secret if you think you are only doing it because you want to. And the thought of using it and getting it wrong was unbearable, almost as bad as the thought that I might be doing wrong because I wanted Maree back so much. I took some of my feelings out by shouting at Stan. "Intended! Then why have they gone through all this trouble if it was what they Intended anyway? Why bring *me* into it at all?"

"You know they can't work directly," Stan said reproachfully. "It's not allowed. You can have my verse when you want it. It won't be the same as yours."

"I hope you realize just what you're asking, both of you!" I said. I think my voice cracked like Nick's. "You're asking me to do a risky major working, a working that can *kill*, in a place where I've got another major working already set up, and a wounded centaur to hide from two murderers, one of whom keeps tampering with the node. And the node's so strong that, even with Will to help, I'm not sure I can do all the rest *and* keep the road open *and* look after Maree on the way—"

"*I'll* look after Maree," Nick put in. "I'm the one doing that."

". . . and then there's Andrew as well as everything else!" I finished. "Yes, I think you'll have to, Nick. I can't do it all!"

"You're forgetting what I always used to tell you, Rupert," Stan said. "Take things one by one, as they come.

245

There's no need to load yourself with the lot. You just get your knickers in a twist."

"I'll do everything I can to help," Nick said. "Anything. I promise."

"All right," I said. "All right." I sat back, feeling a clean blast of relief. "As soon as we get loose from this bloody bus shelter then."

We waited. It was not really long. Once anything is growing, it doubles in size steadily. The metal rails had taken on the segmented look of bamboos and were spreading, gracefully, out and up, carrying the fluted, leaf-like plastic canopy with them. This had turned darker and buds in it were thrusting long, half transparent fronds up. We could hear them rattle in the slight wind. The shelter was quite quickly taking on the aspect of an arcade of interlaced trees. My hands shook on the steering wheel while I waited for it to finish growing. Nick truly did not know what he was asking, of himself or me. But Stan *did*. The fact that I had wanted Stan to ask it only made me all the more nervous.

"About ready to go?" Stan suggested at length.

I turned on my headlights again and restarted the engine. The shelter was suddenly green, and not only green overhead. Spear-shaped green plastic leaves were actually beginning to sprout from the joints in the rails, translucent in the headlights. The whole growth rustled and creaked and swayed as the car crawled along inside it. I was rather impressed. The whole thing was so graceful that I felt quite regretful, when we came sliding out through the end of it with long shining leaves brushing the windows, because I then had to turn and suggest to the shelter that it went back to its former shape. I had to suggest with precision and concentration in order to leave Maree out of this part.

"Pity," Stan remarked as the green foliage began to wilt. "I'd love to have seen their faces when they found it."

"Are you going to do the working now?" Nick asked.

"In the hotel, in my room," I promised him. "I need to talk to Will first."

I drove to the hotel as fast as the one-way system would let me. My poor car rattled and seemed to limp a little, with a clank underneath in the chassis somewhere. As we rattled into the market street, Nick said, "They keep a wheelchair behind the reception desk. Shall I get it?"

We stopped outside the main entrance for Nick to do that. His door would not open. I had to do a small working to spring the lock, and after that the door would not shut. We limped into the staff car park with the offside door swinging and stopped beside Will's pseudo Land Rover. I was heartily glad to see it there. I needed Will. I could not even express to Stan how much. I sent off a strong call to Will to meet me by the lifts and then set about forcing the other doors open.

"You need my verse?" Stan asked.

"Please," I said, with one foot up on the driver's door. It took a severe kick to open it.

"Here it is then," Stan said. His craking voice recited:

> "How do I go to Babylon?
> Outside of here and there.
> Am I crossing a bridge or climbing a hill?
> Yes, both before you're there.
> If you follow outside of day and night
> You can be there by candle-light.

"There," he said. "Does that make any sense with what you've got?"

"Quite a lot," I said. "My verse suggests it's like that too, but mine's got a warning in it as well. I'm hoping Will's verse is going to be the missing link."

I had just wrenched the rear door open (bent, dented and scratched) when Nick arrived with the wheelchair. Together we manoeuvred Maree out of the back seat and sat her in it. I could tell that my accidental working was still operating on her. She seemed heavier than she had been. She sat slumped in the chair, looking very small, waving her hands and muttering. I made Nick walk ahead in case she

247

fell out, waved to Stan, and wheeled her cautiously and carefully into the hotel.

As soon as we were under the lights and among the ubiquitous mirrors, I saw what a weird trio we made. Nick was covered with golden dust, hair and all, with streaks of it on his face, and he had a ragged, slightly bloody hole in both knees of his jeans. I was not much better, and I was charred into the bargain. My good suede jacket was black and crisp in front. Holes had been burnt randomly in my trouser-legs. The front locks of my hair had frizzled off short and my face was red and blistered, except for white rings where my glasses had kept the heat off. As for Maree, she was like a mad little dowager over whom someone had emptied a bag of flour.

Then Nick pushed open the doors into the Grand Lobby and we were not out of place at all. I had forgotten the Masquerade. There were people wandering about there in every conceivable kind of dress, including a large shiny caterpillar with at least five sets of human legs. There were Vikings, aliens of all sorts, Grim Reapers, people in cloaks, several blood-soaked corpses, and scores of stunning girls in robes with strategic holes in them. Some were in next to nothing. One, whose costume consisted of two leather straps and thigh-high red boots, caused Nick's head and mine to whip round after her. We nearly lost Maree over that.

The sudden laughing, vivid crowd seemed to make Maree very restless. She stirred from side to side of her chair and made several attempts to get out of it. While Nick and I were distracted by the straps and red boots, she succeeded. Nick ran after her frantically, diving among aliens and tripping on the train of a queen. He caught her beside the caterpillar.

We had just got her back, coaxed her into the chair and set off again when we found ourselves face-to-face with Rick Corrie, as himself, and two young gentlemen tightly laced into bright silk crinolines, each carrying a fringed parasol.

"Those are interesting costumes," one of them fluted at us. And the other asked, in a strong counter-tenor, "What section are you three entered in?"

Nick, who appeared to know them well, answered airily. "Extra-terrestrial, of course. We're victims of a mining disaster out in Tau Centauri."

"Oh," said Rick Corrie. "Maybe that accounts for the rumour. I heard you were coming as a centaur, Nick."

"Er," said Nick. "I was. But—but the legs wouldn't work. We did this instead at the last minute."

Nick was sweating as we finally pushed Maree out into the corridor beyond. He wiped golden dust around his face with his sleeve and said he hoped we didn't meet anyone else. Naturally the next turn in the corridor brought us slap up against Ted Mallory and Tina Gianetti, who both stared.

"Nice idea, shame about the execution," Ted Mallory said. "You all look terrible. What have you done to yourself, Maree?"

Maree recognized him. She mumbled and shifted. I said hurriedly, "She's the Moon Dowager from that short story by H. C. Blands."

Mallory of course had never heard of the story but, as I had hoped, he did not like to admit it. He took Gianetti's arm and moved on, saying, "Well, on with the motley, Tina." But he was faintly suspicious, enough to turn and look at us over his shoulder and to add in a slightly puzzled way, "I like that costume even less than the centaur get-up, Nick. Don't expect me to award you any prizes."

We rounded the corner to the lifts, feeling limp, both of us. Neither lift was there. Nick pounded his thumb on the call buttons. "This is almost worse than everything else!" he was saying, when both lifts arrived together. "I can't bear to meet anyone else I know," he said, watching a crowd of people surrounding an angel with a harp surge out of the lift on the right.

The lift on the left contained Janine.

NINETEEN

If Janine was disconcerted, you could have fooled me. She stood in the doorway of the lift and stared pleasantly down at Maree. "Dear, dear," she said. "What can have happened to my niece?"

She was still wearing that bloodstained jumper. I noticed it the way you do notice things, vividly, when something this shocking happens. The apparent blood, from this close, resolved itself into a cluster of moistly shiny red strawberries. I tore my eyes from them and met Janine's. "I don't know what happened to Maree exactly," I said. "You tell me."

A perfectly horrible little smile flitted on Janine's face, gleeful and secretly gloating. It took in my blistered face as well as Maree's blanched little figure. "I've no idea," she said. "But I think she ought to go to her room and lie down."

Janine clearly thought she was quite safe. She had no notion, of course, that I knew she had been on Thalangia. But surely, I thought, seeing Nick was with me would show her—Here I began to wonder what mixture of feelings Nick must be having. If it was bad for me, meeting Janine like this, it was surely ten times worse for Nick. I looked round for him and there was no sign of him. He seemed to have vanished into thin air. But Will was standing a few feet away, staring at Maree in evident horror. And Maree knew Janine. Her bleached hands were flailing limply and she was trying to say something.

250

Janine, still smiling, cocked her face sweetly down towards Maree. "What's the poor little thing trying to say, do you think?"

Seeing Will standing there made me feel better. I wanted to hurl accusations at Janine. I wanted to show her I knew what she had done. But it would have done no good. She knew as well as I did that there was no kind of Earthly evidence to connect her with Maree's condition. Instead, I leant forward over the handle of the chair, across Maree's head. "She's trying to tell you," I said, "that someone has sewn six rabbit's testicles to your right breast."

Janine's head jerked upright. She stared at me for a second, obviously wondering if I had said what she thought she heard. Then she settled for looking puzzled and distant, turned and stalked gracefully away.

Will pounced forward. "My God, Rupe! What the hell—?"

"Get in the lift with us," I said, "and I'll tell you." I looked round again for Nick, but he was still nowhere to be seen. It was the deftest vanishing trick I had ever come across. I just hoped he would turn up again. Will and I crowded into the lift beside the wheelchair and its drooping white occupant, and I gave Will a summary of events as we hummed slowly upwards.

"Lord!" he said. "No wonder you look such a mess! And I've never heard even you be that rude to a strange woman before! I couldn't think what—and what about the centaur, Rob?"

"We'll get it out of him somehow," I said. "But I think you saved his life by running into him. He was obviously supposed to take them back to Thalangia with him."

"But what are you going to do about Janine and this man White?" Will wanted to know. "There's no evidence against them except Nick's and she's his *mother*!"

"I know," I said. "And I'm going to have to send Nick to Babylon with Maree—if he turns up—so we could lose that evidence anyway." I looked up at the indicator and found we were passing the fourth floor. Nearly there. "Will, tell me your Babylon verse. I need it."

251

"You certainly will," he said. "It's the central one." And he recited rapidly:

> "How hard is the road to Babylon?
> As hard as grief or greed.
> What do I ask for when I get there?
> Only for what you need.
> If you travel in need and travel light
> You can get there by candle-light."

The lift stopped and the door opened as he finished. I pushed Maree out, saying, "Thanks. Yes. That sounds central." As I said it, the other lift opened and Nick stepped out. He was looking so shut-away and non-committal that all I liked to say to him was "Oh, there you are. Come to my room and I'll get us something to eat from Room Service."

"I'm not very hungry," he said.

"Maybe *you* aren't," Will told him cheerfully, "but *I* am. I can eat anything you can't manage."

That was the right approach with Nick, seemingly. Nick came along beside us as I trundled Maree round the first mirrored corner and along the corridor beyond. The node had been tampered with again. We turned another corner and still had not reached my room. It occurred to me to wonder if this happened whenever Gram White made transit to or from Thalangia. I asked Will.

"Not only that," he said, "someone else has been at it too. Your room's been further off every time I've been up here."

This time it was so far off that we reached Nick's room first. Nick said he wanted to get a sweater and would catch us up.

"We'll wait for you," Will and I said, almost in chorus. We didn't want to lose him again. "And where's Maree's room?" I asked while Nick unlocked his door.

Nick pointed to the next door along. "There. Why?"

I didn't like to say that Janine had suggested I take Maree there. "Just want to check something," I said. "Where would Maree keep her key?"

"Top right-hand pocket of her jacket," Nick said. I could tell by his deadpan face that he guessed it had something to do with his mother.

Wincing rather, I got the key from Maree's pallid pocket and let myself into a hotel room much smaller than mine, filled with a surprising number of possessions. At a rough guess, I would have said it contained all Maree's worldly goods. There was a grey and skinny teddy bear on the bed that looked as if it had been carried around by its neck for years, the vet-case on top of a heap of things on the floor, a computer set up on the dressing-table and several boxes of much-read-looking books. And, as I had suspected, something felt wrong. Something felt very wrong, but I couldn't tell where it was. But it felt so wrong that when Will started innocently pushing Maree in after me, I told him to stay out and, at all costs, to keep Maree outside. Will sensed the wrongness too. He nodded and backed out. I climbed about among the heaps, unavailingly searching.

"Try the computer," Nick said from the doorway. He was engulfed in a big furry blue sweater and shivering as if he had only just now noticed how cold and shocked he had been. "She uses her computer a lot."

I climbed over a book box and turned on the computer. As the screen lit, I did almost without thinking what I always do with any computer of my own, and put out a scan for viruses, Magid-style. The result was startling. VIRUS OPERATES, the screen told me. The space behind filled with dry clustering twigs, more and more of them, until the screen looked like dense undergrowth, and there was a sense of something looking out at me from among them. The twigs grew thorns, vicious ones, and with their burgeoning came every feeling of frustration, despair and humiliation I had ever known—and some I had not, particularly the humiliations. And it caught me.

253

I stood and stared at the clustering twigs, writhing with several kinds of shame, thinking I might as well give up and go home and die. I was no good. Nothing was any good. Nothing was even worth fighting for because everything I touched was going to go wrong. Nothing—

An exclamation from Nick snapped me out of it. He was pointing to the bed. A shadowy thornbush seemed to be growing upon it. It was sending spiteful sprays up through the pillow, thrusting clumps of spines up through the duvet, and several spiky shoots were even pushing through the grey teddy bear. My shame and despair were wiped away by anger. So this was why Janine wanted Maree to lie down! No doubt the original intention was to have left Maree stripped in the lane for Dakros to find along with the other murdered heirs—and she must have been quite annoyed, Janine, to find I had retrieved Maree. So she had suggested this instead, knowing that in Maree's present condition these spectral thorns would finish her off. Somehow it angered me particularly to see them attacking that evidently loved teddy bear.

"It's the Thornlady," Nick said. "Maree had dreams about it. That's why we did the Witchy Dance in Bristol. To get rid of it."

"It wouldn't have worked," I said. "It's a damned goddess. Her computer's rigged so that every time Maree used it the manifestations get stronger." My respect for Maree increased, now I knew she must have been fighting this all the time.

"Can *you* get rid of it?" Nick asked me.

"Yes, but it'll be a long job," I said. Any kind of theurgy and workings connected with deities always take long strenuous hours to undo. Sometimes you have to request the help of another god. I sighed. This was another item in the stack of things accumulating for me to do tomorrow. "We'll just lock it up for now and keep well away."

We did that. I felt drained. Those thorns were powerful. We went on down the corridor and round another corner, with me only wanting to get to my room, clean up and rest before starting on the next part. And there was my room at last. There was something stuck to the middle of the door, just below the number.

"Yuk!" said Will. "That wasn't there when I last came up."

It was one of the foulest of the foul sigils. It made me frankly retch. Its foulness was such that it was perceptible to Nick and even to Maree too. Nick's shivering increased to shudders. Maree gave a mumbling cry and tried to cover her face. I had no doubt that Janine had just been putting the thing here before she came down in the lift. I clenched my teeth and went to get rid of it.

"No, not you," Will said, shoving me aside. "It's aimed personally at you, you fool!" He scooped at the sigil with both hands—hands that were used to scooping farmyard muck every day—and almost instantly threw the double handful down on the carpet with a yelp, where he stamped on it and ground it in with his substantial shoe. For a second or so there was a truly filthy smell. "As I said—yuk!" Will said, wiping his hands hard on his coat.

There was now a smooth rounded hollow in my door, but at least it was a clean hollow. I unlocked the door and we all trooped in. Will had left lights on. I could see Rob as a large mound under my duvet and a spread of fine black hair on my pillow, apparently asleep. Once I had made sure that he was breathing and unharmed by the foulness that had been on my door, I quite deliberately left him alone. I simply pushed Maree in her wheelchair to where Rob could see her if he deigned to open the one beautiful black-fringed eye that was visible, and went to the phone.

"Hamburgers and chips all round?" I asked Will.

"Two cheeseburgers for me," said my brother. Years of the two of us winding up Simon paid off. I didn't even have to wink at him. He went on innocently, "What do centaurs eat? They're all vegetarians, aren't they?"

"I don't know," I said, which was true. "Perhaps I'd better order a vegeburger and a bit of lettuce for him."

"Vegeburgers are full of additives—could do damage to

his stomach—you'd better not," Will said callously. "But on the other hand the meat in most hamburgers could be horse."

Here Nick tumbled to what was going on and nearly gave the game away by laughing. Will and I both glared at him. I said anxiously, "So he's faced with a choice of two things he can't eat. I don't think I'd better order any food for him at all. He seems to be asleep anyway."

Will capped this with, "There's probably nothing on Earth he *can* eat, you know. He'd better not have coffee, and I'm sure milk's bad for him. Even water's full of harmful chemicals."

Here Rob could take no more. He rose up on one elbow, looking surprisingly healthy considering what he had been through. "Oh please!" he said. "I'm very hungry. Isn't there really anything I can eat or drink?"

"That depends," I said. "Do you eat meat?"

"I love it," Rob said frankly. "And cheese and bread, and I'd even eat lettuce. And I do drink milk."

"All right," I said. "Cheeseburgers, chips and coffee all round then."

I picked up the phone, leaving Rob confronting Maree and, beyond her, Nick staring gravely and wonderingly at Rob. I took my time over the order, which was not difficult to do, since the Room Service waiter I spoke to showed signs of stress and kept asking me to repeat things. "And can you assure me, sir," he asked, "that the member of staff who delivers this meal will be spared the sight of—er—eccentric costumes?" I looked at Rob, who was very clearly trying not to look at Maree and as a result kept meeting Nick's eye, and assured the man that everyone in my room was perfectly normal. "And can you give exact directions, sir, as to the whereabouts of room 555?" the harassed man continued. "Staff have unaccountably got lost tonight and we are trying to avoid—er, further complaints."

Here Rob tried to solve his problems by lying down again and pulling the duvet over his face. As I wanted him

256

to remain off balance, I was forced to turn from the phone and ask, "Rob, do you eat hay?"

"Hay?" Rob said, rising up aghast.

"One bale or two?" I asked.

"What?" cried Rob and Room Service almost simultaneously.

"Sorry," I said into the phone. "We convention people have a strange sense of humour. Tell the staff member it was round three corners from the lift to room 555 when we came here just now."

I turned from the phone and pulled up a chair so that I could sit facing Rob, beside Maree. "Right," I said. "We'll have to wait for the food, so you can answer me a few questions while we wait."

"I'll be happy to do that," Rob answered warily.

"I doubt it," I said. "I'm going to want you to answer each question in one word only. Who sent you here?"

"Knarros," Rob said, wide-eyed, sincere and rather hurt.

"And who told Knarros to send you?"

"I don't really see Knarros taking orders from any—"

"Rob," I said. "One word. Who?"

"I—I can't tell you," Rob said. His face paled and he began looking so unwell that, despite what Stan had said, I felt a brute.

"OK," I said. "Who were you sent to fetch? One word."

"I . . ." Rob's voice failed. He slumped back on to my pillow.

"Not me?"

"No," Rob admitted, and his voice failed further. His eyes closed.

"Perhaps you'd like to tell us, Nick?" I said.

Nick was now lying face-down on the carpet. He looked up at me ruefully. "Maree," he said. "Rob said his uncle had to talk to her."

"Not you as well?" I asked him.

Nick shook his head. "But I wasn't going to miss something like that."

Janine, I thought, couldn't know her son very well if she

257

thought she could keep him away simply by not inviting him. But this sort of ignorance seems to be a failing in most mothers. My own mother obstinately fails to notice the queer things I do as a Magid—the queer things all three of her sons do.

"The conversation you and Rob and Maree had in the lift must have been quite interesting," I said.

Nick and Rob looked at one another. There was both exasperation and complicity in the look. "I hadn't thought you'd noticed," Nick said irritably.

"Like to tell me about it?" I asked.

There was a fairly long silence, broken only by a mutter from Maree. In it, I picked out the words "tell him," but I had no idea if she was instructing Nick to come clean or if the words were in fact "don't tell him." But it proved she was attending. That impressed me. Even allowing for my accidental working, she was showing far more resilience than I expected.

At length, Rob looked at me limpidly and said, "Well, I told Nick we were cousins of course. But I thought I was going to pass out—"

"And there wasn't time to say very much before you two hauled the lift back down," Nick cut in quickly.

"Did Rob explain how a centaur and a human could conceivably be cousins?" I asked. "It seems a little unlikely."

"Oh, by adoption of course," Rob said. His beautiful features blazed with innocent sincerity. "My Uncle Knarros adopted Nick's mother as his sister."

"When was that?" I asked him. I needed also to ask *why*, but I knew Rob would not tell me that.

"Fifteen years ago, before she left the Empire," Rob replied.

"So Janine is definitely a citizen of Koryfos?" I said.

Rob nodded, eager to oblige. "She was born in Thalangia."

This, from a centaur, would be the truth. We had got somewhere. But I couldn't see us getting much further with Nick there, not if I was to have Nick's help with Maree.

Will was looking at me anxiously, trying to convey this. All at once, I felt deathly tired. I nodded at Will, suggesting he had a go at Rob now and, fetching clean clothes out of a drawer, I went into the bathroom to wash and change. That felt a great deal better, even with the front of my hair missing. I put salve on my burns and came out.

Will had made no headway, I could see at once. Rob was still shining with sincerity. Nick looked sulky. I went to the cocktail fridge and sorted myself out a little bottle of brandy. "Want some, Will?"

Will is never a great drinker. "Not with a big working coming up," he said, "but you look as if you could use it."

I turned round after the first heavenly, pungent, warming swig, wishing I could confront Rob with the death of Knarros—he ought to be told anyway—but with Nick there I thought it safest to confront him with Maree instead.

"Do you know what's happened to her?" I said, pointing to the wheelchair.

Rob's eyes reluctantly travelled to the little bent, blanched figure. "She's been stripped, hasn't she? I heard they go pale like that."

"That is correct," I said. "Maree was stripped. Furthermore, the gate opened into the heart of a volcano. And that wasn't an accident. The other half of her was destroyed." I took another swig from the little bottle, watching Rob across it, hoping this might make a dent in his huge, false innocence. Perhaps it had. He was looking pale and ill again, but this time I thought it was genuine.

Unfortunately, the Room Service waiter arrived just then, with praiseworthy promptness, bearing a vast tray loaded with cheeseburgers, an outsize basket of chips and an enormous pot of the hotel's excellent coffee. I gave the guy a large tip. The way the node was behaving, he deserved it, although I shuddered a little at how much this extended weekend was costing me. When I had leisure to look at Rob again, the colour was back in his brown cheeks and he had the slightly smug look of someone who thinks he has successfully wriggled out of an unpleasant situation.

I haven't finished with you yet, my lad! I thought.

But for that time we were all preoccupied with food, even Nick, who, as I expected, found the smell of it irresistible and tore into the chips. Maree, to everyone's distress, seemed unable to eat. Nick induced her to drink some sugary coffee at least, leaning over her with surprising patience, coaxing and encouraging, while Will and Rob cheerfully demolished Maree's share of the food. It was quite a sight to see Rob sitting up and munching into a cheeseburger, his dark eyes sparkling, and a hoof or so trailing out from under my duvet. Centaurs not only recover quickly: they need to eat a lot.

So too, it seems, do quack chicks. I had clean forgotten them and I couldn't think what was happening when two fluffy yellow bundles emerged from under my bed, cheeping urgently. Will fed them pieces of bread and a chip or so. And their effect on Maree was quite startling. She sat up, leant forward and followed the little birds with her eyes, avidly. There was even a faint smile on her pinched, colourless face. Of course, I remembered, she was going to be a vet. She had clearly been led to it by a love of small creatures.

Before she could lapse again into mumbling semi-life, I cleared the tray away and tipped every scrap and crumb left on to the carpet in front of the wheelchair. The chicks sped eagerly to the heap, and Maree leant over, watching.

"Right," I said. "Time for serious stuff. Rob, we are going to perform one of the deep secret workings here and you are going to witness it perforce. I must ask you to swear not to speak of it to anyone."

"You could put a *geas* on him," Will suggested.

"Ah, please!" said Rob. "I swear not to say a word. I'll make myself sleep if you like."

"No need, as long as you swear," I told him.

He swore, formally and devoutly, by the name of Koryfos the Great. Will winked at me. "Got enough candles, Rupe? Mine are all down in the Groundraker. Shall I get them?"

Just as Maree seemed to travel everywhere with her vet-case, I never go anywhere without a bag ready packed with the things I might need for a working. I fetched it from the stand and checked. I had eighteen plain white candles and a stack of wire stands for them. "These are enough," I told Will. "I don't want anyone leaving this room until we're through. There are at least two powerful hostiles out there. You start setting up the strongest wards you can. I'll find the road and explain to Nick."

We both stood with our backs to the door, concentrating. I could feel Will building something so thick and strong that I began to feel as if I was working in a vault. He was doing it very carefully, separating us from the node and keeping us that way. I was grateful for that. It meant that I could put my entire mind to thinking through the Babylon verse that was mine, my piece of the deep secret.

> Where is the road to Babylon?
> Right beside your door.
> Can I walk that road whenever I want?
> No, three times and no more . . .

Nick and Rob were staring at us with nearly identical awed respect. Nick suddenly said throatily, "I need to pee. Is that all right?"

"Get it over with now," I said. "Rob too. Go on."

Nick sped to the bathroom. Rob slid all four hooves carefully to the floor, tossed aside the duvet and heaved upright. *"Yow!"* he said. His hand clapped itself to Maree's numerous stitchings along his side. Maree's eyes turned to him with blurred professional interest. She was definitely more alive than she had been. She watched Rob as he tottered gingerly around the quack chicks and across to the bathroom. I supposed there was just space in there for him. Nick could help him. I turned my mind back to the rhyme again.

The road was there in the room, of course, more or less at my feet. It always would be, for me or anyone, since it was, in some sense, life itself. This Babylon working was old, old basic magic. I ignored Nick coming back, and then Rob, and paced out the part of it that lay inside the room. It lay in an odd slantwise way. I had to move Maree's wheelchair against the bed in order to follow it right. When I had it, I came back towards the door, putting down a candle in its holder to the right of it, every few steps. The first two candles were only a step apart, the others had to be more, and then more, until there were nine laid in a line. Then I went back again, putting another candle opposite the first ones, until there were nine again that side, a foot or so away from the first nine. Then I went back to the door and looked to see if I had it right.

I had. Although I had put the candles down in two parallel lines, from where I stood at the door the lane of candles appeared to narrow sharply towards the further end. The illusion of perspective made the room seem suddenly twice the size.

I beckoned Nick over. "Listen carefully," I said to him. "You and Maree are going on a journey. She has to walk. That's why you have to go with her to help her. I can't tell you much about the journey, because nobody knows much. But I know it won't be easy. You'll have your work cut out to get her there—and back. It's just as important to get her back here as it is to get her *there*. Have you got that?" Nick nodded. "When you get wherever the end of the journey is," I said, "it may look like a city, or a tower, or something quite other. We don't know. But you'll know when you get there. When you do, you are each allowed to ask for *one thing only*, and that thing has to be something you need very much. Make sure Maree asks to have the other half of herself restored. Keep telling her. You can ask for anything you like for yourself, but make sure Maree asks for the other half of herself or you'll have wasted the working. OK?"

Nick nodded again, very seriously. "And we walk down there?" He pointed to the double row of unlit candles. He sounded as if he was trying hard not to seem incredulous.

"When the candles are lit," I said, "you should be able to see the road. I hope so, but I'm not sure. This isn't a thing we do every day. There is one other very important thing, though. You have to complete your journey—there *and* back—while the candles are still burning."

"That's only a few hours," Nick said. "Isn't it?"

"I'll be working hard to force them to burn as slowly as possible," I said. "But, yes, you can't afford to hang about. Try to keep going, whatever happens. Have you got all that? Are you ready?"

Nick nodded. I went and helped Maree out of the wheelchair, small and tepid and light in my hands. She stood all right. She even walked when I tugged at her, but she went in a slow, tremulous shuffle, with her head bent limply sideways, watching the quack chicks still. Nick took hold of her firmly by her other arm.

"Come on, Maree," he said. "You've got to walk. You've got to *fight*. You know how strong you can be when you get fierce. Get *fierce*—come on."

Maree responded to this. Her head went round to look at Nick and I saw her lips mumble what seemed to be the word "fierce." One hand made a small, vestigial gesture, trying to push her glasses up her nose.

"That's it!" Nick said. He led her up beside the door, to the start of the two lines of candles. "What do we do now?"

"Will and I light the candles," I said, "and we'll say the words while we do. You join in with the part you know. And the moment you see the rest of the road, start walking. Ready?"

Nick, with Maree draped against him, gave a forced smile. "Going, ready or not."

Will and I hurried to the far end of the line of candles. We both had petrol lighters. Candles are harder to light with those, but you do all old magics by striking flint with steel if you can. As soon as we had the first two candles alight, we went on to the next pair and began speaking the well-known part of the secret. Like all old spells, it contains its own instructions.

263

"How many miles to Babylon?
 Three score miles and ten.
 Can I get there by candle-light?
 Yes, and back again.
 If your feet are speedy and light
 You can get there by candle-light."

Rob was saying the words too, I noticed. Interesting.
Maree seemed to be murmuring them along with Nick.
Nick spoke them out with a will, until I saw him realize
that he was going to have to coax Maree along through
seventy miles—no, a hundred and forty miles—before
these candles burnt out. He faltered a little and stared at
me in some horror, but he kept on speaking the verse.

I spoke my own verse next. That seemed to me to be
where it should come.

"Where is the road to Babylon?
 Right beside your door.
 Can I walk that way whenever I want?
 No, three times and no more.
 If you mark the road and measure it right
 You can go there by candle-light."

Halfway through this verse, Nick's eyes widened. I could
see him focus on something well beyond the walls of the
room. He pulled at Maree and they both began slowly to
walk forward, between the two rows of candles. We moved
towards them, striking light from increasingly hot lighters,
lighting a candle, moving on. I said Stan's verse next.

"How do I go to Babylon?
 Outside of here and there.
 Am I crossing a bridge or climbing a hill?
 Yes, both before you're there.
 If you follow outside of day and night
 You can be there by candle-light."

By that time we were on the last two candles. Even at Maree's slow shuffle, she and Nick had nearly reached the wall of the room. Will struck a light. It burnt him and his face pursed up with pain as he said his verse.

> "How hard is the road to Babylon?
> As hard as grief or greed.
> What do I ask for when I get there?
> Only for what you need.
> If you travel in need and travel light
> You can get there by candle-light."

We lit the last two candles, both stifling exclamations of pain from hot lighters, crouched in the awkward space beside the door. From there, to my awe and relief, we could see the road. It wound into undulating dark distance beyond the two candles at the end, and it seemed to be made of, or picked out in, faint grey light. There was a sketch of a countryside out there, but awesome because it was on a different plane from the carpet and curtains surrounding it. As Stan's verse stated, it was entirely outside here and now. I was relieved, because the old magic had worked and, thanks to Will, worked without so much as nudging the node, and because it is so much easier to hold open a road you can actually *see*. And whatever plane it was on, the physical presence of the place out there was undeniable. There was a sharp downwards slope in the road just beyond the two final candles. Nick and Maree were going down it, only visible from Maree's head upwards as they went. This meant they were going out of earshot. I was glad. There was still one more verse to say and I hoped they would not hear it. Rob again joined in as Will and I recited it.

> "How long is the way to Babylon?
> Three score years and ten.
> Many have gone to Babylon

265

But few come back again.
If your feet are nimble and light
You can be back by candle-light."

Nothing could have been less nimble and light than Maree's faltering feet. It seemed an age before the two of them came into view again in the dark distance, going slowly up the next looping incline in the dim grey road, a large dark figure and a small bleached one, the large figure most gently and solicitously helping the small one along.

"Whew!" said Will, sucking his sore fingers. "How come," he asked Rob, "you know that last verse too?"

"It's a nursery rhyme," said Rob. "Everyone on Thalangia knows those two verses."

"But you *are* mage-trained, aren't you?" Will said.

"Yes," Rob admitted.

He would have to be, I thought, for Knarros to have sent him here. And I was very glad that we on Earth only know just the one verse. Nick would have been far less willing to go.

TWENTY

I took the wheelchair over to the awkward space by the door and sat in it while I concentrated, first on keeping that road established and in sight, and then on slowing the candle flames into eighteen small twinkling flamelets. After that, I checked the node—it was still undisturbed—and Will's warding, which was in place like rock around us. It all took a while. Nick and Maree had traversed the next slope, and become too small to see in the dimness out there, before I felt I could release any of my attention from it. When I did, I found that Will had established himself in the frilly chair we had pushed against the bathroom door, and the quack chicks had gone to roost under it. Rob was very studiously asleep.

"Rob," I said. *"Rob!"*

He woke up artistically. "Yes?"

"Rob," I said, "there are one or two things I couldn't talk to you about with Nick here. First, I'm afraid that your Uncle Knarros is dead—"

I had to stop there. Rob cried. He cried like the centaur Kris had cried, tears swelling from his eyes and pouring down over his brown cheeks and shapely mouth, while he stared piteously from Will to me. He seemed unable to speak for some time. We did not like to interrupt his grief. At last he shakily wiped his face with his hands and managed to say, "How?"

"Someone shot him with an Earth-style gun," I said. "I'm sorry. I should have prevented it, but I was stupid. I had no idea what was going on." I felt terrible, because Rob had so clearly loved that old granite statue of a centaur. And I had not seen, even though I had realized that the youngsters at the gate had not been waiting for me, that Knarros was deep into double-cross and danger. I had bungled everything I put my hand to lately, from the trial of Timotheo onwards, and it took the tears of a centaur to make me see it.

"How old are you, Rob?" Will asked kindly.

"Eighteen," Rob said, on a deep groaning sob.

That was old enough for Rob to find a life of his own, I thought, so long as his outlook had not been permanently narrowed by his austere upbringing in that colony.

"And you did say you had other family to go to?" Will asked.

Rob nodded. Rob took to Will, I could see. Will was the rough, but subtle and kindly, countryman type that centaurs most appreciated. "My mother's still alive," Rob said, with another sob. "But—but she's never been well since she had me."

I could see he felt guilty about this. I sighed, both because the guilt was so pointless and because I saw I was going to have to be the hard man of this interview. I opened my mouth to speak, but before I could Will said, "And your father, Rob? Is *he* still alive?"

Rob's chin came up. His hand went to that gold medallion of his and his still tear-filled eyes stared proudly into Will's earnest ones. "My father is dead," he said. "He was the Emperor."

That confounded me. I had been thinking along quite other lines and this threw all my ideas about. Will looked as confused as I felt. "Then," Will said rather feebly, "your mother and Knarros must be from a very good family."

"From the highest bloodlines," Rob agreed proudly.

We sat and stared at this hurt and desolate centaur prince for a moment. Then I said, "Rob, there are some other things connected with your uncle's death that I think you ought to—"

There was a strong thumping from behind me, from outside my door. Whoever it was could not get through Will's warding and was not able to knock on the door. They seemed to be pounding on the carpeted floor of the corridor instead. Presently there were shouts, muffled and distant at first, then stronger and clearer as the man outside discovered how to project his voice through the layers of protection.

"Venables, Venables! Venables, do you hear me?"

The fact that I *could* hear him was alarming. He seemed to have done it by sliding his voice through Will's working and latching on to my own, more normal, warding beneath. That took great skill and a *lot* of power. My first thought was to pretend I hadn't heard. One often only knows that a magic has worked when people react to it. I looked at Will, and then at Rob, to warn them to keep quiet. And it was clear Rob had recognized the voice. His head was up. He looked as if he was about to shout back, then thought better of it.

"Venables!" It was a strong yell.

"Who is it?" Will asked Rob, genuinely not knowing.

"Gramos," said Rob. He was surprised and puzzled. "He lives in Thalangia. Why is he here?"

"Gram White," I said. "He lives here too, Rob."

"Venables! I know you're there! *Answer* me!" White yelled. "I shan't go away until you do!"

"Answer him. Get rid of him," Will muttered.

I projected my voice back, pretending to be sleepy. "Hello. What is it?"

"You've got Nick Mallory in there, haven't you?" White shouted.

"No I haven't," I replied, with some truth. "Why?"

"His mother's worried about him," yelled White.

I shouted back, again with some truth, "I don't know where Nick is. Why the hell *should* I know? But tell Janine I'll tell Nick she wants him if I see him."

White did not believe me. He made some kind of threat, in a lower voice, about what he would do if I was lying.

Then he stood outside the door muttering for a bit. After that he seemed to go away. I felt through the warding after him, and it seemed to me that he did genuinely walk away down the corridor. But I didn't speak until I was sure.

"Rob," I said, "was it Gram White your uncle was expecting this afternoon? The kids at the gate were waiting for someone. And Knarros didn't come and speak to me until he'd had time to take the magework off the path."

"Yes," said Rob, beginning to look alarmed. "Gramos was expected."

"And Janine too—Nick's mother?" I asked.

Rob gave me one of his limpidly honest looks. "It was the Empress Jaleila who was expected," he said. "She is my aunt. Gramos is her brother."

"But this Empress is Nick's mother," I insisted.

"Yes," Rob admitted.

"Hang on. I don't get this!" Will said. "The Koryfonic Empire doesn't ever have an Empress."

"The title is taken, in the event of the Emperor's demise, by the Emperor's sole surviving consort," Rob told him, evidently reciting a law.

"Then I think the title should be taken by the High Lady Alexandra," I told Rob. "Janine—Jaleila—is merely a Lesser Consort, isn't she?"

"I had no idea the High Lady had survived!" Rob prevaricated.

"Isn't she?" I insisted. "Jaleila, Nick's mother, a Lesser Consort?"

"Yes," he said. "But—"

"Rob," I said. "Please. Listen to the rest. These two came into the compound and one of them promptly cut the throats of the two lads and then the little girl, while the other tried to shoot me and then shot your uncle. Then—"

"Was Kris all right?" Rob asked urgently.

"They sent him away," I said. Rob visibly relaxed. I went on, "And after he and I discovered the bodies, Kris went off down through the wood, where he seems to have come upon Gram and Janine a moment or so after they stripped Maree. I gather Kris raised an outcry . . ."

Rob all but smiled. "Yes, Kris is so very honest. Nobody told him anyth—" He stopped and looked anxiously at my face. "What else happened?"

"Kris was next seen," I said, "running for his life, with Janine chasing him in Maree's car, while Gram fired at him out of its window."

"What?" Rob's front hooves hit the floor and he was half upright before the pain of his side checked him. *"What?"* Tears welled from his eyes again. "But Gramos is Kris's *father*! Gramos *shot* him?"

"It's all right," I said. "We think Kris escaped. Stan— the witness—says Kris jumped like a bird into the nearest vineyard."

Rob subsided slowly back on to the bed. "Well, thank all the gods for that!"

"Hang on. Here's another thing I don't get," Will put in. "Why are you so worried about this Kris? You didn't turn a hair when Rupert told you the three kids you were brought up with had had their throats cut."

"You didn't bother much about Maree either, did you?" I said. "It doesn't seem to mean anything to you that she sewed you up." I said it much more angrily and bitterly than I had expected to. I had to gulp back a sob as I said it. It took me by surprise.

Rob was taken by surprise too. "But," he said, bewildered, "why should I care? None of them was our blood-line."

Will was—spontaneously and totally—disgusted. He got up, he kicked the frilly chair aside and he shot Rob a look of sheer contempt, and then turned his back on him. The quack chicks picked up on Will's feelings and scooted for cover under the wheelchair. Will said, "Of all the—the— the—I can't think of a vile enough word, frankly!"

Rob stared at Will's back. I could see dismay growing in him. He had, as I thought, very much taken to Will. "You

271

mean," he asked huskily, after a moment, "you think I *should* care?"

Will whirled round. "Of course you should bloody well care!" he yelled. The force of it made the tiny flames on the candles flicker. "What kind of a way have you been brought up? Three kids and a young woman get murdered and all you can say is they weren't your bloody bloodline! And damn it all, that's not even *true*! The Emperor was their father as well as yours! They were your *brothers and sisters*, Rob!"

Rob flinched and looked down at the duvet. After another pause, he said, "Yes, I suppose they were."

"Hark at him!" Will said to me. "He supposes they were! That's accessory to murder talking, that is!"

The whole of Rob shook with a sudden deep sob.

"You *do* cry easy!" Will began again. "You—"

"Give him a break, Will," I said. We seemed to have changed roles, Will and I, me to the soft man, Will to the hard. "He's been brought up to consider only the offspring of Knarros's two sisters, as I see it. And Janine as White's sister, I imagine, with the Emperor linking them again. Is that right, Rob? You consider Nick's the next Emperor, don't you?"

Rob nodded. He clearly could not speak.

"Gah!" said Will. "Upbringing *nothing*! He's got a mind. He's mage-trained. That means he's got to have a mind of his own. Come to that, why doesn't he consider *himself* as the next Emperor? He's the Emperor's eldest surviving son, isn't he?"

Rob looked up in genuine, huge astonishment. "But I'm a centaur!"

"So?" said Will. "Racist, too, are we, as well as conniving at murder?"

"I—" said Rob. He swallowed, and the gold pendant bobbed on his smooth throat. "I didn't see it that way. I swear."

His wonderful features were twisted with sincere misery. I could see he really had not, before this, considered his part in today's horrors. Well, neither had I. I hadn't done so well either. I had contrived to keep Dakros away from the colony so that White could do his dirty work in peace. Rob and I had both been manipulated. "You might as well," I said, "tell us what you really did say to Nick and Maree in the lift."

Rob shrugged. "I said we were all the Emperor's children, of course. I knew Nick because he looks like me, only paler. And he was wearing his medallion under his shirt, so there was proof. Maree said hers was somewhere in the junk in her room. She—" He was beginning to look happier, talking around and beside the actual message he had been sent to give. I coughed, to remind him. He shot me a look which, to do him justice, was full of sober guilt. "I—I had to tell Maree that Knarros wanted to see her," he said, "because she was the Emperor's eldest child and ought to take the throne."

"What did *she* say?" I asked with strong curiosity.

"She said she'd go and tell Knarros to get stuffed," Rob said.

I could imagine that. "For what reason? No, don't tell me. Because she was going to be a vet."

Rob grinned, a wondrous, rueful smile, on one side of his mouth. "No. She said she wanted to be a Magid." Will and I both stared at him. "Honestly," he said. "We were arguing about that when you pulled the lift down. I said she could be a Magid *and*—"

His head jerked round towards the far end of the rows of candles.

There were sounds there, from out of sight where the road dipped downhill. Will and I shot one another tense, incredulous looks. This quick? We could hear pebbles clinking, panting and fast footsteps, coming closer. Someone was definitely coming up. We waited, staring at the spot where we thought we might first see that person's head come into view. We had all been far too preoccupied to have noticed anyone approaching along the more distant parts of the road, but I thought, from memory, that when

Will had exploded my eye *had* been catching a faint flicker of motion out there.

We were all watching the wrong spot. It took us all by surprise when Nick hurled himself between the candles and along the carpet and stood there, bent over, panting like a train.

"What happened?"

"What's wrong?"

"Where's Maree?"

I think we all spoke at once, but Nick answered me. "Left—left her at the bridge," he gasped. "Too far for her—here and back. She's OK. Livelier—you know." He stopped and panted loudly. "There's this bridge," he said, when he was breathing easier, "and it's got these rather weird guardians. They won't let us through because we didn't—didn't bring the right stuff. They said go back and find another verse. So I came."

"Damn!" said Will. "Another verse? How?"

"Zinka!" I said. I jumped up, much to the consternation of the quack chicks. "I'll go and find her."

"The candles," Rob said.

Nick, now kneeling between the rows like a spent Olympic sprinter, echoed Rob. "Yes, the candles."

They were right. The candles would be burning lower every minute we took finding the missing verse. But we dared not blow them out while Maree was still out there. "Suppose," I said, "we were to put them out all but the two nearest the road? Do you think that would be enough to keep the road still there, Will?"

"Might work," Will agreed. "If we start from the end by the door and keep checking. I'll do it. You find Zinka."

I left at once and pelted to the lifts, which White's recent activities outside my door had now set four corners away. The lift which arrived first was the one where Rob had been. It was not working very well. It went down in fits and jerks and stopped entirely at Floor Two. I could sense Zinka further down, but I had not the time to spend working on the lift. I stormed out and set off down the stairs at a gallop.

The roar of voices and singing hit me at the first landing. As I barged aside the fire door and swung on down, I saw why. There was a party going on. Almost the entire last flight of stairs was full of people, partying busily, drunkenly, uproariously and, in some areas, orgiastically. It looked rather fun.

Sitting on the top stair, more or less beside where I stood and detached from the rest, was Kornelius Punt. He raised a toothglass to me solemnly. "I am trying," he told me, "to sort out one body from the next on these stairs and not succeeding."

"They are rather entwined," I agreed. I looked at the party. I looked down at him sadly. One of the underlying reasons why I had assumed that Punt might make a Magid was that he held himself apart from the rest of humanity. In fact, he was just a voyeur. I was the one who held myself apart, and it was not necessary, or right. It was probably why I had made such a mess of things. "Why don't you join in?" I said to Punt.

"I am always aloof," he told me. "I am going for Loof of the Year Award."

Zinka was down on the stairs somewhere. "You'll probably win it," I said. I started picking my way down the packed and roaring stairs. I could only advance most of the time by holding on to the wall while I worked one foot, then the other, between thighs and arms or under hands and torsos. I caused several yelps of pain. I knocked over several glasses and a china bottle of the strongest liquor I had ever met. The fumes made me gasp and cough, but left the six people packed in beside it quite unmoved.

I apologized. One of the six said, "Damn, I think the stair carpet's dissolving!" as I was making a long stride to a tiny space two stairs down, and they all laughed.

A hand came out of the writhing bodies lower down and passed me a full glass of rum. I accepted it politely and realized as I did so that the hand was the much-nicked mauve hand of Milan Gabrelisovic. Good. Great, in fact. But I did not trust him not to try poisoning me as a witch. I clambered through a nest of twining legs and passed the glass to the hand that came waving out from among them. Possibly it was Tansy-Ann Fisk's. Below this, a vastly tall and shapely young man was spread out over at least eight stairs, with girls attached to him at intervals. The young man was wearing nothing but a leather loincloth and seemed to be asleep. The girls were drawing on him with felt-tip pens. Two of them were giving him a sunburst on his chest, in a riot of reds and yellows. His arms were being given hearts and anchors on one side and diagrams on the other. Zinka was at work on his left thigh, twining it with delicately drawn vineleaves. She was wearing a slithery silk gown that shone two delicious shades of rose and tended to slip fetchingly off her plump left shoulder, and she was wholly preoccupied. I could tell that, while the other girls were just drawing on the man, Zinka's vine trellis was intended, gently and temporarily, to make the fellow hers later that night.

It seemed a shame to spoil her fun, but the candles were burning down. I bent and took hold of her warm, slithery shoulder. "Zinka, I'm sorry to—"

She jumped and looked up. "Oh God, it's an emergency, isn't it? Rupert, I *am* sorry—I *had* meant to check before I . . . I could tell something was up. Come on."

She stood up and took my hand, towing me on downwards. I would rather have gone up, but down was nearer and easier. Together we negotiated a fairly extreme orgy and then forced our way between a row of ten people swaying on the lowest step and singing. Then we had only to stumble among glasses and bottles into a clear space by the fire door.

"Tell me," said Zinka.

I was aware of Kornelius Punt, up above, doing his trick of amplifying our voices. So was Zinka. She glanced up there and frowned at me and we both cast up at him the illusion of a different conversation—*two* different conversations. We were too hurried to co-ordinate them. Them Up There alone know what Punt thought we were talking about.

"It's like this," I said, and gave Zinka a rapid run-down of events.

"Babylon!" said Zinka. "Oh my lord, Rupert! You should have called me in *hours* ago. Here's my verse for a start—"

The fire door beside us whammed open. Mervin Thurless lunged through and stood looking up at the crowded stairs in huge disgust. "What a revolting display!" he said to us, as if he thought it was our doing. "And the lifts aren't working. How the hell am I supposed to get upstairs?"

"Terrible," I agreed, remembering in time that I was supposed to be a fan of his.

"Just pick your way up," Zinka told him cheerfully. "Kick people. They're all too drunk to notice." She pulled me the other way, out through the fire door, adding, "Or some are. With any luck someone will kick you back!" By this time, we were in the relatively open space beside the lifts. "It's all right," she said, seeing me staring anxiously back at the doors. "I laid it on Thurless to go up through the party. And I think we need to be down here anyway for the kitchens. Here's my verse:

> "What shall I take to Babylon?
> A handful of salt and grain,
> Water, some wool for warmth on the way,
> And a candle to make the road plain.
> If you carry three things and use them right
> You can be there by candle-light.' "

"Ah, of *course*!" I said. "They should have been carrying the elements of life! I should have thought!"

"Kitchens," said Zinka. As we sped that way, she panted out, "I've plenty of candles. Wool's easy. So's water. It's the grain that's going to make problems."

After some blundering about in the hind parts of the hotel, we barged our way through steel doors into a vista of steel appliances, smelling strongly of fat that was not quite hot enough. I let Zinka take the lead here. Every Magid has a special feeling for his or her particular secrets and, besides, the only person on duty here was a weary fellow in a tall white hat. He would obviously respond better to Zinka than to me.

She set about him briskly. "It's very important we have something with whole grains in it," she told him. "Have you got any unmilled cereals?"

"Muesli?" suggested the bewildered chef.

"Too many extras in it," Zinka said. "Wheat or oats or barley in *grains* is what we're looking for."

He did his best, poor fellow. His first offering comprised a packet of frozen sweetcorn, a bag of flour and a carton of porridge oats. Zinka smiled up at him, pink and silky, with her shoulder slithering bare, and made him try again. He came up with brown rice. "It might do at a pinch," Zinka told him. "But we need it *European* if possible." He came up with sesame seeds and groundsel, wholemeal bread and pumpernickel. Zinka took him kindly by the hand and led him away among the cupboards.

While they were gone, I found some plastic bags. There were cruets lined up by the hundred on a shelf near the door and I cavalierly emptied salt out of them until I had a bagful. Then, furiously conscious of the candles dwindling on the top floor, I found a big strainer and attempted to sieve the porridge oats. Most of the grains were crushed, but I had succeeded in getting a couple of ounces of whole, uncrushed oat grains out of it when Zinka came hurrying back with a tin clutched to her chest. In it was a sparse rattling of wheat grains which the chef gloomily opined must have come off the outside of something.

"Oh good," Zinka said, seeing what I had been doing. "If we combine yours and mine and top it up with ground-sel, sesame and just a little of the rice, we should just about have two handfuls. Thanks, chef. I love you. Come on, Rupert."

We sped back to the centre of the hotel, clutching our two plastic bags.

"I'm not sure what's wrong with the *other* lift," Zinka gasped, "but I'm afraid the far lift is my fault—and yours. You sure do put stasis on when you put it, Rupert. I *couldn't* get it off."

"Oh, is that all it is?" I said. That was a relief. I hadn't fancied wading upstairs through that party again. When we reached the lifts, it was an easy matter to whip the remains of my stasis off the lift where Rob had taken refuge and haul it down. We shot up to Floor Three in it, where I waited with it while Zinka picked up her rosy skirts and pelted off to her room for candles.

That wait was horrible. My watch said I had only been gone half an hour and I couldn't believe it. I was afraid it had stopped. I was increasingly convinced that something had gone wrong, but whether it was something wrong in my room two floors above, or some terrible thing that had happened to Maree waiting semi-lifeless in a land of shadows, I had no idea. I just wished Zinka would hurry.

To do her justice, she did hurry. Two minutes later, she pelted up from the opposite direction with her arms full of candles—genuine beeswax: I smelt the honey—gasping out that the node seemed to have gone do-lally and her room was nearer *this* way now. I clapped us into the lift and we shot upwards.

More node activity, I thought. Gram White again. A thought struck me.

"By the way," I said, as we whirled past Floor Four, "which of them do you think did which killing? They were both in it, I'm sure. There wasn't time for one of them to do it all."

"Women very seldom cut throats," Zinka said decidedly. "She did the shooting."

That fitted. Whoever shot at me had been slow, as if he— she—was not entirely used to handling a gun, whereas Gram White, who ran a factory making small-arms, must be quite an expert. "Thanks," I said. "Then he's the more dangerous of the two."

"Don't bank on it," Zinka said, as the lift slowed. "She's pure poison, to my mind."

The door went back. We stormed out and ran again. And ran. And turned corner after corner, running.

And there was a vista of corridor, with my door open halfway along it and Will out in the corridor beside it, making a stooped and swooping chase after a madly running quack chick. Beyond him, in the distance, three people were walking briskly away: Gram White and Janine, with Nick between them.

TWENTY-ONE

Zinka and I stopped and looked at one another. "Someone's done a working out here," she said. "I can feel it."

So could I feel it now. It was what White had been doing after he shouted outside my door. I knew I should have felt it when I left, but I had been in too much of a hurry. I had slipped up again. I cursed. The working had been designed to fetch Nick out of my room the next time the door opened. Will told us the way of it when we walked slowly up to him and he stood up, red and exasperated, after shooing the quack chick back inside.

"I thought the damn door was shut," he said, "but you must have left it open a crack."

"No I didn't," I said. "Gram White left a working on it."

"Oh I see!" Will said, and ran his hands through his woolly hair in the manner of Dakros. "I couldn't understand it. Both bloody chicks got out. Nick and I were out here rounding them up when those two came marching up. And she said, 'Come along, Nick, I need you,' and he obviously couldn't think of a reason not to go with them. Didn't even argue, just went."

We watched Gram, Nick and Janine turn the corner out of sight.

"Not much to be done," Zinka said. "She *is* his mother, that's the problem. So what do we do now? You've got a major working half finished in there. You can't just leave it."

"I'll go," I said, "if you can keep the road open."

281

It was what I had been aching to do anyway. I could barely credit it when Will and Zinka both sternly shook their heads. "It was *your* working, Rupert," Zinka said, and Will added, "You can't start a working on the outside and then go *inside*, Rupe. You must remember Stan telling you that. It's basic."

"Magids have been lost that way," Zinka said.

Will said, "But Rob says he'll go. He was wanting to go back with Nick anyway. I was trying to tell him how dangerous it is to alter a working halfway through when those damn chicks got out."

"It's altered anyway!" I snapped, and flung inside the room.

And here was further trouble.

In the odd-shaped space left between the roadway of candles and my bed, Rob was half on his feet, supporting himself painfully on the bedside table with one hand. His other hand was pointing to the road itself. "I couldn't stop them! I was too slow!" he said.

I followed his pointing finger. And I saw the two quack chicks scurrying between the only two lighted candles, off the carpet and on to the hillside beyond. I confess my first thought was, Good riddance! My second was to wonder anxiously what damage this would do to the working. Will and Zinka crowded into the room behind me, just in time to see the chicks scuttle down over the shadowy brow of the hill and disappear.

"Oh no!" said Will.

Zinka's eyes scanned the dark landscape lying at such a queer angle to the rest of my room. I could see she was awed. But she said drily, "Our Mr. White has done even better than he expected, hasn't he? I don't think you should fetch them back now. What do you want to do, Rupert?"

"We carry on regardless," I said. "Maree's out there waiting."

"In that case," Rob said, "I have to go, don't I?"

Will and Zinka edged down beside the frilly chair by the bathroom. I shut the door of my room and we all looked at Rob. Zinka looked at him with frank lascivious admiration. You could see why. Even ill and pale, with his horse-coat dull and staring, Rob was a magnificent sight.

He stood himself cautiously on all four hooves. "I do owe Maree," he said. "She can't manage alone. And you made me see . . . I see I've done a lot of damage and I ought to try to put it right."

"He is mage-trained," Will said.

"But you're ill!" I objected. Besides, I still wanted to go myself.

"I can manage," Rob said. His beautiful features twisted a little. "If it hurts, it probably serves me right, doesn't it?"

"I think you'll have to send him," Zinka said decisively. "It fits."

After that, I couldn't argue any more. The two candles burning on the edge of the dark landscape were each nearly a third gone. We had wasted enough time. "What does he need to take?" I asked Zinka.

"Water's easy," she said. "I see you've got four little empty bottles. Now, for wool . . ."

"I've got a cashmere sweater," I offered.

"Then you'd better get it unravelled," Zinka said.

"What?" I said.

"The feel of the verse is for raw wool," she explained. "In a hank. You know."

Will stood in the bathroom doorway with a fistful of little bottles, laughing at the look on my face. "Not to worry," he said. He fished in the pocket of his coat and came up with a big handful of fluffy white goat's hair. "This do?" he asked Zinka.

"Perfect," she said.

The last of our hasty preparations had to be done with the door of my room open, mostly in the passage outside. Rob, being so much longer than a human, could not fit into the space in front of the road when the door was closed. He was forced to hop, wincing at the jolt, across the first pair of candles, then out through the doorway and on into the corridor, where he turned himself to face into my room.

There Zinka handed him a candle and Will's belt pouch, with the four little bottles of water chinking in it despite being packed round with the goat's wool.

"There you go," she said, lovingly fastening the belt around Rob's muscular waist-parts, while I stood waiting impatiently with my lighter and the plastic bags of grain and salt. "There. Do try to come back, Rob. You're too stunning to lose."

Rob had been looking ahead, very tense and determined, but at this, he flung back his sheet of black hair and turned his face down to Zinka's. "You think so?" he said. His whole pose turned amorous. So did Zinka's.

I more or less ground my teeth, but before I could say anything I heard the thud of sprinting feet on the carpet. I whirled round. Nick came flying up to us and caught hold of me to stop himself. "Oh good," he said. "Rob's going too."

We stared at him. "I thought your mother—?" Zinka said.

"I told her I was going to bed," Nick said. "That's all she wanted me for anyway. OK, Rob. Let's get going, shall we?"

Will and I looked at one another and grinned, remembering how deftly Nick had avoided Janine before. "Hold out your hand," I said, advancing on Nick with my grain and salt.

"Both hands," Zinka corrected me, and thrust a candle into Nick's other hand.

I had filled Nick's hand with mingled salt and grain and was just about to tip grain into Rob's outstretched hand when I thought I heard footsteps again. Again I whirled round. Gram White was coming round the corner, from the same direction as Nick. Almost certainly he had been following Nick. I saw him in the mirrors first, reaching into his armpit under his robe in a way that could only mean he was fetching out a gun.

Things seemed to go in slow motion. I had time to realize that, if I could see him, then Gram White would have a distant view of us too, including Rob, and that Rob would be the one he shot first. I had plenty of time to plant the plastic bags on the floor. I had what felt like half an hour's leisure to build a thick shield across the corridor, and then to check the other way, in case Janine was coming from the other end. But White was on his own.

He came round the corner and fired. He aimed, I think, at Rob's head. The *boom* and the *crack* of the rebound shook floor, walls, air, everything. At least I got something right! I thought. I watched a rather large slice of the ceiling slowly unhitch and crash down on the carpet.

"Quick work," Will said shakily.

Before White could fire again, Zinka trod the fallen plaster to flakes as she marched down the passage. "Gram White!" she said. Her voice rang as loudly as the shot. Instead of getting smaller as she marched away from us, her rosy figure actually seemed to grow bigger. White backed away as she advanced on him. "Gram White!" she said. "You do anything like that again and I'll make you sorry you were ever born!"

She was magnificent, but we didn't, even Rob, dare wait and watch. I hurriedly filled Rob's hand with grain and salt and stowed the remainder in the belt bag, along with a candle for Maree and my spare lighter. Will meanwhile lit Nick's candle and then Rob's. Then we both bolted into my room to the far end and began relighting the double row of candles and saying the rhyme. Since Nick and Rob could see the road, they started forward at once. I remember looking up between the third and fourth pair of candles and seeing them go past, both in profile and surprisingly alike, not only in the actual classic shape of their faces, but also in their expressions. Both looked thoroughly determined, and with both you wondered how long that would last. Rob's resolution might survive pain, but not if something offered him an easy way out. Nick would probably scorn an easy way out, but I knew I would not trust him if he were asked to sacrifice something he wanted. And I had a

285

strong feeling that both the easy way and the sacrifice were waiting out there on that hard-to-see grey road.

We had reached the end of Will's verse when, to my relief, Zinka came back, expressively dusting her hands, in time to say her own verse. She shut the door and leant against it while we all recited the last one. By that time, Nick and Rob were visible down below, as two dark shapes and two pricks of light, crossing the level towards the next hill. Making good time. We watched them wind up that hill, and went on watching until it was clear that the pin-pricks of light did not carry far enough for us to see them on the next rise. It was all dark out there.

"Right," said Zinka. "I got rid of White for the moment, but I'll tell you what I'll do. There's a party somewhere on this floor. I wasn't going to go, because Thurless invited me there, but I think I will go now. I'll make sure to be there at least until dawn, and I'll be listening. If White comes back, or anything else happens, one of you two just call me or phone Room 509. OK?"

"Before you do," I said, "would you mind terribly checking Nick's room for us? It worries me that his mother wanted him there."

"Good thought," said Zinka.

She went off to do that. I said to Will, "I'm going to risk putting out all the candles but the last two again, and then relighting the next pair as soon as the end pair begin to gutter. That way they'll last nine times as long."

Will rubbed his face, thinking about it. "The only trouble with that—now we know the road stays there as long as there *are* two candles burning—the trouble is that some-one's going to have to sit and watch them and relight the next lot."

"I was going to sit and watch anyway," I said.

"In that case," said Will, "would you mind if I got some sleep? I was up near dawn milking the goats."

"Go ahead," I said.

So Will climbed under my slightly bloodstained duvet,

286

uttering a great weary yawn. He was asleep almost at once. He never even stirred when Zinka came back.

"You were right," she told me. "And here was I thinking you were being paranoid. I take it back. There was a really strong slave spell in there. I mean *strong*—about ten times the strength of whatever you did to that lift. Even a selfish kid like that Nick would find himself doing anything they wanted after five minutes in there with that thing. I scotched it, but I made it look as if it was still there. Is that what you wanted?"

"Yes," I said. "Thanks, Zinka. Unless . . . has he got a computer?"

"Nice little laptop," she said. "But I don't know about computers."

"I'll take a look at it tomorrow," I said wearily. After what had been done to Maree's computer, there was almost certainly something wrong with Nick's too. The list of things I had to do tomorrow seemed to stretch out like a supermarket bill.

After Zinka had gone, I moved the frilly chair round with its back to the door and folded the wheelchair up. It had occurred to me that the wheelchair, though more comfortable, could get shunted forward between the lines of candles if someone like Zinka, to whom locks meant nothing, came in suddenly behind me. I could then be willy-nilly in the midst of a working I should be outside of. Will and Zinka had been right about the dangers of that. If it hadn't been Maree out there, I would never have dreamt of suggesting it.

I turned out the lights and sat in the frilly chair. With only the two candles alight, down to a small, small glimmer, the landscape out there was slightly easier to see. It was as if someone had drawn on black paper with the faintest of faint grey luminous airspray a rolling moor-like distance and a faint road looping across it. Far, far off, there may have been the loom of something else beyond the horizon. But I couldn't see it. I couldn't go there. There was no point trying to speculate on what was happening to the

287

three people journeying out there. All I could do was hold the road and watch the candles.

After a while, the party made itself heard from down the passage outside, muffled by the wards round my room. I was glad of it. I was by that time thoroughly enmeshed in the kind of thoughts I had been warning myself not to think, and it helped to have the noise. It reminded me there was life beyond my room. I thought of Rob, buoyant, flashy, flimsy young centaur, with that sort of slave-child mentality that whines when things go wrong, "It's not my fault! I didn't mean to!" Rob expected adults to scold him. He preferred that, I suspected, to accepting a fault and blaming himself, but he would duck out of both if he could. Smiling limpidly the while, of course. It was probably the result of being brought up by that kingly granite statue, Knarros. Will had shamed Rob into better behaviour, but Will had only been at work on Rob for an hour or so, and Rob had had Knarros all his life. If the journey proved as hard as the rhyme suggested, I knew Rob would be the first to crack.

Then I thought of Nick. Nick's personality seemed to me to run deeper, stronger and more complex than Rob's. When Nick ducked out of things, he didn't signal it in advance like Rob did. He just vanished. He was, I suspected, quite ruthless about it, and about what he himself wanted. I had no idea what Nick did want, really—except I was sure it was not to rule an empire—because Nick had a dark private core. Possibly he didn't know what was in there himself yet. But he knew enough to duck out if that core was threatened. And he would. I knew that. Rob and Nick shared, deep in their genes, a very strong selfishness. It was the same selfishness that had made their common father set up the whole mad mess in the first place.

Maree seemed to me to have escaped that selfishness. It was one of the things I had come to like about her. One of the many things. I wished I dared hope there were things she had come to like about me. But I couldn't think of any. I thought of Maree instead, fierce, droll, unhappy little fighter as she was. She saw deep into things. I wondered, though, if she saw deep enough into herself. It could be that, in that way, she was not selfish *enough*. People who regard themselves as sacred—like Nick and his father the Emperor—know when fighting is worth it and when it is not. I doubted that Maree did know. She could well hurl herself uselessly into something out there, and lose. She could equally well lose by not defending herself when she should do. And with only half of herself present, the loss could be fatal . . .

As I said, I was glad that the gruff roar and distant music of the party kept forcing itself on my attention. I made a strong effort to think of something else.

I thought of Janine and her brother Gram White, and of their intentions. Long ago, Janine must somehow have persuaded Timos IX to let her go into exile in a strange world as guardian of her own son and of Maree, where Janine must rapidly have married Ted Mallory and equally rapidly got Maree adopted by Ted's brother Derek. The Emperor let her go. She was only a Lesser Consort, and someone as paranoid as Timos must certainly have known she had ambitions. Furthermore, Janine's son and Maree (whose mother must also have been a Lesser Consort, I imagined) were both embarrassingly older than the children of True Wives. The Emperor must have sent them off Naywards out of trouble with relief. He could not have realized, when he took care to become the brother-in-law of Knarros, and so ensure the centaur's loyalty, that Gram White had then done the same three years later. The birth of the centaur Kris involved Knarros in a little dynasty and a further loyalty, to Janine this time. No, obviously the Emperor had not known, or he would never have put Knarros in charge of the other children.

So what happened then? Janine seemed to have waited until Nick was old enough to make a credible Emperor (though not old enough to defy her, one supposes), while White learnt to make and use projectile weapons. Before that, he must have been trained as a mage. They must both have been in constant touch with other people on Koryfos, and bided their time until they could organize that explosion in the palace. When the time came—

At this point I said, "Oh, *God*!" out loud. *I* had caused the timing of it. *I* had brought it to a head. I had started looking for Maree. I had told Janine's two sisters-in-law that I was looking for Maree in order to give her a legacy. The one with all the children had actually phoned Janine and told her in front of me. On top of that I had written to Maree and told Janine herself! She must have known me for a Magid at once. People from Ayewards can always tell. I could imagine how that had struck Janine. For "legacy" read "birthright." A Magid looking for Maree because Maree was now the Emperor's eldest child. I had precipitated the explosion and caused the deaths of those three children, not to speak of countless others all over the Empire!

I groaned—howled, more like—with such force that Will rolled about grunting in his sleep.

I was about to make more noises when I fortunately remembered that there had, all along, been a strong smell of these things being Intended. In other words, I thought bitterly, those ruthless bastards in the Upper Room wanted certain things to happen in the Koryfonic Empire. So they set two connecting chains of action going and make sure the Magid in charge of both is a self-confident little bungler. Me. R. Venables. Led by the nose by everyone. Mistakes guaranteed to order. Gah.

The question was, *what* was the Upper Room Intending precisely? Did they really, truly want Gram White for the next Koryfonic Emperor? Because that was what they were going to get. Janine would reign as Empress Regent for a short while. White would establish himself as her indispensable sidekick until he was accepted as a fixture. Then it did not need Janine even to have an accident. It just took Nick to have one. Bingo. Gramos I. Or was I supposed to prevent this?

For the first time, I stopped feeling uneasy that I had so

blithely—with the help of two living Magids and one disembodied, no less—sent all three remaining heirs to Babylon. I had no doubt that they *were* the only three living. White would never have left those two older girls alive if they had been a threat. He knew what he was doing, did White. After he had stripped Maree, he went after Rob. He had coaxed Nick out of my room in order to get Rob out too and get a shot at him. Janine would have told him Rob was in here. Ted Mallory told her. Probably half the convention told her. Smart operator, White. Doing better than R. Venables here.

Still, although it was an accident, I *had* sent Maree, Nick and Rob to the safest place there was. Except that they might not come back. With the working changed and disrupted halfway through, their chances of returning had halved. Heaven knows what mischief those two quack chicks had done.

Even if all went well . . . Here I saw the two candles threatening to flicker out. I was only just in time to light the next two. Since there was no way I should tread in the road marked out by the candles, lighting them involved running frantically down outside it to light the first, then back up in the near-dark to squeeze past the frilly chair, and down the other side to light the other one. A little parable of my activities to date, I thought. It was a great relief to find the dark sketch of landscape was still in existence, even so. But now the two furthest candles were out, it was nearer. The stony path and the sharply shelving hill had advanced a couple of steps into the room.

Hm, I thought. I squeezed round to the kettle and made coffee more or less by touch.

While the second pair of candles burned out, I thought mostly about what the hell I was going to tell Dakros when he came through on my carphone on Sunday morning. I seemed to specialize in letting Dakros down. I still hadn't thought what to say to him when I lit the third pair of candles and made more coffee.

The party down the corridor took a new lease of life

around the time I lit the fourth pair. I heard someone come out of another room and yell for quiet. It made no difference. The stony path now stretched halfway across the room, night dark and slightly luminous, and I was glad of any interruption. I had been considering my faults. *Not* pleasant. I seem to combine a degree of self-confidence and extreme pride in my abilities as a Magid with a slightly pathetic tendency to rely on other people—Will and Stan for a start. I couldn't decide whether my mistakes were worse when I took advice, or when I went my own brash confident way. Maree's ex-mother, Mrs. Nuttall, had probably got me summed up right, even if she *had* thought I was someone else.

I wished I could relate to people more. But then I let them down. I hated that.

I relit the fifth pair of candles with rather more time to spare. Thoughts like these make you want to rove about, restlessly. The party had died to a mere mumble by then.

I sat down again and found myself thinking wretchedly about those three murdered children. I could have prevented that. True, I had been distracted, with magics to overcome and magics to perform, but I should not have *been* distracted. And if this was Intended, I thought the worse of the Upper Room. I kept seeing the kids' clumsy sandals and their long, not over-clean hair so severely in pigtails. I saw their tense, puzzled, ignorant faces. There were minds behind those faces that had never had a chance to work. You could see that their minds had been kept as chilly, comfortless and walled in as that courtyard where they were made to live. It was a double prison. They had, almost certainly, never been allowed even to imagine any bright, warm, extraordinary thing beyond the little penned-in world they knew. It was like Maree's Uncle Ted over his wobbly windows—here I found myself smiling at Maree telling me of this, angrily, over the bookstalls—except that these kids had not *chosen* to see only the distorted old glass. The glass was all they had been given. And, just when they might have had a chance to choose to look beyond, their lives had been ended.

For a short while there, I confess I cried like Rob.

Then I thought that Maree at least had had her chance to look beyond. I was glad of that. I took comfort from thinking of her and hoped she would forgive me for it. If she came back—if, if, if—something would happen because Maree had looked beyond. She was that kind of person. She would thrust her way beyond with angry fingernails. She had been confined, too, by the same dreary bush-goddess, but she had soldiered past. I hoped her life would be better now. I ached to let her *have* something better. I wanted her to come back more than I have ever wanted anything. Ever.

But the hours passed. The fifth pair of candles guttered down, and nobody came back.

I was definitely asleep in the frilly chair when I heard a noise.

TWENTY-TWO

It was inside the room. I heard a pattering, a sharp chink, and the sound of a stone rolling. I jumped awake.

The sixth pair of candles were well down, but not yet guttering. By their light I could clearly see the path stretching across the room and then the brow of the hill, tantalizingly at the dark end between the burnt-out candles. I could still see into the dark stretch of landscape beyond. I stared avidly at the spot where the path tipped downhill, clutching the sides of my chair, my legs braced ready to spring up.

There was a bit more pattering, slow and sedate. Then, to my utter astonishment, two birds walked over the brow of the hill and paused to stare around with bright sapphire eyes. Seeing the room, they turned to one another in evident satisfaction. Each gently nibbled at the broad blue bill of the other. Then they turned again and solemnly advanced. They were as big as geese. I could see they had large webbed feet, so they were aquatic birds, but no kind that I knew. I simply did not understand what they were doing here, until they came within the full light of the candles. Then I could see the blue plumage, glossy and dark on the wings and a shiny gentle azure on the breasts. They were Thule quacks, outsize Thule quacks. I had never seen quacks so large, or so healthy, or so obviously full of intelligence.

They came right up to me, where each solemnly stropped a beak on my trouser leg in token of friendship and then looked up at me with bright, distinctly humorous round eyes. How about *this*? they seemed to say.

"Good God!" I more or less shouted. "How about *that*!"

Will woke up at once. It was probably milking time by then anyway. "What?" he said slurrily. "Vendela been sick again?"

"No," I said, laughing. "The quack chicks are back. Take a look."

Will surged up, looked, rubbed eyes, grated hands on bristly face, looked again. "I don't believe it!" he said. "How did they get so big?" He got up and came closer. The quacks turned to him and each dipped a head, almost as if they bowed. "Aren't they *glossy*!" Will said. "What beauties! They look clever too. I think I shall have to make pets of these. I couldn't possibly sell them."

"No, I want them," I said. "Can I, Will? Please?" The return of the chicks—and their metamorphosis—struck me as the best of good omens. I wanted the quacks for that, and for the fact that they had acknowledged me their friend. And if they were not an omen—well, I wanted them anyway. They were beautiful.

"Well, they're not an Earth species," Will said dubiously. "Still, you've got a breeding pair there. And they seem to like you. Why not?" He looked out into the dark land. "No sign of anything else out there?"

"No," I said.

He surveyed me, and the remaining candles. "Get some sleep," he said. "You look whacked. And you've still got nearly six hours' worth of candles there. Or you should have. You've been letting them burn too high."

I didn't want to sleep. I didn't want to say I had superstitiously let the flames burn higher in hopes that this might help whatever went on out there. I didn't want anything. I felt sick with anxiety and lack of sleep.

"Go on," said Will. "I'll watch."

Reluctantly, I left the chair and took Will's warm place in the bed. The quacks, to my pleasure, followed me and roosted on the duvet.

"That's better," said Will. "Mind if I use the last packet of tea?"

That was the last I heard for a while.

When I woke up, it was getting light outside. Will had left the curtains drawn, the better to see the road and the landscape. The room looked squalid and very strange, with bars of one kind of light coming round the curtains, two minute glimmers on the ends of the seventh pair of candles, and the grey, nebulous luminosity of the stony path, now reaching more than two-thirds of the way to the door. Light of day showed the landscape no less dark, but weirdly skewed, floating at an angle to the room. The quacks were asleep, each with its head tucked under its wing.

"I woke you because I think I saw something out there," Will said tensely. He was leaning forward, staring.

I got up quickly and scrambled round beside him. The landscape looked straighter and more real from here. But I couldn't see anything living out there.

"There," said Will, pointing so that I could sight along his arm. "Coming down the hill."

There was a glimmer. By God, there was a glimmer, steadily moving this way! I watched it crawl round a loop of the road, and then pelted to the bathroom, then to the kettle, where I discovered Will had drunk the last packet of coffee too. I could hardly grudge it him. When I got back to the frilly chair, the glimmer was out of sight.

"Coming pretty steadily," Will said. "Shouldn't be long now."

We waited. Five minutes became ten. Became fifteen. Finally we began to hear the slow scuff of footsteps coming up the hill. I had to hang on to Will's shoulder, or I would have run between the candles and peered over the hillcrest. Another minute passed, and panting breath could be heard above the footsteps, and the roll of stones. At length a dark head topped the rise. Surged into a tall body. And became Nick, grey-white with exhaustion, moving at a loping trudge between the burnt-out candles. He was looking at the burning stub of his candle and so intent on that and on his journey that he did not at first realize he had finished it. He looked bewildered when we both bellowed, *"Nick!"*

I looked at the empty hillcrest behind him. I could hear no more footsteps. "Nick," I said. "What happened?"

Nick's shoulders slumped. "Can I blow this out now?" he asked, raising his candle stump.

"Come on out by the chair first," Will said. "That's it. Want to sit? No? OK." He shepherded Nick quickly into the space by the bed, shooting a look at me to convey that Nick was out on his feet. "Now. What happened?" he asked very gently.

I don't think I could have said or done anything. I was too desolated.

"We got there," Nick said. "Maree and I did. We lost Rob. The last bit, that was. I don't know what happened, not to Rob. Oh, and before that we met your friend, Rupert. The one who Maree thinks is fabulous and Nordic. He said to tell you where he'd gone."

Nick ran down here and stood staring at the carpet. Will said, "And?"

"We got there," Nick repeated. Then, with a sudden access of energy, he added, "And you'll never guess what Maree went and did! When we were at—at the—at the right place anyway—and you were supposed to ask for just one thing. I couldn't believe it! She went and asked for her Dad to be cured of his cancer!"

I couldn't look at Will, though I know he was staring at me. "So what happened then?" I managed to say.

"What? Oh, I had to ask *for* her, of course," Nick said, rather irritably. "I had to use mine up and now I'll never be—" He shut his mouth resolutely on whatever ambition that had been and, I suspected, on the tears that went with it. "I asked just like you told us," he said. "Every word, carefully."

"Well done," said Will. "Didn't it work then?"

Nick seemed surprised. "Yes, of course it worked."

"Where is Maree then?" I dared to ask.

297

Nick hunched his shoulders. "How should I know? Isn't she coming?"

"Not that we can see," Will said.

"Well, I don't know. I didn't dare look," Nick said. "I remembered those stories—that man who went to hell to get that girl—you know—and I thought I heard her behind me, but I didn't dare look, in case, in case . . ."

"That was well done too," I said quickly. "We may even be missing a verse about it. I'm sure she'll be along."

"Could I go to bed now?" Nick said. "I'm so tired."

"Of course," we said, and we bundled him over to my bed. I swear he was asleep before we got him there. He was a big lad and very heavy. It was difficult to get him on to the bed, even with two of us, and he lay like a log once we got him there.

"What do you make of that?" Will murmured.

"Typical Maree," I said. "*Not* typical Nick, though. I didn't know he had it in him."

"Just what I thought," Will said. "You'd think with a mother like his—well . . ." He saw me vainly staring out into the increasingly nebulous landscape. Daylight was strengthening all the time. I hoped that accounted for the grey pallor out there, but I very much feared that the road was now fading. "She'll be along," Will said. "He asked right and he didn't look behind, even though he heard her. He *heard* her, Rupe. And it was clever of him not to look. I shouldn't wonder if you're right and Si or someone hasn't got another verse about that, or some Magid we don't know. And it's a long way and she's small. Short legs. She'll turn up. Why don't you go and find us both more coffee? I'll stay and keep the candles going. I've got really good at keeping them down to just a spark."

Bless Will. A fine piece of bluster that was. He could see I could hardly bear to be in the room just then. I was sure Nick had been lying. I could see Will thought so too. Lying not about what Maree had asked for—that rang true—but about what he himself had asked for. I couldn't see Nick sacrificing something he really wanted, not even

298

for Maree, not in a month of Sundays. I tried to smile at Will as I made for the door, but it felt more like bared teeth. I said, almost normally, "Coffee. Yes. And while I'm down there, I'd better put Stan in the picture and talk to Dakros. I'll be about half an hour. All right?"

Then I broke and ran. I ran until I got to the stairs. A lift was too confining. I went down the stairs slowly, a pause from step to step, Rob gone, Maree missing, each step those words. My head pounded. My mouth felt vile. Coffee was essential. Rob gone, Maree missing, down and down. Otherwise I didn't think much, except to be surprised when I got to the part of the stairs where the party had been, to find so little trace of it: just a litter of tinsel, a cigarette end or so and a smell of body and stale drink that reminded me of the inside of my head. Rob gone, Maree missing . . .

I decided I needed fresh air at once. Even before coffee.

I pushed through the fire door, which thumped out *Rob gone, Maree missing*, into a smell of polish and the muted sound of the place being cleaned. Business as usual. Hotels are marvellous places. The end of the world is coming and breakfast is served from eight to ten. I could smell toast distantly and it made me want to gag. The only thing to do was to cut out through the foyer, avoiding all smell of food, and go round to the car park from there. Instead of turning towards the dining room, I hurried down the steps towards the big glass doors.

Gram White, robed and carrying a staff, was waiting for me in the middle of the foyer.

It was another of those occasions when time stretched. I know my first thought was an ignoble inner cry of *Oh, not before breakfast!* which told me, even as I made it, that I had been caught in a summoning from the moment I decided on fresh air. R. Venables does it again! I also had time to look round the calm, palm-decorated space of the foyer and to notice, in the overhead mirrors, that besides the robed and foreshortened figure of White in the centre I could see the foreign receptionist, Odile, at work behind the desk. On Sunday! They exploited her. But that told me that whatever White intended, it was something quick and hard for the uninitiated to see. Something he was well in practice with. That told me *what*.

I don't think I paused. I went down those stairs and towards him in a rush.

That threw him. He tried to open the gate as I came, but I was now going so fast that he was too late. I caught his gate as it spread and dragged upon its edges with both hands. He yelled with contemptuous fury and tried to force it open again. Fire thundered up between us, smoking the overhead mirrors black. I had been right. He had opened it into the heart of a volcano again. We hung there together for endless seconds, burning and equally balanced.

Meanwhile the node went mad around us.

As I fought the triple fight, trying to get that opening to elsewhere closed, trying not to fry, trying to get the upper hand of White, I had sideways helter-skelter sights of the foyer whirling round us like a merry-go-round, potted palms, glass doors, the desk with Odile crouching behind it too scared even to scream, going around and around in a crazy vortex. But mostly I was simply conscious of White and his heavy pale eyes and his pouchy, bearded face, working away in front of me with flourishes of his staff, full of hate and contempt. He hated the whole Magid kind, that was clear. But it was also clear he hated me, personally, with particularity, not just for getting in his way, but physically too, for being myself. And I hated him the same way. I felt pure contempt for his melodramatic hands-off magic with the staff and the stupid robe.

I was also angry, angrier than I have ever been in my life. This pernicious man, with his mad ambitions, had probably destroyed Maree. He had tried to shoot a centaur who was his own child. He had killed three unoffending children and tried to kill Rob. I wanted to destroy him. I wished, with frustration enough to scream at it, that a Magid was allowed to destroy. And he had no such prohibitions. He drew back in the whirling foyer and lashed through me with his staff a blast of noxiousness. It was intended to give me cancer. I rinsed it aside. As I did so, I recognized it as another thing he had done not long ago. And I thought, You did this to Derek Mallory too, didn't you? And my anger was like sheets of flame.

I thundered a whip-crack of pain at him, truly savage pain—at least that was allowed—and when he yelped, winced and staggered, I followed it up with extreme stasis.

Everything stopped, slightly skewed from where it had been, with Gram White frozen and leaning to one side in the centre. I should have done this straight away, I thought. My stasis had stilled the node, but the gate was still open as a writhing smoky slit. I closed it, and sealed it firmly. I cleansed the overhead glass. I restored the melted marble paving by my feet. One of the potted palms had fallen over. I put it upright. Then I turned to Odile, who had been caught in the stasis too. I released her and she stirred and looked at me as if she was sure I was mad.

"Bear with me," I said. "I have to lay a *geas* on this man. Then it will be over."

"You must take your complaint to the Manager," she replied.

I gave up on her. "In due course," I said. The trouble with a *geas* is that it has to be laid aloud, in the hearing of the recipient. Gram White was not likely to stand around for me to do it any other time or place, except here, right in front of Odile. Ah well. Wondering what Odile was going to make of this, I retreated to the steps as a vantage point and broke the stasis on White sufficiently for him to be able to stand upright and listen to what I said. I said:

"Gram White, I hereby lay *geas* upon you, that you may not now or ever use magic of any kind on any being or thing, alive or dead, inanimate, disembodied or between states. From now onwards, the use and practice of magic will be as far from you as the sun is from this world, and any approach to it will be your instant death. Furthermore, if you invoke or use the magic or other powers of your goddess of the bush, or of any other deity, the *geas* will be

301

your instant death. And by reason of your abuse of the powers you have had at your disposal, this *geas* is now laid upon you, to abide by, on pain of instant death."

Having said this, I released the stasis completely. White looked up at me in total hatred. "You *do* think you're clever, don't you?" he said, and turned and went out through the glass doors.

Someone behind me said laughingly, "That sounded very impressive!"

The landing above the stairs seemed to be full of people, probably all on their way to breakfast. There was Wendy, raising fat hands in silent clapping motions, Kornelius with her, grinning feverishly at what he had overheard; and Tansy-Ann Fisk, looking compassionately at me. She was no doubt forgiving me for being in the grip of a grey psychic blanket. Behind her was a scared-looking Tina Gianetti and her besuited boyfriend, who obviously thought it was all just some more nonsense, and beyond these were Rick Corrie and Maxim Hough, both of whom had the air of hoping that what I had just said was not going to cause trouble for the committee. There were also numerous other people I didn't know by name. One of these asked me, "Are we talking Magicians' Battle here? Are you going to do it for the Swords and Sorcery tonight?"

"That was the idea," I said weakly, "but I'm not sure Gram White wants to co-operate."

At this they all gave various cries of encouragement and enthusiasm and went on along the upper level towards the dining room, leaving me face-to-face with Ted Mallory, who must have been at the back of the crowd.

"I see you've made the acquaintance of my esteemed brother-in-law," Mallory said. "Nasty bit of work, isn't he?" I nodded. He said judiciously, "But I very much liked what you just said to him. You wouldn't think of letting me have a copy of it, would you? It would fit in perfectly with the thing I'm writing at the moment."

I thought of Maree, and the wobbly windows. I felt I

owed it to Maree to say, "What I just said was a very powerful *geas*—but you don't believe that, do you?"

He gave a great jovial laugh. "My dear fellow! I'm a rational man! I may write some pretty strange stuff, but it stops there, you know, stops there."

"A *geas*," I said, "is a magical prohibition."

Mallory looked at me expectantly for a second. "I know that," he said. "I know my trade. Well, if you won't give me a copy, I dare say I can do it from memory."

I gave up on him and watched him stroll away to breakfast. He was worse than Odile.

After that, I simply could not face going that way myself. I found the staff door behind one of the mirrors and went off by back corridors to the staff car park. I felt awful. By the time I reached my poor battered car, I was shaking all over and could hardly get the door open.

Inside, the gentle tinkle of Scarlatti faded out. Stan said, "What's up now, lad?"

"Reaction," I said. "I think." I flopped into the driver's seat and told him.

"Oh dear," he said. "Oh dear. It doesn't get any better, does it? I'm sorry about that girl. And that centaur lad. But on the bright side, if the Upper Room *do* Intend this Gram White for the next Koryfonic Emperor, at least you stopped him from being an Emperor Mage. They're always bad news. Though he sounds as if he'd be bad enough as just plain Joe Emperor, this one. Talking of which, your phone keeps on going. I think Dakros wants you."

"I'm sure he does," I said. "I'd better get it over with." I got through to Dakros, still without the least idea what I was going to say to him. "Venables here," I said.

"Ah. Magid," he said. "I was just going to call you again. Half a second while I secure my cubby." He was evidently aboard one of the troop carriers. I could tell by the machinery noise and the distant military voices in the background. These were abruptly cut off. "There," he said. "Are you secure for serious stuff your end?"

"Yes," I said. "Look—"

"Good," he said. "Now, listen to me, Magid. We finally found that young centaur. Nice naïve fifteen-year-old, name of Kristefos, scared witless and hiding in a stack of vine props. Alexandra, Jeffros and I have had a long talk with him."

"I am extremely relieved to hear that," I said. "Is he wounded?"

"No," said Dakros, "and you might well be relieved, Magid. If it wasn't for that centaur's evidence, I'd have no means of knowing you weren't up there in that colony entirely on your own."

"What?" I said. "Now look here . . . !"

"As it is," Dakros pursued, "I have Kristefos to say that the Lesser Consort Jaleila—whom we all thought was dead—and Gramos Albek were up there too, and the evidence of a hover crew that these two were pursuing Kristefos in an Earth vehicle. At least, we're fairly clear from the timing that it *was* those two and not the pair I found you with in the lane. So the most I'm going to accuse you of, Magid, is of holding out on me."

"Now look—" I tried again.

"Holding out on me," repeated Dakros. "Concealing evidence, if you like. Now I respect Magids and Magid laws, and I do know there is precious little a Magid can do if a thing is Intended. But I have an empire to settle, Magid, and I don't care if a thing is Intended or not."

"I don't follow you," I said hopelessly.

"You will," Dakros told me, "when I tell you that Jeffros, who is no one's fool, spent nearly an hour yesterday with those youngsters who came with you—"

"They *didn't* come with me!" I managed to protest. "I didn't know they were there. They were fetched by Knarros—at least Maree was—"

"Ah," said Dakros. "You didn't say that yesterday, Magid. You let me believe they were with you. And the other thing I have to tell you is that those two girls left alive up there—well, forget them. Blood tests and so forth show they can't possibly be related to the Emperor and

Kristefos claims they were simply servants for the little girl."

"I'd sort of expected that," I muttered.

"Sure you had," agreed Dakros, "because you knew, and I didn't, that when I was standing in that hedge talking to you, the youngster I was looking down on was Nichothodes, our next Emperor."

Now the fat was in the fire. "I didn't *know*. I only suspected," I said.

"And made sure I didn't," Dakros replied. "Well, Magid, I've had enough of this. I want two things of you, and I want them *today*. First I want Nichothodes, handed over, in one piece, ready for coronation. Second, I want Gramos and Jaleila Albek handed over, also in one piece, ready for justice. I give you until dinnertime, Magid. By dinnertime today, you give me these three people, regardless of what's Intended or what isn't, or I take serious action. Is that understood, Magid?"

"Yes," I said limply. He rang off. I sat staring at the phone, thinking that I supposed I should be grateful that Dakros was not accusing me of murder. He had obviously thought about it. Finally, I said, "Stan, when the hell do they eat dinner in the Empire?"

"Eh?" said Stan. "Well, has to be after six or they'd call it tea or something instead."

"Six," I said. "Six. That gives me about ten hours to think of something. Thanks, Stan. See you."

I got out of the car and locked it like a sleep-walker. I simply couldn't think what to do. Or, let's be honest, what to do about Nick. Janine and White I would cheerfully hand over. It was just a matter of thinking *how*. But Nick. It was no use pretending Nick was my favourite person since he had left Maree in Babylon. As Emperor he would be nothing like as badly placed as those poor dead children. They would have been snatched out of next to nothing into almost everything, where Nick would come from the complex culture of Earth and merely have to adapt to a life of high ceremony. Teenage boys do adapt, though I couldn't

305

exactly see him enjoying it. In fact, the way I felt at the moment, I almost felt that would serve him right.

Except, did it serve even the most selfish boy right to be pitched into the situation that had made Dakros lose his hair and Jeffros still look like walking wounded?

The question was, really, was Nick Intended to be the next Koryfonic Emperor? Normally, if a thing is intended, you have a very strong sense of it, and you know equally strongly if it isn't. At that moment, I simply could not tell. I felt a total, weary blank.

Oh damn it! I thought, getting into the lift. Maree valued Nick. You had only to see the way she looked after him at breakfast, when the kid couldn't get his eyes open, to see how much she valued him. I dwelt on that. Maree and Nick may not have known they were brother and sister, but they were friends, all the same. Maree would certainly not want Nick condemned to the inevitable early death when the Empire fell to pieces in his hands. There was my decision, then. No matter what was Intended, or what was not, I was going to respect Maree's wishes. A pity that I had no idea how, I thought, as the lift door opened on Floor Five.

Here I realized where I was. Well, no point in going back down again. I could get coffee from Room Service. My recent fracas inside the node seemed to have put everything back more or less where it had been on Thursday. Room 555 was now only a short way down the corridor. I went there.

The door opened on a rich smell of coffee. The eighth pair of candles was now alight. In the skewed distance they led to, the landscape was grey and cloudy, but still nebulously there. Will and Zinka were on the floor by the bathroom, just beginning on a hearty breakfast.

"Zinka plays Room Service like an artist," Will announced through a mouthful of croissant. "She's got us things that aren't on any menu."

"I got the pancakes and bacon for you," Zinka said to me. "Sit down and eat and tell. Someone messed with the node again. Is that all? I see not. Tell us."

306

I sat and ate and drank ravenously and told them. In the course of it, my quacks woke up. Each took a glorious near-indigo head from under a wing, saw me, saw food, and spread their dark blue wings to glide to the carpet. Then, most circumspectly, they picked their way round the outside of the road by the door and arrived politely for their share of croissant.

"Those birds are intelligent beings," Zinka said respectfully. "They've been to Babylon. I don't know what to advise about Nick, Rupert." Here we all took one of many cautious looks towards the bed, but Nick slept on, on his back now, snoring faintly. "There's no chance he'd make a success of the Empire, is there?" We all examined Nick again as he slept. Zinka and Will both shook their heads slightly. It seemed that they, at least, had sufficient precognition to know this was impossible. Zinka frowned as she plastered marmalade upon cinnamon toast. "I don't know about you two," she said, "but my sense is that Nick is actually supposed to be something quite different."

"That makes one of us," I said glumly.

Zinka fed the toast to the quacks, who accepted it with grave pleasure. Will said, "You could forestall Dakros by putting a *geas* on Nick."

"Ah, come on, Will!" Zinka said. "That's how to have the Upper Room hopping mad at him."

Privately, I thought Will had hit on the best idea yet. But I said, "Dakros has got to have someone, you know."

"He can have himself," Will said. "He's had a lot of practice by now. If you leave him no alternative—"

"He'd never deal with me again," I said.

Zinka laughed. "Oh, the secret relief on your face when you said that! Poor Rupert. No one wants Koryfos. But Koryfos wants Janine and Gram and I vote they should have them. Let's plan."

We spent the next half hour planning. We hatched what seemed to us a perfect, foolproof way to deliver the two of them to Dakros by six that evening. Then Zinka said she would get some sleep. Will said he would go down to his

Land Rover: he needed to phone through to Carina to let her know he was going to be here for the rest of today. I was left alone. I sat in the frilly chair with a quack roosting companionably on each shoe and waited. I don't think I thought any more. I don't think I expected anything any more. I simply stared into that increasingly fogged land-scape at the end of the burnt-out rows of candles. And waited.

Will took his time. He tells me he suddenly felt an over-whelming need for some exercise and took a walk by the river. He was still away when the eighth pair of candles began to near their ends. I watched them anxiously. The slight draught from the door meant that one was burning ahead of the other whatever I did. I was going to have to light the seventeenth candle well before the last one, and the Lord knows what effect that was going to have! In an effort to preserve the fast-burning one, I leant forward and cupped my hand round the flame and tried with everything I knew to slow it down. I worked on it so furiously that I never heard footsteps. I didn't hear a thing. I simply looked up and saw Maree coming over the brow of the hill.

She was the old Maree in every way. She was the right colour again, though pale, and her hair was once more brownish and possibly even bushier. Anyway it seemed to frame her small serious face in quantities, in tendrils and in fine frizz, as she bent earnestly over the tiny lighted stub of candle she carried. And she was the old Maree in another way. For some reason, she was now wearing the woefully ragbag skirt and top in which I had first seen her, and large soft shoes that put me in mind of the children on the hill. Even her fingernails had grown long and spiked again. She was using them to grip the candle with, by its very end.

With all this, she was a whole new Maree. It was hard to say how, but I knew immediately that the same change that had overtaken the quacks had overtaken Maree too. It was not that she was older. It was not that she was more, or larger. It was as if she had not been filling her proper

308

outlines before this. Now she did. A small, small measure of the change was that she now looked good in her woeful old garments. She looked astonishingly good.

As I saw all this, Maree looked up and saw me. A look I had not seen before—one of pure delight—filled her face. I don't think she had ever been truly happy in her life before. Now she was, because she had seen me.

I forgot prudence. I forgot the danger of intruding in one's own workings. The quacks spilled off my feet with indignant honks as I took off like a sprinter and raced down the road of candles. I picked Maree up in both arms, hugging her crazily tight, and swung her round and round. Her candle went out and went flying. I heard her laugh. Nothing mattered. The dark landscape went away in a blink, between one mad rotation and the next. When I put Maree down, there was nothing there but two rows of wax-filled holders. The candles by the door were out too.

Maree's face was a glowing heart-shape of pleasure. She looked up at me and said, "Really?"

"Yes," I said. "Really."

At this, she stepped back a bit and pushed at her glasses in her combat-manner. "I'm not a very good investment," she said, with that sob in her voice. I had missed that sob. "I warn you."

"Neither am I," I said. "Wait till I tell you."

"That's all right then," she said. "But you'll have to wait. I'm out on my feet. I have to go to sleep." She folded over as she said this and I only just put my arm out in time to catch her. "Need sleep," she said.

"Here," I said, and guided her over to the bed where Nick was.

Maree threw herself on it. Her fist pounded at Nick's shoulder. "Move over, lump!" This Nick, without waking, instantly did. Maree was at her most irresistible. I thought that, like Nick before, she was asleep at once. I was just turning away, with a lightness of mind I could not have imagined five minutes before—Nick had *not* lied, all would be well, all problems solved—when Maree's arm shot up, holding her glasses. "Put them somewhere," she said. "And please wake me in time for Uncle Ted's speech. I promised him."

TWENTY-THREE

We woke Nick and Maree just before two. Maree, looking at Nick's still-unopened eyes, was inclined to think we had left it too late. "There's no *way* he'll be alive by three—and I must go and get changed. These clothes are frightful," she said.

Zinka said quickly that she would fetch Maree some clothes. We did not want Maree going into her room yet. I had spent the morning attempting to delouse her computer and Nick's. Nick's was easy—only a matter of cleaning out an enslavement programme—but Maree's computer was woven through and through with thorny, sterile growths from that wretched bush-goddess. I was thinking of junking it and offering her one of my own computers instead, except that, so far, I could not see a way to do it without Maree knowing that I had looked at her files. There was quite a lot in the latest ones about me, none of it complimentary.

Nick surprised Maree by opening both eyes and eating the lunch we had brought. Then he too said he needed to change. I looked at him properly for the first time and saw that he was wearing clothes as ragged as Maree's, very short and tight, as if he had grown out of them, and shoes through which his toes showed. Something to do with Babylon, evidently, although neither Nick nor Maree said so. In fact, they both behaved as if there was an embargo on their talking about their time in the dark landscape. When I tried to discover why Maree had been so far behind Nick,

311

she and he looked at one another, sharing some knowledge, and did not say anything.

Will, Zinka and I exchanged glances and tried not to ask any more.

Before we left to hear Ted Mallory's speech, Maree asked if she could use my telephone to get news of Derek Mallory. She referred to him as her "little fat Dad" and her manner made me wonder if she even knew he was not her father, let alone knowing who her real father was and what had happened to her because of him. I really do not think she remembered being stripped. But some of the rest she must have known. She turned from the phone with her face a heart-shape of delight and looked at Nick, full of meanings.

"It's gone down almost to nothing already!" she said.

Nick, understandably, looked a little dour. He had made a genuine sacrifice and, whatever it had been, it clearly still hurt. I was sorry about that. I almost wished he had been selfish enough to ask for what he wanted. Whatever it had been, I was certain it would have been in direct conflict with the plans of Dakros and, since this was the Babylon secret, Dakros would not have got his way. Now I was going to have to do something. While I worked on the computers, I had come to the conclusion that Will's idea of laying a *geas* on Nick was probably the only way to stop Dakros. But only as a last resort, I thought. There must be some other way.

Just before three, we were all smartened up, except Will, who is uncomfortable in any but the oldest clothes. I had got round to shaving at last. Zinka, when she fetched Maree some clothes, had changed into a flowing green velvet gown, which made her by far the most striking member of the group. We left my room in a body. And, I see in retrospect, that was the last moment when events were in any way within my control.

In the corridor outside my room was a large crowd of people, all of them concerned and agitated. Mr. Alfred Douglas, the hotel manager, was prominent among them and so was Rick Corrie. The rest seemed to be the entire convention committee, with the exception of Maxim Hough. As we came out of my room, Mr. Douglas was pointing to the large brown pebbly area in the ceiling where Gram White's bullet, deflected by my shield, had brought down the plaster. One of the committee was saying huffily, "Yes, of *course* we'll pay for it, if you can prove it was a convention member who did it. Frankly, I don't see *how*—"

"Uh-oh!" said Zinka. "Let me handle this. You go. I'll catch you up." She took hold of Rick Corrie's arm. As we edged past towards the lift, she was saying to him, "You'd better send the bill for this to Gram White. He loosed off with a gun. I saw him do it. Want me to speak to the manager for you?"

And Corrie replied frantically, "Well, don't tell him *that*! He'd never let us hold the convention here again!"

"Trust me," Zinka said and walked demurely up to Mr. Douglas. Goodness knows what story she was preparing to spin, but I felt I could trust her to say something convincing. We went on without her.

Zinka had still not caught us up when we reached the main function room. It was largely full already. The seats on the far side of the aisle were packed. I saw fat Wendy over there and one or two people I knew, but a surprising number of them were either concealed in grey capes or wearing armour. Chain mail and horned helmets predominated, but plate armour was in there too, from every conceivable era of history. I heard Nick explaining to Will— both of them looking rather wistfully at the costumes—that a lot of people arrived on the Sunday specially for the tournament. New arrivals or not, these people were certainly having fun. Most of them had tankards or bottles to hand and, from time to time, a sort of clanking Mexican wave was in progress, accompanied by huge shouts and much waving of a long white banner with SWORDS AND SORCERY painted on it.

The nearer side was nearly as full, mostly with people I had come to know over the first day or so. I saw the lady with OOOK on her, my world-sharing American friends, the singers who had interrupted my tête-à-tête with Thurless, and the three folk with the baby, now dressed quite normally in jeans. In fact, almost the only empty seats were in the front row on this side. It is curious the way nobody likes to sit in the front row. The only people in it were Tina Gianetti and her boyfriend, near the centre aisle. It seemed that Gianetti was keeping to her vow never to chair anything involving Ted Mallory.

I saw Kornelius Punt rise from his seat somewhere in the centre in order to stare at us avidly as we filed into the empty front row, but this was so much his usual behaviour that I thought nothing of it. I could sense also that the crowd in the armour were raising power, but this is something an excited crowd does anyway. I thought little of that either, except to make sure that we had the usual protections around us. Most of my attention was on the half-laughing argument I was having with Maree. Both of us were enjoying the sense that so much more was going on between us, behind the argument.

As we were sitting down, most of the men in horned helmets broke into low, lilting song. One of the three ladies-and-gentlemen with the baby remarked, "They will keep doing that. I suppose it keeps them happy."

I grinned at him-or-her and said to Maree, "But I've got a big yard at the back. They'll have lots of exercise."

"They'll need to swim," Maree said. "It's bad for aquatic birds not to."

"I tell you what," I said. "Andrew, my neighbour's, got a pond in his garden just up the road. I know he'll let the quacks use it."

"They'll probably find it anyway," she said. "Is it clean?"

"Good question," I said. "As Andrew is an inventor and the most absent-minded man I ever knew, probably not. I'll make him have it dredged. Or perhaps I should change houses with him."

"I still think you should dig a pond in your kitchen,"

Maree said. "People who keep pets have to make sacrifices."

"Wouldn't it do," I asked, "if I simply went and stood in Andrew's pond? Day and night, of course."

"Oh yes," she said. "In your nice suit and Will's green wellies."

We were laughing at this image when we looked up to find Janine standing over us, in a new jumper that looked as if she was being eaten by a lettuce. Little green beads like caterpillars danced on her left shoulder. "How did you get here?" she said to Maree.

Maree looked up at her, and pushed at her glasses. All the expression went out of her face. "I went," she said, in a calm and level voice, "to Babylon. And don't think you can try anything like that with me again."

"All right," Janine said. "There are other ways. And don't you think you can spoil Nick's chances, because I'm not going to let you."

"I never did want to spoil his chances," Maree said. "I just want to make sure that *you* don't."

While Will and I stared, frankly appalled by how naked it was between them, Janine turned away from Maree, smiling sweetly, and said to Nick, "Come along, dear. Mother wants you sitting beside her for once. It's your father's finest hour and we don't want to let him down, do we?"

"In a moment," Nick said placidly. "I just need to finish asking Rupert about my computer games first."

Janine's eyes passed across me like a scythe. "Then don't be long, dear," she said and walked gracefully away to the front row on the other side of the aisle, with the little beads chittering on her shoulder as she went.

Nick leant to me across Maree. "You did look at the games, didn't you?" I nodded. They had been prominent in the files I had cleansed that morning. "Then talk about them," Nick said. "Spin it out."

"Well actually, they do have possibilities," I began. "What I liked about the Bristolia game . . ."

Here Maxim Hough, followed by Ted Mallory, climbed

315

on to the platform in front of us. The Viking song, which had been beginning to irritate me, died away and everyone clapped. Nick sank back in his chair, exuding satisfaction. He had avoided Janine and he knew I would not have praised his game unless I meant it. He caught Ted Mallory's eye and they grinned at one another.

Ted Mallory was looking jovial and composed. I would not have believed he was as nervous as Maree said he was. But I saw his eyes search for Maree. Maree leant earnestly forward in her seat until her uncle saw her. She gave a slight nod as his eyes found her. Mallory seemed to sigh with relief. He smiled at Maree and shuffled composedly at the papers in front of him. All was now well.

And all seemed well still while Maxim Hough pushed his blond Egyptian hairstyle behind his ears, coughed into the microphone and introduced the Guest of Honour, ". . . who needs no introduction from me as the best living writer of serious comic horror . . ."

All *seemed* well, but I could sense growing hostile magic. It was coming in cold waves, stronger and stronger, and each wave seemed to lap round me, squeezing at my heart, compressing my lungs and turning my kidneys to blocks of ice. It was so powerful, and its aim was so astutely disguised that, for a minute or so, I actually wondered if I was being egotistical in thinking it was aimed chiefly at me. By this time I was having a struggle to breathe. I glanced at Will and found him giving me a glare of concern. No, I was not being egotistical then: it *was* aimed at me.

I pushed it back sharply and began to wish that Zinka would hurry up and get here. This was *strong*. The sending, or whatever, was being done by that block of folk in hooded robes. Now I looked, I could see them swaying gently to it. But they were using power that had unwittingly been built up by the guys in armour—at least, I hoped it was unwitting. Damn it! The whole thing was orchestrated! I looked searchingly that way. Gram White was leaning smugly against the far door beyond the cowled figures. He saw me look. As Ted Mallory stood up to speak, White blandly spread both hands out, empty. Look, no hands. He had simply organized a good hundred people to do his dirty work for him.

I fear I heard little of what Ted Mallory said. I was struggling with more and stronger cold waves and thinking, But White can't be doing this! The terms of the *geas* would mean he was dead if he even organized something like this! What's going on? I vaguely heard Mallory starting with his favourite premise that writing a book was "just a job like any other job," at which Maree sighed sharply and clicked her teeth in annoyance, and some of his first remarks must have been amusing, because I remember people behind me laughing and clapping. But nobody was laughing on the other side of the hall, not even the men in armour. The robed ones swayed gently—including fat Wendy, to my sorrow—and waves of binding, choking malevolence poured over me. Will had joined in to help me by then, which helped me hold it off a little, enough to think what I could do.

Damn it, White must be *delegating*! I thought. He has told someone lies about me and got this person to organize this for him. The best thing seemed to be to get that person. I tried aiming a massive stasis that way.

That was truly terrifying. Something promptly drank the stasis. It had no effect at all. Or worse, the stronger I applied it the faster it, and my own strength with it, vanished. Like water down a plughole. I was nearly completely thrown by that. Stasis is one of my great skills. In nearly total panic, with no Stan to tell me to stay calm, I found myself being sucked towards whatever was drinking my strength. Will put a hand on my arm then, and thank God he did. It calmed me enough to show me that I could use the sucking to divine what it was.

It was Tansy-Ann Fisk. Or rather, it was that grey psychic blanket she accused everyone else of bearing. It was a great pall of negative power, and it could go on drinking as long as I cared to go on throwing stasis at it. Now I had

317

it tagged, I could even divine what Fisk thought she was at. Someone had told her I had ambitions to be secret ruler of the world. Well, that figured. As Maree had realized earlier, Magids can seem to want just that if you don't know enough to know better.

"Stop pushing and just build a wall," I gasped to Will.

We did that. That was Will's special strength. But there were so many of them over there, and so strong, that it was precious hard work. We both sweated with it. But the cold waves rolled back a little.

Then, to our extreme irritation, Kornelius Punt leapt into the aisle and excitedly beckoned to the folk in robes. Ted Mallory stared from him to them and frowned as he talked. Kornelius then swung round, like a conductor, and beckoned to Will and me.

"I'll wring that fellow's neck!" Will snarled. "This isn't a *game*!"

Kornelius thought it was, though. He saw everything as a game. I gave up the momentary idea I had had that Kornelius was acting as White's lieutenant and probed among the grey cloaks to see who it really was. It had to be someone there.

By this time, Maree and Nick were aware that something was badly wrong. "Can we do something to help?" Maree murmured, still staring attentively at her uncle.

"Just hold my hand and grab Nick's and both of you think strength," I panted.

Her firm small hand instantly folded itself round mine. I heard her whisper, "Come on, Nick!" and I felt the result with gratitude, as an access of energy and, in Maree's case, pleasure at being able to do something. Nick's help was electric with excitement. He knew he was in a genuine magic battle and, in his quieter way, he was almost as high on it as Kornelius was.

Kornelius saw we had co-opted help. He beckoned the other side of the aisle again. Gram White was laughing. He thought this was really funny. His lieutenant was not so amused. With the new help from Maree and Nick, we were

318

strong enough, Will and I, to build one of the stone-hard domes of protection Will is so good at. The lieutenant found himself forced to stand up and yelp some kind of command at the massed men in armour. They began to sway in their seats, *clank, rattle, clank*, and to hum a note deep in their throats.

Damn! I thought. That was a power song.

Ted Mallory stopped speaking and coughed into his microphone. "Do you *mind*?"

The deep note faded to a whisper, but it did not stop. Nor did the shuffling, rattling clink of armoured bodies swaying. Mallory shrugged. "Suppose the constellation of Orion became animated . . ." he continued, looking irritated.

From then on, things got really vicious. While Ted Mallory elaborated his fantasy about Orion—and Will and I both wished he would't: it verged on a deep secret of the Magids and distracted us—the lieutenant flung his worst at us. Power built so from the hum and rattle that all I could do was hold my share of the protective dome and make jabs at the grey-robed figure of the lieutenant, trying to find out who he was and where his weakness lay. His minions, being mostly amateurs, found the increased power difficult and lost their hold on it somewhat. Physical manifestations began. First it was filthy smells, and then lurid green smokes. When half-seen things like Chinese dragons flared and floated overhead, the baby behind me burst out crying and had to be carried out of the hall. Quite a lot of people left around then, and I didn't blame them. Shortly, blue sparks began to sputter across the metal of all that armour. I saw horned figures leaping out of their seats in order to beat at themselves. This disrupted the power-build just enough so that my latest jab at the lieutenant caused his grey hood to fall back. It was Thurless.

I suppose I should have expected that, I thought ruefully.

The manifestations absolutely delighted Kornelius Punt. He began leaping about in the aisle, cheering both sides on. He annoyed Ted Mallory thoroughly. Mallory could ignore the smells and the shapes, it seemed, but he could not ignore a leaping human figure. "Oh, will you sit down, man!" he snapped.

Punt, not very chastened, went back to his seat and sat there jigging.

By this time, I knew that the only thing to do was to leave. Thurless had power that made him a potential Magid, and he had evidently been trained by White. Fisk was another. We could have handled them, but not with the backup of several scores of others, and not if Fisk was simply going to drink up any stasis we tried to impose. I whispered to the others. Nick and Will agreed fervently, but Maree said, "Oh, poor Uncle Ted! I promised I'd hear every word!"

There was no way I could go away and leave her there alone with Janine and White. I shrugged helplessly. We could probably hold out.

"Oh, don't be a fool, Rupe!" Will said. "Pick her up and carry her out. Or I *will*!" And he got up, pounced on Maree and swung her up out of her seat. She gave a surprised squeal.

Ted Mallory's irritable face turned to Will, then shot round the other way as Janine sprang upright in the front row further along. Janine had no intention of letting Maree be removed. She flung her head back and gave a long, howling cry:

"Aglaia-Ualaia!"

I recognized the name of her unpleasant bush-goddess. So evidently did Thurless. He swung round, nodded at Janine and swung round again to wave at his helpers. They all gave out the same cry. *"Aglaia-Ualaia!"* Like a pack of dogs. There was a strong rush of ozone smell, meaning that the level of power had been raised yet again.

"Oh, *really*, Janine!" Ted Mallory said reproachfully across the noise.

"Be quiet, Ted!" Janine said to him. "Can't you see this is far more important than your stupid talk?"

She came walking towards us along the space beside the

320

platform. She came accompanied by a growing, thrusting, rapidly spreading thicket of dry grey thorny brushwood. We were by then also in the space, trying to retreat, but the thicket sprang up behind us, and through the chairs we had just left, and there was nothing Will and I could do but stand where we were and do our best to double the strength of our protective dome. The cries of White's followers had brought the growth beyond the brink of reality. The stuff rustled and crackled as it grew, spreading out into the aisle—where I had a glimpse of Tina Gianetti, backing away in panic, dragging her disbelieving manfriend by the collar of his suit—and then growing in a rush through the speaker's table as Janine passed along it. Maxim, who was reaching for the microphone in an effort to restore order, found the dry twigs rooting on his hand and then actually thrusting through his arm. He snatched his hand back and batted at it, frantically, his mouth open and his head up in despair and pain. Ted Mallory got up and backed away. His face was greenish-white.

The despair and pain were what the goddess brought. Janine had the same look as Maxim. She was almost entirely bush herself as she reached our protected space.

Maree said, "Witchy Dance, Nick, quick!" and wriggled out of Will's hold on her. "You two do it as well, *quickly!*" She snapped her fingers, sprang into a pose and began the absurd dance that had so maddened me twice before. Nick, although he was as green-white as Ted Mallory and I could see him shaking, instantly joined in. And it worked. As they did the first idiotic flick, flick, flick of the fingers, the brushwood stopped advancing. We were in a tiny circular clearing, just big enough for the four of us, with dry grey thorns pressed against the invisible wall. Will and I made haste to join in. "Luck, luck, luck!" we all chanted. Flick, flick, flick. Silly as it was, it was fun too.

The second time we did it, however, I had a sideways view among the grey thorns, of the armoured men getting out of their seats and drawing their swords. Foremost among them was Gabrelisovic, snarling and dressed in armour at least a size too small. The rest were following his lead. They were doing it in a puzzled and reluctant way, but they were doing it, unsheathing weapons and beginning to advance on us. Thurless had thrown them at us as a help to Janine. I remember exchanging a hopeless look with Will. The aim of all this was to eliminate both me and Maree. With us gone, Dakros would have no case against either Janine or White and he would probably accept Janine as Empress out of sheer need.

We danced on, ridiculously and despairingly. There was no way Will and I alone could hold off the dry goddess and the folk in cowls and sixty or so men with swords as well. So far, all that the warriors were doing was walking forward, waving their swords. But each time our flick, flick, flick brought me round so that I could see them, the armed men were nearer and waving weapons with greater conviction—big, heavy, unpleasantly useful swords, they were. Foremost among these warriors was Gabrelisovic, towering in his borrowed armour. Each time I had a sight of him, he was swinging his sword more fiercely and evidently nearer to a pure battle-rage. The look on his face brought me out in chilly, useless sweat. Each time I swung round to the part of the thorny hedge that was Janine, she was more of a goddess. I could see the vast lineaments of a sardonic old woman building around and above the shape of Janine inside those thorns. She was simply leaning against our protective wall, waiting to become manifest enough to send her spiky growths through it and stop us as we danced.

And she was getting through. Dry grey spines were popping their way in towards us when the whole thicket went up in a crackling roll of flame. For an instant, fire washed over the dome of our defences, blinding and scorching us all. We stopped dancing, coughing.

By the time I could see and hear again, nothing was left of the dry growth but a broad black swathe, which stretched over the white cloth of the speaker's table, down the aisle and along the first row of chairs. Janine's body was lying

322

in the exact middle of the blackness. Her hair was gone and her face was flayed to purplish meat.

Funny! I thought. She has the look of someone killed by an Empire beam-gun.

TWENTY-FOUR

Rupert Venables concluded

The room was full of soldiers in grey and blue. Some were efficiently herding men in armour or folk in robes among the disordered chairs to stand in little huddles, each guarded by two soldiers. Others were on guard at all the doors. I wondered how many corners the troops at the far doors had had to turn in order to get there. I could feel the node whirling wildly about us. The first thing I did was to slow it down. I was too weak to do more. Then I looked round at Dakros. He was just beside us, slowly holstering the handgun that had undoubtedly saved our bacon.

"Oh God!" I said idiotically. "You have your dinner in the middle of the day!"

He shot me a look as sarcastic as that of the thorn goddess. "Of course. When else would one have it? Where is Gramos Albek?"

I pointed. "Against that far wall there. Or he was." There was no sign of White there now.

Dakros unhitched his communicator and spoke into it briefly, keeping the sarcastic look and one raised eyebrow on me while he did so. Across the hall, a captain waved acknowledgement and a posse of soldiers moved in among the chairs there, guns at the ready. Dakros turned to face me. "Well, Magid, I promised to take action and I have. When I didn't hear from you, I brought a troop carrier up Naywards as soon as Jeffros could get a gate open. And don't tell me this isn't Intended. I don't want to hear."

"I'm very glad you came," I said humbly.

"Yes, it does rather look as if you might be," he agreed. His eyes flicked over Will, registering him as a Magid, and then on to Nick and Maree. He looked at Nick with considerable satisfaction. I could see him thinking that Nick made a fine, tall, handsome heir. "I believe," he said, "that I address the Imperial Highnesses Nichothodes and Sempronia."

Nick nodded and then looked down again at Janine's body. You would have said there was no expression at all in his face, except that the corners of his eyes had pulled into wrinkles, like an old man's. Maree's face had gone orange-red with embarrassment. "Please," she said. "At least call me Marina."

"My pleasure, Highness," answered Dakros. "I'm very glad to see you restored to health. We've a troop carrier waiting to escort you both back to your rightful home. Prince Nichothodes, you are aware, are you, that you will shortly be crowned Emperor?"

"All right. If that's what you want," Nick said.

Oh well, I thought. I suppose this is what had to happen. Nick, for a moment, almost had me fooled. Then I remembered the smoothness with which he had three times ducked out and evaded Janine, and I realized that he intended to do it again. From the Empire this time. It was his placid, agreeable manner that gave it away. Goodness knew what he meant to do. Probably he did not know himself how he would manage it yet. But, somehow, I knew that when it came to the coronation of the new Emperor Nick was going to be missing. The way Maree came and gripped my arm warningly only confirmed it. Maree knew too.

I risked a major row with Maree. I shook her hand off my arm. "You just can't *do* that!" I said to Nick.

"I realize you don't think he's Intended to be our Emperor," Dakros said, misunderstanding me, "but he's the only male heir I've got, Magid, and I'm damn well going to get him crowned!"

"I don't think my brother meant that," Will said. "Did he, Nick?"

325

"Didn't he?" Nick said guilelessly.

"It takes one to catch one," Will said. "When Rupert was your age, we used to call him Houdini."

"I don't follow—" Dakros was beginning, rather irritably, when two things interrupted him, almost simultaneously. From across the hall came the snarl and flare of a beam-gun—aimed, I think, in the air as a threat—and some shouting. Soldiers were dragging a struggling robed figure out from under the chairs there. Dakros had scarcely time for an "Ah!" of satisfaction before he found himself confronted with Ted Mallory.

"You!" said Mallory. He was still pale, but firm and angry. "Yes, you, sir! What do you mean by shooting my wife?"

"It was necessary," Dakros said.

"That's a bare-faced admission of murder, if ever I heard one!" Mallory said.

"The woman was a murderess," Dakros explained, "and a sorceress."

"I bear witness to that," I said.

Ted Mallory stared at us both, blankly. I was wondering what else one could say, when Maree seized her uncle by his arm. "You *do* know!" she said. "Come on, Uncle Ted. You didn't even *like* her! Admit what you saw her do. Admit it, just for once in your life, Uncle Ted! Come on."

Mallory looked down at her. "Admit to . . ." he said. "Oh all right. I do admit I thought I saw Janine as a most unpleasant—she was part of a most unpleasant sort of bush, I think."

"Bravo!" said Maree. "Well done, Uncle Ted. Nick, you're going to have to look after him rather after this."

"I can't if I've got to be this emperor, can I?" Nick said hopelessly.

"Take him with you, I meant," said Maree.

"He'd go mad," Nick said.

I was inclined to agree with Nick, and I was again wondering what I could say, when the soldiers arrived with their struggling prisoner. His beard was jutting. His robe was half off and being used to wrap his arms in by his captors, and he was yapping, "I tell you I am *not* Gram White! You have no business laying hands on me! Let me go this instant! I am an eminent writer!" I must say I was glad to see Mervin Thurless having a bad time, even though it was evident that Gram White had done a quick substitution as a prelude to a quick bunk.

Will and I exchanged looks. With those troops guarding the doors, White had to be in the hall still. He must have done the classic thing and hidden himself among the other people dressed just like him. We set off at a run towards the nearest grey huddle. Thurless screamed after us, "Stop those two! Stop them, I tell you! They are trying to rule the world!"

There were disarranged chairs and frightened people all over the place. Will and I had only made it as far as the central aisle when a trumpet pealed out from behind us. It was a strong fanfare, incredibly loud, and joyous, and ceremonial. It meant something. It heralded things. We spun round. Every one did, people of Earth and troops of Koryfos alike. Every one of us stared.

The trumpeter was Rob.

He was alive after all—or more than alive: triumphantly and vibrantly alive. He had that same glow to his eyes and his coat that I had seen in my quacks when they returned, and that poise to his body, full of life and health. More than that, he gave you that sense that he was now filling his true outlines, the same way as Maree and even Nick now did. Rob's outlines were unequivocally the outlines of a prince. His mass of black hair was formally tied back. He had on a royal blue uniform coat, braided with gold, evidently borrowed from someone in the élite troops, and it sat on him like a royal robe. He looked magnificent. As far as I could see, there was no sign of the wound in his side now.

He finished blowing the fanfare and brought the trumpet smartly down to rest against his right flank. "Silence!" he called out. "Silence for the Emperor Koryfos the Great!"

One forgets what lungs centaurs have. Rob's ringing

shout caused every movement and murmur to stop—except for the irrepressible Kornelius Punt, who was hugging himself and muttering, "A centaur now! A *centaur*! Now I have really seen it all!"

More soldiers entered the room behind Rob. They wore the uniforms I had always associated with an Empire honour guard, the royal blue and gold of Rob's jacket, and bore themselves very smartly and formally. I heard one of the troops holding Thurless whisper, "They're from the Twenty-Ninth! I thought we'd left them holding down Iforion!" They were followed by four splendidly dressed people. Zinka in her green velvet was one. Next to her was Lady Alexandra in full court dress, train, fan, coronet and all, and beside her was Jeffros as a Mage of the Empire in full panoply, and the flared cloak with Infinity shining on it in gold. The fourth was a Magid in ceremonial robes: white damask, fluttering purple bands, everything. Infinity shone on his breast too. Will and I both exclaimed as we recognized our brother Simon.

Following them, the Emperor came in.

There was no question he was Koryfos the Great. He was exactly like every statue I had ever seen, in the palace or around Iforion. There was also no question that he was my neighbour Andrew as well. His hair was maybe yellower and his face a touch browner, but I was nevertheless astonished that I had never seen the likeness before. The *distrait* and unassuming bearing of Andrew must have misled me. There was no question now that he was indeed Emperor. He came in wearing, like Rob, a borrowed uniform and he even had his customary vague and modest look. And you realized you had never seen majesty before. People on Earth, particularly, are not used to real kings any more. But this was such a real king that your throat caught with awe.

At least three-quarters of the people in that room acknowledged his royalty by bowing. I saw fat Wendy thump to her knees in an utterly sincere attempt to curtsey. She looked very ashamed of the mess she had made of it.

My erstwhile neighbour stopped and looked round at the confusion of tumbled chairs and beam burns. "I'm looking for General Commander Dakros," he said.

Dakros hastened between two crooked rows of chairs, and when he reached the space formed by Rob and the honour guard, he went down on one knee. It looked perfectly natural. "Here, sire," he said. "Forgive me. I would never have forced you to come Naywards if I—"

"I have heard the facts. You needed to be here," Koryfos said. "I am here to confirm your actions and to reappoint you as General-in-Chief of the Empire. But we must finish this business quickly. I need a second coronation, General. And this centaur is my heir. His status must be ratified as well. So please stand up and then tell me whether you have found the criminals you came to catch."

Dakros got up quickly. "Jaleila was found and put to death," he said, "but Gramos Albek is probably hiding—"

The new Emperor stopped him with a small gesture. "Thank you. Where is Gramos Albek?"

He looked across the scattered groups of awed people and the force of it literally dragged Gram White out of hiding. I have never seen anything like it. I wish I had half that much power as a Magid. Gram White came out of his hiding place under a row of chairs, scrambling, toppling the chairs, and utterly unwilling, but he came. He came shuffling along the rows of seats and among people who all backed away from him, with his head bent and protest in every motion and line of his body, but he was quite unable to resist the desire of Koryfos. About halfway, he managed to put his hand in his robes for his gun. Koryfos simply shook his head slightly. White's face puckered with fury, but he took his hand away. He came stumbling unwillingly on until he was level with me. There, with an effort that made veins bulge beside his eyes, he stopped and glared at me.

I saw what he was thinking. I said, "Don't be a fool!"

White had nothing to lose, I suppose. Trembling with the effort it took to stand there and not walk towards Koryfos, he tried, once again, to open a gate and strip me. The *geas*

329

took instant effect. It looked like a massive coronary to me. The man's face turned bluish-purple, lips and all, his arms jerked and then he clutched at his chest as if the pain was so bad he could not help it. He doubled up slightly. But he managed to keep his eyes on me, staring at me tauntingly. *"See?"* his look said. "See what you made me do!" He hoped I would carry the guilt of his death for years. Sometimes I have to work very hard not to. But he did it to himself really. Besides, I noticed that Koryfos did nothing to prevent him. It was, in its manner, an execution.

White pitched down by my feet. While I stared at him, thinking what a small thing—and how absolute a one— separates a live person from a dead one, I heard the Emperor say, "Both bodies are to be taken to the further carrier and incinerated. I shall be talking to the necessary people in the nearer carrier. Rupert."

I looked up to see my sometime neighbour looking at me, with the same courtesy he used when he came to borrow sugar, but with all the difference in the multiverse. It was a politeness strong enough to stun.

"I want to see you shortly," he said. "For the moment I'll just say thank you."

He turned and left. The hall seemed dimmer without him. As the others, including Dakros, followed him, Rob touched my arm and said quietly, "Thank you," too. I could not think what on Earth or elsewhere either of them should thank me for. I had done nothing but blunder about. In the end, I concluded that Koryfos meant all the driving about I used to do for him. The power of Koryfos was still apparent two hours later. The convention—probably—was still going on. At least the armed men, along with Fisk and Thurless, had vanished to take part in various events, to my great relief. But somehow all those who might have business with the Empire were drawn towards the hotel entrance, where Odile still worked, with her fair head down, resolutely ignoring all the strange activity around her.

The foyer was less bright than usual because of the great shiny bulk of the troop carrier outside. Behind it, you could just glimpse the second carrier in which Koryfos had arrived, further down the market square. But Koryfos was now in the nearer one and the foyer became his waiting room. We all sat or stood about in there. Lady Alexandra was there most of the time, acting as a sort of Emperor's aide, soothing or explaining to those who felt they had waited long enough, or else simply walking about talking to Tina Gianetti. From what I overheard, the two of them were comparing notes, ardently and inwardly, on what it really felt like to be a public figure. Meanwhile, as further aides, Jeffros, Zinka and Simon were moving people in and out of the carrier.

Zinka spared a moment to lean down to Will and me. "Do forgive me for not turning up to help," she said. "I'd just got loose from the manager when Si came through on my portable phone, saying he'd got a centaur and someone he was sure was Koryfos asking him for help, and saying if I didn't get myself to Iforion to help him sort it out he was in serious danger of screaming. And of course I had to go belting off there at once. It was all a huge rush after that."

"How did they end up in Iforion?" Will wanted to know.

"I wish I knew!" Zinka said and hastened away.

Will and I sat on in the foyer. Various members of the hotel staff kept coming there to stare wonderingly out of the glass doors at the carrier. "Is it a UFO?" most of them almost invariably asked me.

"Yes, you might say that," I told them. It always seemed to make them happier. "Why is it," I asked Will, after the seventh or eighth time, "that they see a thing and don't know what it is, and I tell them that it's an unidentified flying object, and they go away perfectly satisfied?"

Nick laughed. "*Everyone* knows what a UFO is!"

This was shortly after Ted Mallory had come away from the carrier, looking bewildered, and saying, "I don't get it. I've just been offered a chance to live in this Empire, wherever it is. Of course I said I couldn't. I have Nick to care for after—now that . . . as things are."

Nick, at this, looked much happier. He had seen Koryfos among the first, just after Maree, and I gathered from the way he looked after Mallory said this, that Nick too had declined to live in the Empire and had been wondering quite what he would do if Ted Mallory did not want him.

Maree, sitting between Will and me, was very quiet. She just sat there with her chin mutinously bunched.

Soon after that, Will was called to see Koryfos. Maxim Hough came in through the glass doors from the carrier with his arm bandaged and sat down next to me. "People!" he said. "Can you believe this? The Southampton Convention committee have just asked me where I hired the soldiers and the troop carriers. They want them for their con too! And that idiot Punt keeps getting himself thrown off both carriers. I suppose he's harmless. But he must be the nosiest man in this world. He's going to live in my mind as part of a con I shall never forget!"

"Bad memories?" I asked. I felt responsible, particularly for his arm.

"Well," Maxim said, considering, "I've never seen anyone die before. Perhaps one should. It's part of life, after all. But if you had told me a week ago that any of this could happen at a convention, I'd have laughed in your face."

"I didn't know it was going to happen," I protested.

Here my brother Simon came up and said I was needed. I got up and followed him out of the glass doors and up the enormous, clanging ramp to the entry near the front of the carrier. Inside, it was all rather like a submarine. There were lots of narrow metal passages with curt groups of letters and numbers stencilled at every corner in various colours, colour-coded, I gathered. Simon took me by the red codes, deep into the murmuring heart of the great vehicle, and finally to a little steel cubby-hole open at one side of a corridor. We sat on a narrow steel bench at the end of it. The bench was designed, I think, to keep a sentry awake. It was certainly darned uncomfortable.

"Waiting room?" I said.

"After a fashion," said my brother and sprawled his legs, robes and all. Simon is the most restless man I know. He looks more like Will than me, since he is tall and sturdy, but fairer than both of us, with sharp cheekbones. "I wanted to have a word with you first, because I seem to have got pitchforked into a business that ought to be yours."

"Yes, how *did* you get mixed up in it?" I said.

"Zinka phoned me in the middle of last night," Simon said. "And I'd been getting a feeling anyway that you, or Will, were in a bit of trouble. So, as she'd woken me up, I thought I might as well come here and see what I could do. And I was in transit and quite near the Empire when I came across a centaur and somebody who was obviously Koryfos the Great, blundering about on a hillside, not quite sure whereabouts in the Empire they needed to go. Things had changed a bit since Koryfos was last there. So I took them in tow and led them along to Iforion and then found myself having to organize the restoration of Koryfos as Emperor."

"As was Intended," I said.

"I'm afraid so," Si said, tossing legs and robes about as he sat. "I need to talk to you because of that. I seem to have got your job with the Koryfonic Empire now. Sorry about that. Koryfos will tell you about how it happened. But there's no doubt that that's Intended too. The Upper Room has been in touch. You'll be getting confirmation from Senior Magid any time now. She'll be confirming that, and that you've selected Maree Mallory as the newest Magid."

"I hadn't actually quite—" I began.

"The Upper Room seems quite clear that you have," said Si. "They say you can sponsor her, but they want her to come to the Empire for now so that I can teach her."

My stomach sank. "In other words," I said dismally, "I'm being relieved of all my responsibilities, pending reprimand. Am I suspended for incompetence, or something else?"

"It's not really like that." Simon surged to his feet,

having sat still for actually slightly longer than he usually did. "You talk to them," he said, roving around in front of me, "and you'll see. I think they may even be slightly ashamed of themselves—anyway, they were discussing giving you something slightly easier after this."

"Like a violently science-ridden world Naywards of here," I said bitterly.

Simon paused in his roving and tried to pick some of the trim off the doorway of the cubby-hole. It was firmly fixed, so he left it and roved about again. I knew that if he had got it loose he would have played with it for an hour and then tried to weave it into the ceiling grating. I smiled, in spite of my growing depression. It was good to see Si again. "No. Don't talk nonsense," he said. "You see, what seems to have gone on is that they were Intending to work the Empire round to the point where all the prophecies said Koryfos would return, and as far as they knew, that meant more or less destroying it first. Koryfos says he doesn't think that was right, but there you go. The Upper Room do this sometimes. Anyway, Will says and Rob says that *you* thought they Intended to get the Empire saddled with a boy Emperor and then let it collapse around him. Rob's sure you worried about that and tried to keep Nick away from Dakros because you were so worried. But in actual fact, Rupert, *you* were the Upper Room's boy Emperor yourself. *You* were the one it was supposed to all fold up around."

"Thank you *very* much!" I said.

"Well, you *have* only been a Magid for just over two years," Si said. "I think you've done damn well, considering you had the Upper Room working against you most of the way. I think it's only thanks to you encouraging Dakros that there's still an Empire for Koryfos to rule, frankly."

"I haven't done well," I said. "I can see any world that's offered me as Magid in charge in future screaming, 'No! Not *R. Venables*! Anyone but R. Venables! He lets all those people die! He lets children get their throats cut!'"

"They Intended that," my brother said. "You know how

334

ruthless they can be. They're not going to blame you for that, or let it give you a bad name. They're fair, as well as ruthless. I think they're really quite pleased with you."

"So why aren't they letting me instruct Maree?" I said.

"Oh that's different." Simon came and plunged down on to the bench again. "They wouldn't let *me* instruct Zinka— Zinka says I just confused her with long explanations anyway. They never let you teach someone you're married to, and they seem sure you're likely to marry Maree—"

"Hang on," I said. "Are you and Zinka *married*?"

"These last three years," Si said, grinning merrily. "It's nice."

"But—" I said, in some consternation.

"I know what you're thinking," he said. "She may draw sexy pictures of alien life forms, but I make damn sure it's only Art."

"Sure," I said, though that was not what I had in mind at all.

Luckily, Will came striding down the corridor just then and fetched up with a clang against the cubby-hole doorway. "Family reunion," he said. "Wow, that was an interview and a half! Koryfos seems to think I reformed Rob overnight."

"Well you did shout a few home truths at him," I said. "Rob needed someone to do it." I stood up nervously. "Does he want to talk to me yet? Or not?"

"Oh yes," said Will. "Show him, Si. I'll wait for you here."

Simon showed me up the rest of a short passage to a steel door heavily stencilled in red. It slid aside to let me in and slid closed again behind me, shutting me in a big steel box with the almost overwhelming presence of my one-time neighbour.

He was sitting on a bench rather like the one I had just left, but he got up to meet me. "Forgive me keeping you waiting so long, Rupert," he said. "I wanted to get the other things sorted out so that I could talk to you properly."

He had somehow contained his kingliness, pushed it

down to a more domestic level, but he was still not an ordinary man. You know how thunderclouds produce those shining white towers above the main cloud, full of energy? What he was showing me was like that, a smaller energy pile above the main one. Being in the same room with a thunderhead is a fairly stunning experience.

I was feeling fairly dejected one way and another. I said, "Thanks."

He smiled at me, in the way that had always astonished me. This time it astonished me by making me feel more like a viable human being again. "I want to thank you," he said.

"I don't understand why," I said. "A bit of driving. A tin of beans and a bag of sugar or so . . ."

"Yes, but you see you did those kindnesses to a person who was, on a rough estimate, only a twentieth part of me," he said. "Most people would have avoided me as plain mad. Let me explain.

"At the end of my last reign, I was in your world, in a city called Babylon which no longer exists, trying to negotiate an alliance with the ruler there. The ruler refused any kind of treaty, so I meant to leave. But the Babylonians attacked as I left with my party and the Magid with us tried to open a gate for us in too much of a hurry. And he accidentally opened it right through me."

I was glad to hear that some Magids besides me made mistakes. "You were stripped?"

He nodded. "And assumed dead, and buried on both sides of the gate. That area, as you know, is a mass of nodes. The gate had been opened at a node. The stripping was very violent and it took me a good many years to come round from it. When I did, I found I was having practical experience of part of your Babylon secret. Changes had occurred in the worlds on both sides and worlds had divided and multiplied. As I had been buried at the point of division, I had multiplied also." He laughed slightly, making the room electric. "There were ten of me in normal

Infinity and another ten existing as anti-matter. I've spent all this time trying to come together again."

"But I don't see how you—" I began. Koryfos shook his head slightly and I stopped.

"This is where you come in," he said. "I was always, without understanding why, trying to settle near a Magid. I had a sense that Magids knew something about nodes that I didn't and that I needed a node to help me in some way. You would hardly believe how many times, in this world and in others, I achieved proximity to a Magid, only to have that Magid realize that there was something strange about me and move away in a hurry."

"I moved in after you, in Weavers End," I said. "You'd been there six months when I bought my house. That was pure luck."

"Maybe," he said, "but it was not pure luck that you were unfailingly kindly and helpful. You drove me to one node after another, even though neither of us knew what we were doing, until you brought me to the extremely powerful node here in Wantchester. And I would not have understood how to use this node, any more than any of the others, if you had not happened to include me in your fateline working."

"How *did* that happen?" I said.

"I sensed the working," he said. "I always sensed any powerful working and I always came along to them, like a hungry animal, not knowing what I needed. Every Magid before you promptly turned me out. You let me stay. And I half consciously linked my fateline in as you worked. Believe me, it was like a revelation. Quite suddenly I felt and knew four times as much. I knew I had to come to this powerful node here and I knew what to do when I got here. For nearly three days, I was collecting the other parts of myself. I'm afraid I disturbed the node somewhat."

"Yes, you did rather," I said. "But other people were at it too. And you got all the pieces?"

"No," he said. "Some were dead, and those who had become anti-matter were impossible to reach on this plane of Infinity. In order to become complete, I found I had to go outside the material planes entirely, to the place that is another part of your Babylon secret. No doubt this was Intended. For while I was on my way there, I encountered three heirs to the Empire and learnt more or less what was going on there. Rob came with me. He asked for his birthright, you know. He said that you and your brother had made him ashamed to be without it. He told me a great deal on the way back."

I couldn't help smiling. "Our Rob likes to talk. So you'll be followed by a line of centaurs as Emperor? Good idea. Centaurs have never been the force they should be in any world."

"I'm glad you agree," Koryfos said. "But I feel I have deprived you of your office. Rob and I got lost on the way back. We were trying to do two incompatible things, trying to get home and to find you. And we found your brother instead. The Powers Above promptly installed your brother as our adviser instead of you."

"Si's a good deal more competent than me," I said ruefully. "He seems to have got you recognized as Emperor in no time at all."

"He knew just what to do, certainly," said Koryfos. "And he tells me that he is Intended to become Magid to the Empire from now on. But I would have preferred you. Your brother's habit of striding about and fiddling with things perturbs me."

"You mean even you can't make him sit still!" I exclaimed.

"I doubt if anyone could," Koryfos admitted. "It seems to be part of the way your brother functions."

. I could not help smiling. Nothing is ever perfect. Koryfos was obviously an exceptional man, but all the same . . . All the same, one thing about Koryfos was plain impossible. "How is it," I asked him, "that you managed to get stripped so often and still be alive after more than two thousand years?"

He looked at me with his golden head tipped to one side and a slight smile on one corner of his mouth. In that pose, he looked exactly like all the statues of himself. He answered me with a question that shook me to the core. "How many members of the Upper Room are there?"

"You know I can't tell you that!" I said. "You shouldn't even know there *is* an Upper Room!"

"Precisely," he said. "So I will tell *you*. There are presently seventy-one. There should be seventy-two, but there are not, because I am missing."

"Oh!" I said. No one but an Archon could have Koryfos's sort of vitality, or choose a centaur as his heir, for that matter. "Then greetings, great Archon."

"Greetings to you too, Magid," he replied. "I had to come here to do something that would stop Infinity drifting entirely Naywards. The Empire was supposed to do that. But I had not established it properly when I was stripped. I must now finish what I started. Because of this, can I ask you to do two things for me?"

"Probably," I said. "As a neighbour, or as a Magid?"

"One of each," he said. "Sadly, I must desert my house and my inventing. Would you, Magid, consent to become the owner of my house, to look after or to sell as you see fit?"

I thought of my quacks and Maree's notion of me standing in Andrew's pond and I was filled with pleasure. His house is bigger than mine too. "I'd be delighted. What was the other thing?"

"I would like," he said, "if it is not too difficult, that when you make your report for the Upper Room, you give a copy to me for the archive I shall found in Iforion."

I considered. He was asking me something much dodgier here. I could see by his head-on-one-side hopeful look that he knew perfectly well he was. It is not just that the Upper Room do not like the reports of Magids to go anywhere but to them: they also take steps to make sure of this. It would take a bit of contriving to get round their usual methods. And I would need to add a few explanations for lay readers. Still, it could probably be done. It could be regarded as a challenge. "Yes, all right," I said. "But don't be too disappointed if you don't get it."

"I have every faith in you," he said.

Our interview was over with that. He gave me a strong, electrical handshake and I wandered forth into the metal passageways again. Will and Simon seemed to have gone from the cubby-hole. I walked on, with the steel resonating faintly around me, to the entrance and down the great ramp. I did not feel like going back into the hotel. I went to the staff car park instead, thinking of how to tell Stan about all this.

I unlocked the bent driver's door on the faintest tinkle of Scarlatti. "Stan?" I said.

There was nothing. No one. My tape-deck was still going, but the car inside was without a presence. Stan had gone. The Upper Room, with customary brusqueness, had decided that Stan's job was now done and recalled him. I rested my forehead against the roof of the car, near tears.

"I don't know whether your car or mine is more of a mess," Maree said, with the gloomy sob prominent in her voice. "If you think this is bad, you should see what Janine did to mine."

I looked up to find her with her chin resting on the other side of the roof. "I thought you'd gone to the Empire!"

"Not yet. Not permanently," she said. "I stuck out for going twice a week for lessons, and I'm not seeing that other brother of yours until the end of this week anyway. And I've made it clear that it's not going to interfere with my vet's degree. No way. Otherwise . . ."

"Otherwise?" I said.

"There's all this week and then a lot of time round the edges," she said.

"Yes," I said. "Isn't there." I felt a great deal better.

TWENTY-FIVE

Nick Mallory   Upperom Doc
Printout for R. Venables

[1]

Rupert wanted me to write this. He said it was for something called the Upper Room. He said they needed a full report and he was having to make one as well, and would I mind very much? Even they don't know the things about Babylon that I do. They wanted it for their records. Kind of a debriefing, he said.

I didn't much want to. I don't like writing things and when I try to think about Babylon I sort of think I don't know what happened. I tried to get Rupert to bribe me to do it at first. I know he's been transferred to a project in another set of worlds now, and it sounds *fantastic* and I said I'd do a report if he would tell me what he was doing now. But he wouldn't. Well, it was worth a try. He told me to do it anyway.

Anyway I started. It was difficult at first, but then there was a breakthrough and it got quite easy. That part is on the rest of this disk. *This* part is the bit I'm adding to the disk I'm giving Rupert and copying to the one for Maree to take to Koryfos. Koryfos really seems to want it.

When I'd done the report I copied it on all the disks I'd got. I'd got quite a lot. I can't get used to having so much *money*. I do things wrong, like buying a hundred ready-formatted disks and forgetting that what I really want is a modem. The money is because my mother didn't make a will and I count as her next of kin, and Gramos Albek *did* make a will, leaving everything to Mum. So I got the clothes business *and* the arms factory. I haven't got the factory yet. Rupert and Dad are doing stingy stuff about setting up a Trust for that, but they sold the clothes shop to Mrs. Fear, who used to run it really anyway, and now I have an allowance in the Post Office and humongous amounts in a building society and money to burn. I said I didn't think it was fair on Maree or Dad, but Dad says he has his pride and his books do bring in a pittance after all. Maree says she wouldn't touch anything belonging to those two with a bargepole as long as the Cabot Tower. But I think Maree's all right for money. Koryfos has given her some kind of estate over there. She says she and Rupert are having fun laundering the money so that she can use it on Earth.

We persuaded Dad that there was enough money to pay someone to do the cooking. Maree can't, Dad won't learn, and I only know spaghetti. So Dad goes and gets Mrs. Fear's sister Yvonne, because she was the last person Mum sacked from the shop. This is carrying charity too far. Yvonne cooks worse than Maree. I spend £100 a week buying food I like instead. What I mean is that there is money for things. I bought all these ready-formatted disks. I put my report on all of them and then hid the disks in all sorts of different places before Maree drove me over to Rupert's place in her new car.

Rupert's house is quite small, but it's really good inside. You should just see his roomful of computers and the sound system in his living room. They're trying to persuade my Uncle Derek (Maree calls him her as-it-were-Dad these days) to move in there. Maree and Rupert want to live in the bigger house just along the road where the pond is, as soon as Maree's qualified, but that won't be for a while yet, and she wants Rupert to keep an eye on my as-it-were-uncle. I think Uncle Derek is too independent-minded for that. If he stays in London, *I* shall buy Rupert's house. I really like it.

When we got there, his latest lot of quack chicks had just hatched. You couldn't go in the kitchen for fear of treading on them. The Lady Quack always nests under the sink. Lord Quack comes in through the cat flap Rupert's put in the back door for them, and then goes out again in a hurry when all the chicks rush at him. He came and sat in the living room with us while we had lunch. Rupert is a really good cook. I wish he'd give Yvonne some lessons.

When we'd finished eating, Rupert said, "Ready, you two?" and when we said yes he told me to have my printout ready and to hold it in my hand. Then he said, "Whatever you may *think* happens, you must remember that you're never really going to leave this room where we are."

I keep wondering why he said that. I had a sort of feeling that it was what he was supposed to say to outsiders (meaning me). And I don't believe it was true. Magids seem to have to lie quite a lot. I like that, personally. I know that when we'd finished it was hours later and my feet ached from having to stand up all that time. But we started by sitting round in three chairs facing the bookcases and the sound system.

After a while, though nothing much had changed, Rupert said, "Right," and got up and went to the bookcase. He swung a piece of it back like a door. Inside there was a foggy-looking staircase. "Follow me," he said, and started to climb up it. It was wooden and it creaked. Maree went next. She was very nervous. You can always tell when Maree's nervous because she looks extra fierce and gloomy and keeps pushing up her specs and blinking. I went last, and I wasn't nervous at all at that point.

The stairs went up and up and round in a spiral for quite a long time. After about half the climb, I realized that we'd already gone higher than Rupert's house by a long way. I got *very* interested. And the higher we climbed, the foggier the stairs got, until everything was sort of milky—or just a bit like a film negative—but the stairs were still made of wood. They still creaked. I could smell the dusty wood-smell of them and I *know* they were as real as I am. It was quite warm, too, and that made the wooden smell stronger.

When I reckon we had climbed at least as high as the top of the church spire in the next village, or maybe higher, we suddenly came under an open arched doorway, on to a bare wooden floor made of very wide boards that creaked worse than the stairs. And I saw we were in the Upper Room. It was pretty big, but I never saw how big, even though I could see the walls and see that they were plain and whitewashed, because it was all the same milky, film-negative whiteness as the stairs. The people there were like that as well. There were lots of them. Half of them were sitting against the wall on benches that looked built in there, and the other half were sitting in chairs round an enormous wooden table that filled most of the room. They seemed to stretch off into the distance. I could see the ones up the other end bending forward or leaning right back in their chairs to look at us.

It was odd, with these people. You got the feeling they were from all different times and places, even though they all dressed the same. Some of them had the kind of faces you only see in very old paintings. And there were two kinds of them. I can't describe how I knew that. It had nothing to do with where they were sitting or how they looked. I just knew that some of them had been alive once and some of them never had.

The only one who wasn't sitting down was a little man with a half-bald head and rather bandy legs, who came skipping up to Rupert, grinning all over his face. He was as real as everything else. Rupert bent down and hugged him and then kissed him on both sides of his face like a European politician. I thought the little man must be French or Russian or something. Then he started speaking and I recognized the croaky voice. He was the ghost who was in Rupert's car. Even then I wasn't nervous, though Maree was, worse and worse. It was so warm and quiet there.

"I've given my evidence already, lad," the little man croaked. "I'm staying on to confirm yours."

"Great," Rupert said. I thought he was a bit nervous too. "I was afraid I wasn't going to see you again. You remember Nick and Maree, don't you? This is Stan."

We shook hands. It was all normal, except that Stan croaked, "Pleased to meet you face to face, if you see what I mean."

Then Rupert sort of ushered us all forward to the end of the table. There was no one sitting at that end. It was wide enough for us all to stand in a row along it. Even in the milkiness, I could see that the table was thick black oak, and under our feet, where we were standing, the floorboards were worn in a dip from other people standing there.

And then suddenly I was nervous. It was all those faces, all looking. I could see Maree shaking. Stan patted my arm. I looked down on the top of his head, half bald, half curly grey hair, and it made me feel a bit better. But those faces. Some of them were—well, like Koryfos. Even the normal ones looked like judges do without their wigs on television. You know the way they have mouths that don't seem to smile in the same way as normal people's. And it made it worse that they were all rather hard to see in the milkiness.

Rupert said, "Magids and Archons of the Upper Room, may I sponsor to your presence Sempronia Marina Timosa Euranivai Koryfoides, as the latest Magid of our number?"

Now I knew why Maree was so nervous. I had noticed she was wearing smart clothes, whatever she says, but I'd thought they were just because she was meeting Rupert. She always dresses up for him. I hadn't realized it was her day for being sponsored. She bowed.

Someone halfway up the table, a man with a dry sort of voice, asked her if she felt ready to be a Magid, and she pushed at her glasses and more or less snapped, "As ready as I'm ever going to be."

Then they started asking her all sorts of questions. It was an oral exam really. And I can't say anything about the questions. I heard them quite clearly at the time, but they seem to have arranged to have them all blurred in my mind when I try to think what was asked—rather like what I thought had happened over Babylon. But Maree did quite well answering. Everyone asked her things, but the chief askers were halfway up the table on both sides. I think that's where the important ones sat.

And I can't say anything about the next bit either, because Maree says she'll kill me if I do. I know she *could* kill me too, but she says how to do it is a deep secret. She'll let me say that what she had to do next was a sort of ceremony of magic, like the Tea Ceremony in Japan, and that's all. That was because she went wrong in the middle. She had to go back three stages and do it again from there. But I was impressed at what she could do. And envious. I can't make light in the shape of the Infinity sign float over my head. I've tried.

She finished properly in the end. One of the people on the benches came and gave her a bundle of robes like the ones they were all wearing, and she put them on and went all milky like they were. That frightened me. It was so like when she was stripped. Stan saw and patted my arm again. Then they told her by all her names that she was now a Magid. She stopped looking nervous and she beamed, all white and foggy.

After that it was Rupert's turn. He was really nervous by then. He had gone stringy-faced. One of the ones in the middle of the table asked if he had made a full report "of Koryfos, the heirs of Koryfos and the matters associated." He said he had. And he laid a thick bundle of papers on the end of the table. I couldn't help trying to read the first page, but all I saw in the milkiness was the first line. That said: "About a year ago, I was summoned to the Empire capital, Iforion, to attend a judicial enquiry." I think he's done what I did and added some more later.

All the faces turned to the papers. There was a long, long, thoughtful sort of pause. It was rather horrible. Rupert got out a handkerchief and wiped at his face.

Then, all at once, they seemed to know all about what he'd said in the papers, and they began asking him about it. Really hard questions. Did he know the Emperor was going to beam Timotheo? Did he even suspect it? Why had he taken such a casual attitude to the Empire and its affairs? Was he acquainted with the nature of the bush-goddess? Had he looked her up in the Magid database? On and on.

Rupert explained what he'd done and his reasons, carefully each time. Sometimes he even defended himself, but he didn't make nearly such a good job of it as I would have done. I kept thinking of excuses he could have made. Twice I made excuses for him. Maree and I both chipped in when they asked why he had let us go after him to Thule and then Thalangia. Maree got really angry, the second time.

"We made sure he didn't know a thing about it," she said. "We only followed him because Rob was hurt and couldn't take us. Damn it, how else were we going to find the way? You can't just sit there and blame him for something *we* did!"

I expected them to get angry with her for that, but they were quite polite. Someone right down the end of the table that I couldn't really see said, "My dear, there's no need to get so heated. We are not *blaming* the Magid. We are trying to find out truly how and why these things happened."

"You could have fooled me!" Maree said. Some of them even laughed.

But that didn't stop the questions.

After a while I realized why Rupert was not making excuses. Every time he explained something truthfully, in a way that seemed to clear things up, it *was* cleared up. The pages they were asking the question about just sort of filtered away from the end of the table. I noticed it first when Stan was croaking out about some of the advice he had given Rupert. Quite a chunk of pages vanished after Stan had finished. But if the people were not satisfied, the pages stayed there. Sometimes they even spread out in a row along the end of the table. This happened when they were asking why Rupert didn't prevent the murders on the top of the hill. And I began to see that if you didn't tell these people what happened and why, exactly honestly, you were going to have to stand there for days—weeks maybe—until you did. Around then, I started wondering if it was as much fun being a Magid as I'd thought.

The pages spread out again when they were asking about Babylon. They were *really* interested there. To begin with the questions were the important sort of things you'd expect, like, why had Rupert sent all three Empire heirs to Babylon? (you know, I hadn't realized he had!), and, had he considered what he was doing? Did he know how few people came back? Had he attended to the rhyme, where it said this?

Rupert suddenly cracked. "No I *didn't*!" he said. Well, he almost shouted really. "It was the only way I knew to get Maree back! I felt as if I'd just been stripped myself, if you must know!"

Nobody said anything. The pages just gathered themselves back into the pile, and they started asking other questions, much calmer, detailed sort of questions. The things they wanted to know surprised me. Had the flock of goat's wool disappeared? Rupert went calm again and said it had, and so had the bottles of water and our clothes. And could he say more what the landscape looked like? He said he couldn't. Then they asked about the quacks. They were really interested in them. Nothing like that had ever happened before, they said, and could Rupert account for the way the quacks came back as mature birds? He said he couldn't, but they weren't just mature, they were clever now. Quacks are normally rather stupid birds, he said. And Maree spoke up and said *she* thought the quacks had dimly known they were foolish and hadn't liked the idea. But how had the quacks managed to ask for what they needed? someone along the benches wanted to know.

Maree said, "We haven't the faintest idea. They got there long before we did. And I don't know how that happened any more than I know why I was so long after Nick coming back."

At that, that chunk of pages vanished, but slowly, as if the people were regretting not knowing more, and they went on to the last part and asked about when Dakros appeared. I hadn't known Rupert was worrying about me so much. I'd have told him not to. I can get out of most things.

Then all the pages were gone. Rupert looked nervous again. A lady right near our end of the table said to him, "Didn't you realize Charles Dodgson was a Magid? I thought that was quite generally known."

Rupert was just going to say something to her, when a man further up the table waved at him for attention and said, "You're not quite right about the Roman augurs, you know. They were mostly pretty stupid. I was actually the chief surveying engineer, and I often had real trouble persuading the blessed augurs to let me put the camp on the node. There were at least three sites where they forced me to miss it. It still annoys me. I wanted you to know it wasn't my fault."

Rupert laughed and said, "Thanks!"

After that there was a bit of a pause, full of wood creaking and robes rustling. Then the dry-voiced man leant forward from his place halfway along the table and asked, "What is your assessment of your performance, Magid?"

"Pretty awful," Rupert said. "If I *could* make a mistake, I *did*. Sometimes I think I invented new mistakes to make. And I don't think I'll ever forgive myself for the deaths of those children."

Long silence.

Then I heard the person I couldn't see in the distance. He had a voice you remember though. He said, "Not that bad, Magid. Until today, you were the youngest Magid among us, and we were guilty of throwing you into the midst of one of our riskier and more tangled Intentions. To tell the truth, we expected you to go to pieces. The most we can blame you for is that you were often too pleased with the workings you were able to perform, and did not always remember *why* you were performing them. All of us have felt the same in our time. Archon or human, we have all once been new to our abilities. We now hope you will accept some less arduous assignments for the next year or so, in order to profit by and assimilate what you have learnt on this one."

"I hope so too," Rupert said. I could see he really meant it.

Then it was my turn. Rupert had explained to me that, because I wasn't a Magid, I was going to have to read my report aloud. I still don't quite understand why. He said things about the Upper Room wanting to respect my integral autonomy. Or something. Anyway, all the faces turned to me. I held up my print-out to read it. And I hadn't any voice at all. What came out was huskier than Stan's, and I had to push to get that much out. I had to cough hard. I could feel my knees shaking. The edges of the papers fluttered like mad moths.

"Come on. No one's going to eat you, lad," Stan said.

"That's right," Maree added in. "They've just consumed Rupert. They're not hungry any more."

"Er—*hum!*" I went. I felt a fool. Then I did read it out.

(2)

"The first part of the way was not too bad. We could have got on quite quickly if Maree hadn't been so slow and weak. I had to hold her up by her elbow and pull her along. It was quite easy to see the road. It was very stony, and all the stones were faintly lit up from one side as if the moon was shining on them from somewhere, but when I looked round the way the light was coming from, there was nothing. The sky was dead grey-black. I couldn't see much of the land around. But I could hear it. There must have been dead grass growing all over, because it rustled faintly all the time, in gusts, as if there was a wind blowing across it, only there was no wind. It was the kind of dead, warm calm that makes you sweat a lot. And there was a smell coming off the land that made me think there must be acres of peaty bog out there.

"The way looked quite simple when I was standing in the hotel room looking out at it, but when you got out there it was all ups and downs. It was really hard, getting Maree along it. When we'd got over the first big hill and down into the valley beyond, it began to get to me. It was the way you couldn't see anything except the road curving about in front, and all the rustling, with no wind to make it. Then, in the bottom of that valley, the road broke up. It was suddenly all big stones, and boulders with sharp corners and sides. I think it was an old riverbed. There was no water, but I could just make out the dry dip winding through the valley on both sides of us, choked with these big rubbly stones. And on our left were square stone lumps and a bit of curving stone that looked like an old broken bridge. Something had destroyed it. We had to clamber about beside it.

"While we were crawling through this bit, Maree seemed to get very eager. She began to struggle around with excitement. I didn't know what to do with her. I supposed she was anxious to get on, but I didn't know really, and suddenly everything got to me and I wanted to scream. She was like someone mentally handicapped. I started thinking that maybe the road was destroyed worse than this further on, and maybe what destroyed it was waiting for *us*, and there was only me to keep Maree safe and get her along it, and I didn't think I could. I'd never been in charge of someone this way before. And the two of us were utterly alone. I realized I had a very bad feeling about this trip.

"But I had to get Maree to the end somehow, so I sort of squished my mind back together and kept on pulling at Maree, and we got across the dead river and up the next hill somehow.

"After that it wasn't so bad, mostly because Maree began to be more like a person. She still wasn't speaking very well, but as we went winding over more ups and downs, she sort of chanted, 'Up and down, up and down, all the way to London town. On and on, on and on, all the way to Baby*lon*.' And when I asked her what *that* meant, she

said, 'Skipping rhyme. You do bumps on the "*lon*." ' I
didn't know what she was on about. Then she said, 'Did
you put anything like this in Bristolia?'

"I said, 'It's a bit like the Unformed Lands.'

"She said, 'Talk about it.'

"So I talked about Bristolia all through the next bit, and
I felt a lot better, and then we were suddenly coming down
a long slope towards another river.

"There was water in this one. I could see it glinting.
Otherwise it was dead black. It was enormously wide and,
from the way the glints rushed along, it was flowing really
fast. There was a huge long bridge over it. I could see the
bridge faintly lit up like the road, arching away into distance. The near end had tall sort of gateposts on either side
that seemed to be carved into statues. When we got nearer,
I could just pick out that the statues were creatures with
wings. But I never saw them clearly. By the time we were
near enough to see, the whole gateway and the path in front
of the bridge turned out to be in black shadow.

"We had just walked into the shadow—and it was cold
in there—when the statue on the left spoke. That gave me
such a fright that I thought for the moment I might pass
out. It had a big hollow voice, a bit like the noise you make
when you blow across the top of a milkbottle, and it said,
'Halt! In the name of the maker of forms!'

"Then the one on the right spoke too and said, 'Halt! In
the name of the maker of force!'

"And I thought at first that both of them spread out a
wing to block the way on to the bridge. But when I looked
closely, it was more like a grille, in spidery, feathery
shapes, like the crystals you get in rocks. I pushed at it,
and it felt dead cold—and it wouldn't budge.

"Then someone else came and looked at us through the
middle of the grille. I never saw him clearly, but he was
pretty terrifying. He said, in a sharp, cold voice, 'What do
you think you're doing here?'

"My teeth were trying to chatter by then. I bit them together and said, 'We need to get to Babylon.' And I backed away pretty quickly.

"He said, 'You can't get to Babylon as you are. Turn back.'

" 'No,' I said, 'I can't go back because of Maree. What do we need so that you'll let us through?'

"I swear he smiled. He said, sort of amused, 'Much less than you've got, or a certain amount more."

"I couldn't see how we could have much less, so I said, '*What* certain amount more?'

" 'You'll have to go back and ask the ones who sent you for that,' he said.

" 'Oh God!' I said. 'Look, isn't there any chance of you letting us through as we are?'

" 'No,' he said. 'Go back and ask for another verse.'

" 'All right then,' I said. I was annoyed and in a panic, because the candles would be burning down, and Maree was so *slow*. 'Then I'll have to leave Maree here while I go back,' I said, 'or we'll be all night. You won't hurt her while I'm gone, will you?'

"He was furious that I thought he might hurt Maree—I could tell, sort of feel it raging through the grille at me like cold wind. 'Nothing will touch her,' he said scornfully. 'Go away.'

"So I made Maree sit down just outside the shadow where it was warmer, and I wasted a lot of time telling her to stay there and not to wander away, and then getting her to *promise* she wouldn't move from the spot. In the end she said, 'You run. I'm fine,' as if she'd understood after all.

"So I turned round and ran. That part, going back, was awful. I hated being all alone, and I was scared stiff Maree would wander off, and I kept thinking how this was wasting the candles, and I was afraid I wouldn't see the hotel room and go straight past it or something. I went as fast as I could, but I had to go slower after I twisted my ankle down in the dead river. And in some ways I remember it as endless. Yet at the same time it was over quite quickly. It was really only a few minutes before I saw a spreading, winking light at the top of the hill in front, and when I was down at the bottom of this hill, I saw that the light was two of the candles. They looked surprisingly big from there.

"I went panting up that hill and there I was, inside the room again.

"They looked pretty stunned to see me. I could tell Rupert thought at first that we'd *been* to Babylon and Maree hadn't come back. So I told them how they wouldn't let us across the bridge without something more. Rupert kind of sagged with relief that that was all it was.

"He wants me to tell what happened while he was off fetching Zinka.

"Not a lot, at first. I went round to the three-cornered space by the bed. I meant to sit on the bed beside Rob, but I was so impatient that I just kept walking up and down and fidgeting with the bottles on the fridge and so on. Rob went up on one elbow and watched me anxiously. Will said to sit down, I was disturbing the quack chicks, but I couldn't. So they began running about and cheeping, and I think Rob caught the restlessness too, because he sat up and slid his hooves to the floor and asked me what it was like out there.

"Rob is someone I can talk to. There aren't many other people, bar Maree, that I can tell real stuff to, but Rob's always going to be one. I've been over to see him quite a lot since all this happened and we've talked of *everything*. (Rob wants to come to Bristol to see me, but we know he'd cause a bit of a sensation there.) This time I told him a bit of what I've put down here, mostly about being down in the stones of the dry river, because it was the worst. I didn't say much. I could tell Will just thought, Oh, it's hard going out there, but Rob understood what it was like being all alone with Maree behaving strangely and not being able to *see*.

"Next thing I knew, Rob was out of bed. He said, '*Yowch!*' because his side hurt, and trampled with his

354

hooves and made faces. His face went all white and twisted for a bit. Then he found his shirt and started putting it on.

"Will said, 'What the hell are you doing, Rob?'

"Rob said, 'Getting ready to go to Babylon with Nick. They need my help.'

"'Don't be a damned fool!' Will said. 'You've got one side stitched up. It's hard going. You'd tear it open again. And it's dangerous in other ways.'

"Rob stuck his head up proudly, hair flying all over, and said, 'Bother the danger!' He said he owed it to Maree. She'd stitched him up and he'd lured her into getting stripped in return. And Will said, really very snidely, I thought, that oh yes, Rob had gone from worm to hero in one bound, and why didn't he stop posing and lie down? And Rob more or less roared, 'I am *not posing!*' After that they really yelled at one another and the chicks got pretty frightened.

"I didn't say anything. I wanted Rob along. It was a real relief to think I'd have company, as long as Rob could stand it. And I could see his wound was beginning to feel easier as he trampled about shouting. In the midst of it, Rob whirled round on me and asked if I had a piece of string. I found a rubber band in my pocket. Rob took it and put his hair back in it. For a second it looked exactly like a horse's mane, until the rubber band snapped and his hair all came tumbling round his face again.

"Rob twiddled the broken rubber in his fingers gloomily. 'Centaurs always tie their hair back when they're going into battle,' he said.

"Will laughed. That made Rob so mad he turned round and went back to bed again. I was feeling really depressed and wanting to hit Will—only he's bigger than me all over—when Will realized that the door had come open and the quack chicks had run away out into the corridor. Will went leaping after them, swearing a blue streak, and shouted at me to come and help round them up. So I climbed over the candlesticks and went out there.

"The chicks were really frightened. They were running

every which way, and I could have sworn there were at least twenty of them, instead of just the two. And you know how when you're chasing something that small you run all bent over with your arms out like a baboon. Well, I was doing that when I ran slap into Gram White. *Thunk.* I looked up and found Mum was with him.

"I remember thinking, I *wish* she wouldn't go around with him! They don't make a nice pair.

"Mum said, 'Oh, there you are at last, Nick! I want you go come along with me now.'

"I shooed one of the chicks back in round the door and said, 'OK.' I tried to give Will a look under my arm to tell him I wouldn't·be long, but he may not have seen. He was into serious chick-chasing. Then I went along the corridor with Mum and Gram.

"You see, after Maree's parents-as-it-were took her off to London, I was left on my own and I had to work out a way to deal with Mum. I know that sounds unfeeling. But I had to. I used to sit and blame myself about it, and then go on and work it out quite coldly. The week after Maree left I realized I wasn't going to be able to call my soul my own unless I did. Mum wanted me to do everything with her—not *my* things, *her* things—and to tell her everything I was thinking. And she looked through my pockets and read my computer files and all my school exercise books. Another thing about Mum is that she enjoys it if you fight her. Maree always went wrong there, fighting Mum. It gives Mum a real buzz to get you under. But she gets— no, I mean '*enjoyed*' and '*got*,' I keep forgetting—she got bored if you gave her her own way, and even more bored if you told her lots and lots of thoughts and stuff that was not her kind of ideas.

"My very first cold thought after Maree left was: Mum isn't interested in *me*, she's only interested in me *belonging* to her. So I invented Bristolia. She got more and more bored with that, though I got more and more into it. Stupid really. I'd only invented it to cover up other things I wanted to think about. I filled my computer with Bristolia and she

356

very soon stopped looking at it. Then I worked out how not to fight her. I just said OK quite pleasantly whenever she wanted me to do anything with her, and waited until she stopped noticing me and then went away. She almost never checked up on what I was doing. She wasn't interested enough.

"That was what I did that evening. Only they were marching along on either side of me like police and the candles were burning down and Maree was waiting out there, and I was still scared she'd wander off, so I thought I'd hurry it up a bit. I said, 'What did you want me for then?'

"I hope that was not what sent Gram White following after me. It *was* out of character for me. I usually wait quite patiently for Mum to issue her orders once she's found me. But Rupert thinks Gram was after Rob really. Could be. After the fuss and the trail of blood Rob left all through the hotel when he came, *everyone* knew there was a centaur there, even if most of them seemed to think it was me in disguise.

"I could see Mum hadn't actually got any orders. She just wanted me where she could see me. Gram White said, 'We don't want you consorting with those people in that room, young man. They're not nice to know.'

"I said they were harmless in there, only rather boring. I yawned a bit.

"Then Mum said, 'Go to bed, darling. Have an early night. You were up till all hours yesterday.'

"So I said I would go to bed (and I did in the end, didn't I?) and went slouching off. It wasn't hard to look tired after all the pulling at Maree I'd done, and all the running to get back. They stood watching me. I had to go all round all the corners on the top floor. Seven right-angles. I ran as soon as I was out of their sight, but I still only just made it back to Rupert's room before they sent Rob off without me. Rupert says I must have broken a fairly strong compulsion-working in order to come back, but I didn't notice. I think I may have been quite used to breaking compulsions put on me.

"I know it gave me an awful shock when Gram White suddenly came round the corner and shot at Rob. Rob too. Neither of us had ever had anything like that happen to us before. We couldn't wait to get our handfuls of seeds and our candles lit. Then we pushed off at once. I knew the room door was open behind us, and I kept expecting Gram White to come through behind us, shooting. I didn't relax until we were well down the first hill.

"Carrying those candles made a lot of difference. The road was far easier to see. You could even see vague, shivering grass on both sides. And it didn't seem to matter how fast we went. The candles didn't blow out. There wasn't any wind, even from moving. The flames just went straight up. Rob went at a fast walk and I sort of trotted. And in no time at all we were through the dead river and going down towards the bridge where they'd sent me back. I asked Rob if it had seemed a long way and he said no. He was limping a bit, but not badly. It was mostly the stitches dragging, he said.

"When we came down to the bridge, my heart did strange things—sort of hopped up into my throat and then kicked in down in the right place but going like crazy—because I couldn't see Maree. But she was there. She was in the black shadow at the gate, hanging on to the grille with her fingers and talking to the guardian on the other side.

" 'It's the frustration that does it,' I heard her saying. 'Everything went wrong lately.' Then she heard Rob's hooves and turned round slowly, as if she couldn't believe it. 'Rob!' she said. 'And candles! Jack be nimble, Jack be quick, Jack jump over the candlestick. Are they important?' From then on, she was talking almost normally, except that nearly everything she said was peculiar.

" 'Candles, water and a handful of grain with salt,' Rob said.

" 'What about air?' Maree said.

358

" 'Our own breath,' Rob said. Being mage-trained, I suppose he knew better than me what Maree was on about.

"We tried to fix her up with her candle and grain, but she insisted on checking Rob's side first. She said she hoped he wouldn't have to put too much strain on it. But finally we got her to put a bottle of water into her jacket pocket—I took one too—and take the grain and the candle. It was creepy when we lit her candle. She went whiter all over, and a bit luminous, as if the candle was lighting her from inside, not outside.

"When we looked away from Maree, there was no grille across the bridge and no one standing there. Not even the two statues. We shrugged at one another and walked out across the bridge. Rob's hooves didn't make as much noise there as you'd suppose. In fact, everything was nearly noiseless. That big full river rushing below didn't make a sound. The bridge was as broad as a main road and it arched uphill, and it all seemed easy enough until we'd come to the top of the arch and were going down the other side.

"Then it all went weird.

"For a start, the bridge only seemed to be *there* where the candles lit it. Everything was like that from then on. After a while we got used to taking our own lighted space of realness with us, and it was just the way things were, but then, not having seen anything like it before, we were pretty frightened. You looked up, and there was black nothing beyond a few feet of perfectly good road. You had to keep your eyes on the lighted bit. But you couldn't look straight down. The candles spread a ring of shadows round your feet, and the shadows were black nothing too. It was worst underneath Rob's body. He seemed to be walking on an oblong of emptiness. When he saw he was, he braced all his hooves and just stood there, panic all over him. His tail at the end of him lashed. But Maree and I were nearly as bad.

" 'We—we have to keep going,' Rob said at last.

" 'The only way to go on is to go on,' Maree said.

359

"So we got going, creeping along, afraid we were going to go down into the emptiness every next step.

"As if that wasn't enough, there was a feeling from under the lighted part as if the emptiness was waiting for us to fall through. It was an emptiness that was alive. I can't describe it, though I knew it was black and pointed—it was worse than any of Dad's demons. We all knew it was alive. We heard it shifting and creaking and felt cold breathing up from it. It kept level with us under our feet.

"Rob said, sort of inching along sideways, with his teeth shut, 'I don't think I've ever been so frightened in my life.'

" 'Good,' said Maree. 'I've been dying to say that too.'

"I couldn't speak.

"Then it got worse because, the nearer we came to the other side, the more broken up the bridge was. It was in pieces like ice-floes. Down in between the pieces the emptiness waited for us to fall. And we only saw each new piece as our candles came near enough to light it. Some of this was worse for me and Maree, like the time the next floe was a huge stride away, and we had both hands full and couldn't hold on to one another for balance. You just more or less shut your eyes and stepped long and hoped. Some of it was worse for Rob, when the pieces were small and irregularly spaced. He had to sort of tiptoe, hoof by hoof. Once or twice his eyes rolled and I thought he was going to go berserk. But we all managed, piece by piece, and after what seemed miles of it, we saw the carved pillars at the end of the bridge. We went between them and on to firm ground with a rush.

"It was no better there, just different.

"The road we lit up with our candles was really only a path, partly overgrown with gorse bushes or brambles or something, and some of these were taller than Rob. The spines were fierce. Rob had a bad time there, because he couldn't turn sideways like Maree and I could. Then, when there were gaps in the bushes, there was a vicious wind. The candle flames fair roared sideways in it. Even so, the candles never blew out. We gave up trying to shield the flames after a while. It was very awkward anyway with the hand you were trying to use full of grain. Besides, we needed that fist, all of us, to push the thorns back with.

"I can't remember when our clothes disappeared, but they went, shoes and all, at some stage. At first I just felt perishing cold. Then a dirty great bramble went clawing straight across my belly and I realized I was stark naked. Maree was naked too, up in front of me, looking more luminous than ever, and when I looked round, I saw Rob had lost his shirt. I was absolutely freezing by then. I could hear Rob's teeth chattering. Maree was chanting out, 'This is so embarrassing, this is *so* embarrassing!' but actually I thought having no shoes was worst. The stones in the path were sharper than the thorns, and there were dead thorns down there too. It was so awful, I did wonder about turning round and going back, to tell the truth. But I remembered the bridge.

"After an age, the path ran through a sort of clearing in the bushes where the wind was worse than ever. There was something pale there, sort of darting and fluttering at us just ahead. We all saw it at once. I yelled. Maree stopped. Rob nearly gibbered, 'What's *that?*' It looked demonic.

" 'It looks like the week's washing coming for us to kill us!' Maree said. '*Oh!*' And then she went rushing towards the flapping things, crying out, 'This aye night, this aye night!'

" 'What *is* it?' Rob shivered.

" 'Fire and flete and candle-light!' Maree yelled up ahead. 'Come on, idiots, it's *clothes*!'

"We went over there and—well, I know we weren't anywhere ordinary, but I could hardly believe it all the same— the clothes caught on the bushes were Maree's old skirt and sweater, and the jeans and sweatshirt I'd given her to take down to the charity shop. It made me think a bit. Down on the ground were quite a lot of old shoes. There wasn't much point wondering how they'd come there. We stuck our candles in the ground and got into the things one-handed. I used a sharp stone to make a hole in the toes of

361

the biggest pair of trainers. That was so awkward that I didn't care about rhymes and spells any more. I stuffed the grains in my pocket so I could work on the shoes with both hands. Then I realized that my little bottle of water had gone with my other clothes. I looked round to tell Rob, and there he was, shaking all over, with his arms wrapped round his top half, and no clothes in the bushes to help him get warm.

" 'Didn't you ever give away any old clothes?' Maree asked him.

" 'No,' he shivered. 'Knarros made us wear everything until it fell apart.'

" 'Have you still got your pouch?' I asked. 'Will's pouch, I mean.'

"I was going to say that if he hadn't got it, then we'd lost all the water, but he looked at me as if I'd just had the brainwave of the century. 'Of *course*! Thanks!' he said. He got the pouch open and then stuffed his handful of grain inside it and pulled out the lump of goat's wool. He passed me his flaring, streaming candle to hold and tore a piece off the lump. Then he set to work pulling and teasing out that small bit. It kept opening up. In no time, it was big enough to flap about in the wind, but Rob caught the edges down and went on pulling.

" 'Oh, a horse blanket,' Maree said.

"It ended up bigger than that, a fine fluffy thing, like mohair. Rob tied the ends round his neck. Maree told me to spread it right across Rob, down to his tail. So I did, and it clung there. It seemed such a good idea that I took half the rest of the wool and made a sort of shawl with it. Maree said she was warm, but when I touched her, she was icy. I made a shawl for her too. We knotted them round our necks and set off again. I was feeling a whole heap better, but Rob and Maree seemed to get more and more tired from then on.

"That thorny path went on and on. I think it was sloping uphill all the time, but you know how hard it is to tell things like that when all you can see is the little ring of light

362

you're walking in. But when we came to the end of the thorns at last, the way in front was *really* steep. It was all bare rock, eaten into hundreds of spikes and ledges and edges, like a stack of knives. I was surprised Rob could get up it, but he said there was plenty of traction. It was Maree who had trouble with it. She almost couldn't climb it. In the end, Rob stopped and said we'd never get up like this and Maree had better ride on his back.

" 'But it'll hurt you!' we both said.

"Rob knew it would. He answered in the really irritable way you do, when you know you have to do something nasty, 'Put her up on me and don't argue!'

"He held all three candles while I heaved Maree up on to him. It was lucky she had gone so light. I'd never have managed her normal weight. And it did hurt Rob. He stamped and winced and got more irritable than ever. Maree lay down on her face on his back because that seemed to hurt him less. And while I had both hands free, I took the spare bottle of water out of Rob's pouch and put it in my pocket. I was glad I did later.

"Then we went on, toiling up across the sharp edges, until suddenly Rob gave a yell and all his hooves slithered. I thought his side must have torn open again, but it wasn't that. There were three kids standing at the edge of the light, on the other side of Rob from me. I couldn't see much of them except their white, peaky faces. They were just standing there, sort of staring, two youngish boys and a girl. They didn't do anything, but Rob got in a real state.

" 'Oh don't, don't, don't!' he said. 'I always liked you!'

"We were all looking at the kids when birds started coming out of the dark at us. You've no idea how frightening it is, great big birds coming whipping and whirring into your face out of nowhere. They were black birds and white ones. First they dived at us. We shouted and batted them off, so they left us and started trying to peck bits off the three kids. The kids didn't seem to know what to do about it.

"Maree shouted, 'Quick, quick! The grain, the grain!'

And she leant off Rob and scattered some of her handful on the rocks at the kids' feet.

"The birds swooped down on it at once and began fighting one another for it. They behaved as if they were really starving. I was trying to get my grain back out of my pocket when Rob took hold of the plastic bag with the spare grain in it and poured the lot out in front of him. The birds dived on that too. The black ones—they were mottled brown in the candle-light really—threw the grains aside and went for the salt, but the pale birds gobbled down the grain.

" 'Run away. Now, while they're busy,' Maree told the three children. They looked at her as if they didn't understand, but after a bit they backed off into the darkness. They didn't seem with it at all.

"We went on before the birds could get interested in us again. Maree said, 'But we ought to stay and help those poor stupid kids!'

"Rob said, 'There's nothing any of us can do to help them.' He sounded so wretched about it that Maree didn't say any more.

"Beyond that was what felt like half a century of climbing and slithering. At least the wind had died down a bit, but it was still blowing, cold, sudden gusts. None of us got too hot. And at last we came out on what felt like the flat top of a hill. For a few blissful seconds, we thought we had got where we were going. There were what seemed ruined buildings all round us. Then Rob held his candle up beside the nearest ruin, and we saw it was really a weird pinnacle of rock. Very black rock. The path went down to the size of a rabbit run and went winding this way and that among hundreds of these spikes of black rock. Some of them were low—knee-high—and some towered like church spires. And each one was a peculiar shape. Every so often, the path seemed to stop, and we all thought we had arrived at last, but then one of our candles lit a white gleam of it winding away between more of the pinnacles.

"Rob had trouble squeezing through. Maree got down to make it easier for him. She said she was rested, but she looked pretty weak to me. But she went marching ahead, holding her candle high, with the wind gusting the flame to show new black spires each side. The wind made strange sounds in these rocks. At first we thought that was *all* it was. Then the sounds were definitely voices.

"Most of it was just murmuring and mumbling. That was creepy enough. Some of it sounded to be in strange languages. But I nearly jumped out of my skin when someone said, just by my shoulder, 'You won't get away. I'll be waiting for you outside after school.' It seemed like a real threat. But there was no one there.

"After that, we were all hearing voices, but I don't think we heard the same things. Whatever Rob was hearing, it made him try to cover his ears. Candle-grease ran into his hair and his hair sizzled sometimes, but I could see he preferred that to listening. Maree was going along with tears running out from under her glasses. I mostly got more and more annoyed after that first scare. There was one voice that kept saying in a bored, self-satisfied way, 'No need to worry. Consider it done.' It really got up my nose. The worst of it was, it sounded like my own voice. I yelled back once or twice. I yelled, 'Oh, shut up! I do say nice things sometimes!' But it didn't stop. In the end, I was so fed up, I shouted at Rob to tell me what the voices were saying to *him*.

"He turned round as if I was salvation. He shouted back that they were telling him his looks would be ruined if he went on. 'They keep saying I've only got to squeeze between the next gap this side and I'll be home,' he said. At least, I think that was what he said, but my voices kept drowning him out and muddling everything else.

"And it went on, like bedlam, until we wormed between two last pinnacles of rock and the voices, and the wind, just stopped.

"Then there was a long, long straight stretch. Rob and Maree were fine in this bit and they walked side by side, talking. Rob didn't know what to ask for in Babylon, would you believe! He said that Will had made him see he badly needed to ask for *something*, but he couldn't see what. He told Maree some of the things Will had said.

"While they talked, things got to me again. It was the way there was only darkness in front and behind and to the sides. Particularly at the sides. I felt as if I was walking on a tiny ribbon of land with a void all round. That cold, hungry void with sharp points in it that was under the bridge. While Maree was saying tó Rob, 'You sound as if you ought to be asking for a new soul,' I went to the side of the road and held my candle out to see what was there.

"There was nothing there. Truly. There was just an enormous precipice. Like a fool, I went scuttling over to the other side of the road and held my candle out there. And it was just the same. Another precipice. We really were walking along a ribbon in the middle of nothing.

"After that I didn't hear a word Rob and Maree said. They walked along, seriously discussing Rob's soul, and I shuffled after and had the purple shaking-cold nadgers of sheer terror. I was so scared I wanted to get down on my hands and knees and crawl—I *did* crawl coming back— but I was ashamed to crawl in front of Rob and Maree when they didn't mind at all. I didn't feel better until we got to the hanging gardens.

"We called them the hanging gardens almost at once, and I think that is what they were, but they were not at all like you'd expect. The first we knew of them was that we were walking on spongy, tufty stuff that gave off a lemony smell and seemed to sway a little under our feet.

"Maree said, 'Lemon verbena! Nice!'

"The tufty surface went up quite steeply, swaying more and more as we went, and after a bit our candles picked out a tower half buried in growing things. It looked like the rook from a chess set, only easily house-sized. After another bit, there was another tower on the other side, and this one looked like a pagoda made of china. The growing things draped everywhere. The candles lit up flowers and the smell was too sweet, worse than a Body Shop. Then there was a tower on the near side again, like a pyramid

366

with too many steps—or maybe that was one of the later ones. Anyway, after the first three towers, the path was going up nearly vertically and the flowery, scented ground was not just swaying, it was swinging about. By then it was quite obvious somehow that all the towers were tall as lighthouses, with their bottoms way, way down in an abyss, and that the gardens were hung from the towers high in the air. As soon as you realized that, the swinging ground felt really *flimsy*.

"Maree panicked and froze. From then on I had to drag and haul her along. Rob couldn't help me. If he hadn't had hands to pull himself up with, he would have been really stuck. As it was, there were times when his front hooves were on one swinging bit and his back hooves were on another, and he was just helplessly spreading apart. Before long, I was having to help Rob as well as Maree. I took my shawl off and tied it round my waist. Then I hauled Maree up as high as she would go before she started crying and begging me to stop. I tried to park her near one of the towers most times, where the ground didn't swing so much, and then I went back down for Rob. I did that over and over again, one-handed, holding the candle up to see my footing and Rob's. The flower scents kept changing, to sweet, to spicy, to herbal. They made me hot and annoyed. I crunched flowers underfoot to get a purchase while I heaved at Rob, and I lost count of all the towers and the different pretty shapes they were. I just climbed grimly up and down, hauling Maree, parking her, going back down for Rob, until I was exhausted.

"We got to a part that was more open because it was made of thousands of hummocks of pale moss. It was so pale, you could actually see it ahead and to the sides, looking as if it went on forever. It swung about here worse than any part we'd been through. Maree was happier there in spite of the swinging, but Rob was in real trouble. Some of the trouble was that he could see better here and see his hooves being swung apart. Most of it was just the swinging.

"He was doing a really bad spread, with his front hooves

almost under my chin while I hung on to his hand, and his hind hooves right down below, so that he was more or less rearing up, when the whole hillside began swaying, hard.

" *'What's doing it?'* he screamed.

"I suppose I shouldn't have told him. But I was panicked too. I looked down past Rob and I saw a candle lighting the leaves below us into that bright green you get when the colour's too bright on your telly. Whoever was down there was coming up fast, with great leaps, pulling on the plants to help himself up, and that was what was making the swaying. 'Someone else is coming,' I told Rob.

"Rob swore and struggled. We were both sure it had to be an enemy. Rob glanced down over his shoulder and saw the light too. 'I'm no help to you like *this*!' he said, and he tried to jump. His back parts sort of bunched and pushed, but he was sore and stiff from his wound and the bunching just spread him worse than ever. Then his hind hooves slipped on the moss and the entire horse-end of him went right through into the space underneath. In no time he was frantically dangling. He dropped his candle and grabbed for a clump of moss. I saw the candle falling, under the moss, and falling and falling and falling. That was when I knew I had better not let go of his other hand. I sat on his front hooves to anchor them, even though that hurt him, and I hung on like mad to his hand. It was awful. I was so tired anyway that my arms felt like string.

"Maree was a house-height above us. She screamed and came scrambling down. And the person below shouted out, 'What's the matter?'

" 'He's falling *through*!' Maree screamed. *'Help!'*

" 'Hang on!' the man shouted. And he came up like a train, making the mosses surge about worse than ever. By then I didn't care who he was or whether he was friendly, or anything. Rob and I stared at one another by the light of my candle that I'd stuck in the moss so as to hang on with both hands, and I just willed the man to *hurry*.

"Then he arrived and he was the strange man who had worn different clothes in the mirror. I didn't even care about that. I was just glad he was strong. He took one look at Rob, stuck his candle in beside mine and knelt down to grab Rob under the arms. 'You pull too,' he said to me. 'One, two, *three*!' I almost couldn't pull. The man did it all himself really, hauling backwards until he was more or less lying up the slope, while Rob came slowly, slowly, up through the moss, then scrambled and found a purchase with a back hoof and pushed himself. And finally he was out on top.

"For a bit, we were all folded up beside the two candles, panting. Tears were running down Rob's face and Maree was sitting up above us saying, 'Thank you. Oh, thank you,' over and over again.

" 'I won't say "Think nothing of it." It was hard work,' the man said, when he'd got his breath. 'But I'm glad I was here. This is a vile spot for a centaur.'

" 'Worse than some,' Rob agreed. He found the spare candle Zinka had given us and lit it with Rupert's spare lighter.

"I said, 'I saw you. In the Hotel Babylon.'

"Maree said, 'So did I.' I remembered then that she thought he was fabulous and I looked up in case she was fainting or anything. She wasn't. She was looking at the man in a way that was puzzled but sort of understanding as well. 'Who are you?' she said. 'Rupert Venables knows you.'

" 'I'm not sure who I am yet,' he said, rather ashamed about it. 'But I used to be the next-door neighbour of Rupert Venables. You know him, do you?'

" 'Met him six weeks ago. Hated him. Met him again at the hotel and feel as if I'd known him for years,' Maree said.

"I said, 'Yes, we all know him quite well.'

" 'Then,' the man said, 'if you see him before I do, tell him I'll be in touch.' He stood up and looked ruefully at the palm of one of his hands. 'Three grains left,' he said. 'The rest went down the way you nearly went, centaur.' He put the grains carefully in his pocket.

" 'We can give you a few more,' Rob said.

" 'Three should be enough,' he said, and he held the hand out to Rob. 'Come on. I'll help you up the rest of the way, and these two can help one another.'

"So we set off like that. Rob did much better with somebody helping him all the time, saying things like, 'Don't stretch. Use this tuft, it's bigger. Now jump up to here, but steadily.' But Maree was really tired and I felt weak as a kitten. Rob and the man got further and further ahead. At last, when their candles were just little twinkles high above, they shouted down that they would wait for us at the top.

"That was the last we saw of them. At the time, it was upsetting. But Koryfos explained to me, back at the hotel, inside the troop carrier, that they *had* tried to wait, but the place at the top wasn't arranged for that. Whether they stood still or whether they walked, they went where they were going. And coming back, they found they were going a different way. 'And believe me,' he said, 'it was much worse than the way we came. Rob was lucky to survive it.'

"This was because it really was Babylon at the top of the hanging gardens. As soon as we got to it, Maree and I, we knew. But I don't think I can describe it. Partly this was because it was so many things at once, somehow. I can remember it as just the dark flat top to the mountain, or I can remember it as an absolutely huge tower—that we were inside *and* outside of, both at once—or I can remember it as just standing in an incredibly bright light. But when I think of it as the light, I think, No, there were *colours* in it, and some of the colours were ones you don't see anywhere else and don't have words for, and they were in ripples like the Northern Lights, except they were like moving signs, too. Then I think, No, again, they weren't ripples, they were pillars. And I simply don't know. And the oddest thing, which makes it even harder to remember than not knowing the colours, is the way everything had at least twice as many directions it was in as normal. I mean, when I think of Babylon as the tower, I know it went through ten or twelve right-angles, up and down as well as around, just like the hotel, only in this tower I could *see* all the different directions and it was really *strange*. And there were other things.

"Maree doesn't even remember this much. All she can recall is the last bit, when we both think we arrived beside a thing like a stone trough—only it was as strange as everything else because it had all the other directions too, which made a queer shape for a trough. And we thought about it a bit. I said, 'We can't just stand and ask. They have to tell us it's all right to ask first.'

"Maree said, 'Give me a bottle of water.' I'd only the one, but I passed it to her, and she carefully poured about half of it into the trough—and you had to be careful, because the water went round all sorts of directions too and made it hard to aim. Then she passed the bottle back to me and said, 'Now you pour some. Then scatter grain.'

"I did, and it was even harder with the grain. It went all over the place and round all the corners and only a few seeds went in. But as soon as the seeds had gone into the water it all began foaming and sort of growing, until it was rushing like a river at the brims of the trough.

"Then I *think* a voice spoke. But I'm not sure, because if it *was* a voice, it was more like notes or chiming. And it seemed to me to tell us Maree could ask first, provided she was in great need.

"I nudged at Maree. She sort of jumped. I whispered at her what to say. She nodded happily and I thought she understood. She pushed her glasses up and said, 'I ask that my little fat Dad should be cured of his cancer.'

"I couldn't *believe* it. It was a total waste. I knew I was going to have to ask for the other half of Maree for my own wish and I could have screamed. There was no chance of getting her back if I didn't, and I would have wasted everyone's trouble. I think I cried at the waste. But it was pointless to have come all this way and *not* ask. So I asked for her.

"And there was a sort of chiming. Maree suddenly went the right colour. She even looked heavier. And she seemed to have her mind back properly. Anyway the shape of her face was right again. And I suppose I was glad. Well, yes, I *was* glad.

"Then there was another chiming, and this one meant we had to go. But I think it gave me a hint too. Anyway, I thought of the stories, Orpheus and so on, and I didn't look at Maree again. I just turned round and started to go back.

"I've no idea how I got so far ahead of her. Maree doesn't know either. She thinks she had my candle in sight most of the time. I heard her behind me quite often. I heard her scrambling down the moss after me, and I felt it swaying under her. I heard her walking while I was crawling along the ribbon of rock with the precipices on either side. I just don't understand it.

"Going back was awful. The worst of it was, you knew just what you were in for. The one thing that wasn't the same was when I was coming down the rocks like the stacks of knives. I never saw the children or the birds there. But the rest of it was all there, waiting. Another difference, now I think, was when I got to the thorns. I kept expecting my clothes to vanish again, but they didn't. The only thing that did vanish was the shawl made out of the goat's wool. And when I got to the bridge, there was nothing at the other end, no gateway and no statues. By then I was so tired I almost didn't notice. I was just glad that nobody tried to stop me, and trudged on. I was so tired that I almost didn't know I could stop when I got back to Rupert's room at last."

[3]

They all listened hard to me reading, leaning forward, attending to every word. I was so busy reading at first that it took me a while to notice that the sheets of paper were sort of filtering away as I read them. Almost every time I put a page underneath the pile after I'd read it, it went. By the end, I was holding three sheets of paper. I looked. The top one was the part about the birds and the children.

Someone quite a long way down the table asked, "Do you know who those three children were?"

I said, "Yes. They have to have been the Emperor's other children who were killed."

"And what do you think the birds were?" another distant voice asked.

"I don't know," I said. "I thought maybe *you* did."

"I wish we did," the person right beside me at the end of the table said. "This is as strange to us as it is to you."

Then I had only two pages. The top one was now the bit after I'd come back and we were chasing the quack chicks. My stomach wobbled.

It was one of the people on the side bench against the wall who asked me about that. She was an old, old lady with sucked-in cheeks. She said, "What are your feelings about your mother now?"

I couldn't answer. I simply didn't know how—and I'd been trying to work it out ever since Dad and Maree and I went back to Bristol.

The old lady said, "Try to answer. It might help."

The only way I could manage to answer was to talk about something else. I said, "Last year, I had a boil on my neck. It was quite impressive. It grew and it grew and it was a sort of purple-red. And all the time it was growing it was wonderfully neat and well shaped, quite round and pointed and regular, with a funny little dip in the middle at the top. When I looked at it, I used to think it was such a perfect shape that it almost seemed as if it was a proper part of me and meant to be there. But it hurt more and more, in a dull sort of way, and it made me hold my head on one side. In the end, Dad marched me off to the doctor with it. The doctor took a short look, then he lanced it. That made the most appalling mess and it hurt ten times more. When I got home it looked even more of a mess. It was not even a good shape any longer, and it kept running and felt horrible, but the pain was a much better sort of pain, even though it went on for a long time and I've still got quite a mark."

"Fair enough," said the old lady.

That left me with only the one sheet. I looked down at it and I sort of clenched. It was the last sheet, and I was absolutely *not* going to tell them what I'd wanted to wish for. But I wasn't sure how I could stop them making me.

Somebody right along the table asked. He said, "You've left out your motive. You haven't said why you went through with this."

"What do you mean?" I said, defending for all I was worth.

"I mean," he said, "that you've made it clear why you hung on to the centaur and asked for the other half of your sister, but there was at least one occasion where you wanted to turn back, and your account shows that you *could* have done. Why did you go on?"

"Oh," I said. I tried not to show them how relieved I was. "I went on because I was *interested*, of course. I wanted to know what would happen."

That seemed to amuse them all. There was quite a ripple of laughter round the room, and when it stopped, all my papers had gone. Rupert seemed to think we were going to leave then, but they hadn't quite finished. One of the stern ones in the middle of the table said to me, "One moment. This account of Babylon contains substantial parts of the deep secret of the Magids that is called Babylon. For this reason, we are going to have to expunge all trace and memory of it from you. Please understand and forgive this assembly for it. It is necessary."

That is just what they tried to do. I really didn't remember a thing—though I was puzzled to see that Maree was the right colour again, and couldn't think why—until I got home and found the note I'd left for myself. *Look for disks*. So I looked all over and found about twenty of the hundred disks I'd hidden. The rest were gone, and the file wasn't on my hard disk. But I don't think the Upper Room realized how cunning I'd been.

You see, after Rupert told me that the computer games people didn't want my Bristolia game after all—they said it was too complicated!—I decided I'd do a Babylon game instead. Blow that about deep secrets! Rupert and Maree say that the basic job of a Magid is to gradually release all the special knowledge anyway. And besides, I want to re-member. It strikes me as one of the best ways of forcing that Upper Room to make me a Magid too. That was what I'd been going to ask for, until I had to ask for Maree instead. Now I'll have to get to be one another way round.

TOR
BOOKS The Best in Fantasy

ELVENBANE • Andre Norton and Mercedes Lackey
"A richly detailed, complex fantasy collaboration."—Marion Zimmer Bradley

SUMMER KING, WINTER FOOL • Lisa Goldstein
"Possesses all of Goldstein's virtues to the highest degree."—*Chicago Sun-Times*

JACK OF KINROWAN • Charles de Lint
Jack the Giant Killer and *Drink Down the Moon* reprinted in one volume.

THE MAGIC ENGINEER • L.E. Modesitt, Jr.
The tale of Dorrin the blacksmith in the enormously popular continuing saga of Recluce.

SISTER LIGHT, SISTER DARK • Jane Yolen
"The Hans Christian Andersen of America."—*Newsweek*

THE GIRL WHO HEARD DRAGONS • Anne McCaffrey
"A treat for McCaffrey fans."—*Locus*

GEIS OF THE GARGOYLE • Piers Anthony
Join Gary Gar, a guileless young gargoyle disguised as a human, on a perilous pilgrimage in pursuit of a philter to rescue the magical land of Xanth from an ancient evil.